Penguin Book 2940
The Mimic Men

V. S. Naipaul was born in 1932 in Trinidad.
He is the author of *The Mystic Masseur*
(1957; John Llewelyn Rhys Memorial
Prize), *The Suffrage of Elvira* (1958), *Miguel
Street* (1959; Somerset Maugham Award),
A House for Mr Biswas (1961), *The Middle
Passage* (1962), *Mr Stone and the Knights
Companion* (1963; Hawthornden Prize), *An
Area of Darkness* (1964), and *The Mimic Men*
(1967). *A Flag on the Island* (1967) is a
collection of his short stories.

V. S. Naipaul

The Mimic Men

Penguin Books

Penguin Books Ltd, Harmondsworth,
Middlesex, England
Penguin Books Australia Ltd, Ringwood,
Victoria, Australia

First published by André Deutsch 1967
Published in Penguin Books 1969
Copyright © V. S. Naipaul, 1967

Made and printed in Great Britain by
Cox & Wyman Ltd,
London, Reading and Fakenham
Set in Intertype Baskerville

grey sky roofs were white and shining black in patches. The bombsite was wholly white; every shrub, every discarded bottle, box and tin was defined. I had seen. Yet what was I to do with so complete a beauty? And looking out from that room to the thin lines of brown smoke rising from ugly chimneypots, the plastered wall of the house next to the bombsite tremendously braced and buttressed, looking out from that empty room with the mattress on the floor, I felt all the magic of the city go away and had an intimation of the forlornness of the city and the people who lived in it.

A mattress, a writing-table. Had there been more while Mr Shylock lived? Such a distinguished man, so carefully dressed; and this his room, the scene of his pleasure. I opened the drawer of the writing-table. An identity card, fuzzy at the edges. Mr Shylock's: his neat signature. A creased photograph of a plumpish girl in a woollen skirt and a jumper. The photographer's hand had shaken, so that the photograph, like the photograph in some magazine article on great events, seemed rare, as of a person who would be photographed no more. An innocent, unarresting face, untouched by the wonder which vice and the word 'mistress' ought to have given it. She stood in a back garden. The house behind her was like its neighbours. Her familiar home: I sought to enter it in imagination, to re-create the moment – an early summer Sunday afternoon perhaps, just before lunch – when the photograph was taken. Not by Mr Shylock surely? Brother, father, sister? Here anyway it had ended, that moment, that impulse of affection, in an abandoned room among the chimneypots of what to the girl from the back garden must have seemed like a foreign country.

I thought I should preserve the photograph. But I left it where I had found it. I thought: let it not happen to me. Death? But that comes to all. Well, then, let me leave more behind. Let my relics be honoured. Let me not be mocked. But even as I tried to put words to what I felt, I knew that my own journey, scarcely begun, had ended in the shipwreck which all my life I had sought to avoid.

A sombre beginning. It could not be otherwise. These are

7

not the political memoirs which, at times during my political life, I saw myself composedly writing in the evening of my days. A more than autobiographical work, the exposition of the malaise of our times pointed and illuminated by personal experience and that knowledge of the possible which can come only from a closeness to power. This, though, is scarcely the book to which I can now address myself. True, I write with composure. But it is not the composure I would have chosen. For, so far from being in the evening of my days, I am just forty; and I no longer have a political career.

I know that return to my island and to my political life is impossible. The pace of colonial events is quick, the turnover of leaders rapid. I have already been forgotten; and I know that the people who supplanted me are themselves about to be supplanted. My career is by no means unusual. It falls into the pattern. The career of the colonial politician is short and ends brutally. We lack order. Above all, we lack power, and we do not understand that we lack power. We mistake words and the acclamation of words for power; as soon as our bluff is called we are lost. Politics for us are a do-or-die, once-for-all charge. Once we are committed we fight more than political battles; we often fight quite literally for our lives. Our transitional or makeshift societies do not cushion us. There are no universities or City houses to refresh us and absorb us after the heat of battle. For those who lose, and nearly everyone in the end loses, there is only one course: flight. Flight to the greater disorder, the final emptiness: London and the home counties.

There are many of us around living modestly and without recognition in small semi-detached suburban houses. We go out on a Saturday morning to do the shopping at Sainsbury's and jostle with the crowd. We have known grandeur beyond the football-pool dreams of our neighbours; but in the lower-middle-class surroundings to which we are condemned we pass for immigrants. The pacific society has its cruelties. Once a man is stripped of his dignities he is required, not to die or to run away, but to find his level. Occasionally I read a letter in *The Times,* a communication on a great topic from a mean address; I recognize a name and see with enormous sympathy the stirring of some chained and desperate spirit. Just the other day I was in the West End, in the basement of one of those department stores where the assistants carry their names on little plastic badges. I was among the unpainted kitchen furniture. I required a folding wooden clothes-airer, which I thought I might introduce at nights into the bathroom of the hotel where I now live. An assistant had her back to me. I went up to her. She turned. Her face was familiar, and a quick glance at the name pinned to her blouse left no room for doubt. We had last met at a conference of non-aligned nations; her husband had been one of the firebrands. We had seen one another in a glittering blur of parties and dinners. Then she had worn her 'national costume'. It had given her a seductive appearance, and the colours of her silks had set off her own rich Asiatic complexion. Now the regulation skirt and blouse of the department store converted her breasts and hips into untidy bundles. I remembered how, when we were saying our good-byes at the airport, the third secretary of her embassy, breaking the precise arrangements of protocol, had run up at the last moment with a bunch of flowers, which he offered to her, the personal gift of a man desperate to keep his job in the diplomatic service, fearful of being recalled to the drabness of his own background. Now she stood among the unpainted kitchen furniture. I couldn't face her. I left the purchase unmade, hoping that she would not recognize me, and turned away.

Later, sitting in the train, going past the backs of tall sooty houses, tumbledown sheds, Victorian working-class tenements whose gardens, long abandoned, had for stretches been turned into Caribbean backyards, I wondered about the firebrand. Was he pining away tamely in some office job? Or was he, too broken to take employment, idling on a meagre income in a suburban terrace? Many of us, it must be said, are poor. The tale is there in the occasional small paragraph on the financial page which tells of the collapse of some little-known Swiss bank. Too much shouldn't be made of this, however. Most of us were too timid to make a fortune, or too ignorant; we measured both our opportunities

9

and our needs by the dreams of our previous nonentity.

They talk of the pessimism of the young as they talk of atheism and revolt: it is something to be grown out of. Yet less than twenty years after Mr Shylock's death, with this journey to London which I feel is final, sealing off such experience and activity as were due to me, my present mood leaps the years and all the intervening visits to this city – leaps the Humbers, the hotels, the helpful officials, the portrait of George III in Marlborough House; leaps my marriage and my business activities – leaps all this to link with that first mood which came to me in Mr Shylock's attic; so that all that came in between seems to have occurred in parenthesis. Which is the reality? The mood, or the action in between, resulting from that mood and leading up to it again?

I last saw Mr Shylock's boarding-house some years ago. I wasn't looking for it; the minister with whom I was dining lived nearby. The heavy panelled front door with its studs and its two panes of patterned glass had been replaced by a flush door, painted lilac, on which the number was spelt out in cursive letters; it suggested the entrance to a ladies' underwear shop. I felt little emotion: that part of my life was over and had been put in its place. I wonder whether I would be as cool today. Kensington, though, is not the part of the city I live in or care to visit. It has become a little too crowded and is, I believe rather expensive. It has also become a centre of racialist agitation, and I do not now wish to become involved in battles which are irrelevant to myself. I no longer wish to share distress; I do not have the equipment. No more words for me, except these I write, and in them the politician, chapman in causes, will be suppressed as far as possible. It will not be difficult. I have had my fill of political writing. My present urge is, in the inaction imposed on me, to secure the final emptiness.

I have seen much snow. It never fails to enchant me, but I no longer think of it as my element. I no longer dream of ideal landscapes or seek to attach myself to them. All landscapes eventually turn to land, the gold of the imagination to the lead of the reality. I could not, like so many of my fellow exiles, live in a suburban semi-detached house; I could not pretend even to myself to be part of a community or to be putting down roots. I prefer the freedom of my far-out suburban hotel, the absence of responsibility; I like the feeling of impermanence. I am surrounded by houses like those in the photograph I studied in Mr Shylock's attic, and that impulse of sentimentality embarrasses me. I scarcely see those houses now and never think of the people who live in them. I no longer seek to find beauty in the lives of the mean and the oppressed. Hate oppression; fear the oppressed.

The christening was at three. At about five to I went down to Lieni's room. It was in a greater mess than usual: assorted haberdashery on the mantelpiece together with bills and calendars and empty cigarette packets; clothes on the bed and the lino and the baby's crib; old newspapers; a sewing-machine dusty with shredded cloth. Beyond the grilled basement window the small back garden, usually black, was white: snow lay on the weeds, the bare plane tree, the high brick wall. It added to the dampness inside and seemed to add to the chaos. But the baby was ready, and Lieni herself, filing her nails before the fancy mantelpiece mirror, stood clean and polished and almost ready. It was a transformation that always interested me. She was in the habit of talking of the 'smart London girl', a phrase I had first heard her use in a discussion with the fascist and others, mostly disapproving, about the marriage of an English girl to the chief of an African tribe. Lieni saw herself as a smart London girl; and whenever we went out together, sometimes with the young Indian engineer with whom she had a relationship, she spent much time on the creation of this smart London girl, whether we were going to the cheap Italian restaurant round the corner, or to the cinema, which was not much farther. It was like a duty owed more to the city than herself.

The christening party had assembled in the front basement room. Now, as three o'clock came and went, they began drifting into the bedroom to make inquiries and to remind

Lieni of the time. She calmed them; they stayed in the bedroom to talk. One couple had come up from the country.
I had met them before. She was Italian; she had bitter memories of the war and especially of the greed of priests. He was
English, the tiniest of his race I had seen. This wartime
romance, and the fact of children, had given him a good deal
of confidence; but his eyes remained dark and creased with
suffering. From his new security he saw himself 'standing by'
Lieni; he was in fact to be the godfather. Another guest was
a thin middle-aged Italian lady I had never seen before. She
had a square jaw, very tired eyes, and was slow in all her
movements. Lieni said she was a countess and 'in society' in
Naples; in Malta she had once been to a ball which Princess
Elizabeth had attended. 'The Countess is thinking of buying
this crummy house,' Lieni said; the American slang word
fitted her Italian accent. I smiled at the Countess and she
smiled wearily at me.

At last we were ready. The tiny Englishman ran out to
get a taxi. After a little time Lieni, now impatient, took us all
out to the portico to wait. The street was already brown and
squishy. But the snow still lay white on the columns of the
portico, obscuring the name of the hotel. Presently the taxi
came, the tiny Englishman sitting forward on the tip-up seat
overcoated and absurdly diminished but spry and restless.
The church was not far. We got there at about twenty past
three. We were in good time. No one was ready for us. The
church had been bombed out and the christening was to take
place in an annexe. We sat in an ante-room of sorts with
other mothers and children and waited. Lieni was smiling
all the time below her hat, the smart London girl. A baby
squealed. A box of candles had a card: *Candles twopence.*
Two young girls went to the box, dropped coppers, lit candles
and fixed them in a stand. The mother of the girls looked
round at us and smiled, inviting witness and approval.

At half past three an unshaven man with a dirty collar
entered in a rush and said, 'Christening?' 'Yes, yes,' the
mothers said. He went out again and reappeared a second
later. 'How many, how many?' He counted the babies himself and said, 'Three.' He disappeared once more, returned

as quickly as before, opened the door and asked us to follow him. We followed him up the stairs, candlestands all the way, candles twopence, and came into a large room with ochre walls. He took a white gown off a hook and forced himself into it. A priest came in silently, smiling. He went to a rack, picked up a purple scarf with gold crosses and arranged the scarf carefully over his shoulders. The unshaven man scuttled about, seeking the three godfathers to hand them little cards in transparent glossy sheaths. The christenings began. At last it was the turn of Lieni's baby.

'John Cedric, what doest thou ask of the Church? Say Faith.'

Our godfather didn't like being told. He hunted out the response on the card he had been given. Then he said, 'Faith.'

'What does Faith give you? Say everlasting life.'

'I know, father. Everlasting life.'

The priest hallowed the baby with his saliva, his thumb and his fingers. With his nose he made the sign of the cross over the baby. I believe – my memories of the ceremony are now a little vague – that at a certain stage he put a pinch of salt into the baby's mouth. John Cedric made a sour face and worked his tongue. Through his godfather he renounced the devil and his works and accepted God instead; and presently the ceremony was over. Lieni grew grave towards the end. She was almost in tears when she went to the priest and offered money – I believe – which was rejected. No longer the smart London girl; and for the first time that afternoon I remembered that she was an unmarried mother. It was left to the tiny godfather to revive our spirits in the taxi, and even Elsa, his wife, passionately anti-clerical, agreed that it had been a beautiful ceremony of forgiveness.

There was to be a party afterwards. Lieni had invited all her friends. At about six they began arriving, some coming straight from their jobs. Lieni was in the kitchen, her afternoon grooming partly abolished by a very dirty apron. The tiny godfather acted as host in the front basement room. Several damp, macintoshed Maltese came in together and talked glumly in English and their own language. I got the impression they were talking of jobs and money and the current London prejudice that turned every Maltese into a white slaver. The Countess smiled at everyone and said little. Johnny the fascist came in with his wife. He wore his black shirt, a sign that he had been 'working' some district. His wife was drunk as usual. All the Maltese greeted him warmly. 'Hi, Johnny-boy! Where you been operating tonight, Johnny?' 'Notting Hill Gate,' Johnny-boy said. 'Not much of a crowd.' 'The weather,' one of the Maltese said. 'Her ladyship was getting sozzled in the Coach and Horses,' Johnny-boy said, as though this was the better explanation. He wore his usual air of patient exasperation. Her ladyship, hearing herself referred to, blinked and tried to steady herself on her chair. Other boarders came down. The girl from Kenya; her man friend, a blond, vacant alcoholic incapable of extended speech and making up for this with a fixed smile and gestures of great civility; the smiling, mute Burmese student; the Jewish youth, tall and prophetic in black; the bespectacled young Cockney who had as much trouble with his two Italian mistresses, according to Lieni, as with the police; the Frenchman from Morocco who worked all day in his room, kept to Moroccan temperature with a paraffin stove, translating full-length American thrillers at speed – he did one or two a month. It was always good to see them, familiar in all the unknown of the city. But this was how they always appeared: two-dimensional, offering simple versions of themselves. Conversation, apart from that conducted by the Maltese group, was not easy. We sat and waited for Lieni, whom we could hear in the kitchen.

Lieni's brother came. He had got time off from the West End restaurant where he worked as a waiter. He was pale, handsome, fatigued. He spoke little English. Lieni came in with a scuttle of coals. The room had been cold at the start of the evening; now it was getting a little too warm. Putting the fresh coals on, killing the heat a little, Lieni said to her brother, 'Rudolfo, why don't you tell them about the time I asked you to go and buy a sheet of paper.' Rudolfo sucked his teeth and made a gesture of impatience, as he always did when he was asked to tell this story. The gesture itself aroused laughter. Then the story came. Rudolfo, just arrived in London, knowing virtually no English, had been sent out by his sister to buy a sheet of writing paper: some momentous letter had to be dispatched. He had gone to the W. H. Smith bookshop and asked for 'a sheet paper'; he had been directed by an imperturbable assistant to Boots the chemists and had returned, flaming with anger, with a roll of toilet paper.

Her ladyship rocked on her chair and fell forward on to the floor without a cry. Johnny-boy, like one used to these happenings, set himself first to arrange her clothes and then to raise her and lead her out of the room.

'Hi, Johnny-boy!'

This was from Paul, entering the room as Johnny-boy and her ladyship left it. We had heard his shoes crushing the ice and cinders on the basement steps. Paul was short, thick-set, almost bald, and wore glasses. He was gentle; his English accent was rich; he was a homosexual. In Lieni's basement rooms this was his 'character'. He liked wearing an apron and doing household things. He liked sweeping up dirt, storing it and, before throwing it away, gloating over its quantity. He liked smoothing out tablecloths and bed sheets; he was frequently to be seen ironing. The first thing he did whenever he came to Lieni's was to express horror at the disorder and to set to sweeping. This was what he did now. He went out to get his broom and apron. Lieni came back with him, carrying another scuttle of coals for a fire that was now scarcely bearable.

'Poor Johnny-boy,' Paul said.

'Tell them, Paulo,' Lieni said.

Paul made a face.

'Go on, Paulo. Tell them about one tit this way and –'

The glum Maltese laughed.

'I wenta one day to see Johnny-boy, you see,' Paul said, picking up his accent. 'They was sleeping. Ladyship was naked. That is all.'

'Rubbish,' Lieni said. 'Go on, tell them.'

'She wazza sleeping, you see. And she wazza naked. And – she hadda one titta thisaway and one titta thataway.' He wrinkled up his nose and made the requisite face of disgust.

The fire had stupefied most of us. The young alcoholic mechanically passed around cigarettes. The Frenchman sat blank and quite still in the American army tunic he always wore in the boarding-house. Elsa and her husband went in and out of the kitchen. The Countess sat and smiled. I don't know what Lieni was preparing for us; but she was determined that we should do nothing to spoil our appetites. She had no more stories for us; but whenever she came in, with yet another scuttle of coals, she stopped to make us sing or do dances or play a game. We did as she directed; we became hotter. At the end we were all hugging the damp walls.

The basement bell rang. Lieni ran out to the passage. We heard conversation. A male voice was subdued: we guessed it was her engineer. We waited for her to bring him in. He was shy and had little English, but the occasion was also partly his. We waited. We heard the bedroom door slam; we heard it locked. There were footsteps in the passage; the basement door gently opened and gently closed; and there were footsteps outside climbing up, crushing the cinders and frozen snow like dry leaves. Lieni didn't return.

Elsa told us what had happened. The engineer had brought his laundry; this was his custom. Once, on Lieni's birthday, he had left a gift, a piece of jewellery, in the pocket of his white coat; and had said nothing. Now Lieni, seizing the laundry, went through the pockets of the coat. She came upon a letter. It was from the engineer's home in India; he was married, with children. It might have been a deliberate act of brutality, or bravery; it might have been accidental. The engineer denied nothing; he made no attempt to defend himself or reassure Lieni. When Lieni locked herself in her bedroom, he simply took back his laundry and went away.

That was the end of the party. One by one and two by two the Maltese and the boarders left. Rudolfo went back to his restaurant. Johnny-boy was trying to revive his wife in the kitchen; he was succeeding; she was becoming obstreperous. Elsa and her husband were getting ready to catch their train back to the country. Lieni kept herself locked in her room, out of the chaos of which a few hours before she had arisen, the smart London girl. The Countess sat and looked. Paul, still in his apron, cleaned up and offered food.

I went to a dance at the British Council in Davies Street. I fell into a flirtatious, mock-witty conversation with an idle French girl. These conversations with French women always wearied me. Still, at the end, I prepared to do what was expected of me. I said, 'Do you dance?' She at once rose. It was then that out of nowhere the impulse of cruelty came to me. I said, 'I don't.' And I left. I walked back across the park. Snow was sharp below my shoes; it astonished me to find that in spite of the cold I was thirsty.

I was in bed that night when I heard someone sobbing outside my door. It was Lieni, red-eyed in the cold passage. I let her in. I sat on the edge of the bed and she sat on my lap. She was not a small woman and I thought beyond her unhappiness to her weight, to the pressure of her bone on my flesh. I had an idea where her tears were leading. But I was unwilling. I shook my cramped legs; she clung to my neck. I stood up and she glided down to the floor. She sat on the chair and cried, her big fingers beating softly on the padded arms of the chair. I told her to be silent; she sobbed more loudly. I asked her to leave. To my surprise, she got up and left without a word. I felt foolish and uncomfortable. She had once told me that Lieni was the Maltese for Helen, and had added: 'Have you ever seen a Helen so fat?' But she was not fat. I thought of the incidents of the day; they seemed so far away. I thought I would go to her. Down the dark stair-well; past the frozen musty smell of the ground floor, where were the public rooms nobody used; to the cooking and baby and scorched smells of the basement. A night-light was on in Lieni's room, sufficient to show, through the frosted glass, the clothes hanging on her door. I tried the knob; the door opened. A chaos of weak light and deep shadow: clothes and paper and boxes, wash-basin and crib and sewing machine and wardrobe. Lieni was in her bed, fast asleep.

This was my first snow.

2

How right our Aryan ancestors were to create gods. We seek sex, and are left with two private bodies on a stained bed. The larger erotic dream, the god, has eluded us. It is so whenever, moving out of ourselves, we look for extensions of ourselves. It is with cities as it is with sex. We seek the physical city and find only a conglomeration of private cells. In the city as nowhere else we are reminded that we are individuals, units. Yet the idea of the city remains; it is the god of the city that we pursue, in vain.

So quickly had London gone sour on me. The great city, centre of the world, in which, fleeing disorder, I had hoped to find the beginning of order. So much had been promised by the physical aspect. That marvel of light, soft, shadowless, always protective. They talk of the light of the tropics and Southern Spain. But there is no light like that of the temperate zone. It was a light which gave solidity to everything and drew colour out from the heart of objects. To me, from the tropics, where night succeeded day abruptly, dusk was new and enchanting. I would sit in Lieni's basement room, in the clutter, and study the light, not willing to risk losing any gradation in that change. Light was slowly withdrawn; a blueness remained, which deepened, so that before the electric lights began to make their effect the world seemed wholly aqueous, and we might have been at the bottom of the ocean. Then at night the sky was low; you walked as though under a canopy; and all the city's artificial lights, their glow seemingly trapped, burned intensely; and sometimes the wet streets threw up their own glitter.

Here was the city, the world. I waited for the flowering to come to me. The trams on the Embankment sparked blue. The river was edged and pierced with reflections of light, blue and red and yellow. Excitement! Its heart must have lain somewhere. But the god of the city was elusive. The tram was filled with individuals, each man returning to his own cell. The factories and warehouses, whose exterior lights decorated the river, were empty and fraudulent. I would play with famous names as I walked empty streets and stood on bridges. But the magic of names soon faded. Here was the river, here the bridge, there that famous building. But the god was veiled. My incantation of names remained unanswered. In the great city, so solid in its light, which gave colour even to unrendered concrete – to me as colourless as rotting wooden fences and new corrugated-iron roofs – in this solid city life was two-dimensional.

At the lecture halls there was the young English student who, out of his own insecurity, had attached himself to me, an outsider. Shrouded in his college scarf now, he was doomed to later nonentity; but I listened. His ambition ever changed. It was poetry one week. He had a thing, he said, which he did not expect me to understand, about Nature and the English countryside; I remember that 'the green of grass not grown' was one of his lines. It was philosophy the next week. 'Tell me, do I *look* like a Christian? I do? Aha! That's what they *all* think.' And the week after that: 'Look at me. Do you think I will become Prime Minister?' He was like me : he needed the guidance of other men's eyes.

From the lecture halls and canteen of the School to the boarding-house, where the Frenchman always typed, Lieni always chattered in her basement room, and Duminicu, also from Malta, talked of escape. Duminicu was short and fat; he worked in a department store; he saved his money. Once a week he went to the cinema; the rest of the time he stayed in his room, stripped to vest and pants, reading newspapers and magazines and working out crosswords. He often had tinned meat or tinned fish for dinner, eating straight from the tin with a knife. He said that in Malta his family was of some standing, and he didn't get on with Lieni, whom he considered his social inferior. He resented being bossed around by her in London. But he didn't leave. His reaction to his humiliation was kleptomania. He stole incessantly from shops and stores, and always had some new trifle to show. He would say, 'I am not like some people I could mention who would buy something for five shillings and then say that they paid five hundred shillings. I will be honest with you. I stole this.'

And from the boarding-house to the halls of the British Council. Trying out my French, finding myself committed to difficult light conversation, whose velleities I couldn't always grasp, with a series of young girls and women, domestics who said perhaps with truth that they came of good families. Hilariously practising Norwegian crossed o's with Norwegian girls and Swedish j's with Swedes. All the preliminaries to the invitation to the cinema, the book-shaped room, the fumbling with clothes and breasts, the lips first averted, then offered, the intense expression of the young girl who prepares to be wooed.

In London I had no guide. There was no one to link my present with my past, no one to note my consistencies or inconsistencies. It was up to me to choose my character, and I chose the character that was easiest and most attractive. I was the dandy, the extravagant colonial, indifferent to scholarship. In fact my income was small, and the allowance I had fixed for myself was half of this; I didn't think I could be happy spending without earning. But I let it be known that on my island my family were the bottlers of Coca-Cola. The fact impressed less than I had expected. But the respect with which I was treated by boys from the island – to whom the fact was significant – was a help, as was Lieni's willingness to play the game. Lieni. I had no guide, I said; and so it seemed to me at the time. But there was Lieni in her basement. I saw her every day. I thought she accepted the character as a character and sought merely to heighten it. But she it was – it is so obvious now – who, by suggestion and flattery, created the character of the rich colonial. We become what we see of ourselves in the eyes of others. She pretended that I was richer than I said. She made me aware of my looks, to which up to then I had paid little attention, content with the knowledge that I was no monster. It was Lieni who told me that my eyes might disturb and that my dark, luxuriant and very soft hair might be a source of further disturbance. It was Lieni who led me through the stores and chose my clothes, and suggested the red cummer-

20

bund. Her background was the war, whose glamour, fading as the peace dragged on, was more and more concentrated in her memory of an affair with an Indian officer in Italy. This was how she explained her interest in me. It was disquieting, yet at the same time oddly flattering, to be cherished as a substitute; and it imposed no obligation. I became her apt pupil.

It became a pleasure to get ready for an evening at the British Council, and with arms loosely held aloft to spin into my cummerbund. I exaggerated the dancer's movements if I had an audience – some poor scholar from my island, for instance, who, seeking company, had brought me his complaints, and whom my frivolity, I could see, was reducing to despair. It was Lieni who told me that I ought to spend the extra half-crown two or three times a week to arrive at the School in a taxi, having travelled by public transport the better part of the way. It was Lieni who dressed me, approved of me, and sent me out to conquer. I delighted in my act, and the boys of my island of Isabella, I was glad to see, with their feeling for the stylish, their tolerance of what they felt to be absurd, which, however, if well carried off, they were prepared to admire, the boys of Isabella approved of me. I exaggerated the role they admired. 'My dear fellow,' I said to a young man, wrapped in a college scarf, whom I met as he was coming out of a teashop, one of a popular chain, 'my dear fellow, never, never, never let me see you coming out of those doors again. And remember that the sole purpose of your college scarf is to shine your shoes.' This is not of course how it occurs in my memory; I was probably no more than flippantly reproving. I give the story as it circulated in Isabella some years later, when I had gained a little local celebrity. And I must confess I was pleased then that the character Lieni created had in its own small way become a legend.

But Lieni, with the woman's limited view of the world, had sent me out to conquer. She wished to share or at any rate witness my conquests; she expected me to bring back women to her boarding-house. And because she expected me to do so, I did. It was not hard. In the halls of the British

Council there were always women to be picked up. Those halls could be disagreeable, with acrid-accented Africans in stiff white collars and gold-rimmed glasses nursing racial grievance like a virtue and righteously seeking sexual reward from the innocent. But I preferred the halls of the British Council to the halls of the School. I could not separate those earnest scholarship girls from their families, from the bitterness and mean ambitions that had been passed on to them; I knew their language too well. It suited me better to have a relationship with someone whose language I couldn't speak. From the halls of the British Council I wandered off on occasion to the art galleries. I thought that with their vast intercommunicating rooms, their excuse for movement backwards, forwards and sideways, any number of times, they provided the perfect hunting ground. It grieved me to find out that I was not the first to have seen the possibilities. But the excursion trains to provincial centres of culture were, I flatter myself, a discovery wholly original.

To the town of Oxford, for instance, there used to run in those days a Wednesday excursion train. It left Paddington station at a quarter to twelve; it arrived at Oxford at three minutes to one; the return fare was seven shillings and sixpence. The Continental girls were easy to pick out. As I remember, in the late forties these girls went in for very pale, bloodless colours; they wore flat-heeled tan shoes and their macintoshes were nearly always of a fawn colour. I would try to choose my compartment sensibly; but in the end I always surrendered to instinct and luck; in these matters they are as good a guide as any. I would not attempt any conversation immediately. I would wait until the ticket collector came round. The excursion ticket was, suitably, fawn-coloured, contrasting with the regular ticket, which was green. If the girl proffered a fawn ticket I would put her down as a tourist like myself. I had taken care to provide myself with magazines, notably *Punch*, published as it still is on a Wednesday. *Punch*, then, I might offer; it would always be accepted. The way was then open for that type of conversation at which I was becoming adept. The slow French; the question about the Norwegian crossed o or the

Swedish j; followed by the suggestion that we might do our exploring of the cultural centre together. At any one of three or four stages the encounter might have been rendered futile. But when one is in vein, as the French say, when dedication and commitment are total, mistake is rare. Will I be believed if I say that on four successive Wednesdays I made lucky strikes on the Oxford train? A Norwegian – what a country, Norway, its reputation in this respect dimmed by the somewhat inflated reputation of its vulgar neighbour Sweden; a French girl and a French woman; and a German Swiss. After the disturbance of this last adventure I transferred my attentions elsewhere.

It had been disturbing indeed. No walks up the twisted wooden steps of colleges on vacation, no exploring of the spacious sitting-rooms of undergraduates and their cramped bedrooms. We had just walked and walked, pausing occasionally for refreshment; and the day had ended with us back in London, in St John's Wood, past one in the morning, still walking, after innumerable cups of hot tea from stalls, though excitement, of a sort never before experienced by me in London, would have been enough to give me energy. In the deserted streets – and a detail like this enables us to judge change, for today streets are as noisy at two in the morning as during the day – in the deserted streets a declaration had been made to me, and it had moved me in spite of myself. Beatrice had decided that I was to be her friend. She explained the significance of the word, and I was afraid that some invitation to my book-shaped room was expected. But no; we walked round and round the house in St John's Wood where she was staying; and when at last we stopped in front of the house and the moment for separation came, I saw with relief that nothing was expected of me. She kissed me lightly on the lips – observe how I had surrendered all will – and for a little pressed her hand on the side of my face as though learning its shape. She said it had been a good beginning.

I returned to the boarding-house in an agony of disturbance. I doubted whether I even knew what she looked like. I had fallen in so completely with her mood. She had led; I had followed. When she made her declaration I had felt called upon to respond. I had been careful not to perjure myself – it had never been my way in these encounters – but I had given her an Isabella dollar-note which I kept in my wallet and which had served me in the past as a useful topic of conversation when the hilarity of the Swedish j had faded. At the time the surrendering of this dollar-note seemed important – how we flounder when emotion overtakes us. Now, however, out of this emotion only disturbance and threat remained. The threat of the 'good start'; the threat, frequently expressed, of a father arriving from Basle in a fortnight, a 'man of culture', to whom she desired passionately to present me since we had so much in common.

Luck intervened. The day remained whole, unsullied. Was it luck, though? Mightn't I have found that order I looked for, mightn't order have come with this complete break from the past, if I had pursued where I had been so moved? But I had my doubts then; I didn't know whether during that day I had simply become what she had wanted me to be. Still, I wonder: wouldn't it have been better, or at any rate more amusing, if I had met the father, the man of culture – these European phrases: how quaint they are when turned into English – and if I had gone away with that girl and we had milked our cows among mountains and snow and rolled our cheeses down the hillsides?

But my luck – let the word stand – intervened. The next afternoon a letter in a small envelope came. *I want to give you your dollar back. Please take it.* No more; no *dear*, no *love*. The clear-sighted Swiss! The mystery had been too much for her; she preferred to avoid it. She had sensed more than the absurdity of our relationship; she had sensed its wrongness. And, perhaps, she had seen the absence of virtue.

Let me explain. *Virtus*: how could anyone who had gone through Isabella Imperial and studied Latin with Major Grant fail to know the meaning of that word? Let me take you to the book-shaped room; let the scene not dissolve as we close the door and the face of the girl, already growing serious and blank, is averted and still. It was a logical moment. But it was the moment I dreaded. Both of us adrift in London, the great city, I with my past, my own darkness, she no doubt with hers. Always at these moments the talk of the past, the landscapes, their familiar settings which I wished them to describe and then feared to hear about. I never wished even in imagination to enter their Norman farmhouses or their flats in Nassjo, pronounced Neshway, or their houses set atop the rocky fiords of geography books. I never wished to hear of the relationships that bound them to these settings, the pettinesses by which they had already been imprisoned. I never wanted our darkness, our auras, to mingle. Understand the language I use. I am describing a failure, a deficiency; and these things can be so private. I had spent all my life among women; I could not conceive of an existence away from them or their influence. Perhaps the relationship into which I had fallen with Lieni was sufficient; perhaps all else was perversion. Intimacy: the word holds the horror. I could have stayed for ever at a woman's breasts, if they were full and had a hint of a weight that required support. But there was the skin, there was the smell of skin. There were bumps and scratches, there were a dozen little things that could positively enrage me. I was capable of the act required, but frequently it was in the way that I was capable of getting drunk or eating two dinners. Intimacy: it was violation and self-violation. These scenes in the book-shaped room didn't always end well; they could end in tears, sometimes in anger, a breast grown useless being buttoned up, a door closed on a room that seemed to require instant purification.

But there was my 'character'. I took to retaining trophies from the girls who came to the book-shaped room: stockings, various small garments, once even a pair of shoes from a girl who had thought of staying the night. Not for fetichist reasons, I give my word! Though even now I cannot understand my motives. I believe I had read or heard that it excited some men to think of girls going back to their rooms and travelling on underground trains without certain garments. Nor can I understand why I began keeping a sexual diary. I began it, I remember, out of boredom and idleness;

but soon it developed into a type of auto-erotic enterprise. It was myself, my minutest reactions, that I sought to analyse. Ridiculous! Vile! So it was to me too, even at the time. Yet I persevered, and stopped only when I discovered that Lieni, who had been sending me out into the world to conquer, read this diary as regularly as I wrote it. I was not annoyed. It was the sort of relationship I had with her: it seemed to me no intrusion that she should come into my room at odd hours or read my letters. I welcomed this sort of participation. But I stopped the diary. She spoke about it to some of the boarders in the front basement room one evening; it was considered a great joke, suited to my 'character'. The Frenchman said, 'You should go to France and marry a French girl.' But his thoughts must have been elsewhere, perhaps on the dinner of Lieni's he had just eaten, for he added: 'She will make you the most wonderful dishes with a little piece of bread and a little piece of cheese.' After this Lieni became freer. Sections of the diary, which she had apparently memorized, she would quote at me in the presence of others; and in her playful Maltese way she would grab at my crutch, threatening to bite 'it' off. In moments of especial hilarity she even attempted to unbutton me. So to my boarding-house character was added this humorous modification.

The warnings signs were so clear. Yet at the time I thought I was simply playing, that in the keeping of trophies and writing-up of experience I was expressing a non-existent side of myself. As though we ever play. As though the personality, for all its byways and wilful deviations, all its seeming inconsistencies, does not hang together. There are certain states into which, during periods of stress, we imperceptibly sink; it is only during the climb back up that we can see how far, for all the continuing consciousness of wholeness and sanity, we had become distorted. Coming to London, the great city, seeking order, seeking the flowering, the extension of myself that ought to have come in a city of such miraculous light, I had tried to hasten a process which had seemed elusive. I had tried to give myself a personality. It was something I had tried more than once before, and waited for the response in the eyes of others. But now I no longer knew what I was; ambition became confused, then faded; and I found myself longing for the certainties of my life on the island of Isabella, certainties which I had once dismissed as shipwreck.

Shipwreck: I have used this word before. With my island background, it was the word that always came to me. And this was what I felt I had encountered again in the great city: this feeling of being adrift, a cell of perception, little more, that might be altered, if only fleetingly, by any encounter. The son-lover-brother with Lieni, the player of private games in public rooms, the sensitive young man with a girl like Beatrice; the brute with the girl who, undressed, had revealed a back of irritating coarseness and had then, in tearful response to my disgust – how inconsequentially people act in extremity – shown me a picture of her Norman farmhouse. This last remained a memory of shame for some time; for I had actually shouted at the girl. I have been guilty of three or four acts of pure cruelty in my life, no more. I have now recorded two; they occurred close together, during a period of stress.

In the great city, so three-dimensional, so rooted in its soil, drawing colour from such depths, only the city was real. Those of us who came to it lost some of our solidity; we were trapped into fixed, flat postures. And, in this growing dissociation between ourselves and the city in which we walked, scores of separate meetings, not linked even by ourselves, who became nothing more than perceivers: everyone reduced, reciprocally, to a succession of such meetings, so that first experience and then the personality divided bewilderingly into compartments. Each person concealed his own darkness. Lieni; the English student in his scarf; Duminicu, forever in my imagination sitting in vest and pants on the semen-stained magenta spread of his narrow bed, spearing ham from a tin and, moustache working above weak mouth, speaking between and through mouthfuls of his imminent escape; and myself. Little twinges of panic too, already. Not the panic of being lost or lonely; the panic of ceasing to feel myself as a whole person. The threat of other people's lives, the remembered private landscapes, the relationships, the order which was not mine. I had longed for largeness. How, in the city, could largeness come to me? How could I fashion order out of all these unrelated adventures and encounters, myself never the same, never even the thread on which these things were hung? They came endlessly out of the darkness, and they couldn't be placed or fixed. And always at the end of the evening the book-shaped room, the tall window, myself sitting towards the light or towards the mirror.

The signs were all there. The crash was coming, but I could see this only when the crash had come and when the search for order had been abandoned for something more immediate and more reassuring. And the need for reassurance was constant. I began, as the saying is, to frequent prostitutes. Instinct alone didn't suggest this; I was also influenced by what I had read. I became an addict of what these women offered, which was less and more than pleasure: the quick stimulation of fear, followed by its immediate dissipation. But it was a grotesque business, not the least grotesque part of which was the vocabulary. Personal service; correction; domination; thirty shillings dressed, two guineas undressed. The first occasion was a failure; it was an occasion of unrelieved fear. I remember a very warm ante-room with a gas fire, a wallpaper of flowered, country-cottage pattern, and an elderly cigarette-smoking maid in an upholstered armchair reading the evening paper by the light of a dim ceiling lamp. In the room beyond there was the manageable talk of money and something extra for the maid; then the humiliation. After some time the body threw me off, rearranging its stiff, evil-smelling hair. But the cruelty and cheating were, as I discovered later, exceptional; I never experienced them again. The occasions that followed are a blur: of encounters less with individual bodies than with anonymous flesh. Each occasion pressed me deeper down into emptiness, that prolonged sensation of shock with which I was every minute of every day trying to come to terms. Still the cummerbund, though, still the well-brushed hair: in those days my only act of heroism.

I write as though Lieni is in some way to blame. This is not my intention. Lieni might even have saved me. I was not with her when the crash came. I had left the boarding-house, and the move had been a climax to disturbance. The house had been sold to the Countess and we had all, Lieni as well, been given notice. So we scattered. I made no attempt to look up Lieni. Presently I had my own private fight; I didn't think I could face her. I saw her, from a taxi, twelve years later. It was in that same area, on a Sunday afternoon, sunny, the street littered with paper. She was in a party of macintoshed Maltese, perhaps the very men I knew: small, pale, worried, with bodies and faces that carried the signs of childhood deprivation. Her own style had changed little. Her heels were still very high, her lipstick still a little too bright on her wide mouth: not the smart London girl, but a full-bodied woman who could be recognized at a glance as an immigrant, Maltese, Italian, Cypriot.

Six months after I moved I saw both the Countess and the boarding-house mentioned in the *News of the World*. The house had been turned into a brothel. I cried out to Mrs Mural, my landlady, when I read the item, delighted to recognize an address with which I had been connected. It was the Murals' paper and it was the sort of item they relished. But they did not care for the connexion. The Murals were on their postwar rise; they were breeders of boy scouts; they grew more grave as they grew more acquisitive. Mr Mural once had a suit made to measure by a firm with many branches; for a full week the card advising him that his suit was ready lay on the letter tray in the hall. He was a scrupulous bill-maker. The bill which followed a minor illness, during which they had had to feed me, began: *Telephone call to Doctor 3d.* I paid without comment. Folding my cheque, not putting it away, he became genial; he told me that once, during the war, he had seen the Emperor Haile Selassie. 'Standing by himself on Swindon station.' Poor Emperor! Mrs Mural nourished her family with care, and my ration card was not without its uses towards this end. Some little portion fell to me, it is true. My breakfast,

29

with its little pat of rationed butter and its little dish of rationed sugar, was brought up to me in procession every morning: Mrs Mural, her daughters, aged five and seven, and the dog.

One morning the elder girl hung back in my room. She had something to say. She said: 'Shall I show you my rude drawings?' I was interested. She showed me the drawings: a child's view of unclothed dolls. I was greatly moved. She said: 'Do you like my rude drawings?' 'I like your drawings, Yvonne.' 'I will show you some more tomorrow. Would you like to keep these?' 'I'd rather you kept them, Yvonne.' 'No, you can have these. I can always do some more for myself.' I became the patron of her assiduous art; so at any rate she represented me when the story came out. You couldn't blame the Murals then for wishing, as the saying now is, to keep Britain white.

From room to room I moved, from district to district, going ever farther out of the heart of the city. Those houses! That impression of temporary, fragile redness, of habitations set superficially on trampled fields! Those shops! Those newsagents! Quickly each area was exhausted. I remember the total tedium of a summer Sunday – once, in my imagination, a photograph of a girl had been taken on such a day: the purest anthropomorphic sentimentality – during this day I drew the backs of all the houses I could see from my window. I was restless. I travelled to the provinces, taking trains for no reason except that of movement. I travelled to the Continent. I used my savings. Everything of note or beauty reminded me of my own disturbance, spoiling both the moment and the object. My world was being corrupted! I didn't wish to see. But the restlessness remained. It took me to innumerable tainted rooms with drawn curtains and bedspreads suggesting other warm bodies. And once, more quickening of self-disgust than any other thing, I had a sight of the prostitute's supper, peasant food, on a bare table in a back room.

With Lieni and Mr Shylock's boarding-house one type of order had gone for good. And when order goes it goes. I was not marked. No celestial camera tracked my movements. I abolished landscapes from my mind. Provence on a sunny morning, the Wagon-Lit coffee cup steadied by a heavy tablespoon; the brown plateau of Northern Spain in a snowstorm; an awakening clank-and-jerk in the Alps and outside, inches from my window, a world of simple black and white. I abolished all landscapes to which I could not attach myself and longed only for those I had known. I thought of escape, and it was escape to what I had so recently sought to escape from.

But I couldn't leave right away. There was the degree; and then I wished to go back as whole as I had come. It was two years before I felt strong enough. And then I did not leave alone.

We left from Avonmouth, a port set in a grey-green wasteland. It was August but the wind was chill. Gulls bobbed like cork amid the harbour litter. We headed to the south and sailed for thirteen days. One evening the wind began to blow. We felt for pullovers; but there was no need; this wind was warm. Butter melted in the dishes; the salt didn't run easily; the officers changed from black to white; the stewards served ice cream instead of beef tea on deck in the morning. The wind whipped the crests of waves into spray and the spray was shot with a rainbow. Then one morning, waking to stillness, we looked out and saw the island. Each porthole framed a picture: a pale blue sky, green hills, brightly-coloured houses, coconut trees, and green sea.

So already I had made the double journey between my two landscapes of sea and snow. To each, at the first parting, I thought I had said good-bye, since I had got to know each in my own way. The island before me now: the Technicolour island of *The Black Swan*, of cinema galleons and men-o'-war, of rippling sails and morning music by Max Steiner. But my rejoicing was not complete, to tell the truth. It was forced, it was tinged with fear; it was a little like the tourist trying to summon up a response to the desired object of pilgrimage which, because it is so well known, leaves him cold. So too it was with London later : even from the centre, of six-guineas-a-night hotels, of helpful doormen and chauffeured Humbers, of Lord Stockwell's drawing-room and Lady

Stella's bedroom, that other London which I had just left remained like a threat. Well, as you know, what was threatened came, from both places.

3

In that period of my life which was to follow, the period between my preparation for life and my withdrawal from it, that period in parenthesis, when I was most active and might have given the observer the impression of a man fulfilling his destiny, in that period intensity of emotion was the thing I never achieved. I felt I had known a double failure, and I felt I continued to live between their twin threats. It was during this time, as I have said, that I thought of writing. It was my hope to give expression to the restlessness, the deep disorder, which the great explorations, the overthrow in three continents of established social organizations, the unnatural bringing together of peoples who could achieve fulfilment only within the security of their own societies and the landscapes hymned by their ancestors, it was my hope to give partial expression to the restlessness which this great upheaval has brought about. The empires of our time were short-lived, but they have altered the world for ever; their passing away is their least significant feature. It was my hope to sketch a subject which, fifty years hence, a great historian might pursue. For there is no such thing as history nowadays; there are only manifestos and antiquarian research; and on the subject of empire there is only the pamphleteering of churls. But this work will not now be written by me; I am too much a victim of that restlessness which was to have been my subject. And it must also be confessed that in that dream of writing I was attracted less by the act and the labour than by the calm and the order which the act would have implied.

It would have been, as I said, in the evening of my days. Life lived, endeavour past, the chances taken. My place of retirement an old cocoa estate, one of our rundown former slave plantations, blighted by witchbroom, not bringing in an income likely to revive any acquisitive anxiety. Myself installed in the old timber estate house, grey, its corrugated roof painted in stripes of faded red and white, the wide, low-eaved verandas hung with cooling ferns, the floors dark and worn and shining. Everywhere there would have been the smell of old timber and wax; everywhere the eye would have found pleasure in fashioned wood, in the white fretwork arabesques above doorways, the folding screen between drawing-room and dining-room, the tall panelled doors. There is no finer house than the old estate house of the islands. Few survive; I doubt whether there are now four in Isabella.

And cocoa: it is my favourite crop. It grows in the valleys of our mountain ranges, where it is cool and where on certain mornings your breath turns to vapour. There are freshwater springs that make miniature waterfalls over mossy rocks and then run clear and cold and shallow in their own channels of white sand. The floor of the cocoa woods is covered with broad brown-and-gold cocoa leaves; and between the cocoa trees, stunted, black-barked, as nervously branched as the oak, there are bright green coffee bushes with red berries; the whole sheltered by giant *immortelle* trees which at their due season lose all their leaves and set every hillside ablaze with bird-shaped flowers of yellow and orange which then, for days, float down on the woods. You hear the murmur and gurgle of streams everywhere, mountain streams which after rain turn to torrents that occasionally flood the depressions. Walk through the woods then at five. It is a walk from grotto to grotto; the level flood water is the colour of mud; it sucks and sighs and crackles in the gloom; and from this level water the tormented black trunks of the cocoa trees rise, their shining cocoa pods, in all the colours from the lime green through scarlet to imperial purple, attached to them individually, by the shortest of stems, without leaves.

In the deep valleys of the cocoa woods the sun comes up late. I would have gone riding in the early morning. The labourers would have been at their undemanding tasks;

cutting down the pods with gullets, hand-shaped knives which are like the weapons of medieval knights; or sitting in the shade, arcadian figures, before a multicoloured heap of pods which they were splitting open. Words would have been exchanged, about their jobs, their families, the progress of their sons at school. Labourers of the olden time! Not yet 'the people'! Then back for breakfast to the estate house, where fresh morning cocoa was mingling its aroma with that of old wood. The true cocoa, such as Montezuma and his court drank; not the powder from which all virtue has fled, but the cocoa made from roasted beans pounded to paste, imbued with spices and dried in the sun, releasing all its flavours in simmering milk. Cocoa and papaw and fried plantains, freshly baked bread and avocadoes; all served on a tablecloth of spotless white, still showing the folds from its ironing; the clean napkin on the polished plate; the glass-ware catching some sparkle from the light filtered through ferns and that fine wire netting which, barely visible, kept out tropical insects while permitting a view. The rest of the morning would have seen me at my desk, slowly patterning the white paper with the blackest of inks; and the late evening too, when there would have been no sound save that of the generating plant, set some little way from the house, or, failing that, the hum of the pressure lamp. So the days would have passed, literary labour interdigitating with agri-cultural; and that word agriculture would have acquired its classical associations and lost its harsher island significance.

It is so my imagination now fills out the scene. I linger over it, because I write in circumstances so different! I work at a rough, narrow table, acquired after a little trouble, since it is in excess of the regulation hotel furniture. The room is in the new wing of the hotel. It has a metal window of a standard size and pattern; the flush door, equally of stan-dard size and pattern, is made of a composite material so light that it has already warped and, unless bolted, swings slowly to and fro. The skirting board has shrunk, with all the woodwork. Nothing here has been fashioned with love or even skill; there is as a result nothing on which the eye rests with pleasure. The window looks out on the hotel's

34

cutting green, where on sunny days our middle-aged ladies, mutton dressed as lamb, as our barman says, give themselves a tan. Beyond, a mass of pale red brick; and from beyond that — answering the wallpaper in my room, which has a pattern of antique motorcars — there is a ceaseless roar of traffic; the tainted air vibrates. No cocoa trees! No orange-and-yellow *immortelle* flowers! No woodland springs running over white sand in which dead golden leaves and fresh red flowers have become embedded! No morning rides!

I leave the hotel every lunchtime to go to a public house a few hundred yards away. The hotel does not serve lunch on weekdays; and, apart from an appalling restaurant, the public house is the only place within two miles or so that offers food; we are in that sort of area. The public house has to be approached through its vast car park; the gardens this asphalt replaced are commemorated inside in photographs which hang between advertisements of the humorous variety. It is my custom to take a cheese sandwich and a glass of cider; I do not feel I can risk more. The barmaid, cutting ham or beef with that appearance of relish which explains her success, forever wipes her hand on her apron, while the pimply boy dips dirty glasses in dirty water. The talk is of crowded roads and foreign holidays. A chattering churl on a barstool asserts that the aeroplane is 'no way for a gentleman to travel'; he is impressed by what he has said; he says it again. Everyone does everything too assertively or too noisily; glasses are banged down too hard, knives screech too often on plates, the talk is too loud, the laughter too hearty, the clothes too vulgar. I do not believe in the chum-miness; I do not believe that there is communication be-tween these people any more than I believe in the hilarity of the advertisements by which they are surrounded: those irritating drawings in which the mouths of funny men are too wide open, to denote humorous speech, those beer-mats whose circular legends I know by heart. *Who comes here? A Grenadier. What does he want? A pot of beer.* And the other, attributed to Charles Dickens: *Oh, I'm slain! I'd give a pot of beer to live again.*

It is a relief to get back from this to the hotel. Here at

35

least there is decorum and calm; no one insists on an impossible communication. The management is unobtrusive but vigilant. If nothing pleases the eye, everything works; everything has that gloss and warmth which comes from daily use and daily cleaning. Impersonality is softened by little touches, such as the fresh flowers on my table in the dining-room. This room is like a great hall. It is panelled and dark; it has a large decorative fireplace with a high mantelpiece. We dine below oil portraits of our lord and lady. The originals eat with us, separated not by the height of their table but, in this technological age, by a sliding partition of plate glass which permits the same mutual inspection and maintains the same respectful distance. We do not think this distinction is unsuitable; we are grateful for what they provide and we look to them for a continuation of order.

For here is order of a sort. But it is not mine. It goes beyond my dream. In a city already simplified to individual cells this order is a further simplification. It is rooted in nothing; it links to nothing. We talk of escaping to the simple life. But we do not mean what we say. It is from simplification such as this that we wish to escape, to return to a more elemental complexity.

But observe the contradictions in that dream of the run-down cocoa estate. It was a dream of the past, and it came at a time when, by creating drama and insecurity, we had destroyed the past. The Agricultural Society and the Chamber of Commerce were not our friends. The commonest type of political ambition is the desire for eviction and succession. But the order to which the colonial politician succeeds is not his order. It is something he is compelled to destroy; destruction comes with his emergence and is a condition of his power. So the legitimate desire for succession is neutralized; and drama ensues. I feared drama. My dream of the cocoa estate was not the dream of eviction; and it was more than a dream of order. It was a yearning, from the peak of power, for withdrawal; it was a wistful desire to undo. Scarcely the politician's drive. But then I never was

36

a politician. I never had the frenzy, the sense of mission, the necessary hurt.

Politicians are people who truly make something out of nothing. They have few concrete gifts to offer. They are not engineers or artists or makers. They are manipulators; they offer themselves as manipulators. Having no gifts to offer, they seldom know what they seek. They might say they seek power. But their definition of power is vague and unreliable. Is power the chauffeured limousine with fine white linen on the seats, the men from the Special Branch outside the gates, the skilled and deferential servants? But this is only indulgence, which might be purchased by anyone at any time in a first-class hotel. Is it the power to bully or humiliate or take revenge? But this is the briefest sort of power; it goes as quickly as it comes; and the true politician is by his nature a man who wishes to play the game all his life. The politician is more than a man with a cause, even when this cause is no more than self-advancement. He is driven by some little hurt, some little incompleteness. He is seeking to exercise some skill which even to him is never as concrete as the skill of the engineer; of the true nature of this skill he is not aware until he begins to exercise it. How often we find those who after years of struggle and manipulation come close to the position they crave, sometimes indeed achieving it, and then are failures. They do not deserve pity, for among the aspirants to power they are complete men; it will be found that they have sought and achieved fulfilment elsewhere; it takes a world war to rescue a Churchill from political failure. Whereas the true politician finds his skill and his completeness only in success. His gifts suddenly come to him. He who in other days was mean, intemperate and infirm now reveals unsuspected qualities of generosity, moderation and swift brutality. Power alone proves the politician; it is ingenuous to express surprise at an unexpected failure or an unexpected flowering.

But more often we see the true politician in decay. The gifts, unexpressed, the skills, undiscovered, turn sour within him; and he who began as wise and generous and fighting for the good cause turns out to be weak and vacillating. He abandons his principles; with every defeat he becomes more desperate; he loses his sense of timing, changing too early or too late; he even loses a sense of dignity. He turns to drink or to fine food or to women coarse or superfine; he becomes a buffoon, contemptible even to himself, except in the still hours of the late evening, when he has no audience save himself and his wife who, though embittered, remains loyal because she alone knows the true man. And through everything he never gives up. Here is your leader. Here is your true politician, the man with the nebulous skill. Offer him power. It will revive him; it will restore the man he once was.

I do not seek to describe myself. For me politics remained little more than a game, a heightening of life, an extension of the celebratory mood in which I returned to my island. Someone better equipped, someone who had paid more attention to the sources of power and had more of the instincts, would have survived. Celebration: after London this was what I wished to maintain. Power came easily; it took me by surprise. It filled me with a degree of tremulousness which more than anything else unfitted me for the position I found myself called upon to hold. I remember so well – how far away that emotion seems now, though I know that, given power again, it will come back – I remember so well the pity I felt for people of all conditions. All were so far below me; and my inexplicable luck made me fearful.

At my secretary's slightest summons the barber would leave his little shop and come running to my house. His joy in this house exceeded my own. I had built it a few years before, when my marriage was breaking up; it was modelled on the house of the Vetii in Pompeii, with a swimming-pool replacing the *impluvium*. The happy barber would run his hands through my hair and say, 'Your hair very soft, sir. What you use? Something special?' It was the sort of thing Lieni might have said; and I would grieve for the man. It was naturally fine hair, it was true, and Lord Stockwell himself complimented me on it at our first meeting: 'You'll never grow bald, that's for sure.' But that was at an awkward moment; it was during our little nationalization crisis,

38

and Stockwell's estates were at issue. By this sentence Lord Stockwell not only removed tension but also, as I could not help noticing with admiration, dismissed his own immense, clumsy height, from which he could no doubt see little more of me than my hair. For Lord Stockwell there was an excuse, and for Lieni. But not for the lowly barber; and I thought, 'How can this man endure? How, running his hands daily through the hair of other people, can he bear to keep on?' And not only the barber and the ridiculous shoeshine men, applying themselves with vigour and a curious feminine pleasure to the removal of the last speck of dust and dirt from my shoes, and inviting me to commend their work. How could the newspaper men endure, 'meeting me at the airport' – words which occurred, deliciously, in their printed reports? They ran so eagerly to meet me, as full of the importance of their jobs as the girl apprentice at the hairdresser's. They had lost their sense of their place in the scheme of things. How did they preserve their self-esteem?

To everyone I sought, secretly, and from the height of my power, to transmit my sympathy and above all my admiration for a courage which I thought I could never myself have. So that in the very midst of power I came upon a centre of stillness within myself, a centre of detachment, which my behaviour in no way revealed; for the confident, flippant dandy that was my character in Mr Shylock's house was the character I retained and promoted, almost without design now, as soon as I spoke. To encounters with people of all conditions I gave much; they exhausted me quickly; the effort of sympathy was so great. And yet, when the time came, I was accused of arrogance and aloofness.

I remember one interview. It was at the time our bauxite royalties were about to be renegotiated. This was a personal triumph and I was, as the saying is, the man of the hour. It was with the eye of pure compassion that, while we spoke, I studied the reporter's clothes, his shining tie, his young face fussy and tired with worry, his uncertain voice attempting bluntness, his slender weak hands. At the end, putting away his notebook, he became momentarily abstracted, a man with problems of his own. I thought he was going to

39

speak about himself. I had found this to be the pressing need of those whose business it was merely to report the views of others; I never discouraged it. How startling it was, then, when without malice and as though seeking personal solace, he had asked: 'And, sir, if all this were to come to an end tomorrow, what would you do?' It was my technique instantly to begin a reply to any question. But now I hesitated. So many absurd pictures came to me. Relief: this was my first reaction, and it was a reaction to the man in front of me. Not in any unkind way, for with the word there came a picture of myself in some forest clearing, dressed as a knight, dressed as a penitent, in hermit's rags, approaching a shrine on my knees, weeping, performing a private penance for the man in front of me, for myself, for all men, for whom in the end nothing could be done. Relief, solitude; penance, peace. Words and pictures came confusedly together. For a tremulous instant I felt a suffusing joy: to suffer for all men. Do not misunderstand; do not accuse me of presuming. Understand only that centre of stillness, that withdrawal, that compassion which was really fear. Understand my unsuitability for the role I had created for myself, as politician, as dandy, as celebrant. But it was in this role that, recovering quickly, I replied. Why, I said, I would return to my business affairs and the life I had led before, in the days of my marriage; it had been a pleasant enough life.

And I spoke sincerely. As though, in the drama we had created, it was possible simply to step down and return to the order of the past! As though I hadn't seen the point of the reporter's question! What made the reporter ask, I wonder. Some personal insecurity, perhaps; the weak man's wish to tease. Whatever it was, he has had his revenge. The doers come and go, the recorders go on. And my reporter now doubtless runs to interview others, while for my own views the world cares not at all. Be kind to those you meet on the way up, runs the saying; for they are the very people you are going to meet on the way down. Frivolous; and very safe; and very smug. The tragedy of power like mine is that there is no way down. There can only be extinction. Dust to dust; rags to rags; fear to fear.

4

In the active period of my life, which I have described as a period in parenthesis, marriage was an episode; and it was the purest accident that I should have entered politics almost as soon as this marriage came to an end. Cause and effect, it seemed to many; but the obvious and plausible is often wrong. At the time my marriage and the circumstances of its break-up won me much sympathy; later these very things were to win me much abuse. It seemed a textbook example of the ill-advised mixed marriage. I was seen as the victim, the exploited, offering comfort and status to a woman who was denied these things in her own country. There is something in this, but it is not the whole story. I never thought of myself as the victim, and even now all I have against Sandra is her name which, whether pronounced with a short or long first vowel, never ceases to jar on me. Hostile comment would have it that, for reasons of glamour, I pursued her. Sympathetic comment makes her the pursuer. And in fact marriage was her idea.

It was during the time of breakdown and mental distress when, as I have said, I travelled about England and the Continent with no purpose, not even pleasure. After each of these journeys I came back more exhausted than before, more oppressed by a feeling of waste and helplessness; and it was in such a mood that one afternoon in the last week of the vacation, having nothing to do, I drifted into the School and, discovering nothing to do there either, stood in front of the notice-board and dully read the last notices of the previous term. Those student associations! Playing at being students, playing at being questioning and iconoclastic, playing at being young and licensed, playing at being in preparation for the world! The dishonesty of the young! I belonged to none of their associations. The confession, I know, will surprise those who try to link my subsequent career with my membership of this celebrated School. Its reputation, I have since seen, lay especially heavily on those who were to sink without a trace into their respective societies.

I read the badly typewritten notice of something called the Turkish League or Turkish Association: the Annual General Meeting was being indefinitely and apparently quite arbitrarily postponed. Below, scrawled right across the sheet in ink of a vivid blue, was *PS Rigret Inconvinience!* and under this exclamation was a flamboyant, extensive signature. The exuberant, defaulting Turk! I had reason to remember him, for it was while I was idly examining his notice for further absurdities that I was aware of Sandra coming down the corridor towards me. We exchanged glances but for some reason did not speak. She came and stood directly beside me. She looked at the Turk's notice and pretended to be as absorbed in it as I was. Waiting to be greeted, she did not herself speak. It was I, after some seconds, who broke the silence.

She seemed to be in a particularly bad temper. Perhaps it was exaggerated for my benefit; I believe I was the only person outside her family who noted and assessed her moods. In response to my question about the holidays she mentioned the serial quarrel with her father. The latest instalment had occurred only that morning; it had kept her seething and had at last driven her out of the house in the afternoon. 'A father,' she had said to me at our first meeting, 'is one of nature's handicaps.' She had also said on that occasion that she wanted to be either a nun or a king's mistress. I had been impressed by this and made to feel not a little inadequate; but awe had been converted into sympathy and something like affection when I came across the sentence in one of Bernard Shaw's plays. To a similar source I attributed her remark about fathers, though I had never been able to trace it. She had another remark for me now, as we stood in front of the Turkish notice. 'Do you know what I said to him this morning? I told him he was arguing like a crab. Do you like that? Arguing like a crab.' I said I liked it. She said, turning away from the board, 'I can't stand the big-and-busy public-lavatory smell of this damned place.' I said I had been told it had something to do with the type of disinfectant used. She asked me to give her tea. Snappy, inconsequential: the way she liked her lines; and I had acknowledged the two remarks she had made. But it did not dispel her gloomy irritation. We left the School and walked out into the Aldwych and down to Bush House, to the canteen of the British Broadcasting Corporation's European Services. I had used this canteen so often that no one now stopped me.

Sandra, I can see, will not be everyone's idea of a beauty; few women are. But she overwhelmed me then; and she would overwhelm me now, I know: her looks were of the sort that improves with the strength and definition of maturity. She was tall; her bony face was longish and I liked the suggestion of thrust in her chin and lower lip. I liked her narrow forehead and her slightly ill-humoured eyes – perhaps she needed glasses. And there was a coarseness about her skin which enchanted me. I liked a quality of graining in the skin; it was to me a sign of a subtle sensuality. There was firmness and precision in her movements, and always a slight bite to her speech. Women were continually provoked by her manner, which gave the impression of irony even when none was intended. She affected a very old and grubby khaki-coloured macintosh, which it was always a pleasure to help off, for below it, and always as a surprise, were soft, cool colours, and a body fresh and scrupulously cared for. Not even the macintosh could hide the fullness of her breasts, to which I had for some little time been admitted. They were not the self-supporting cut apples of the austere French ideal; but breasts curving and rounded with a weight just threatening pendent excess, which the viewer, recognizing the inadequacy and indeed crudity of the cupping gesture, instinctively stretches out a hand to support; breasts which in their free state alter their shape and contour with every shift in the posture of their possessor; breasts which in the end madden the viewer because, faced with such completeness of beauty, he does not know what to do. No one loved her breasts more than Sandra herself. She caressed them in moments of abstraction; and indeed it was this ritualistic, almost Pharaonic,

43

attitude – right hand supporting and caressing left breast, left hand supporting right – which had first brought her to my startled if delighted attention in the dreary library one morning and had encouraged me to pen an invitation to coffee on one of the library's borrowing slips and slide it towards her across the polished table that we shared. Pure joy it was later, at the assisted uncovering, to discover that she painted the nipples of her breasts. So absurd, so pathetic, so winning. I kissed, caressed, stroked with hand and cheek; inadequate speech was dragged out of me. 'Lovely, lovely,' I said. And Sandra had replied, 'Thank you.' A cooling thing to hear, as I lay between her breasts; and head and hands for an instant went still. But it was a revealing reply, in its humourlessness and confidence. The adoration of none could equal her own; and even at that first encounter I could feel her own sense of self-violation. Self-possessed at one moment, she became frantic at another that the fumbling should go no farther.

Language is so important. Up to this time my relationships had been with women who knew little English and of whose language I frequently knew nothing. These affairs had been conducted in a type of pidgin; they were a strain; I could never assess the degree of complication we had arrived at after the sexual simplicities. Once this had been glamorous and had suited me; now it was like entering an imperfect world, some grotesque tunnel of love, where, as in a dream, at a critical moment one is denied the use of arms or legs and longs to cry out. With Sandra there was no such frustration; the mere fact of communication was a delight; to this extent I had changed. And for all the recurring checks that occurred in my rooms, our relationship developed. It was with surprise that I discovered that, though of the city, her position in it was like my own. She had no community, no group, and had rejected her family. She saw herself alone in the world and was determined to fight her way up. She hated the common – her own word – from which she nevertheless freely acknowledged herself to have sprung and about which she therefore claimed to speak with authority; no one knew 'them' as well as she. To the end she had a cruel eye for the common, and she passed on to me the word and the assessing skill. No family, two or three school friends, now scattered: it was easy to see how she felt imprisoned and fearful and how important it was to her to be free of the danger of that commonness which encircled her. The king's mistress! I saw the magnitude of her ambition and the matching difficulties of her struggle, and sympathized, not yet knowing the part I would soon be called upon to play in their resolution.

The war had also left its mark. No one was more sensitive to anything that savoured of the luxurious; no one had a greater capacity for creating occasions. A bottle of wine was an occasion, a meal in a restaurant, a seat in the dress circle. She took nothing for granted. Was I exploited? I never misunderstood her interest; but no one offered himself more readily. She was rapacious. It was in her social ambitions, in her diligent reading of approved contemporary authors and her pursuit of culture, for which at home she willingly – perhaps even gratuitously – carried the cross of being considered odd; it was in her walk, in the bite of her speech, even in the way she ate food which she considered expensive; in all these things, not least in the adoration of her body, there was a consuming self-love. But how could I resist her quick delight? Her very rapaciousness attracted me. To me, drifting about the big city that had reduced me to futility, she was all that was positive. She showed how much could be extracted so easily from the city; she showed how easy occasions were. Her delight strengthened me; often, in public, I pretended to be seeing her for the first time: those close-set, myopic, impatient eyes, that jutting lower lip. In those days in London, when a decision had to be made every morning to dress, to go through the day, when on numberless nights I could go to sleep only with the consoling thought of the Luger at my head or the thought of retreat on the following day, the degree and the School abandoned, in those days at the darkest moments I was strengthened by the thought of Sandra. I would say, 'I am seeing her tomorrow. Let me delay decision and last until then.' And the day would come; and we would create, out of the drabness that surrounded us both, an occasion. It was the perfect basis for a relationship.

She was at her lowest that afternoon as we walked down into the basement canteen for tea, her grubby macintosh belted around her waist. The last few weeks at home had been difficult; she had had to put up with a good deal of mockery. She had failed a qualifying examination for the second time. That was the end of her government grant, the end of the School. No degree for her now; no escape by that route. And as we sat in the low, airless basement she outlined a life so destitute of glamour or point, a life which now, with the failed examination, neither imprecise ambition nor the pursuit of culture could enhance, that my own disturbance was sharpened. She reflected my own mood exactly. Her despair worked on me; we acted and reacted on one another, there in the canteen of a radio service which, when picked up in remote countries, was the very voice of metropolitan authority and romance, bringing to mind images, from the cinema and magazines, of canyons of concrete, brick and glass, motorcars in streams, lines of lights, busyness, crowded theatre foyers, the world where everything was possible; there now, at the heart of that metropolis, we sat, at a plastic-topped table, before thick cups of cooling tea and plates with yellow crumbs, each drawing out the frenzy from the other. What awaited her? The secretarial course, the librarian's course, the common employer. She went on, railing at her society, bitter at her lack of protection and patrons within it. A job in the bank; the typing pool; the Woolworth's counter. She was working herself up to a pitch of hysteria. Tears of anger came to her eyes. Then suddenly, fixing those moist eyes on me, she said, almost ordered, with a look of total hatred: 'Why don't you propose, you *fool*?'

I have gone over this moment more than once in my mind; I do not think my recollection of it is wrong. The tone of Sandra's request, so odd considering its nature, seems to me to have come from a number of causes. The idea, I feel, had occurred to her on the spur of the moment, the one clear flash in dark panic; she was impatient with herself for not having thought of it before, impatient because she wished to see it instantly realized; and impatient because she had broken down and shown weakness. And I suppose that if the idea had been put to me as a plea rather than as an order, if there had been the slightest suggestion that it issued from uncertainty rather than firmness and lucidity, I might have reacted otherwise. But, and always my mood must be borne in mind, I had such confidence in her rapaciousness, such confidence in her as someone who could come to no harm – a superstitious reliance on her, which was part of the strength I drew from her – that in that moment it seemed to me that to attach myself to her was to acquire that protection which she offered, to share some of her quality of being marked, a quality which once was mine but which I had lost. So I did as she asked; and even added, strange to think of it now, an apology for not having done so before. Her anger vanished; just for an instant she looked a little abashed and apprehensive. We sat silent in the clattering canteen. And it was a second or two before, for the first time since our talk had begun, I thought of her painted breasts.

There were moments of stillness and awe later, of course. But Sandra gave me little time. Just two days later she moved in with me, to the delight of old Mrs Ellis, my landlady, whom by a display of exaggerated manners I had completely under my thumb. To Mrs Ellis, I discovered, Sandra had represented us as already married; and to Mrs Ellis, as to many others later, this marriage contained the elements of dark and stirring romance. Some little concern for my sake Mrs Ellis showed, however; she expressed the hope, with tears in her eyes, as she gave me a china dog, her wedding present, that I had made the right choice. The words struck me as odd in the circumstances. Sandra, on the other hand, spoke of the difficulties with her father, who argued like a crab; and for an instant, if only she knew, I was totally on his side. Apparently he too had been told that we were already married. I objected, but not as forthrightly as I might have done, contenting myself with wondering why, since nothing had happened as yet, she had told him any-

47

thing at all. Even at that late stage I was still trying, feebly, to play for time. She said, 'I haven't got the patience either to give him a blow-by-blow account or to lie to him.' This won me back; she had the gift of the phrase. She said that we would soon 'regularize the position' so far as Mrs Ellis was concerned. This was another aspect of her speech. She spoke of workmen as 'operatives'; she often linked unconnected sentences with 'with the net result that . . .'; my two-roomed flat became our 'establishment', for which there had to be 'catering'. Perhaps it was the influence of the School.

So now, in the shiny brown wardrobe in my bedroom, there appeared the grubby macintosh; and on satiny pink and blue hangers the dresses and blouses of soft cool colours which once it had taken away my breath to behold. The moment seemed to me profoundly tragic. Sandra, recognizing my mood, offered me her painted breasts later that evening. Where before she had been endlessly passive, accepting all strokings and kissings as part of a rightful homage, now she made an effort to take the lead. She laid me on my back and pressed her breasts on my chest, my belly, my groin. She hung over me and, holding her breasts, traced lines on me with her nipples; she brushed her breasts over me, and skin felt tickling smooth. In all this there was a good deal of determination and dutifulness; I was grateful nonetheless. She also did certain things which puzzled me. She painted my own nipples; then she bit them, really hard; then she held them with her nails as though they were things to be severed. Even through the pain – killing passion, I regret to say: my first concern afterwards to see whether she had in fact wounded me and to check that what looked like lipstick, was not really blood – even through this I thought I could sense the experimental, assessing nature of these attentions and I put them down to some too hastily consulted handbook of sex, as I had once attributed all her *mots* to Bernard Shaw. I wished neither to hurt her pride nor to turn her away from these studies. Accordingly I assumed naturalness and behaved as one to whom these attentions were not novel. I suppressed the urge to cry out and slap her hand away. Eventually – for me it was a matter of urgency, as will be understood – we achieved success of a sort. She appeared tired but pleased.

It has since occurred to me that the art of physical love is in the keeping of women, and depends to a considerable extent on the position of women in society. As this position improves, so the art of love declines. Woman becomes neither server nor served; and with this emancipation prudery, the fear of the erotic, the fear of fear, has to be restated. The absurd view is promoted that sex is neither vice nor mystery. So we arrive at slot-machine or peasant-sex; and the praise of profane love gives way to the farm-yard lyricism about pregnancies and lyings-in. But enough of this. It was my intention to say no more than that, in this matter of sex, Sandra and myself were well matched; and to register my wonder at the frequency with which, in our imperfect world, through every type of accident and arbitrary decision, like noses out like.

We were married at the Willesden registry office. We travelled there on a number eight bus with our two witnesses, fellow students. The details of the absurd ceremony are too well known to be recounted here. The registrar, I remember, was concerned about Sandra. He warned her that in certain countries women could be divorced just like that; with his own hand he wrote out the address of an association which offered information and protection to British women overseas. To me he offered neither advice nor consolation – his manner, in fact, was one of controlled reproof; and in that largish room, full of empty folding chairs, the awful deed was done. Now I was truly appalled. I wished to get away at once, to reflect, to be alone again. But I was detained by one of our witnesses: the poet, philosopher, politician, now, as I suspected, sunk without trace in the society he was so mad to master, and even then, with his tweed jacket and the beard he was beginning to grow, getting near to the schoolmaster he has no doubt become. 'Well done, old boy. I say, I know it's a hard thing to put to a chap on his wedding day. But you couldn't advance me a fiver?' I thought that both his language and the sum he had mentioned had come to him from a literary source and that both exceeded his requirements. I gave him ten shillings. I cut short his delighted acknowledgements and, telling Sandra in a garbled, wild way that I had something to do in the centre, ran after a number eight bus, caught it and allowed myself to be taken in a state of near stupefaction to Holborn where, habit reasserting itself, I got off and went into a public house, already, though only a husband of some minutes, feeling like the cartoon man who knows that the storm will presently break over his head for some dereliction of marital duty.

The dark romance of a mixed marriage! Think of me sitting in the Holborn bar, drinking Guinness for strength, holding an evening paper for the ordinariness it suggested – cheatingly, the greyhound edition, it being too early for the others – and being really very frightened. So at the time I thought of myself. I stood away from the pensive figure and considered him and his recent, terrible adventure. *Quantum mutatus ab illo!* The words ran through my head until they were meaningless, until they became the emotion of loss and sadness and sweetness and apprehension. So nemesis came to the dandy, the creation of London, the haunter of British Council halls, art galleries and excursion trains. *Quantum mutatus ab illo!*

I have spoken of the mood of celebration with which I left London and which for the next ten years I sought to maintain, never ceasing to savour each day the pleasure of the whole mind. I have also hinted at the uneasiness with which on the morning of arrival I saw through each porthole the blue, green and gold of the tropical island. So pure and fresh! And I knew it to be, horribly, man-made; to be exhausted, fradulent, cruel and, above all, not mine. Yet I pretended that it was, and stood against the rail with the camera-clicking visitors who threw pennies into the clear water and watched the Negro boys dive for them, the pink soles of their feet like luminous fins. The boys also dived for oranges, apples, anything thrown into the water. The grey-green bay was still and in shadow; far away, in the early morning haze, fishing boats were going tinily about their tasks. Below us the diving boys rocked on their rafts; they giggled and laughed, all teeth; water glinted in beads on their seemingly dry heads; they invited us to throw more things for them to retrieve. Someone threw a rotten orange; the boys dived. It struck me as intolerable; it was one of the things I had stopped later. Not for long, needless to say. Distress can be shared only up to a point, to go beyond that point is to presume. In the recent tourist publicity for Isabella I see that the diving boys are again presented as a feature.

I linger now on this moment of arrival more than I did at the time. This return so soon to a landscape which I thought I had put out of my life for good was a failure and a humiliation. Yet this, together with all my unease, I buried away. I am no great believer in justice, but I think there is a moral balance in all human events; if only we look down deeply enough, we can spot the beginning of the misfortunes that eventually overtake us in just such a small suppression of the truth, in just such a tiny corruption. On that first morning I should have said, 'This tainted island is not for me. I decided years ago that this landscape was not mine. Let us move on. Let us stay on the ship and be taken somewhere else.'

In my own mind I have the excuse of the mood of celebration, of the failure so recent and damaging. Also, it might have been that as a result of my marriage to Sandra I had begun to surrender the direction of my life, not simply to her, but to events. So dishonesty linked to dishonesty, unease to unease: to have examined my reactions more closely would have meant making myself open again to that feeling of drift and helplessness, the nightmare I had combated on so many evenings by the thought of the Luger at my head. I suppose it is also the excuse I must put forward for my behaviour in the subsequent years. And to me it is strange that it is only now, as I write, that I see, like the sympathetic historian of a revolution who detects the seed of disaster in some minor and unregarded action, it is only now I see that all the activity of these years, existing as I have said in my own mind in parenthesis, represented a type of withdrawal, and was part of the injury inflicted on me by the too solid three-dimensional city in which I could never feel myself as anything but spectral, disintegrating, pointless, fluid. The city made by man but passed out of his control: breakdown the negative reaction, activity the positive: opposite but equal aspects of an accommodation to a sense of place which, like memory, when grown acute, becomes a source of pain.

But for the moment I trusted to Sandra's luck. It was soon tested. As we drew nearer the docks the island of the travel poster vanished. Hills, palms and fishing boats in the morning grey gave way to the international paraphernalia of a dockside; tall warehouses bounded and shadowed our view of cranes, asphalt and a small old locomotive. Here and there a near-naked Negro in spectacularly ragged khaki shorts lounged in a parked lorry. Thoroughly, tropically futile he might have seemed to a sight-hungry visitor; but I knew that his garments were his so-called working clothes, that he was a docker, and that he belonged to a particularly cantankerous trade union whose go-slows and general wilful inefficiency had been the subject of innumerable fruitless inquiries.

As yet, though, it was a scene of peace: cranes at rest, the violent dockers in attitudes of repose, everything awaiting the heat and dust of the rapidly approaching working day. But then, even before that came, there rose the most fearful clamour.

I hadn't, I must confess, informed my mother of my marriage; nervousness had always been converted into fatigue whenever I sat down to write that letter. Sandra believed that my mother knew; and the mutual dismay of the two women – precipitated by my easy remark to Sandra: 'Oh, look, there's my mother' – might easily be imagined. Yet not easily: we are a melodramatic race and do not let pass occasions for public display. Picture, then, Sandra in her carefully chosen disembarkation outfit coming face to face with a conventionally attired Hindu widow. Picture her mistaking the raised arms and the first wail for a ritual of welcome and, out of a determination to meet strange and ancient customs half-way, concealing whatever surprise and bewilderment she might have felt; then, with the wail broken only to be heightened, the gestures of distress converted explicitly into gestures of rejection, realizing the nature of her reception, hesitating in her already tentative approach to the frenzied figure of my mother, and finally standing still, the centre now of a scene which was beginning to draw a fair audience of dockworkers roused from their languor, passengers, visitors, officials, the crews of ships of various nations.

I was very calm myself. I paid no attention to my mother's interjections that I had killed her and went about the business of looking after luggage, nodding to customs officials whom I recognized, exchanging words with the newspaper reporters who interviewed every returning student. Poor old Eden, whom I had known at Isabella Imperial College, was the *Inquirer*'s man. (He played fair: his story stated simply that my wife and I had been met at the docks by my mother.) I was calm because I felt that the situation was not important. The suspicion – later confirmed – had come early to me that with the steady traffic between London and Isabella my mother had some idea of my marriage and had prepared for the scene she was now so successfully making. It was a grand scene, perhaps the grandest that had been granted her, and was recompense of a sort for the ridicule I had exposed her to, particularly from those families with marriageable daughters by whom, during my absence, she must have been courted. I say it myself, but I was a catch! Not only one of the heirs to the Bella Bella Bottling Works fortune but also – unlike the common run of our business people – educated, degreed, travelled. In the circumstances I had given my mother a blow. But I also knew that silence and passivity on her part would have been the true danger signs. They would have betokened a lingering rebuke; and this might have taken the form of suicide by slow, secret starvation. This dockside scene, on the other hand, was pure self-indulgence; it augured well.

Complicated: Sandra could not have been expected to make my swift assessment, nor could it be transmitted to her in a few whispered words. She came and stood next to the gathered luggage. She looked quite bad-tempered, and I thought that this meant she was in control of herself and the situation; I expected nothing less of her. I told her that I thought it would be unwise if we went to my mother's house. She said snappishly, in university jargon, 'That's an interesting approach to the subject. You don't happen to have such a thing as a hotel on this damned island?' I misinterpreted her mood; I thought she was being decisive. It was only later, when regret was valueless, that I saw that the greater callousness of my placidity that day was to Sandra rather than my mother. I relied on her forthrightness and what I thought was her vision; but to her this reliance must have seemed like abandonment at a moment when she was most insecure. I don't think she ever forgave me or the island. Yet I acted from the finest feelings towards her! I remember with what affection I contemplated her as, exhausted by more than the warmth of our Isabella afternoon, she lay stretched out on the bed in the hotel room, in her clean white brassiere and chaste white cotton petticoat, below the electric ceiling fan. She wore the cheap, white-rimmed and I believe damaging sunglasses she had bought in the Azores. She smoked a cigarette, smoking in the factory-girl way, lips bunched wetly over the cigarette set in the centre of her mouth, inhaling deeply as though drawing urgently needed nourishment. It was a mannerism she had picked up in a government agricultural camp in Dorset where she had spent a month and where she had learned to smoke; it was a mannerism that attracted me greatly. The smoke eddied and thinned in the draught from the fan. I was exhausted myself, on the verge of self-pity; and considering the comic, intense, sunglassed figure on the bed, her skin just beginning to be moist, I thought that she was courageous to have come so far to a life of which she knew nothing. Until this journey she had never travelled or stayed in a hotel; and I felt that, catch though I might have been on the island of Isabella, I could not have provided better for a return to the island than by marriage to Sandra.

About a fortnight later – a fortnight, I imagine, of scenes in various drawing-rooms up and down the island – the expected meeting with my mother was arranged through my married sisters. We all had tea at a chipped metal table in the hot, scantily shaded patio of the hotel, brown and green-brown almond leaves at our feet, and decided on a reconciliation. But the damage was done. Just as Sandra exaggerated the importance of the dockside scene, so now she exaggerated her victory. I thought it made her character more pronounced still; it foreshadowed all that was to come.

5

The sanctions my mother had invoked on the docks were not important. We were a haphazard, disordered and mixed society in which there could be nothing like damaging exclusion; and before the end of that first fortnight we had found ourselves attached to the neutral, fluid group which was to remain ours for the next five or six years. The men were professional, young, mainly Indian, with a couple of local whites and coloured; they had all studied abroad and married abroad; on Isabella they were linked less by their background and professional standing than by their expatriate and fantastically cosmopolitan wives or girl friends. Americans, singly and in pairs, were an added element. It was a group to whom the island was a setting; its activities and interests were no more than they seemed. There were no complicating loyalties or depths; for everyone the past had been cut away. In that fortnight we got to know as much about the group as there was to know; all that followed was repetition and ageing. But at the beginning we were dazzled. We had come to the island expecting the meanness and constriction of island life; we were dazzled, as by the sunlight itself, by the freedom which everyone who welcomed us proclaimed by his behaviour. The clothes! So light, so fresh, so prodigally changed! We were dazzled to be among the rich, to be considered of their number; and to get, from this, the conviction that in such a setting a comparable wealth would soon be ours as well. Austerity and prudence were forgotten. In that fortnight we spent! We gave as much as we received. We consumed quantities of champagne and caviar. It was part of the simplicity of our group; we loved champagne and caviar for the sake of the words alone. And after the anguish of London, after the mean rooms, the shut door, the tight window, the tarnished ceiling, the over-used curtains, after the rigged shilling-in-the-slot gas and electric meters, the dreary journeys through terraces of brick, the life reduced to insipidity, I felt revived. And even before the fortnight was out Sandra could be heard disdaining demisec and expressing a preference for Mercier above all others. The splendid girl! Sprung so sincerely from her commonness! It was our happiest fortnight; she was at her most avid and most appreciative. We celebrated our unexpected freedom; we celebrated the island and our knowledge, already growing ambiguous, of the world beyond; we celebrated our cosmopolitanism, which had more meaning here than it ever had in the halls of the British Council.

Celebration; and within it a great placidity. Once, longing for the world, I had wished to say good-bye to the island for good. Now, at a picnic on the hot sand of a beach reticulated with succulent-looking green vines on which grew purple flowers, or at a barbecue around an illuminated swimming-pool, it was possible without fear or longing or the feeling of being denied the world to draw out from one of our group her adolescent secret of cycle rides along a dirt road to the red hills outside her town, in a state west of the Mississippi, to see the sun set; to get from another a picture, in grey and white, of snow and Germans in Prague; and from yet another an English Midland landscape at dusk, a walk among moon daisies on the bank of a stream, an endless summer walk beside water, into a night scene, with swans; these, on the island, becoming pictures of a world now totally comprehended, of which I had ceased to feel I could form part and from which we had all managed to withdraw. I loved to contemplate this fragmented world that we had put together again; and I did so with the feeling of my own imminent extinction. I belonged to a small community which

in this part of the world was doomed. We were an intermediate race, the genes passive, capable of disappearing in
two generations into any of the three races of men, with perhaps only a shape of eye or flexibility of slender wrist to
speak of our intrusion. My mother's sanctions were a pretence, no doubt; but they were also an act of piety towards
the past, towards ancient unknown wanderings in another
continent. It was a piety I shared. But what release to be the
last of one's line! Consider this as an underlying mood,
occasionally coming to the surface in an alcoholic haze when
the music from bands or record-players grown distant, I
considered our group as though for the first time, and Sandra
and myself within it. It was a mood never examined beyond
this point, never revealed. It was the mood of my placidity,
the mood of my new life of activity. Within me, with that
very placidity, with that departure from London and that
total acceptance of a new, ready-made way of life, I felt that
I had changed. I recognized that the change was involun-
tary, so that at last my 'character' became not what others
took it to be but something personal and ordained. This
placidity, at the heart of celebration, I felt to be my strength;
I visualized it as existing within a walled, impregnable field.
I lived neutrally; activity was real, but it was all on the surface; I felt I would never allow myself to be damaged again.

They would say later that I 'worked hard and played
hard'. These phrases that tabulate! I had no profession and
no job. I needed money. I studied my resources and looked
around for a way. On an island where, apart from the pro-
fessions and agriculture, money could be made only through
commission agencies, I must have appeared a little too coldly
adventurous. But at least the School cannot say that the
years I spent in it were wasted. A small part of the Bella
Bella money had come to me; within five years that part had
outgrown the whole. I was one of those who foresaw the
postwar spread of cities, the destruction of the open spaces
between settlements; and on Isabella I was the first. I cannot
claim much credit. What I did was obvious, considering my
resources. I had inherited a 120-acre block of wasteland just

outside the city. It was part of a blighted citrus plantation which had been allowed to go derelict during the depression; had been sold to a racing man who had tried unsuccessfully to breed racehorses on it; and had then been bought by my grandfather for no other reason than that it was land and going cheap. It brought him no money; I doubt whether it paid the wages of the watchman-overseer and the upkeep of his mule. From time to time on a Sunday my grandfather would go and pick a few avocadoes and grapefruit, which he would pretend he was getting free. It was not much of a thing to inherit. A derelict citrus plantation is one of the slums of tropical nature. The soil is not rich; the barks of the trees are mildewed and mossy; the grey branches are thin and brittle-looking and almost bare; the leaves are yellow; and the fruit rots before it ripens, hanging soft and blanched like disease, in a pestilential smell. When it came to me my first thought was to sell. But even in 1945 I could find no buyers.

The feeling still existed, aided no doubt by a poor transport system which had grown even worse during the war, that town was town, and country country; our city, too, had remained the same for so long that we had definite ideas, almost medieval and superstitious, about its limits. The last telegraph pole within what was considered the city was shaggy with posters; the one just two hundred yards away – in the country – was quite bare.

This was the land which I now thought to develop. It was already to a large extent attractively landscaped, with dips and knolls; we were close enough to the city for water and electricity to be available. I divided the land into one hundred and fifty half-acre plots; built roads, laid down services; and offered the plots for sale: $2,000 a plot, a 25-year lease, the ground rent $500 a year. I deal, it must be remembered, in Isabella dollars, five of which at that time were worth three United States dollars. They were not excessive terms. Our city had been built on short leases and even in an unsavoury area you could pay five dollars a month ground rent for half-a-lot, one-sixteenth of an acre. My terms in fact were more than reasonable; my only difficult condition was that every house had to be approved by me and should cost not less than $15,000. Nothing nowadays, when teachers and civil servants buy houses for $20,000; but in the early fifties in Isabella it was accounted a great deal; and for Kripalville – such was the name I gave the development, speedily corrupted to Crippleville, which had its attractions – the residents selected themselves. The scheme required nothing but method, precision and time. I worked at it calmly for two years. My conviction of success was total; in my own mind it never was an issue, not even when I owed the bank $150,000. I handled men as I handled money, by instinct. When it came to employing someone I ignored advice and references and was never swayed by racial considerations. I employed a man, foreman, clerk, labourer, only if I took an instant liking to him; and I gave no one a second chance. The man who lets you down once will let you down again; this is especially true of the man whose dereliction occurs after a long period of satisfactory service. The dereliction of such a man means that his attitude to his duties and to his employer has changed for good; it is the failure of a relationship, and blame one way or the other is useless; the man needs a new employer, a new relationship; and it is better to let him go at once.

And Crippleville worked. There is no drama to record. Within a year a hundred of the plots were taken. People bought but did not always build; and within two years plots were changing hands at five and six thousand dollars. It is simple and obvious now; it was simple and obvious to me then. But when the thing was done, so to say, I held my breath. Not at the risks I had taken, but at the neglect in my own mind of those very factors which made the scheme a success. The absence of mosquitoes was one such factor; two or three other developments, inspired by my own, ended as malarial slums. Then there were the hills around Crippleville. I had never thought of the hills except as landscape; but while other developments were swallowed up in further developments and all as a result speedily declined, the Crippleville hills limited the growth of the city in that direction and the development remained what it was. There was

59

the further point that the road from the city centre to Crippleville led through reasonably pleasant areas; to get to almost every other suburb you had to drive through slums. I considered these factors, I say, only when it was all done; and I held my breath. I suppose it was my single-mindedness and conviction which made it possible for me to get credit so easily; though it was also my good fortune to deal with an American bank anxious to establish itself on the island. I don't imagine any of the older British or Canadian banks would have been so accommodating; and I would not have blamed them.

A man, passionate for security, works and saves for a lifetime and is lucky at the end to have ten thousand pounds. Another, placid with the knowledge of his own imminent extinction, makes half a million dollars in five years. Neither ambition nor design comes into it, I feel. The gift falls on us. When we are in the middle of success nothing seems so easy or natural; in failure, nothing seems so unlikely. Observe how my luck, my intuition served me. With my initial scheme beginning to prosper, I took the precaution of buying up as much of the surrounding land as I could. I was gambling – though it did not seem so to me then – with all that I might have comfortably earned. This land I did not develop in the same way. I left many open spaces, divided the rest into small lots, eight to the acre, which I offered at proportionately lower prices: $500 a lot, ground rent $125 a year, a house for $5,000. Amazing value; the rush might be imagined. Simple again; yet I might so easily have tried to repeat myself, and that would have landed me in trouble, as it landed some of my imitators. Our middle class was small; the number of people willing or able to spend a good deal on a house was limited. As it was, the less luxurious new development reinforced the smartness of the old; and the smartness of the old gave glamour to the new. Each development supported the other; Crippleville acquired an integrity which was to last. It wasn't forethought; it was instinct, intuition.

So success led to success; and it seemed that I could just go on. It was unsettling, this rightness, this sureness over what always later turned out to have been a knife's edge. I did not feel responsible for what had befallen me; I always felt separate from what I did. Time alone has erased the feeling of unreality, violation and self-awe; it is only now that I feel I can truly lay claim to my achievement. I remember a trifling incident; it occurred almost at the beginning. The men were landscaping. In the afternoon the foreman told me that they had run into the stump and roots of a giant tree; three charges of dynamite had been necessary to get rid of it. He showed me the crater: a monstrous wound in the red earth. A giant tree, old perhaps when Columbus came: I would have liked to have seen it, I would have liked to have preserved it. I kept a piece of the wood on my desk, for the interest, as a reminder of violation, as a talisman. Success has its alarms! It was open to me to go on, I said. Soon I began to feel that I had to go on. Between this and inactivity, between the alarm of a world without end and a world without point, there was no middle way. And I was glad, to tell the truth, when the time for withdrawal came. It might seem perverse. But the gift which falls on us is also an intolerable burden. It sets us apart; it distorts us; it separates us from the self we recognize and to which we remain close. Every week in some part of the world a man, starting from scratch, makes a hundred thousand pounds, which he will soon lose. The tragedy and even the chagrin lie only in the eyes of the beholder. The gift is Mephistophelean. It is, however unconsciously, willed away. But even then the taint remains.

On the island, in our group, we were set apart. Jealousy or envy is not a sufficient explanation. See how disquieting we must have appeared on a Sunday morning at the house, say, of the girl from Latvia. Rum-punch time. I am in my dark glasses; the cuffs of my shirt, of Indian raw cotton, are buttoned at the wrist; I am leaning forward, the frosted rum-punch glass held in both hands. Sandra is sitting on a high black-draped settee – possibly a Latvian chest, now happily converted: the conversion of houses or articles of furniture constantly exercised the ingenuity of our women. Sandra is in white trousers. Her legs are apart and her hands, between her legs, are pressed on the edge of the settee; her very thin low-carat Willesden second-hand wedding ring is barely noticeable. Her feet are tapping in time to music from the gramophone; the heels of her gold Indian sandals flap loose setting off her finely-veined, well-shaped ankles, part of the slender elegance of her feet, whose shape and colour are further heightened by the red paint on the nails of her long undeformed toes and by the gold straps of the sandals. The stockings and shoes of London had concealed those feet. They were nervous without being too bony; they were feet one could caress; I frequently did. But I concentrate on the moment. I am looking down through my dark glasses – no pockets to put them in: the recurring inconvenience of tropical dress – at the double spread of the Society Page of the *Isabella Inquirer*, open on the terrazzo floor which is cool here in the shade but which, when it runs into the concrete of the swimming-pool terrace, is glaring white. Things are changing. The society pages are full of pictures of pop-eyed clerks in over-big double-breasted suits, arm in arm with their frilly brides. The people are on the march and the *Inquirer* has latterly become *your* paper. But for us, to whom it is a point of honour never to be mentioned, the society pages still hold a certain interest. Word has got around that the person responsible for the pages offers us a weekly joke: one special, distinguished hilarity: a dead-pan description it might be, to put it at its simplest, of the wedding festivities of a man 'employed by the City Council', this fact being mentioned last. This is the Sunday morning joke we look for and share. It is part of our self-cherishing, the necessary cruelty of a poor country; it is also part of our colonial simplicity. This, of course, is the judgement of today; there is no such self-assessment as my dark-glassed eyes go through each item, trying to spot the week's fiction. I am aware, besides, of Sandra's clean white trousers and those feet which I feel I would like to handle. There is pleasure and avidity in those feet; and I feel that Sandra is working especially hard with the Latvian. The Latvian is new to our group. She is red-haired, mouse-faced, sharp-nosed, and wears glasses; she is really a woman of appalling ugliness, to whom everyone has as a result to be especially nice. There is going to be trouble here soon. The Latvian will take these attentions at their face value and, gaining in confidence, will one day overreach herself; and then people won't be so nice any more. She already strains us by serving all wines from wicker baskets; her pleasure is matched by our embarrassment; this is something we don't know how to handle; example has proved fruitless, for that wicker basket delights her husband as well, a man of simple origins, still exulting in his own emancipation and, like so many people of this type, gadget-mad.

The others drift in. Pampered children, overacting the part, as I always feel when I hear their refined little voices, squeal about in the background; their special little rubber ducks and other inflated and totally unnecessary aids to swimming bob about in the pool. Their parents make their usual half-flippant remarks about Crippleville, which I barely acknowledge, not out of annoyance, but because it is my custom never to talk of business outside business hours. No principle is involved; it is merely part of my placidity, which in this respect Sandra, with her woman's fear of ever being too open about anything, has adopted. After this I begin to be aware of the attention of studied inattention. The talk is a bit too loud, too hearty, too aggressive or too defensive; these people are acting, overdoing domesticity and the small details, over-stressing the fullness of their own lives. Sandra's feet no longer tap as lightly as they did. And it occurs to me that we are straining these people whose welcome meant so much, whose friendship we value, whose pleasures we share. Sandra appears all naturalness, all delight. And perhaps she is. But she is so young! Her husband is so young! Can this naturalness be trusted? Away from this gathering, they are not just earning a living; they are making a fortune; how this must consume them! There, in the making of a fortune, in the management of Crippleville, in the dealings with contractors and banks and solicitors and accountants lies their true interest. It is the bigger and more important side of their life. They are making a fortune and working

63

at it with a dedication that must obsess them. Here they can be natural and relax; but isn't this an exploitation of their friends? All this I can see. I can see how every attempt at friendliness must appear false and insecure and must arouse the instinct to snub, how even my laughter at the fiction just discovered in the Society Page must irritate. This youth, this placidity, this coldness concealing the passion, the money passion, that is truly nameless. All this I see but do not know how to communicate to Sandra. She is still my luck. I leave her as always to fight her own battles; I know that she will win. I still delight in the bite of her phrase-choked speech, that thrust of chin and lower lip.

So we were set apart. And a little above. It is the human instinct for order; and those who so willingly ranged themselves below us required us to display extraordinary qualities. We were required to be kinder, more considerate, less impatient, and above all never to pay attention to the one thing – in our case money – which in the minds of others set us apart. We were constantly challenged, provoked, tested. The extra strength that was attributed to us encouraged our friends to a display of proportionate weakness. And we responded wrongly. It is difficult to be a lord! I sought accommodation where I ought to have imposed authority. And there was Sandra with her gift of the phrase, her North London tongue, battling where she should have succoured and consoled. I encouraged her, I am afraid, by being amused. She often spoke damaging words in public for my benefit alone.

We went one Sunday to see the house which one of our couples had built in the central hills of our island. Everyone else was mad about beach-houses – a house in the hills was original. We had heard a lot about this house; but its details had been kept secret, and were to be a surprise. The road to the house was bad and dangerous and slow; it was raining. Sandra did the driving; she was not in a good mood when we arrived. Almost the first thing she said to our hostess, in response to some light though too self-depreciating query about the house, was: 'I wish you would make up your minds whether it is a country cottage or a country house.' There was an instant chill in the air, more than the chill deriving from the altitude for the sake of which the house had allegedly been built. The thermometer might have dropped to sixty just before sunrise, and the most you might have said was that with a log fire you wouldn't be too uncomfortable. Much varnished pine, I remember; an abundance of knots; very Scandinavian, as we agreed. We were led to the enormous fireplace, brass-and-leather belts or some such studded things hanging irregularly on either side. We stood stunned and hushed; the moment for exclamation and congratulations passed, missing us; we moved away. We stood before an open window which looked out on to lush, dripping greenery; it was sunny now, and steaming after the rain. Sandra said: 'It must get damned cold up here.' Our hostess, who was Swedish, lost control of her English accent. Sandra, though recognizing she had gone too far without being in any way amusing – and perhaps because she recognized this – made no effort to repair the damage, not even when, to exclamations in many accents from the other girls, our hostess brought out open sandwiches, the pronunciation of whose native name had, on so many occasions in the years gone by, served me as the subject of hollow jests. Our hostess's English sounded like Swedish when she said good-bye. Sandra, driving me away, down the damp, dangerous bends, and acting now for me, lost nothing of her self-induced temper or hostility. 'Common little Lapp!' A bitter little explosion, climaxing intermittent speech. I laughed; Sandra smiled, frowning, concentrating on the road. I kissed my finger and pressed it on her lips. The gift of the phrase! Yet pure fantasy on this occasion; for the Swede was splendidly built, and had an impeccable Stockholm background, with a father in publishing.

The gift of the phrase: she relied on this more and more, letting simple words harden into settled judgements and attitudes. She used the gift to render grotesque the girls whose company she had once sought and whose way of life had delighted her. She turned them into a kind of comic chorus, evolving for each a pejorative racial description. A bulky girl from Amsterdam, married to a man from Surinam who had migrated to Isabella, became a 'subkraut'; the Latvian became, rather tellingly, the 'sub-Asiatic'. I accepted these phrases; and in our household, which had of course its own racial contradictions, I might hear myself saying quite naturally, 'Shall we have the subkraut over to *genever* on Sunday morning?' Or: 'It looks as though the Lapp has forgiven you. She wants you to go to a party she is giving for a bearded fellow-countryman. He is over here collecting voodoo songs to play on the Swedish radio.'

An invitation like the last was reconciliation indeed. Among us, cosmopolitan though we were, nothing was prized so much as the visitor from countries reasonably far away. Over such a visitor our women would fight, practising exclusions to indicate disfavour or offering invitations to announce reconciliation. This was the basis of the hospitality on which we prided ourselves, this pampering of the visitor while he remained a visitor, while his foreign cigarettes and shirts and foreign shoes lasted, before he became one of us. Invariably, with such a visitor, there would occur a moment, unplanned, of collective sadness, each girl then seeming to see at the same time the landscape from which she had broken; and in a darkened veranda, from which we offered our visitor the tropical night, there would be soft criticism, anticipating the visitor's judgement, of the narrowness of island life: the absence of good conversation or proper society, the impossibility of going to the theatre or hearing a *good* symphony concert. Why the quality of the symphony concerts we were being denied should have been stressed I don't know. It always was; it was as though on Isabella we were subjected, as a condition of residence, to an endless series of bad symphony concerts. And it was at one such session of soft criticism – at the Indian Commissioner's, Indian Republic Day, such diplomatic or quasi-diplomatic corps as we had on Isabella all assembled, our women in saris, light glinting on silk from Banaras and jewellery from Guiana – it was then that Sandra, in a sari herself, succeeded in antagonizing the entire group, by saying loudly, in the middle of their music complaint, 'The one thing I've learnt

66

to recognize since I've come to this place is a bad symphony concert.'

So Sandra battled on with her North London tongue, responding openly to hostility which was not hostility but only that type of provocation which I have described. Until at last an undeclared state of war existed between the others and ourselves. We continued to meet and to offer and receive hospitality; but it was now accepted that no holds were to be barred. It was our final setting apart. For all this I was to pay later; but then it was Sandra who suffered. Common: it was the word Sandra had given us, and it was the word to which she was now herself pinned. She became a girl from the East End of London, without breeding or education, who had been rescued by myself, besotted by the glamour of her race. But money was the subject of greater fantasies. I don't suppose we could have made anyone believe that to Sandra money had come as no surprise, it being no more than what she had considered her element; that about money she had always been vague, not knowing even as a student what her grant was or how much she had in the bank; that in money matters she lacked the neurotic precision of myself, who was uneasy unless he knew how much he had and how much he could reasonably expect to have in a year's time; and that to me it had come as no surprise that the very girl who before her marriage would have considered fifty pounds wealth should be talking calmly three years later of our overdraft of a hundred thousand dollars. Her feeling for the luxurious, her readiness to create the occasion with very little, never altered from the time I met her; her demands, even during the days of riches, remained small; and when she left me she left more or less as she had come. Not only from pride; nor yet from that sense of tainted fairy money which the money-gift brings; but, I feel certain, from the conviction that money had ceased to be an issue. It is the peculiar madness that comes with the gift; it makes so many unlikely people – to the wonderment of the world – throw away all.

The simplicities! The distortions! The incident at the Indian Commissioner's, for instance, was more than modified in the retelling. The talk, it was said, had turned to music. The Canadian Trade Commissioner had said to Sandra, 'Do you care for music?' To which, the story would have it, Sandra replied in a low-class London accent: 'What do you think I am? I would have you know that I like a good symphony concert.' Then there was the bookshop story, in which I figured. Was it the assistant who spread the hilarious exchange in which he had said to me, 'Oh, your wife likes reading!' and I had angrily replied, 'Look here, I would have you know that my wife reads good books'? This was the dialogue style of these stories: Sandra and I were always 'having people know' things. To these stories and to others, of lasciviousness, betrayal and even sexual quaintness, I reacted not at all; and I thought that Sandra shared that placidity, partly her gift, which had come to me with our marriage. But she suffered more than I knew. It did not occur to me that she was not always able to handle a situation which she had provoked; it did not occur to me that, with the gift of the phrase, she could also be vulnerable to the phrase; and that against a low level of distortion she was helpless, as some children remain helpless against the taunts of their fellows, for all the philosophizing of their elders.

She would cultivate a woman friend assiduously, jealously, someone newly arrived, someone new to the group; she would see this person every day and show her every sort of generosity and favour. In no time every aspect of the relationship would be exhausted; and there would occur the inevitable rupture, the anger that was really hurt. More and more I noticed she cultivated Americans; in our group they were a neutral and variable element; and they were as charmed by her accent as she by theirs. With every new encounter, every new friend, she fashioned a matching myth of racial niceness. She was never content with the individual as individual; she wished to go beyond; it was what remained of her avidity and enthusiasm, which could revive at so little. I wish I had seen then, as I see so clearly now, that she was sinking.

What makes a marriage? What makes a house with two

68

people empty? Surely we were compatible, even complementary. Yet it was this very compatibility that drew her away from me. She had begun to get some of my geographical sense, that feeling of having been flung off the world, for all the landscapes and memories that were locked in the heads of those we met. She spoke increasingly of her childhood, of school, of walks, and of one friend whose wish it was to own a motorcar of pure white. One morning – we had for some time been sleeping in separate rooms – she told me she had awakened in the night with a feeling of fear, a simple fear of place, of the absent world. That she shared a fear I knew so well strengthened me; and subtly my attitude towards her changed. The very things I had once admired in her – confidence, ambition, rightness – were what I now pitied her for; I felt we had come together for self-defence. But there was always morning, always the healing phrase – what a comforting, deceptive thing it is, the gift of words. 'I suppose this must be the most inferior place in the world,' she said. 'Inferior natives, inferior expats. Frightfully inferior and frightfully happy. The two must go together.' I suggested a trip to England. But she was not interested; it remained the country she had wished to get away from. No family or group awaited her; and she was no tourist; she didn't want to see the Tower or do the galleries or go to the theatre; she didn't even need to close her eyes to see what two weeks or a month in London would be like. She said, 'I can take that as read.' She spent more time in the house; in the hot, airless afternoons she often walked about barefooted in her white cotton petticoat and a brassiere supporting breasts she no longer painted. A man came in two or three mornings a week to look after the garden; we had a Grenadian woman cleaner. Apart from these we employed no servants, Sandra having grown to resent them, sometimes hysterically, as intruders. There would have been little for anyone to do anyway. The well-equipped kitchen of our rented house was cold for much of the time. Little came out of it: coffee and toast, hot milk, scrambled eggs, some simple bit of frying. On the shelves were musty, once-used tins and drums of herbs; at night, as soon as the fluorescent tube jumped into dazzle, cockroaches scattered lightly in all directions over bare white surfaces. The women of our group were outraged. On my behalf then; later, of course, it would be different.

But to me as well as to Sandra our house was something to get out of whenever we could. Into that most inferior place in the world. Where could we go? The beaches? We knew them all; we could take them 'as read'. The mountain villages, Negro or mulatto, with their slave history and slave customs? They were more exciting to read about in the Sunday edition of the *Inquirer* than to see: rundown villages of concrete and corrugated iron, set in green, always shining green, like a dozen others elsewhere. At nights we would go out driving, just for the sake of motion. We drove to the airport and sat drinking in the lounge with intransit passengers, listening to the names of foreign cities. We hunted out every new bar or restaurant or nightclub: Isabella was the sort of place where such establishments regularly opened and closed under new management. We were at our happiest outside; it was outside, in a crowd, late at night, the champagne working, that we communed. The sight of Sandra across a room could stir me to a degree that was sometimes disgraceful. Those ill-tempered eyes! That bony face with its jut of jaw. Those feet, as nervous and expressive as hands, but so much more subtle and complex, so much more beautifully made! Those breasts she was always ready to offer me, as to a child. I liked to go across to her and detach her from the man – usually American now – whom those breasts had attracted. And so, in public, we would commune. It was the word we used. I would say, 'Shall we commune?' 'Let's,' she might reply. 'Let me get a drink first.' On a high settee she might then sit, her head and shoulders jammed against the wall, her feet hanging loose over my shoulders as I sat on the floor below the settee; and I would be content, kissing and stroking those feet and legs which twitched and squeezed in answer. As much as by Sandra's cold kitchen the feminine instincts of Europe and Asia were outraged – and perhaps rightly – by these public displays.

But the mood that overcame us seldom came to any consummation. It might have done if we were willing to outrage all sensibility, to do in public what plebeian rumour attributed to our group. But our mood seldom carried us to our house; we could not obliterate the feeling of failure, the feeling of the house's emptiness, the feeling that whatever solution we achieved would be only temporary, would not destroy the night or the morning to come. We had never slept on a double bed; it had always seemed to me unpleasant and, in the tropics, where the body oozes oil, unhealthy; and we had taken to sleeping in separate rooms so that the sleeplessness of the one might not disturb the other. And frequently, on returning, we had simply gone to our respective rooms.

Was it the house? It was one of those large timber town houses of the old colonial period, slightly decaying in spite of its modern kitchen. We both thought it attractive but for some reason we had never succeeded in colonizing it. Large areas of it remained empty; it felt like a rented house, which soon has to go back to its true owner. It had never seemed important to us to have a house of our own. I had no feeling for the house as home, as personal creation. I had no things, no treasures, no collection even of books, no household gods, as Sandra would have said; and apart from a few school prizes, neither had she. Still, to build a house seemed a thing to do; to continue living in an old rented house was beginning to appear ostentatious. I was looking through a picture book about Pompeii and Herculaneum. I was struck by the simplicity of the Roman house, its outward austerity, its inner, private magnificence; I was struck by its suitability to our climate; I yielded to impulse.

But was it something more? Wasn't it that cotton-clad body, with the cleanliness and freshness of the barren, a body without danger or mystery and forbidding for that reason? A body which was no more than what it was, holding no promise of growth, speaking only of flesh and futility and our own imminent extinction.

We violate no body so much as our own; towards it we display the perversity of the cat that constantly rips its wounds open. I saw that there was waste; and I felt, let there be waste. The habits of my student days, which had never altogether died, were now revived. On the island I had become acquainted with a number of women of various races, of the utmost discretion; what had been an occasional extravagance became, as before, an addiction, but now guiltless and clinical. Sometimes I had to stifle my own disgust; sometimes it went well. And it was after a good and successful afternoon – they speak of the sadness of the animal after coitus: but in my experience fulfilment was always followed by a mood of exceptional gentleness and optimism – it was after one good afternoon that I found myself about to say to Sandra as we were dressing to go out – the sentence was fully phrased: delight had been converting itself into reporting words all afternoon – 'Darling, I've had a most marvellous afternoon. I've been in bed with a most skilled and delightful woman.' It was only as I was, I repeat, on the point of saying this, that I realized that perhaps similar sentences had sometimes come to Sandra herself.

And I was amazed at my innocence.

Men in the position in which I now saw myself to have been for some time arouse a variety of reactions. There is ridicule, which I find puzzling. I have never been able to enter into the Sicilian attitude to possession; though I wonder whether this ridicule isn't simply a required attitude, and disingenuous, a covering up for a private fear. But then there is also anger, contempt, pity. And in the special nature of my marriage these things were to fall upon my head in full measure. Was it my placidity which made me indifferent, that very placidity which had dismissed the numerous stories I had had from so many people? Would I be believed if I say that my first thought was not for myself but for Sandra? I was filled, I was overwhelmed, with pity for her; at no time since we had met did I feel such responsibility for her. For myself I felt only a slight, sickening twinge of fear. It was fear of the unreality around me; it was the fear of the man who feels the veils coming down one by one, muffling his deepest responses, and panics at not being able to tear down the unreality about him to get at the hard, the concrete, where everything becomes simple and ordinary and asy to seize. It was my London fear; and now, in addition, I feared for the luck I attributed to Sandra, this luck to which I thought mine was linked. It was then that I began to will everything away: the gift, ambition, everything; and consoled myself consciously with thoughts of extinction, as a vague and general fate, as once, in London, I could get to sleep only with the thought of the Luger at my head. Strange reaction to shattering news! Too good to be true. Perhaps. But certainly too good to be good. I should have fought and created scenes. I should have slapped her on that mouth which it gave me so much pleasure to contemplate. It might have revived us both. As it was, I let the poor child sink. I left both fear and pity unexpressed, and waited in silence for something to overtake us.

And all this while at Crippleville our Roman house was being built. It built itself. We had both lost interest in it, but we both kept this secret from the other. It is a strain to inspect the progress of a house in which you know others will live. A house, though, is one of those things in which the principle of inertia is clearly demonstrated. It is more difficult to abandon the building of a house than to take it to the end. To the end we took ours, through all the rites that go with the building of the house, sacred symbol; until we came to the final rite, the housewarming, the installing of the household gods who convert brick and timber into something more. The lights, the food, the illuminated swimming-pool (our modification of the Roman *impluvium*), the discreet band; the shining faces of those outside the gates who had come to watch; the road choked with motorcars; and even a couple of policemen, like hospital attendants with their white night armbands. In the centre of all this I felt a stranger, as so often happens during grand occasions of one's own. Everyone we had invited had come. I noticed Sandra's American, slightly too hearty towards me, who felt nothing but paternally towards him; though this had been overlaid by what I thought he must feel about me, so that a muted embarrassment now existed between us. And I noticed too how even at this late stage our position was proclaimed; it was still possible for us to accept our rôle, if only we had

73

known how. The women had dressed with unusual care
most of them had clearly spent the morning or the afternoon
at the hairdresser's. Whatever might have passed between
us, our housewarming was still, magnificently, an occasion

There can be no surprise, considering my own mood
that the occasion should have gone wrong or should have
been turned into an occasion of another sort. I was never
sure how exactly it started. Possibly the example of recent
'breaking-up' parties was unfortunate; at an appointed hour
at these parties, usually after drinks and just before food
guests were required to destroy certain things indicated by
the host – glassware and china from sets that had been irre-
deemably decimated, items of furniture that had been overtaken by our racing taste, an old-style radio, toys that had
been outgrown. It might also have been that boredom against
which we all fought; when we did not talk of our children
we talked of occasions that had just passed and occasions
that were to come. And, indeed, after the champagne, the
caviar on buttered toast, the barbecue, what was there to
do? What was the new thing that could hold us? After the
thrill of the campfire preparation of food, what could we
do except eat the food? And there was the swimming-pool
A swimming-pool is a most tedious thing. You get in and
swim twelve lengths and that is fine. But if you are not a
swimmer seeking exercise, if you are nothing more than an
extravagant bather, if you wish to be in a swimming-pool
only to savour the luxury of being in a swimming-pool at
night, with uniformed attendants who at a wave hurry to the
pool's edge with trays of food and drink in appetite-killing
variety, if you wish to do only that, you are soon restless. It
was there, in the tedium of the swimming-pool, that everything began, I am sure. There were calls from the pool for
balls, for games. Was it from the American's hefty hand that
the ball was sent flying among tables, breaking plates and
glasses and cracking a window? I am not sure. But within
seconds the ball was sent from hand to hand, from pool to
house to pool again, and there was a positive destroying
fury. The pool was set centrally, so that damage was satisfying and easy. There rose excited laughter; it seemed that at

the first, releasing sound of breaking glass and china a sort of hysteria had set in among our guests. Everyone pretended to be drunker than he was; everyone was suddenly very active. But for the first time since I had come back to the island I knew anger, a deep, blind, damaging anger. I shouted, I screamed; I did not know where I walked or who I hit or what I said after the presentiment of the anger breaking up through me. Just pictures: of the disturbed blue of the pool, rocking to rest in an instant of stillness, of the splashed edges of the pool, the bright lights, the recessed areas of gloom, the flies fluttering above the caged underwater light, the faces of one or two registering so clearly the thought that I had gone mad, about me the splashings and the spilled drinks and wasted food.

I was in the car then, driving through the gates, past the parked cars of the others, past the faces, women wrapped up against the night air; and I drove through the city and out of it and went on, driving, driving through the dark, occasional lights, houses asleep, not wishing for terminus, until I came to the ruins of the famous old slave plantation, the overgrown brick walls of the sugar factory, the bricks brought as ballast in the eighteenth-century ships from Europe. And, oh, I wanted to cry. The damage to the new house: not that. It was not the rage we feel when something new receives a scratch or dent and we feel that it is all destroyed. I had assessed the damage as superficial; in a morning the workmen could mend it. Not that, not that. I just wished to cry. I leaned over the steering wheel and tried to cry, but I couldn't. The pain remained, unreleased, the nameless pain from which one feels there can be no way out, and one knows that despair is absolute.

Weeping because he had no more worlds to conquer. I can enter into those tears of Alexander. They were real tears, but they came from a deeper cause. They are the tears of children outside a hut at sunset, the fields growing dark; they are the tears of men in the middle of great achievement, men who are made weary by a sense of futility, who long to be the first men in the world, who long to do penance for the entire race, because they feel the lack of sympathy between

man and the earth he walks on and know that, whatever
they might do, this gap will remain. They are the tears of
men at the end of their line, who foresee their extinction.
But the mood passes. Alexander goes back to his generals,
indulgent towards the sensibility they will misinterpret; the
child goes inside the hut and the big world is reduced to a
small warm sphere. So now, over the wheel of my motorcar,
I returned to myself, anger, despair vanished, only a sense
of outrage and shame remaining, and the knowledge that
this slave plantation was a favourite spot for courting
couples as well as rapists and others seeking social revenge.
I drove back to the main road, switched on the car radio
and slowly now, driving to music, to cheap old songs, the
tears rolled down, quite pleasurably.

The cars outside the house had gone; so had the crowd,
the policemen. The house was empty, lights dimmed, the
swimming-pool in darkness, only the two water jets playing.
Everything had been cleaned up – no sign of broken glass
splashed, swept concrete already almost dry in our warm
night – and how affectionately I felt towards the staff! Such
a noble instinct, the instinct to mend, repair, prepare for the
morning. Here and there a cracked glass pane. Simple. The
damage was slight. But I did not go to Sandra's room. I had
willed the gift away; my prayers were being answered. Ob-
liquely, as prayers always are.

6

It only remained now for Sandra to leave. It could not have
been an easy time for her. But the true wound I thought to
be mine, and I believed by saying nothing I was behaving
well. Sandra was after all in a position to leave: other relationships awaited her, other countries. I had nowhere to go;
I wished to experience no new landscapes; I had cut myself
off from that avidity which I still attributed to her. It was
not for me to decide to leave; that decision was hers alone.
We continued to go out together; we continued to try out

new restaurants and nightclubs. But I was waiting for her to leave. The time for quarrels between us was past. A quarrel occurred, though, before she left. It was not with me. It was with Wendy Deschampsneufs.

The name of Deschampsneufs was famous in our island. They were one of our old French families – always a Deschampsneufs on the committee of our Turf Club, always a Deschampsneufs prominent in the *Cercle Sportif* – but their reputation had always been slightly ambiguous since the unexpected emergence of a Deschampsneufs as a leader of the common man, 'the man without', during the Rate Riots of 1877. The challenge to the Colonial Government then had been serious enough for an emergency to be declared and a governor recalled. But just ten years later the Deschampsneufs appeared to have become quite respectable again, respectable enough at any rate to entertain James Anthony Froude, the imperialist pamphleteer, who was visiting. The story of this visit was famous in Isabella. Froude arrived in a state of nerves. A pathologically gloomy man, he had been thoroughly rattled by an Irish telegraph operator in New York who, between items of fact, was transmitting vivid accounts of imaginary British disasters in various parts of the world. On Isabella Froude had little heart for looking over more declining plantations and listening to more tales of imperial woe. The Deschampsneufs offered to take him on an expedition to the Devil's Cauldron, a hot sulphur lake high up in our mountains. It was a difficult three-day journey on foot and mule through forest, rain and mud, and Froude's temper wore very thin. The sight of every Negro forest hut drove him to rage at Negro idleness and to pessimistic conclusions about the future of that race; he saw the bush speedily claiming its own again and reflected bitterly on the abolition of slavery, which he thought the Negroes themselves would live to regret. The only hope for Isabella, he said, lay in the large-scale settlement of Asiatics, who 'to the not inconsiderable merits of picturesqueness and civilization add the virtues of thrift and industry'. Matters reached a head when at the Cauldron itself a solitary Negro was discovered, totally naked, washing some clothes. Froude,

77

exceeding his privileges as a visitor and exceeding, too, the custom of the island, 'most civilly requested the young black to return into his already sufficiently threadbare garment or garments and proceed in any direction of his choice'. The negro grew 'sullen', then 'abusive'; and it was clear, even from Froude's account, that it was only the intercession of the great Deschampsneufs, speaking soothingly in the French patois of the mountains, that saved Froude from violence or a show of violence. Froude was not greatly impressed; the chapter on Isabella in *The Bow of Ulysses* was rounded off with a diatribe against the French, their language, their religion; in the existence of these things on a British island Froude saw the greatest danger to British rule. So that the ambiguous reputation of the Deschampsneufs endured. The family had not done much that was extraordinary since; but it needed very little – a Deschampsneufs championing creole horses, for instance, against English – to revive the reputation of the family as being aloof yet totally committed to the island in their own way.

With Wendy Deschampsneufs, small and ugly and bright and gay, celebrating, as we had all once done, a return to the island – she had been to a school in Belgium or Switzerland – I could never feel at ease. I had seen her once, briefly, when she was a child; then she had climbed over me and my chair and done a little bit of showing-off. Not a pleasant memory for me, that afternoon tea at the Deschampsneufs', when I thought I was saying goodbye to the island; and Wendy grown up revived all my embarrassment. I had never questioned the family's credentials, but I had never felt they were of interest to me. The descendant of the slave-owner could soothe the descendant of the slave with a private patois. I was the late intruder, the picturesque Asiatic, linked to neither. Yet for so many years of my youth – for reasons to be described in their place – I had felt involved with the family of Deschampsneufs. At that tea party I had failed to make my position clear; by failing to do so I felt I had some-how continued to involve myself in the conflict between master and slave, and was as a result leaving the island with the taint which I had wished to avoid, and which was to

78

draw me back. This defaulting, this weakness, was like a shame. If I put down a newspaper with a sense of something wrong, something naggingly undone, and then retraced the steps, I invariably found it was due to the appearance of this unsettling name of Deschampsneufs, whose unimportance to myself I deeply realized yet whose weight I could never shake off. I recognize in myself the attitude I have described in others. With Wendy I moved between the desire to crush and the desire not to hurt. So full she was of the name! What a shock it had been to see her for the first time at one of the houses we went to, to hear her name pronounced a little too casually!

Yet if I was embarrassed, in a way I couldn't explain, Sandra was at once taken; and between the two women there instantly grew up an intense relationship. They saw each other for hours every day; they went out together, for the day, for weekends; doubtless they arranged adventures. In those last days I often had the absurd feeling that I was responsible for two alien women. What was the basis of the attraction between them? Was it the attraction between the ugly woman and the attractive? It might have been; though in such a relationship Wendy would have had the counter-weight of her name. Was it that Wendy recognized in Sandra someone who was about to leave and was therefore in no way a danger? Was it that, starting from opposite ends, they had come to share the same social attitudes? A little of all this, I feel sure. A little, too, of enthusiasm: for in these last days Sandra wonderfully revived. In our island myth this was the prescribed end of marriages like mine: the wife goes off with someone from the *Cercle Sportif*, outside those gates at night the willingly betrayed husband waits in his motor-car. The circumstances were slightly different, it is true. I couldn't believe the story, put about by the women of our group, that Sandra had begun, under Wendy's influence, to frequent the *Cercle*. To these women, with their metropolitan backgrounds, their new money, their wine-basket pretensions, their talk of interior decoration and the books reviewed in the last issue of *Time*, the *Cercle* would have been shabby and a comedown; and I could not think of Sandra,

79

with her gift of the phrase and her attitude to the common, lasting long among the salesmen and bank employees and estate overseers.

The end came, of course. The weekends, the morning coffee with Wendy in our air-conditioned bars and cafés, the trips to the beach, and doubtless the adventures, they came to an end. And it was announced as usual by Sandra wandering about the house in petticoat and brassiere. Once, through the open door of her room, I caught sight of her, late in the afternoon, lying on the bed, her feet together, the toes nervously twitching; I was greatly moved.

There remained a restaurant to do. We went on a Saturday. We were given a table at the front, just a few feet from the platform on which the band and the master of ceremonies stood. From time to time someone went up to the master of ceremonies, whispered into his ear or handed him a bit of paper; a minute or two later a spotlight would play on a table and the whisperer would stand while the band played and would either clown or look offended, as one whose privacy had been disturbed. Sandra and I agreed that the restaurant was not likely to last. There was much coming and going in the area between our table and the dance band, and it was with surprise that we saw that Wendy Deschampsneufs was with a small party three tables away.

I could see that Sandra was drawn. I could see that she was, disastrously, yielding. The music ended. She got up and walked over. And Wendy did not see her. No anger on Wendy's face, no drumming of feet or hands, no humming and slow nodding, no staring ahead or through. Wendy simply did not see. It was as though she had been born and trained for this perfect moment of non-seeing. It was seconds before Sandra began to walk back. Walking back, she became a little more composed. She took her bag from a chair at our table and said, very precisely in the small room:

'The Niger is a tributary of that Seine.'

The island phrase! The cry of the defeated in the war between master and slave! I was sickened. The sentence that had come to me during that afternoon tea at the Deschampsneufs', when Wendy had climbed over my chair and rubbed against me like a cat, now came back, whole: *Why, recognizing the enemy, did you not kill him swiftly?* These emotions of weakness, when we try to frighten no one so much as ourselves with our ability to hurt! So differently it was to turn out. As, even then, it was already too late for action or for speech: going down, past the brand-new 'tropical' decorations on the steps, from the grotesque air-conditioned restaurant into the warm, smelly street.

7

My first instinct was towards the writing of history, as I have said. It was an urge that surprised me in the midst of activity, during those moments of stillness and withdrawal which came to me in the days of power, when with compassion for others there also came an awareness of myself not as an individual but as a performer, in that child's game where every action of the victim is deemed to have been done at the command of his tormentor, and where even refusal is useless, for that too can be deemed to have been commanded, and the only end is tears and walking away. It was the shock of the first historian's vision, a religious moment if you will, humbling, a vision of a disorder that was beyond any one man to control yet which, I felt, if I could pin down, might bring me calm. It is the vision that is with me now. This man, this room, this city; this story, this language, this form. It is a moment that dies, but a moment my ideal narrative would extend. It is a moment that comes to me fleetingly when I go out to the centre of this city, this dying mechanized city, and in the window of a print shop I see a picture of the city of other times: sheep, say, in Soho Square. Just for an instant I long to be transported into that scene, and at the same time I am overwhelmed by the absurdity of the wish and all the loss that it implies; and in the middle of a street so real, in the middle of an assessment of my situation that is so practical and realistic, I am like that child outside a hut at dusk, to whom the world is so big and unknown and time so limitless; and I have visions of Central Asian horsemen, among whom I am one, riding below a sky threatening snow to the very end of an empty world.

Two

On Isabella when I was a child it was a disgrace to be poor.
It is, alas, no longer so. And it astonished me when I first
came to England to find that it wasn't so here either. I arrived
at a time of reform. Politicians proclaimed the meanness of
their birth and the poverty of their upbringing and described
themselves with virtuous rage as barefoot boys. On Isabella,
where we had the genuine article in abundance, this was a
common term of schoolboy abuse; and I was embarrassed on
behalf of these great men. To be descended from generations of idlers and failures, an unbroken line of the unimagi-
native, unenterprising and oppressed, had always seemed to
me to be a cause for deep, silent shame. Sandra's attitude,
of contempt for her origins, seemed to me healthier and more
liberal, being more quickening of endeavour; though it
puzzled me that she too made no attempt to hide her origins.

It was my ambiguous New World background, no doubt.
My father was a schoolteacher and poor. I never saw his
family and naturally suspected the worst; and though it was
through my father that I was later to be dragged into public
life, as a boy I did what I could to suppress the connexion.
I preferred to lay claim to my mother's family. They were
among the richest in the island and belonged to that small
group known as 'Isabella millionaires'. It gave me great
pleasure at school to have Cecil, my mother's brother,
roughly my own age, say that we were related. Cecil was a
tyrant; he offered and withdrew his patronage whimsically.
But I never wavered in my claim.

My mother's family owned the Bella Bella Bottling Works
and were among other things the local bottlers of Coca-
Cola. In Coca-Cola therefore I at an early age took an almost proprietorial interest. I welcomed gibes at its expense

and liked to pretend they were aimed at me personally, though I could not find it in myself to go as far as Cecil, who offered to fight any boy who spoke disrespectfully of his family's product. Though he perhaps never knew the word, my mother's father managed his public relations with skill; there was no one on Isabella, I am sure, who did not know of Bella Bella. We – or they – sponsored two programmes on the local radio station: one, *Songs of Yesteryear*, a request programme, rather dreary, for Bella Bella in general; the other extremely popular, for Coca-Cola, *The Coca-Cola Quiz*, which offered prizes. Tickets for this show were allotted to schools throughout the island; there was always a rush for them. Two or three afternoons a week groups of school-children were taken round the Bella Bella works. My grandfather had put it to the education authorities that such tours of modern industrial plants were educational; and in spite of the passionate but unimportant opposition of my father the authorities agreed. The visits took place during school hours; at the end each child was given a free drink; and again, as for *The Coca-Cola Quiz*, numbers had to be fiercely controlled.

I liked going with these groups to the bottling works, though it was a torment to me then to be anonymous. I longed to receive some sign of overlordship or even recognition from the employees, and had fantasies in which, during an emergency, I demonstrated my familiarity with the complex machinery of the great enterprise. It was easy enough for Cecil. He never stayed with the group but prowled around everywhere, Mister Cecil to everybody. He made stern comments about the clarity or consistency of the syrup – about which the Coca-Cola people were strict – and generally tried to hint that he had come not as a student but as a spy. This was what we sometimes did in the city together, frightening a shopkeeper who had at first taken us for simple schoolboys. Sometimes I tried to be a spy on my own. I was not always successful.

Cecil was so awed by the wealth and importance of his family that anyone might have believed money had come to the family when Cecil was of an age to understand. This wasn't so. But perhaps Cecil remembered, as I remembered, the older house of his family. There was a large covered area at the back of this house, and for a long time I saw there a rusting metal pole of sorts, which was said to have been the first piece of Bella Bella bottling equipment. I believe it had been used for capping bottles manually, one at a time. I also remembered a long wooden gallery in this house. It was divided into dark cubicles and it was possible to find on shelves in these cubicles bottles of coloured concentrates and little packets of powders, imported from England. The labels were oddly scientific and medical in appearance, black and white with fine printing, a contrast with the bright colours and the drawings of fruit on the labels of the drinks these concentrates went to make.

In the new house, of course, there was no sign of home manufacture. I believe Cecil regretted this. He was Bella Bella and Coca-Cola. He didn't like anyone to forget it and he didn't like to forget it himself. He had all the facts and figures about Coca-Cola sales, being admitted even when very young to the family's business secrets; and he was full of stories about Coca-Cola. It was Cecil who told me either that Coca-Cola was an aphrodisiac or that it was regarded as such in certain Eastern countries. And I believe it was Cecil who told me that, to prevent the Coca-Cola secret formula from perishing for all time in a single ghastly accident, the American directors never travelled together, even in an elevator; though this might be a later story, from a different person, about another company. Of Cecil himself it was told that once, going by launch to a children's picnic on one of the islets near Isabella, he became so enraged by the sight of cases of Pepsi-Cola, destined for this very picnic, that he threw them all overboard before anyone realized what he was up to; and sought to justify his behaviour to his bemused hosts and their outraged guests by a prolonged show of temper at what he claimed was their discourtesy to his family. I heard the story many times; it acquired the nature of legend. Cecil himself told it often when he was a young man and already, sadly, looking back to his childhood as to his great days. As a child Cecil was licensed to a degree. He liked to think of himself as eccentric and violent, and in this he was encouraged by his family, who relished the resulting stories. He was naturally aggressive; I feel the passion for real-life story-making permanently unsettled him. He was the only person I knew who even as a child tried to be a 'character'.

My father hated Cecil. It was a lukewarm response to Cecil's contempt; Cecil had no respect for age. My father often said, 'That little brute is going to end up swinging on the gallows, you mark my words.' Hating Cecil he hated Coca-Cola, and made a vow, which I believe he kept, never to touch it. I reported the vow and the abstention to Cecil, who said, 'It's a young man's drink.' I reported this back to my father, who raged. But each was piqued by the other's contempt; each wished to put down the other; and between the middle-aged man and the young boy I acted as go-between.

'Nana,' I said one day, referring in this way to Cecil's father, 'Nana went to America to buy a pipe.'

'Do you really believe that? He probably bought a pipe when he was in America. He didn't go to America to buy a pipe.'

'It was what Cecil said.'

'If you believe that you are a bigger damn fool than that damn big fool.'

On another day, when my father heard that I was going on a tour of the Bella Bella works, he went to the mousetrap and brought out a dead mouse and with a worrying smile whispered into my ear, 'I bet you six cents, a shilling, you wouldn't drop this in the vat or whatever it is they use. I bet you you wouldn't.'

Part of the trouble was that my mother's family had made their money five or six years too late. When my father married my mother the condescension had all been his. He was over thirty, had already made some mark in missionary circles, and was considered a rising man in the Education Department. The proof of this early glory was to be found in my father's bookcase, in a slender old-fashioned volume called *The Missionary Martyr of Isabella*. It was one of a series of *Missionary Martyrs:* the decorated endpapers listed them all, some from places, like Thebaw, of which I had never heard. The martyrdom referred to in the Isabella book was not especially bloody: the missionary had died at an advanced age in bed, in his own country, but of malaria contracted in the tropics. The book was made up of extracts from the missionary's diary, his wife's diary, letters, sermons; and ended with the text of the oration over his grave. There were also many photographs which contrived to make Isabella look exceedingly wild. One of the photographs was of my father as a young man, almost a boy, standing up in a group in front of a thatched wooden hut; the background was simple bush. The reproduction was poor, light and shadow ill-defined; and in the badly-fitting old-fashioned costume, which appeared to force his neck and chin out and up, my father looked faintly aboriginal and lost, at the end of the world, in a clearing in the forest. The impression was not altogether belied by the text, for in the diaries and letters of the missionary and his lady was a startling vision of the world. The centre of this world was their missionary activity; everything led outwards from this and led back to this. Isabella became an almost Biblical land, full of symbols and portents and marks of God's glory, a land of stoic journeys through scoffing crowds, encounters with khaki-clad officials hostile to the work, and disputations with devious Brahmins in oriental robes seeking to undermine the work. It was not an island I recognized. Nor could I recognize my father from the descriptions in the diary of the missionary's lady. It was she who had discovered my father. It was she who saw that, young as he was, he had the marks of grace. I read, incredulously, of the young boy, my father, 'proclaiming the terrors of the law' and urging 'jeering crowds' to 'receive the Gospel of grace'. Again and again he came to the rescue of his patroness when she was 'struggling unequally with a wily disputant'. 'Let me speak,' he said simply. Then she stood behind him; and 'like a war-steed rejoicing in the din of battle he charged in where danger was greatest, and the antagonist was silenced'. One Sunday she was waiting for him at the mission house. He was late; she was getting impatient. Then she saw him in the distance cycling along the bumpy dirt road, and all thoughts of reproach went out of her head. She guessed he had had a puncture; she saw him 'riding on his bicycle, as on an ass, to his Sabbath work'. He came slowly up, and then was cycling beside the tall hibiscus hedge of the grounds. All of him was hidden except for his white turban, which the sun caught and turned to dazzle; and she thought then she saw an angel flying in the midst of heaven, having the everlasting Gospel to preach unto them that dwell on the earth. I found this entry in the lady's diary inexplicably moving. Always at this stage in the book I felt the need for a climax. But after this, in *The Missionary Martyr of Isabella*, there was no more of my father. The missionary's lady, much younger than her husband and, from both their accounts, very frail, fell ill and was sent to her home; and after some years of solitary labour the missionary himself followed her. So that it had all led to nothing, so far as my father was concerned. When I read this book I used to get the feeling that my father was a man who had been cut off from his real country, which in my imagination was as glorious as the Isabella described in the diary of the missionary's lady: nowhere else would people see magic in a white turban, a hibiscus hedge, a bicycle and the Sunday-morning sun. I used to get the feeling that my father had in some storybook way been shipwrecked on the island and that over the years the hope of rescue had altogether faded. The book, of magic, was in his bookcase; but he never spoke of it; I never saw him reading it. Perhaps he too felt that it described another man.

'Your mother and her family can get on their high horse,' he used to say, when the talk turned to Coca-Cola or when I came back from a week-end with Cecil, 'but I remember the time when your mother's mother used to sell milk to *my* mother. Selling and carrying the cow. Milking the milk out – in a pan, in a bottle, in a bucket – and selling it on the spot, just like that, in the road. Carrying the cow with a rope. And I remember the time when your mother's father, never mind the Legco and the Exco' – my mother's father was a nominated member of both the Legislative Council and the Executive Council – 'I remember the time when your mother's father used to full his bottles with a funnel.'

This was far from lessening my admiration for them. In my imagination I saw my mother's mother leading her cow through a scene of pure pastoral: calendar pictures of English gardens superimposed on our Isabellan villages of mud and grass: village lanes on cool mornings, the ditches green and grassy, the water crystal, the front gardens of thatched huts bright with delicate flowers of every hue. She was as brightly coloured a storybook figure as her husband. I imagined him sitting at a wooden table and by the light of an oil lamp scrupulously 'fulling' his bottles with a funnel, bringing to that labour a self-contained, almost religious, stillness, his inward eye fixed on a goal which transcended the frivolity of his present pursuit, the concoction of soft drinks, whose quality and measure yet remained of surpassing importance. The goal, when realized, would astonish the scoffing world. It would not astonish him. Nor would it astonish his wife who, as devoutly as himself, looked far beyond the flowery lanes through which, penitentially every morning, she led her milk-giving cow.

It was, as might be imagined, a slow humiliation for my father to find that he, who had married the shopkeeper's daughter, was forced over the years into the position of the underpaid schoolteacher with whom the family of the rich industrialist had imprudently formed a marriage alliance. And it didn't help that my mother's behaviour was that of someone who quietly accepted her own guilt. My mother had received little English education and so was separated as by a generation from her brother and sisters who came later, at the period of wealth. One result was that she exaggerated her age. She liked to think that she was old-fashioned and had more in common with her parents than with her sisters and brother. In this way she tried to resolve a difficult situation. I think she succeeded. Her old-fashioned upbringing which prescribed acceptance without complaint, was a help to her. She accepted my father's abuse; she accepted her family's tacit – in Cecil, open – disapproval of my father. By a display of perpetual guilt she continued to show loyalty to both sides, even after my father had stopped going to her parents' house.

At an early age, then, I was made aware of the oddity of the arrangement whereby two human beings, who were in no way related, paired off. I suppose it is in this that I must look for an explanation of the scene which took place while I was still in a very junior class at school. We were, I remember, doing masculines and feminines from Nesfield's *Grammar*. The master asked the masculines, the boys provided the feminines. Abbott, abbess; stag, roe; hart, hind; fox, vixen.

'Husband?'

It was my turn. I was mortified.

'Husband, boy.'

An answer was needed, and I knew. I got out of my desk and walked down the aisle to Mr Shepherd's table. He looked puzzled. I went and stood in front of him. He bent down with concern and I whispered into his ear: 'Wife.'

More than thirty years later, the man agrees with the child: it is a terrible word.

For Cecil childhood was the great time; he would never cease to regret its passing away. It was different with me. I could scarcely wait for my childhood to be over and done with. I have no special hardship or deprivation to record. But childhood was for me a period of incompetence, bewilderment, solitude and shameful fantasies. It was a period of burdensome secrets – like the word 'wife', a discovery about the world which I was embarrassed to pass on to the world – and I longed for nothing so much as to walk in the clear air of adulthood and responsibility, where everything was comprehensible and I myself was as open as a book. I hated my secrets. A complying memory has obliterated many of them and edited my childhood down to a brief cinematic blur. Even this is quite sufficiently painful.

My first memory of school is of taking an apple to the teacher. This puzzles me. We had no apples on Isabella. It must have been an orange; yet my memory insists on the apple. The editing is clearly at fault, but the edited version is all I have. This version contains a few lessons. One is about the coronation of the English king and the weight of his crown, so heavy he can wear it only a few seconds. I would like to know more; but the film jumps to another classroom and the terrors of arithmetic. Then, in this version, as in a dream where we wake before we fall – but not always: recently, doubtless as a result of the effort of memory and this very writing, I dreamt that in this city I was being carried helplessly down a swiftly flowing river, the Thames, that sloped, and could only break my fall by guiding my feet to the concrete pillars of the bridge that suddenly spanned the river, and in my dream I felt the impact and knew that I had broken my legs and lost their use forever – but as in a dream, I say, the terrors of arithmetic disappear. And I am in a new school. Cecil is also there. The first morning, the parade in the quadrangle. 'Right tweel, left tweel. Boys in the quadrangle, right tweel. Boys on the platform, left tweel, right tweel, left tweel. To the hall, march! Right and left tweel.' I tweel and tweel. I write what I hear – a tweel to me a very dashing and pointless school twirl. But school is such pointlessness. 'Today,' the teacher says, 'while I full up this roll book, I want you boys to sit down quiet and write a letter to a prospective employer asking for a job after you leave school.' He gives us details of the job and on the blackboard writes out the opening sentence and one or two others for us to copy. I know I am too young for employment, and I am bewildered. But no other boy is. I write: 'Dear Sir, I humbly beg to apply for the vacant post of shipping clerk as advertised in this morning's edition of the *Isabella Inquirer*. I am in the fourth standard of the Isabella Boys' School and I study English, Arithmetic, Reading, Spelling and Geography. I trust that my qualifications will be found suitable. School overs at three and and I have to be home by half past four. I think I can get to work at half past three but I will have to leave at four. I am nine years and seven months old. Trusting this application will receive your favourable attention, and assuring you at all times of my devoted service, I remain, my dear Sir, your very humble and obedient servant, R. R. K. Singh.' The letter is read out to the class by the teacher, who has fulled up his roll book. The class dissolves in laughter. It is an absurd letter. I know; but I was asked for it. Then the letters of other boys like

Browne and Deschampsneufs are read out, and I see. Abso
lute models. But how did they know? Who informs them
about the ways of the world and school?

Of Deschampsneufs, in fact, I already knew a little. Soon
I was to know more. His distinction was vague but acknow
ledged by all. The teachers handled him with care. Uni
formed servants, one male, one female, brought his lunch t
school in a basket and spread it on a white tablecloth o
his desk. He had taken me once to his house to see the grape
vine that grew on a trellis in his drive. He told me it was th
only grape-vine that grew on the island and was very specia
and historical. He had also shown me his Meccano se
Grape-vine and Meccano sets were accordingly thing
which I at once put beyond ambition, just as, until tha
moment, they had been outside knowledge; they wer
things that befell a boy like Deschampsneufs. It was als
part of his developed ability to manage the world that h
had views on the reigning king, preferring the last, whos
portrait hung in our school hall; it was a judgement tha
coloured my view of both kings for years.

Browne of course had no Meccano set and no grape-vine
But Browne too knew his way about the world; his speech t
me was the very distillation of the wisdom of a hundre
Negro backyards. Browne knew about the police and I be
lieve even had connexions with those black men. Brown
knew about the current toughs and passed on gossip abou
sportsmen. Browne was also famous. He knew many funn
songs and whenever a song was required at school he wa
asked to sing. At our concerts he wore a straw hat and
proper suit with a bowtie; people applauded as soon as h
came on. His biggest hit was a song called 'Oh, I'm a happ
little nigger'; his miming during this song was so good tha
people jerked forward on their seats with laughter and ofte
you couldn't hear the words. I deeply envied Browne hi
fame and regard. For him the world was already charted.

So it was too for the young in my own family. Cecil had no
only lived for a hundred years but had a fantastic memory
He constantly referred to his past and already had th
gift of seeing a pattern in events. And there was Cecil's elde

92

sister Sally. She was the most beautiful person in the world. I was in love with her but I felt I made no impact on her. She had a little court made up of young girls from other families; with her these girls were grave and adult. Sally read American magazines for the fashions, which she discussed with these girls. They also discussed films in a way that was new to me. They were less interested in the stories than in the actors, about whom each girl appeared to possess an exclusive, ennobling knowledge. This knowledge disheartened me. Sally was especially interested in actors' noses. This interest had never been mine, had never occurred to me. Was it Peter Lawford's nose she approved of then? No; that came years later. This interest in noses referred us, her hearers, back to her own nose, which was classical Indo-Aryan, the nostrils, as Sally herself told us, being exactly the shape of a pea. How could I get anywhere with a girl like Sally?

My reaction to my incompetence and inadequacy had been not to simplify but to complicate. For instance, I gave myself a new name. We were Singhs. My father's father's name was Kripal. My father, for purposes of official identification, necessary in that new world he adorned with his aboriginal costume, ran these names together to give himself the surname of Kripalsingh. My own name was Ranjit; and my birth certificate said I was Ranjit Kripalsingh. That gave me two names. But Deschampsneufs had five apart from his last name, all French, all short, all ordinary, but this conglomeration of the ordinary wonderfully suggested the extraordinary. I thought to compete. I broke Kripalsingh into two, correctly reviving an ancient fracture, as I felt; gave myself the further name of Ralph; and signed myself R. R. K. Singh. At school I was known as Ralph Singh. The name Ralph I chose for the sake of the initial, which was also that of my real name. In this way I felt I mitigated the fantasy or deception; and it helped in school reports, where I was simply *Singh R.* From the age of eight till the age of twelve this was one of my heavy secrets. I feared discovery at school and at home. The truth came out when we were preparing to leave the elementary school and our records were being put in order for Isabella Imperial College. Birth certificates were required.

'Singh, does this certificate belong to you?'

'I don't know. I can't see it from here.'

'Funny man. It says here Ranjit Kripalsingh. Are you he? Or have you entered the school incognito?'

So I had to explain.

'Ranjit is my secret name,' I said. 'It is a custom among Hindus of certain castes. This secret name is my real name but it ought not to be used in public.'

'But this leaves you anonymous.'

'Exactly. That's where the calling name of Ralph is useful. The calling name is unimportant and can be taken in vain by anyone.'

Such was the explanation I managed, though it was not in these exact words nor in this tone. In fact, as I remember, I stood close to the teacher and spoke almost in a whisper. He was a man who prided himself on his broad-mindedness. He looked humble, acquiring strange knowledge. We went on to talk about the Singh, and I explained I had merely revived an ancient fracture. Puzzlement replaced interest. At last he said, loudly, so that the others heard: 'Boy, do you live by yourself?' So, in kind laughter, the matter ended at school. But there remained my father. He was not pleased at having to sign an affidavit that the son he had sent out into the world as Ranjit Kripalsingh had been transformed into Ralph Singh. He saw it as an affront, a further example of the corrupting influence of Cecil and my mother's family.

I have given a flippant account of this episode. Flippancy comes easily when we write of past pain; it disguises and mocks that pain. I have no material hardships to record, as is clear. But observe how weighted down I was with secrets: the secret of my father, who was only an embittered school-teacher, the secret of that word *wife*, the secret of my name. And to this was added a secret which overrode them all. It was the secret of being 'marked'. From inquiries I have since made I believe this will be understood right away or not understood at all. I felt, to give my own symptoms, that I was in some way protected; a celestial camera recorded my

94

very movement, impartially, without judgement or pity. I
was marked; I was of interest; I would survive. This knowledge gave me strength at difficult moments, but it remained
my most shameful secret.

So many secrets! I longed to be rid of them all. But it
was difficult in Isabella. It was difficult at that school and
with those boys. We had converted our island into one big
secret. Anything that touched on everyday life excited
laughter when it was mentioned in a classroom: the name
of a shop, the name of a street, the name of street-corner
foods. The laughter denied our knowledge of these things
to which after the hours of school we were to return. We
denied the landscape and the people we could see out of
open doors and windows, we who took apples to the teacher
and wrote essays about visits to temperate farms. Whether
we dissected a hibiscus flower or recited the names of Isabellan birds, school remained a private hemisphere.

There was a boy called Hok in my class. I liked him for
his looks, his intelligence, his slightly awkward body, his
girl-like way of throwing a ball. He had long, well-articulated fingers which he was in the habit of rubbing together
whenever he was nervous. I envied him his elegant manner,
and I believe he envied me my manner. With Deschampsneufs I had belching matches. With Hok I had another sort
of competition. The class had decided that we were both
'nervous'; we each decided to be more nervous than the
other. We might gaze at the ceiling during a lesson and not
hear the master's call to attend. We ate paper while we
spoke. I couldn't keep up with Hok here. He was a reckless
eater, and once during a lesson ate a whole page of a textbook before remarking on its absence. I, aware of the
occasional surveillance of my father the schoolmaster at
home, had to be content with the odd corner. I began to
chew my collar; Hok almost ate his off. I ate my school tie
to rags; the end of Hok's tie was never out of his mouth; he
chewed it like gum. Between us was another bond. We were
both secret readers of strange books. We often caught sight
of one another in the Carnegie Library; then we became
furtive or tried to hide, each unwilling to read the books he

was interested in. But I found out about Hok. He was working his way through the Chinese section. His name indicate Chinese ancestry, but he was not pure Chinese. He had som admixture of Syrian or European blood with, I felt, a tinc ture of African. It was a happy blend; it had produced sensitive, attractive boy.

Sometimes our class was taken to the Training College to give the learner-teachers there practice. In our crocodil we were the object of attention of various sorts, to the em barrassment and sometimes fury of our teacher. But in ou crocodile we were also in our private hemisphere, and w walked through the streets of our city like disrespectfu tourists, to whom everything that was familiar to the resi dent was quaint and a cause for mirth: a snatch of conversa tion, the shout of a vendor, a donkey-cart. We were enjoy ing the sights of our city in this way one morning when som of the boys began to titter and whip their fingers, callin the teacher's attention.

One boy said, 'Sir, Hok went past his mother just nov and he didn't say anything at all to her.'

The teacher, revealing unexpected depths, was appalled 'Is this true, Hok? Your mother, boy?'

The crocodile came to a halt. Hok looked down at th pavement and went purple, rubbing his hands together. W looked for the mother, the hidden creature whom Hok sav every day, had said good-bye to that morning and was t see again in two hours or so at lunchtime. She was indee a surprise, a Negro woman of the people, short and rathe fat, quite unremarkable. She waddled away, indifferent her self to the son she had just brushed past, a red felt hat o her head, swinging her basket, doubtless bound for th market.

'Hok!' the teacher said. 'Go and talk to your mother.'

He blew a whistle and we all stood to attention, exag gerating the military posture, the more greatly to impres the onlookers, the native, the ordinary. Hok continued t look down at his shoes and rub his hands, scraping alternat palms with his fingers.

'Hok, go this minute and talk to your mother!'

She was receding serenely.

Hok turned and began to walk towards her slowly. She was almost at the corner. Soon she would have disappeared.

'Hok, *run*! Do you hear me? *Run!*' And the teacher himself ran after Hok, threatening him with his tamarind rod.

Hok shot off, running in his awkward girl's way, and we who were secure and unbetrayed stood to attention and watched. We saw him gain on the dumpy little figure with the hat and the market basket, saw the figure, doubtless disturbed by the sound of running feet, turn in some agitation before Hok had caught up with her, saw the head inclining towards Hok, the black cartoon face of Hok's purple, then saw them separate, the woman going round the corner, Hok turning and coming slowly back towards us, his purple face swollen as if about to burst, Hok the nervous, the secret reader, the eater of paper and ties, now totally betrayed and as ordinary as the street. The poor boy was crying.

It was for this betrayal into ordinariness that I knew he was crying. It was at this betrayal that the brave among us were tittering. It wasn't only that the mother was black and of the people, though that was a point; it was that he had been expelled from that private hemisphere of fantasy where lay his true life. The last book he had been reading was *The Heroes*. What a difference between the mother of Perseus and that mother! What a difference between the white, blue and dark green landscapes he had so recently known and that street! Between the street and the Chinese section of the Carnegie Library; between that placid shopping mother and the name of Confucius her son had earned among us for his wit and beauty. I felt I had been given an unfair glimpse of another person's deepest secrets. I felt on that street, shady, with gardens, and really pretty as I now recall it, though then to me wholly drab, that Hok had dreams like mine, was probably also marked, and lived in imagination far from us, far from the island on which he, like my father, like myself, had been shipwrecked.

I must explain. I cherished my mother's family and their Bella Bella Bottling Works. But in my secret life I was the son of my father, and a Singh. China was the subject of

Hok's secret reading. Mine was of Rajputs and Aryans
stories of knights, horsemen and wanderers. I had even read
Tod's difficult volumes. I had read of the homeland of the
Asiatic and Persian Aryans, which some put as far away
as the North Pole. I lived a secret life in a world of endless
plains, tall bare mountains, white with snow at their peaks
among nomads on horseback, daily pitching my tent beside
cold green mountain torrents that raged over grey rock
waking in the mornings to mist and rain and dangerous
weather. I was a Singh. And I would dream that all over
the Central Asian plains the horsemen looked for their
leader. Then a wise man came to them and said, 'You are
looking in the wrong place. The true leader of you lies far
away, shipwrecked on an island the like of which you cannot visualize.' Beaches and coconut trees, mountains and
snow: I set the pictures next to one another.

It was at these moments that I found the island most unbearable. Study the paradox of my fantasy. I looked about
me minutely; I was pained. And I discovered I was more
pained than most. I was driving with Cecil's father one day
along a country road. We were in the area of swamps
Sodden thatched huts, set in mud, lined the road. It was a
rainy day, grey, the sky low and oppressive, the water in the
ditches thick and black, people everywhere semi-naked,
working barefooted in the mud which discoloured their
bodies and faces and their working rags. I was more than
saddened, more than angry. I felt endangered. My mood
must have communicated itself to Cecil's father, for at that
moment he said, 'My people.'

I wonder why those calm words had such an effect on me.
I hated the speaker. For the first time he had disappointed
me. I had thought of him as ascetic and fair and pious. I
thought that these qualities, which I admired, had come to
him with that money and success to which I was so devoted;
and for a long time, even after this incident, I attributed
these qualities to people who had made their money the
hard way. I admired his lack of show, his separation of his
business life from his home life. I noted his quiet, sincere
taste. In his back veranda, where other people would have

98

had things like thermometers from the tyre companies and calendars from various firms, he had religious pictures and photographs of Indian film actors. He was not interested in the cinema and photographs of Hollywood stars in a private house would have struck him as hopelessly vulgar. But the Indian actors in his back veranda were on a level with the religious pictures: together they were an act of piety towards his past, a reverencing of the land of his ancestors. Details like this had gone towards the making of my picture of him.

And now I was disappointed. I imagine I had expected more passion and more pain. But I kept my thoughts to myself and merely said, 'Why can't they give them leggings?' 'They' were the Stockwell estates, whose overseers' houses, tall concrete pillars, cream concrete walls, red corrugated-iron roofs, presently appeared, rather close together, with no gardens to speak of and as bare of trees as the sugarcane fields in which they were set. Miserable crop! But the pain I felt was my own. Cecil's father said, 'Leggings cost money.'

The fields fell behind. The road ran between shops and two-storeyed houses. Traffic was slower in the main road of the small town and we were driving behind a lorry loaded with floursacks covered by a wet tarpaulin. On this tarpaulin lay two Indian loaders, soaked through. They studied us. Cecil's father had the ability of his age to ignore such scrutiny. I returned the scrutiny; it was the scrutiny of compassion still. There was nothing of compassion in the restless gaze of our driver; he was merely impatient to overtake and get on. His chance, as he thought, came. But he had miscalculated the speed of the oncoming car, and he had to cut in front of the lorry, which braked with a squeal. He was a new driver, glad of the job and anxious to keep it; the silence in our car deepened into strain. At the next slowing-up our driver was too cautious. The lorry overtook us and instantly cut in. The loaders were no longer lying down. They were sitting up. They began to abuse us. I have always hated obscenity; it was doubly hateful to have to listen to it with Cecil's father. We turned up the windows. The loaders turned to obscene gestures and the gestures of threat. They

99

indicated that they had our number and would hunt us down and shoot us and cutlass us. For minutes this went on.

At last we cleared the town and on the open road the lorry pulled away. Our driver made no attempt to keep up. When the lorry was out of sight Cecil's father broke down. As he spoke he lost control of himself. He clenched and unclenched his fists, struck his palms and struck the back of the driver's seat. The driver, out of sympathy and perhaps also because he feared assault, pulled up on the verge and, with his hands on the steering wheel, looked ahead past the clicking windscreen wipers.

'Why you make me suffer like this?' Cecil's father asked the driver. 'Why you make me suffer?'

'I got his number, boss.'

'You got his number, you got his number. What good that will do? You put me in the position of listening to all that.'

'Telephone Mr Mitchell, boss. They will find out about the loaders and fix them up.'

'Telephone Mr Mitchell, telephone Mr Mitchell. Hello, Mr Mitchell, some damn illiterate people insult me for ten minutes on the road this morning, and my own driver was in the wrong.' He went wild. He was Cecil's father and subject to the same somewhat unbalanced rages.

I tried to calm him down. 'They were only loaders, Nana.'

This excited him more than ever. He howled and slapped his forehead. 'They make me shame. They make me shame. Oh, my God!' And in the parked car, close with the windows up, he behaved as though he had just been told he had lost a fortune. The bottler of Coca-Cola, the Isabella millionaire, the nominated Member of the Council.

At first, during that drive, I had felt endangered. Now I thought I saw how easy it was to destroy. A man was only what he saw of himself in others, and an intimation came to me of chieftainship in that island. This was my political awakening. This might be said to have been my first political lesson. A leader of my people? A biter of the hand that fed me? Or simply a Singh, avenging a personal shipwreck?

100

Whatever the impulse, that lesson, so easily learned, so easily carried out when the time came, was an exceedingly simple and foolish one.

2

Cecil sometimes came home with me after school. I was always pleased when he did. I liked Cecil. He was the opposite of Hok but in his own way just as attractive. I liked his confidence and his wildness. I liked his left-hander's gestures, that lift of the shoulder when he walked. He was impulsively generous; his father used to say, with greater truth than any of us then knew, that Cecil was born to give away. I liked to give Cecil things too. But I had little to give him. The only interesting thing our house had was paper, headed or plain, from the Education Department. My father brought home quantities; he said that the stealing of paper was not really stealing. I used to give Cecil some of this paper. His delight puzzled me; I never knew what he used the paper for.

We were going through my father's desk one day, both Cecil and I looking for something I could give Cecil, when we came upon a worn little booklet with photographs of naked women, blurred or depilated in patches. Plump little bodies in foolish attitudes: the weak enticing the weak. I was astonished and as ashamed as when I heard the loaders' obscenities in Cecil's father's car. I told Cecil that the photographs were mine, partly to ease the shame and partly to suggest to him that I had resources of vice he had not suspected. I said he could have them. I had 'used' them – I don't know how the word came to me – and I no longer needed them. He was greatly excited, so excited that he forgot to carry out the threat of nailing a Coca-Cola cap to my father's desk.

He took the booklet to school next day. It created a sensation. It caught the attention of the teachers as well and was passed among them from hand to hand until it rested on the headmaster's desk. Cecil said the book was mine and when I was asked I said this was so. I was not flogged. Instead I was regarded with awe, especially after I had repeated the sentence about not needing the pictures since I had 'used' them. A letter was written to my father, which I delivered. He came to the school and we had a confrontation in the headmaster's room below the neat time-table that was never followed and the board that contained the names of brilliant past scholars. The booklet lay isolated on the headmaster's desk like a thing that could not be of interest to any of the three of us. The headmaster looked from my father to me. My father did not look at me and I did not look at him. I wished all the time to transmit to him the message that I did not think less of him for being interested in these pictures: he after all had a 'wife' and was only yielding to widespread weakness. My father suffered. He was an honest man. The headmaster pressed him but he could not bring himself to condemn me. 'I will talk to him. I will talk to him,' he kept on saying.

He never did. It was only on that Friday, library day for me, that there was something like a sequel. I was in our back gallery reading *The Aryan Peoples and Their Migrations*. It was an old book with an old smell; every time I opened it the spine cracked; I believe I was the first person to take it out of the library. It was not an easy book to read.

My father came in, his bicycle clips still on, his sharkskin jacket sagging and dirty at the pockets, his face tired, his eyes watery behind his glasses.

'What are you reading today?'

I showed him.

'You can go and impress your mother's family with that. They can't read without moving their lips or turn a page without licking their finger. But don't try to fool me, you hear. You understanding what you read?'

'But of course.'

'You are a damned liar. Aryan-waryan, what the hell do you know about that?'

I remembered how at school Browne, being seen with a Tarzan book, explained in his clowning way to the master,

I only read books of commonsense, sir.' So now I said, 'I only read books of commonsense.'

I really believed he was going to hit me. And when he pulled the book out of my hands, so roughly that he tore the brittle cover from its binding, I thought he was going to hit me with that. But he merely opened the book at random and asked, 'What is the meaning of homogeneous?'

We underestimate our strength and throw away our hand. Up till that moment the advantage had been mine; but now faced with the home version of *The Coca-Cola Quiz*, I panicked and said, 'I didn't bring the book home for me. I brought it for you.'

'Damned liar.'

'I won't listen to this. You know that cricket bat you gave me for Christmas? I am going to give it to Cecil. I don't want to touch it now.'

'Give it to Cecil. The poor always give to the rich.'

I brought Cecil home on Monday and showed him the bat. I had left it in the front veranda with a formal note that I no longer wished to make use of this present from my father. In a way this was true, for I had given up as commonplace the fantasy in which, going to the cricket ground during an international match, I had been discovered with his bat, had been instantly picked – one of the batsmen's bats being broken and the batsman discarded with his bat – and had saved the side. I asked Cecil whether he wanted the bat. He read the note and it upset me that he didn't, like my mother, coax me to keep the bat. He simply tore the note off, crumpled it up and threw it into the garden. He said that legally the bat was now his and I was not to touch it without his permission. He was a strange boy, Cecil. I was miserable afterwards.

My father broke a few things when he got home and found I had given the bat away. He went to his room and I heard him talking to himself. Late in the evening he went out. He stopped at the parlour at the corner for a soft drink. Something must have happened there to irritate him, because without any provocation he began to break the place up. It was a simple breaking-up at first, but soon my father

103

began to concentrate on Coca-Cola. He broke bottle afte
bottle; and, being continually armed with jagged Coca-Col.
necks, he terrified the poor shopkeeper. He broke ninety-si
bottles in all, four full cases, breaking one bottle after an
other, methodically, as though he had been paid to do it
he didn't just lift a Coca-Cola case and smash it on the floo
My mother ran out when a neighbour brought the new:
The police had also been called, and the police in this cas
was a young policeman whom my father had often sum
moned in the past to quell disturbances in the street: th
unlicensed butchering of animals in backyards, the playin
of games on the pavement and so on. The matter fortu
nately didn't get into the courts or the newspapers. We com
pensated everyone generously.

The incident brought my father considerable local re
nown and not a little respect among the idlers of the neigh
bourhood. It was the loaders' cursing of Cecil's father al
over again. No one had anything against the shopkeeper
who was always ready to give trust and didn't charg
interest; he would give you a glass of water if you asked fo
it, even if you bought nothing. It was only that the shop
keeper was rich and the idlers were poor and were glad t
see how easily the rich could be made ridiculous. But wha
was most unsettling about this unhappy incident was it
effect on my father. He behaved as though he had had a
access of madness and couldn't be held responsible for wha
he had done that Monday evening. But it was clear h
enjoyed the new renown. He sported his bandages an
plaster with quiet pride – his hands had been badly cu
about, and there were also cuts on his face and chest -
during the fortnight's sick leave he got from the Educatio
Department. He began to presume on the affection of peopl
on the street. He, who before had kept himself to himsel
now had no hesitation in asking a street idler to help hin
mend a bicycle puncture or dig the garden. It was astonish
ing how readily he got the help he asked for. Madness, bu
there was method in it, even if the method came afterwards

My sisters and I spent more of our time with my mother"

family. We went there every weekend and soon our clothes and other possessions were divided between the two houses. My sisters joined Sally's court and so became even more removed from me. This was no loss. They were good-looking girls, but their looks were a source of mortification to me. It was the tradition among schoolboys in Isabella, as perhaps elsewhere, that the brothers of beautiful girls were in some way effeminate, and were to be ridiculed on that account. As much as I suppressed my father, then, I suppressed my sisters. They grew away from me as a result; they never again became close. I thought their attitude to my father extreme. They said to Sally and the others that they were not responsible for him and were generally more severe than Cecil even, who saw some humour in the parlour incident.

Cecil's father built a beach house and decreed a long holiday there. He was one of the first in Isabella to build a beach house. Today of course the beaches of tropical islands have been turned into suburbs and have the same regulated meanness of population and aspect. I have no doubt they will fall into the same disrepute; but by then the work of destruction will have been complete. At the time of which I write, however, it was still held that beaches were to be wild and uninhabited and without even a shed for changing. You took care to put two or three hundred yards between yourself and the next bathing party; and if that was impossible you said that the beach was crowded and went home, hoping for better luck next time. At that time a beach house was a novelty, and throughout the school term we had heard talk about it from Cecil and Sally.

But there was an awkwardness. My sisters and I had not been invited. About a trip to the beach, wild and uninhabited, there was still, among us, an element of venture-someness, as about a voyage itself; and no one was willing to take the responsibility for us during a beach holiday of some weeks. Neither Cecil's parents nor my mother wished to ask my father for his permission, for fear of underlining our separation from him; and we were unwilling to ask ourselves, for fear of being refused. Accordingly, exercising our

105

rights of dual residence, we did nothing. Cecil's parents'
house was going to be shut up; we doubted that we would
be shut up with it or ordered back to our own house. My
mother encouraged us by her silence. The day of departure
found us packed with the others and, still without invitation,
waiting to go. Of course we went.

The sea broke on us almost without warning. Only a
height of sky and a quality of openness behind the tops of
trees suggested that a little way beyond there was no more
land. And then, at the end of an avenue of coconut trees,
was the living, destroying element, almost colourless at this
distance. The trees swayed and rustled and crackled. The
white surf crashed and hissed on the wide beach. Among the
trees, the two-storeyed timber house. No garden, no yard,
no fence: just sand and the unnatural plants and vines,
glittering green, that grew in hot salt sand. Not my element.
I preferred land; I preferred mountains and snow.

Night came, moonlit or black, spectral or empty; and
nothing could be heard except the wind and the trees. Beach
houses were not for me. Not for me this feeling of abandonment at the end of the empty world. Even Cecil appeared
chastened. The girls gathered around an oil-lamp and, in
all the sea din, spoke in whispers. At the end, when it was
not really very late, we played draughts. I was good at
draughts and with every game got better. I played Cecil. He
said 'Aah!' and scrambled the counters when he saw he was
losing. I played my sisters and beat them. I beat Sally. She
offered to play me again. I beat her again and she cried.
She stamped up to bed, shouting that I was conceited.

It was a relief to find in the morning that the world was
still there. As soon as I could I went outside. There was dew
on the vines and the coconut husks. The tide was ebbing;
there was a new tidewrack of wet litter; the wind was fresh.
Far away on the beach I could see the stripped remains of
a great tree, washed up, I had been told, months before,
coming from heaven knows what island or continent, drifting on the ocean night and day for weeks, for months, for a
year, until stranded on our island, on this desolate beach. I
had thoughts, too alarming to pursue, about things existing
106

nly when seen. I went back to the house and found them
getting ready for breakfast. Above the salt of the wind was
the smell of simmering chocolate and fried plantains.

Then Sally came stamping down the stairs in her yellow
seersucker housecoat. Both the garment and the material
had come to Isabella at the same time and had become the
rage; even my sisters wandered about after school in wide-
lapelled seersucker housecoats, showing little bits of slip as
they walked. In her yellow seersucker housecoat, then, Sally
came stamping down the stairs. She was as distressed as she
had been when she went up the previous night. 'Somebody
used my toothbrush!' she sobbed, and waved the tainted
instrument.

The older women were at once concerned – Sally the
beautiful, the delicate – and they hurried to console the
melodramatically outraged daughter of that melodramatic
family. Their concern did not exceed mine. As soon as Sally
spoke I knew it was I who had used her toothbrush. I could
taste the toothpaste again. I felt dreadfully unclean. I ran
up the steps past her to rinse my mouth out. 'It's him! It's
him!' Sally shouted. Her tears vanished even while she
stamped. She giggled; she laughed. At breakfast she didn't
let me forget.

Afterwards I walked by myself along the shining desolate
beach. I observed vines and shells and weed and sand-crabs,
and the almost transparent small fish that each roller
brought right in and very nearly stranded. I wondered
whether I shouldn't take the bus back to the city. I walked
towards the village. It was grey, rusty and rotting: the rust
of old tin, the grey of rotting wood. In a café shack I had a
Pepsi-Cola and a turnover cake with hot sugared coconut
inside. I walked along the bumpy asphalted road out of the
village, away from the sea. I got queer looks from people
behind their hibiscus hedges, people to whom this part of
the island was the world, people who, I had been told, all
their lives never travelled five miles beyond their birthplace.
It was the looks that after an hour or so turned me back
towards the village. It was hot. The leaves were still and
appeared about to quail. The asphalt, laid on in pure,

rippled pats, was already soft underfoot. Here, away from the sea, the freshness of the day had already been burnt off.

In the village shadows had contracted to edgings around huts and to faint glare-shot patterns below trees. On the beach, which I had left empty, there was now a sprinkling of people and activity of a sort. The sand was not fresh. What had been level and shining clean now had the look of something sullied. It had been scuffed and scored, abraded in irregular patches, and littered with red and pale blue entrails already gone flat and lacklustre. Pariah dogs, ribby and of nondescript colour, fawn or pale yellow, wandered about with their long tails between their legs. The heat of the sand penetrated the soles of my canvas shoes. More people appeared on the beach. But being by now part of the activity I had noticed from a distance, it struck me that the activity was curiously muted, without a centre. Some people looked at the sea. Many more stood idly on the sand. Some stood beside the fishermen, who sat mending their nets in the no-shade under coconut trees next to their rough but brightly painted boats. The mixed Carib and African descent of these fishermen showed in their expressionless faces, burnt by the sun and salt and wind to a blackness so pure it had ceased to be a noticeable colour. About me on the beach movement was continuous, but unhurried and undefined. From the refreshment shack where I had earlier had the Pepsi-Cola and the turnover came the gramophone. I remember the song it played. It was *Bésame Mucho*. Words and music rose above the wind and surf and went out ragged over that ragged crowded beach. Then I heard. People were drowning. There in that infernal devouring element people were drowning. The fishermen were being begged to go out and save them. The fishermen sat on the roots of coconut trees and mended their nets and stripped lengths of canes for their fishpots. Their lean Carib-black faces were like masks. I imagined myself drowning. And in this imagining I became detached; feeling no anger against the fishermen who, as I could hear now, were talking among themselves in their patois; feeling only the feebleness and absurdity of any attempt to rescue those persons, already bodies, hidden in that turquoise water beyond the breakers. The visitors, the people on holiday, were frightened; the locals were as calm as the fishermen. To me, standing in my detachment, my overwhelming fear of death, the story came in snatches. A brother had swum out to save his drowning sisters and had himself disappeared. The tide was ebbing fast: they would all be carried far out. So many versions in a short time I heard of that rescue effort by the brother. He had been frantic and foolish and had exhausted himself too soon. He had tried to fight through the breakers and had not swum under them; he had been dashed and twisted and broken on the sea bed. He was a townsman, he couldn't swim. So many stories.

In my fear I turned away and walked back to the beach house. So private a fear it was, so private a sensation of the weakness of the flesh – these poor arms, these poor feet, this vulnerable head – it was shame for the weakness of the flesh that kept me from telling the story to the women. They took my silence for distress at the incident of the early morning and were kind. I accepted their kindness; as though I had taken on for all mankind the weight of the tragedy of flesh and the body I had just witnessed; and this comforting, this service at the hands of women, was fitting.

So it was Cecil who brought the news, and I pretended to hear it for the first time. Then we all ran out, the girls in their bathing suits tripping along the beach, now at low tide very wide, Cecil running far from us through the edge of the foaming water, taking high, splashing steps, an odd celebratory figure. The sand was like the sand of a tainted arena. The fishermen had disappeared. Their boats were out. The cork floats of the seine were in a wide arc on the sea beyond the breakers. Two boats were coming through the breakers in a confusion of white water; suddenly they were clear and driven down and up almost to the limit of the sea; they were being beached. The crowd split and ran to the two boats to take hold of the rope to pull in the seine. The story of the drownings came to us again. It was just before two, the period of stillness between morning and afternoon. The fishermen pulled in their measured way; the visitors and townspeople, already recognizable by their clothes, pulled frantically, as in a tug-of-war contest. And that record still played in the café. Still those words rode over wind and coconut branches. *Bésame mucho, como si fuera la última vez.* The absurd words of popular songs! Then I recognized Deschampsneufs and perhaps members of his family among the frantic pullers. I did not want to be observed. I stood aside. Until then the whole extended incident had been a private moment; now I became an observer.

The arc of the cork floats steadily contracted. It came in closer and closer. It cleared the breakers. Net appeared. Then came shouts. The dragging of the sea! Such an endeavour, so futile, like something in *The Heroes*. Yet it had produced results. The first body appeared, the second, the third. They had all died together, the rolling, drifting bodies, mingled now, as the seine came in to the shore, with fish, alive and silver. There were the fish we called the dogfish, attracted by death, people said. And there were thousands of little fish. And soon everything lay strained and dry on the dirty beach. The fish lay flapping on the sand, curving in brief spasms. The dogfish, threats until a minute ago, lay expiring, and people went among them as though animated by personal revenge and mangled their heads.

The bodies were laid out side by side on the sand in the sun, the bathing costumes still like living parts of them, wet as my own costume would have been if I had been swimming. Away from the group around the stretched-out bodies little arguments had started between the fishermen and some of the people who had helped to pull the seine. The people wanted the fish; the fishermen wanted money for the fish; the people said the fishermen had already been paid, and just for casting the seine. One toothless fisherman continually spoke obscenities. Eventually it was settled. I believe the fishermen got their money. The bodies were taken away; and on the low-tide beach, shining everywhere else, there remained matt marks where the bodies had lain, scrapings and scratchings and scuffed sand to show, just for a few more hours, what had happened. The beach was strewn with small fish so recently whole and now so dull, so like garbage, silver turning to dark grey. The pariah dogs prowled nervously. The vultures watched from the coconut trees. The stingray, on its brown back, its underside bluish-white, showed a bloody stump where its tail had been hacked off.

The beach in this section of our island stretched for more than twenty miles, broken at intervals by the neat channels of streams, fresh but brackish, that flowed into the ocean from the *cocoteraie*. Coconut trees and beach and the white of breakers seemed to meet at a point in the distance. It was not possible to see where coconut turned to mangrove and swampland. Here and there, interrupting the straight line of beach, were the trunks of trees washed up by the sea. I set myself to walk to one tree, then to the other. I was soon far away from the village and from people, and was alone on the beach, smooth and shining silver in the dying light. No coconut now, but mangrove, tall on the black cages of their roots. From the mangrove swamps channels ran to the ocean between sand banks that were daily made and broken off, as neatly as if cut by machines, shallow channels of clear water touched with the amber of dead leaves, cool to the feet, different from the warm sea. On the beach itself the banks of these channels, the tide now rising, were continually undermined, fell off in vertical sections; and then the process of rounding and undermining began again: a geography lesson in miniature, with time speeded up. Here lay the tree, fast in the sand which was deep and level around it; impossible now to shift, what once had floated lightly on the waters, coming to the end of its journey at a particular moment; the home now of scores of alien creatures, which scattered at my approach. Here the island was like a place still awaiting Columbus and discovery.

And what was an unmarked boy doing here, shipwrecked chieftain on an unknown shore, awaiting rescue, awaiting the arrival of ships of curious shape to take him back to his mountains? Poor boy, poor leader. But I was not unmarked. The camera was in the sky. It followed the boy, tiny from such a height, who walked at the edge of the sea beside the mangrove of a distant island, an island as lost and deserted as those which, in films like *The Black Swan*, to soft rippling music, to the bellying of sails of ancient ships, appeared in the clear morning light to the anxious man on deck. Not unmarked. Therefore there was to be no fear. Back through the late afternoon, already turning to night, along the empty beach with its immemorial noise, I walked without fear.

Pinpoints of light, winking, never still, appeared in the distance, like things imagined in the darkness. It was the day of the full moon, when female crabs came out of their holes and went to the waters to wash the eggs they carried on the underside of their bellies, and were surprised by electric torches and captured. I walked towards the dancing lights. I crossed the crab-catchers. They wore hats and were buttoned up against the night breeze. I had exhausted my mood when I came within sight of the beach house, its dim lights diffused more dimly through the tangled coconut gloom.

There was a small figure on the beach stamping on the sand. It was Cecil. He was stamping out his name in huge letters, really enormous letters. It was just the sort of idleness to which he devoted himself with energy. I stood and watched him as the moon came up. We didn't speak. I knew he was expecting me either to help him stamp out his name or to begin my own. I made no move to do either. I left him there and walked towards the house. It didn't surprise me that he abandoned his name and followed me. I heard *When I Grow Too Old to Dream* on the gramophone. Through an open window I saw that the girls were dancing. I went to the window and leaned on the ledge. It was gritty and sticky with sand and salt.

I said: 'Sally, do you know what I think you are?'
She fell into the trap. She said, 'No, what?'
'I think you are a fool.'
I had the pleasure of seeing her stamp.

At school I never mentioned my seaside holiday. I let Deschampsneufs tell of the drownings and his effort with the seine and listened as one to whom it was all new.

So at last, in this matter of relationships at any rate, I

began to eliminate and simplify. I concentrated on school and relationships within that private hemisphere. I did not take to my books or become a crammer: I still retained my pride. Cecil was prepared to admire a brilliant student; and his father often quietly gave money and other help to poor and promising boys of various races. But the feeling still existed among us that education was mainly for the lower classes. I did not go so far myself. My ideal was to be brilliant without appearing to try. But though I thought this was just what Hok brought off, I gave up competing with him in this business of being 'nervous'.

I took up sport. I put my name down for cricket. I thought I would be a bowler and needless to say I wished to bowl very fast. I took a long run and not infrequently at the end lost control of both the run and the ball. I did not last on any side. But the effort was not wasted. I lost some of my self-consciousness. It takes some doing, after all, to put on the absurd garb of the cricketer and to walk with a straight face to the middle! Hok and his supporters scoffed at my new character. I did not mind. I had my compensation in the astonishing number of boys who, in spite of my obvious failures, accepted me as a sportsman. While I was 'nervous' I was in fact unsure of myself. Seeing myself as weak and variable and clinging, I had looked for similar weaknesses in others. This was the cynicism I now arrested. The discovery that many were willing to take me for what I said I was was pure joy. It was like a revelation of wholeness.

I do not wish to claim too much for the playing fields of Isabella Imperial, or rather – to diminish the grandeur and destroy the comparison the plural unavoidably evokes – its somewhat ragged cricket pitch. But it was there that I acquired a certain composure and a certain attitude. I could not at the time formulate that attitude. But it was an attitude, I now see, towards the fact of an audience. And it was this. An audience is never important. An audience is made up of individuals most of whom are likely to be your inferiors. A disagreeable confession; but I have never believed the actor who says he 'loves' his audience. He loves his audience in the way he might love his dogs. The successful public

113

performer in whatever field operates, not perhaps from contempt, but from a profound lack of regard for his audience. The actor is separate from those who applaud him; the leader, and particularly the popular leader, is separate from the led. My later career as a public speaker and handler of men surprised many and was seen by some as a violent breaking out of character. It did not appear so to me. The public speaker was only another version of the absurd schoolboy cricketer, self-consciousness suppressed, the audience ignored, at the nets of Isabella Imperial.

Alas for theory! Alas for abiding fears! Attend to the sequel. A chance for athletic distinction, as I thought, presently offered itself. The occasion was the annual Isabella Imperial sports. It was clear to me that I stood every chance of winning the hundred yards, the two-twenty and the four-forty in my group. The reasons were special and are now not quite clear in my own mind. It had to do with the entry date or my birthday or a combination of both – one day or so either way would have made all the difference; and to this was added the fact that the kindergarten of Isabella Imperial, abolished some years before, then briefly revived, had just been finally abolished and the toddlers incorporated into the main school. For them there were two groups, one under eleven or under ten the other under thirteen or twelve. It was in this last group that a unique chance had placed me. And in this group I was like a giant. Because of the stop-and-start intake of the kindergarten I was competing with children who were fifteen or eighteen months younger. The childish, blotted signatures of entrants on the notice-board confirmed this happy fact.

I took up athletics. I made my mother get me running shorts and I practised assiduously in the college grounds in the afternoons. I imitated the older athletes. After a practice run I did not simply stop. I ran myself down slowly, reining myself in, so that at the end I was like a dancer, elbows high, lightly clenched arms extended and working in rhythm with the high-lifted legs. It amused me to see my juvenile rivals, a scramble of brittle little limbs at one end of the playing field, also practising in this way. They too rubbed themselves down with Canadian Healing Oil or Sloan's Liniment, like me, like the older athletes with developed, hairy legs.

My new character did not pass unnoticed at home. It was put down to the influence of Cecil and aroused distaste in my father, quiet pleasure in my mother, and pride and relief in my sisters who, having given up my father, had no close male to lean on or talk about. The women liked the running shorts, the exposed and massaged limbs, the promise of a manhood which, with my 'nervousness', must have seemed to them somewhat delayed. My father's distaste I interpreted as jealousy; it gave me an unpleasant feeling. Unpleasant too was the interest of the women. Isabella Imperial had been divided some time before, quite arbitrarily, by a head-master fresh from England, into houses, the idea no doubt being that the division would encourage team spirit and competitiveness. The idea had fallen flat. But the houses and their emblems, devised by this same headmaster, had remained. They came to life once a year, on sports day. My mother began to embroider the red emblem of my house on my running vest. She worked on it with love, elaborating in her own fanciful way on an already fanciful design. She worked on it evening after evening, as a woman works on baby clothes. The baby-clothes preparations at home were matched by the week-long preparation of the ground at school: the marking out of lanes, the sticking up of little flags, the erection of tents and marquees. I began to feel that my endeavour was not only unimportant but was being taken out of my hands. I finally lost my temper when I discovered that my sisters had begun to assume that they were going to the sports. I objected. They insisted; they had been making their own preparations. I became abusive. They abused me back. To punish me, they decided they would leave me alone and have nothing more to do with me. I was relieved: it had been a close thing.

The day came. Breakfast astonished me. We usually breakfasted simply, just cocoa or tea with buttered bread and sometimes avocadoes or plantains. Now I was given orange juice, corn flakes, eggs, toast and jam. To me such a breakfast was associated with high days and for this reason was slightly repugnant. All ritual embarrassed me, and I was doubly embarrassed that this day should have been deemed a high day. I was jumpy and it was only when I was alternately crunching and squelching through the corn flakes that I recalled, with shame, the dream I had had. It was a double dream, the dream within the dream, when the dreamer, fearful for the reality of his joy, questions himself whether he is dreaming and decides he is not. I had dreamt that I was a baby again and at my mother's breast. What joy! The breast on my cheek and mouth: a consoling weight, the closeness of soft, smooth flesh. It had been at dusk, in a vague setting, no lights, in a back veranda, all around a blue of dark bush. My mother rocked and I had the freedom of her breast. A dream? But no, I was not dreaming. What pain then, what shame, to awaken!

Seeing her now, the embroiderer of my house colours, so unsuspecting, I felt secret added to secret, weight to weight. But with lucidity and the ordinary light of day the shame passed. Just before lunch I put on the vest with the red badge and covered it with my shirt. And I was surprised by a feeling of high pleasure when, after kissing my mother on the fern-hung veranda of our old-fashioned timber house, I stepped out into the street and was alone, free of mother and sisters, without a father: myself alone. The camera was in the sky. I was a man apart, disentangled from the camouflage of people. The street, usually to me so dull, was now an avenue to wonder.

But when I came to the residential area in which Isabella Imperial was set, something of the Saturday-afternoon lassitude of silent, wide-open houses made itself felt. My jumpiness returned; I was powerless to check it. And as soon as, entering the college grounds by the side gate, I saw the tents and the marquees and the carefully dressed men and women and boys and girls – hundreds of preparations like my own – I felt again the unimportance of my endeavour. My courage ebbed and was replaced by a type of weariness.

The sports began and the grounds were presently a confusion of unrelated and apparently private activities. The patient long distance runners plodded on unnoticed as if fulfilling a vow; there were practice sprints and practice starts and real races at the same time; you turned here and saw the long jump, you turned there and saw the high jump. Scattered about the bustling semi-nude were calm, fully dressed groups conversing or drinking. I saw my rivals. Many had their parents with them. Many were already stripped and displayed embroidered badges as fussy as my own, which was still hidden by my shirt. So many private preparations! When the announcement came, and the boys ambled over earnestly to the starting line and one or two made stylish practice starts, I knew I would never join them, not for that race or the others. They lined up; a master looked them over with a revolver in his hand. My decision was made; my weariness and feeling of unimportance vanished. The revolver was fired and the race was run. It was the hundred yards; it was over quickly and aroused little attention. The master was already himself running off somewhere else, silver whistle in his mouth, his tie flapping, a scribbling pad in one hand and the revolver in the other. I joined the traditional scrimmage for free ice-cream. Then I wandered about the marquees. After some time relief turned to insipidity and at the end, out of boredom as much as anything else, I took part in the four-forty handicap for the whole school – a free-for-all, no entrance fee or signing on required, small boys given a hundred or even two hundred yards' distance – and so with the whole school, a moving multicoloured mangrove of legs, I ran, one pair of legs among many, my house badge still below my shirt. I dropped out and melted unnoticed into the crowd at the centre. Some of the carefully dressed men were now a little beaten up with drink and indulging in a final boisterousness; the girls were tired; the faces of the women were shining. But amid the traditional clowning of the four-forty there was still a pocket of official gravity, much shuffling of papers and comparing of notes: the prize-giving was to follow. The crowd was drifting towards the tent with cups and trophies.

I did not stay. My mother was waiting for me when I got home. She asked, 'Well, what happened?'

'I didn't win.'

And on Monday morning my form master said to me, in front of the class, 'That was a very sporting gesture of yours on Saturday. Though I had no doubt you would do the right thing.'

So the reputation as a sportsman not only endured but was enhanced; and the day became another of my secrets which I feared I might give away in my sleep or under chloroform, before an operation.

I wanted no more secrets like this, no more Saturday afternoons poisoned by a feeling of shipwreck and wrongness among crowds. I had already begun, as I thought, to simplify my relationships. But I had begun too late. I was too far sunk in the taint of fantasy. I wished to make a fresh, clean start. And it was now that I resolved to abandon the shipwrecked island and all on it, and to seek my chieftain-ship in that real world from which, like my father, I had been cut off. The decision brought its solace. Everything about me became temporary and unimportant; I was consciously holding myself back for the reality which lay elsewhere.

I have read that it was a saying of an ancient Greek that the first requisite for happiness was to be born in a famous city. It is one of those sayings which, because they deal with the particular and the concrete, like the instructions on a bottle of patent medicine, can appear flippant, except to those who have experienced their truth. To be born on an island like Isabella, an obscure New World transplantation, second-hand and barbarous, was to be born to disorder. From an early age, almost from my first lesson at school about the weight of the king's crown, I had sensed this. Now I was to discover that disorder has its own logic and permanence: the Greek was wise. Even as I was formulating my resolve to escape, there began that series of events which, while sharpening my desire to get away, yet rooted me more firmly to the locality where accident had placed me.

3

My father became the possessor of a second-hand motor-car. It was one of those baby Austins of the thirties, quaint even at the time, which we in Isabella, more used to American motorcars, called matchboxes. I believe my father bought his car with an interest-free government loan: his duties in the Education Department required him to travel. On the street my father already had the engaging reputation of a bottle-breaker and café-wrecker; the arrival of the baby Austin, emblem of respectability and steadiness, turned him into a type of eccentric squire. They called him a 'radical'. On Isabella this was a word of approval; it described an unconventional person or someone who was a 'character'. With the car and all its attendant dignities and anxieties – petrol-buying, servicing, a constant commerce with inept but impressively greasy mechanics – a change came over my father. His interest in the world revived. He spoke more loudly at home and in public and he became possessed by an odd passion for wit. He repeated your sentences out of context and laughed; he replied to questions by asking absurd questions of his own; he took your phrases and turned them into awkward questions and laughed. It was disquieting. He wore a fixed, ugly grin whenever he was at the wheel of his car, his head slightly raised, his hands in the position recommended by the instructors, his lips parted. He would sing to himself while he drove; he was determined to find humour and interest in everything. It was fatiguing.

At the same time he made some effort to draw his family together and to restore his prestige as its head. To keep us at home at weekends he instituted a 'family lunch' on Sundays. We normally ate in a haphazard but satisfying private fashion, each person helping himself from the kitchen as from a hotel buffet. It was at one of these uncomfortable mass lunches – the last, as it turned out – that he embarrassed us by making a formal little speech.

He said: 'It is good for all the members of a family to be together from time to time, breaking bread. I feel it strengthens the bonds of the family. The family is the unit which is at the basis of all civilization and culture. This was something I learned as a boy from the greatest of the missionaries who came to this island, to whose home, as I believe you know, I was admitted more as friend than student.'

It was bizarre, and not only because it was the first time I had heard him refer to his past. My sisters were on the point of giggling and I was fearful for my father's sake. The mood was too high-pitched and good to last. My mother was enjoying it, though; she liked the sound of the words. She ate slowly, staring at her plate; tears came to her eyes and threatened to fall. Tears came to my father's eyes as well. My sisters noticed and became grave.

'There is no need to tell you, educated one and all, that life is brief and unpredictable. Here today, for example, we all sit, a complete family, each close to the other, each knowing the other well. Do you know that this might be the last time we do so? Do you know that in the years to come you might look back to this very moment and see it as one of the most important moments in your life? One growth reaches perfection and produces another. Nothing stands still. Our meal today is a type of perfection. I would like us all to be silent for a little and think about this moment.'

He was overcome by his own words. He hung his head over his plate and I could see the tears running down his cheeks. We finished our meal in miserable silence.

Afterwards he became sadly gay. It was a continuation of the same unusual mood. He said we should dress; he was going to take us out for a drive. 'Family outing, family outing,' he said, pretending to make a joke of it, applying to his new mood his new style of humour. My sisters and I were not excited. Cars – real ones: our mother's father's – were not unfamiliar to us and we didn't care for a Sunday family outing. That was something we associated with other people: packed second-hand family cars, polished like treasure, going slowly nowhere in particular, with powdered and beribboned girls looking out at pedestrians and fighting

120

back a smile. But there could be no denying my father. We dressed and squeezed into the car and hoped we wouldn't be recognized. There was some trouble about getting the car to start. This gave us hope, but not for long. On my father's instructions we all got out, my sisters, mother and myself, and 'rocked' the little Austin. The engine gave a kick and came confidently to life. We were relieved, though, that my father didn't take us on the usual Sunday afternoon circuit of the city. He drove us out of the city; and then our relief was balanced by anxiety about the ability of the ticktocking little engine to take the hills which, away from the narrow coastal strip, were numerous and steep. We listened to the beat of the engine and to my father's commentary about the areas we drove through.

We drove along narrow rough roads into the valleys of our eastern hills. We went through purely mulatto villages where the people were a baked copper colour, much disfigured by disease. They had big light eyes and kinky red hair. My father described them as Spaniards. They were a small community, exceedingly poor, separate even in slave days and now inbred to degeneracy, yet still distinguished by an almost superstitious fear and hatred of full-blooded Africans and indeed of all who were not like themselves. They permitted no Negroes to settle among them, sometimes they even stoned Negro visitors. We drove through Carib areas where the people were more Negro than Carib. Ex-slaves, fleeing the plantations, had settled here and intermarried with the very people who, in the days of slavery their great tormentors, expert trackers of forest runaways, had by this intermarriage become their depressed serfs. Now the Caribs had been absorbed and had simply ceased to be. We were not far from the city – the little shops stocked familiar goods and carried familiar advertisements – but it was like being in an area of legend. The scale was small in time, numbers and area; and here, just for a moment, the rise and fall and extinction of peoples, a concept so big and alarming, was concrete and close. Slaves and runaways, hunters and hunted, rulers and ruled: they had no romance for me. Their message was only that nothing was secure.

We drove through abandoned, blighted cocoa estates and my father showed us the beauty of cocoa trees. We came out into the Indian areas, the flat lands where rice and sugarcane grew. My father spoke of the voyage, so recent but already in our strange hemisphere so remote, which the fathers and indeed some of the people we saw had made from another continent, to complete our own little bastard world.

'O God, Pa!' one of my sisters cried. 'You knocked that lady's bucket out of her hand.'

He had. The woman was at the roadside standpipe, bucketless, a picture of shock and amazement. My father looked back to see. And at that moment I saw a cyclist, leaning on his bike and chatting on the verge, suddenly, with the briskness of a character in an animated cartoon, twist the handle of his cycle out of the path of the Austin.

'O God, Pa! Look where you going.'

It was the irritation in my sister's voice which annoyed my father, the irritation which broke into his own high-pitched mood and mocked it. He fell silent, and in silence we drove on for some time. He began to mutter to himself and to bite his lower lip. He always overacted, even when his emotions were genuine.

The winding road straightened out on an embankment lined at the foot of each steep slope with poui trees. The sight of the straight empty road seemed to decide my father.

'Bitches!' he said, taking his hands off the steering wheel and accelerating.

We shot across the road and rolled swiftly down the embankment. A split second separated this abrupt deviation from my sisters' screams. We rolled swiftly – but to me it was all in slow motion – towards the trunks of the poui trees. The baby Austin model had its points, though. We went straight between the tree trunks without touching. A series of soft grassy bumps, and the car came to rest, slightly on its side. The engine cut out and there was silence until my sisters remembered to scream again. Abandoning modesty, they scrambled out of the car as fast as they could and climbed up to the road, getting such purchase as they could out of grass and weeds. They said they had no inten-

on of driving back to the city with my father; they would
alk until they found a bus or a taxi. My mother called
hem back, not to make them change their minds, but to give
hem money for the journey. Her manner indicated that it
as her own duty to stay with the Austin, come what might.

It didn't take much to right the Austin. And presently we
ere pulled out by a passing lorry, with whose driver and
river's family – all brilliantly dressed, all in the cab: their
unday afternoon outing as well – my father exchanged the
ghtest of banter. We picked up my sisters. They had al-
eady begun to wilt a little and scarcely needed to be per-
uaded; they also welcomed the opportunity to abuse my
ather. My father ignored them; he sang all the way back.
But as soon as we were home he became morose. His face was
rawn; the pouches under his eyes went dark; and the unusual
hood of the day now showed itself to have been a type of
ysteria. He locked himself in his room, answered none of my
hother's calls, and didn't come out even to have a cup of tea.

So our first and last Sunday family outing ended; and
o our Sunday lunches ended as well. My father withdrew
nce more. The baby Austin ceased to be comic and became
o us a symbol of indefinable terror. We were happier when
t was garaged with some defect. Since then, I might add
ere, I have looked upon the little-man type in his little car
vith feelings which, to say the least, are mixed. My sisters
nd I began spending our weekends freely again with my
hother's family. The suspicion came to me that between
Cecil and one of my sisters there existed an incestuous rela-
ionship. I had nothing to go by, but with these things one
ust suddenly knows.

I was walking home from school one rainy afternoon.
They were laying cables and the roads were dug up. The
bright red clay ran like paint in the gutters. Here and there
n the pavement were enormous cable bobbins. The cables
vere dusted with a white powder and looked like mass-
nanufactured pastry, a type of strudel, produced in enor-
nous lengths and conveyed in this way – on the bobbins,
oushed through the streets by straining barebacked men –

123

to the retailers, who would chop it into small pieces. I heard a fresh shower of rain coming and I began to run. At a corner, as though he had been there a long time, expecting me, was my father. He was sitting on his bicycle with one foot on the pavement; the Austin was in some mechanic's garage.

'Hop on,' he said. 'I think we can take a chance.'

To me towing on bicycles was one of the deep, tempting illegalities. It ranked with cycling at night without a light or riding an unlicensed bicycle; it ranked, in illegality if not yet in temptation, with driving an uninsured motorcar or driving without a permit. It astonished me that my father, a government servant, should choose on a main road so openly to break the law. But his arm was outstretched in invitation, and it was raining.

I sat on the crossbar. I felt the awkwardness of my protruding limbs and the burden of my weight. His arms imprisoned me. We went off shakily. I could hear his tremulous breathing and was aware of the difficulty of every manoeuvre on the muddy, slippery asphalt. I concentrated on the road. The rain was heavy and stinging; we were soon both soaked. People sheltering under the eaves of shops – as still and as meditative as people in the tropics appear when they shelter from a downpour – stared at us. We didn't take shelter ourselves. We didn't say a word to one another. We went on, concentrating on the road and its difficulties. The gutters were full and racing. We sank some inches in water once when the flooded road dipped without warning. We slipped and had little skids. But no accident befell us. When we got home my hair was dripping, my nose was dripping, my books were a pulpy mess, and my shirt was ticklingly stuck in patches to my chest and back. My father's suit was ruined. But still we said nothing; and in silence we separated, to dry ourselves.

I wonder if I would have said anything, if I would have made some statement of gratitude or sympathy, if I had known that that was to be our last contact, that afterwards we were both to follow our separate destinies and that mine, for all my unwillingness, was to be linked to his.

My mother had a theory about the lower classes. She needed one because on our street we were surrounded by them. Apart from one or two very rich areas and three or four very poor areas, all our city was like this, with the slum shack in the unfenced lot next to the two-storeyed mansion. The system or lack of system had its points. Since for most of us there was nothing like a good address or a bad address, everyone submitted to an individual assessment, and this was invariably fair. Everyone received his due and there was harmony. My mother's theory was that the lower classes respected only those who respected themselves. She used to tell the story of a middle-aged white woman who had lived on the street for years, respected by all; but had then so enraged the lower classes by briefly taking one of their number as a lover that she had had to move. Her house was stoned and broken into; when she walked down the street she was insulted by the very people who before would have been delighted to help with the garden or with a heavy box or suitcase. And now, without warning, we found ourselves in the position of that woman. We were not stoned or abused. But we fell definitely into the category of those who had ceased to respect themselves.

Not long after that cycle ride through the rain, my father failed to return home one afternoon. We kept the news to ourselves. The next day he wasn't at the Education Department. We continued to keep the news to ourselves. It was only at the end of the week that we discovered that what was unknown to us and had become our secret was known to a large section of the island. We were waiting anxiously at home; we went out and found we had become notorious. It was like that. We went out and found that my father, so far from disappearing quietly, had become a figure of sorts. He was in the hills, a preacher, a leader, with a growing frenzied following.

We read about people leaving their homes 'one day'. This is the fact, and beyond this we can seldom go. The literal side of my mind has tried a hundred times to work out satisfactorily the events of that day and that week; and a hundred times I am left with the facts minutely established, and their mystery. My father obviously intended to return home when he left for the Education Department that morning. Some of the department files he had brought home were on his desk; his clothes were in the wardrobe; his bankbook was in his drawer. What happened? A fit at the office, a rage, a storming out of the building? Or was it in a lower key? Did he leave the Austin behind because he thought of the city centre, and remembered the traffic congestion there? He was unbalanced, in a temper; he walked. He walked to the city centre, to Waterloo Square. He found himself among the idle and the unemployed. He found himself among the striking dockworkers. They talked among themselves. He broke in and told his own story. He told of his early life, of the missionary and his lady and the aboriginal young man in a clearing in the forest. He told of the years of darkness that followed his abandonment. He told of his marriage and his service with the government. He had never spoken of these things before; he held his audience. He told these men as despairing as himself of his decision, perhaps made even as he was speaking, to turn his back on this darkness. He was aware of his audience: the sons of slaves. Once, he told them, after the abolition of slavery, the ex-slaves had abandoned the foreign city and withdrawn to the forests to rediscover the glory and a way of looking at the world. They were not afraid – fear lay not in the forests but in the regulated city and plantations – and these men had survived. Couldn't the same be done again? His speech would have improved as he spoke. He saw, and his words were vivid. Then they started walking in procession. They went past the docks, where daily for a week there had been scuffles between the locked-out dockers and the equally depressed 'volunteers' who had replaced them. And the procession, taking both dockers and volunteers along with it, had left the area around the dock-gates deserted except for policemen, and in peace. Success is success; once it occurs it explains itself. On the march to the hills food and shelter must have been provided by the poor. Every morning the numbers increased. Witness my father, then, at the end of the week, camping with his followers on crown lands, 'the

126

forests of glory', proclaiming the withdrawal of his flock and asking only that they be left alone.

It was an eccentric lower-class movement, and there were always eccentric movements among the lower classes. On any Sunday in our city you could have found twenty bizarre processions all dedicated to God and glory. In that first week the newspapers spoke only of the silence on the docks. They ignored the beginnings of a movement about which monographs have since been published by the universities of Porto Rico and Jamaica. The monographs tell accurately enough of the rise and withering-away of the movement; they describe its occasionally frightening ritual. But like so many sociological studies, they leave the mystery as mystery; they explain nothing. Twenty people say a thing and they are twenty madmen. But the twenty-first comes along, and he is a hero, a chieftain, a saint. A quality in the man, or a quality of the time? The message, or the fine tuning of responsive despair? A dock strike was being cruelly broken. Who ever believes in the totality of his defeat? Who, seeing this defeat coming and unable to comprehend its horror, does not believe he will in some way be protected or revenged? Today we can see this exodus from our city as a small part of the unrest in the colonies and poorer territories of the Americas just before the war. Each territory produced its own symptoms of disease, its own fantastic growths. We lived with disease; we had ceased to notice. Every day, if you looked, you could find some crazed preacher under a shop awning singing with his little band of the destruction to come. I see these religious excesses, still an aspect of the tourist quaintness of the islands, as an attempt to deny the general shipwreck. Movements like my father's – without that purpose which might have turned them into true revolutions – expressed despair but were at the same time positive. They generated anger in people who thought they were too dispirited even for that; they generated comradeship. Above all, they generated disorder where previously everyone had deluded himself there was order. Disorder was drama, and drama was discovered to be a necessary human nutriment.

The general historical trend can be explained now. But my literal mind goes back to that first day, to the leaving of the Education Department, the decision not to drive but to walk. It goes back to that moment in the square when my father broke into the conversation of the striking dock-workers; that moment when he judged that the time had come to leave the square, and people followed him out. It goes back to the mystery of the widow of the transport contractor who saw in my father a deep distress and sincerity and, from that first day, offered him her devotion. To her he was the man attempting to live the good life as laid down by his Aryan ancestors. He had ceased to be a householder and man of affairs; she saw him entering the stage of meditation before the final renunciation. It was an idea he received from her and exploited; it was an idea which in its essence he lived out with her. I always saw method in my father's madness.

I believe that when he left the Education Department – it might have been after an argument about a minute or a decision to appoint a schools inspector or even after a rebuke from an 'enemy' for having his hair cut in office hours – I believe he had in mind something like a repeat of the bottle-breaking incident, whose triumph had remained with him. But he had gone to the square and fallen in with strikers; a widow, resting her feet after shopping, had seen virtue in him. Ideas had been given him; he had begun to talk. He lost control of himself and events; even at the beginning, I feel, his movement ran ahead of him. What the missionary's lady had seen in him, the aboriginal young man in the high collar, fighting his way up and out of poverty and darkness, was at last about to be fulfilled. The chance had come; he could swear he had not looked for it. It was now or never, and he must have known this. He must have summoned up all his original gifts. But now there was the transport contractor's widow, with her especial piety; and the irony of my father's long-prophesied success was that it came to him as a Hindu. It was the Hindu mendicant's robe that he wore in the hills; and for all the emblems and phrases of Christianity that he used, it was a type of Hinduism that

128

he expounded, a mixture of acceptance and revolt, despair and action, a mixture of the mad and the logical. He offered something to many people; but it was his example and his presence rather than his teaching which mattered. His movement spread like fire. Fire was the word. Sugar-cane fields burned in his path. Calm in the hills, he offered disorder and drama. And at last the newspapers noticed.

I cannot say that the island was alarmed. We – if for the moment I can detach myself from so intimate a phenomenon – were if anything excited. On Isabella we were starved of large events and we secretly longed for the riots and burn-ings to continue. We felt we had at last caught up with the other disturbed territories in the region; we were flattered by the hints, now beginning to be thrown out, that we too were ripe for a Royal Commission. But for us who were of the family of Gurudeva – that was the name my father now took – the matter, as might be imagined, was somewhat dif-ferent. My sisters were especially distressed; style and fashion cannot come easily to the daughters of someone regarded as a lunatic of the commonest sort. In the early days the movement drew most of its support from the three or four very poor areas I have mentioned. There was as yet little publicity, and nothing to suggest that the lunatic was beginning to be seen by some as a great workers' leader, a successor to the revered Deschampsneufs.

The first reports that came to the street suggested only that a family which had for years been treated with respect had suddenly thrown up a type of street-corner preacher. Street-corner preachers had their place and enjoyed their own respect. But the lower classes looked for such people among themselves, and just as, out of that immorality which they accepted as a condition of their own existence, they abused the respectable who lapsed, so now they mocked us. They were tirelessly and grotesquely familiar. My sisters left the house and went to live with my mother's family. The street was pleased; they had 'driven out' someone else; tradition had been maintained. My mother and I con-tinued to live in the house. We were left more or less in peace, until my father's new reputation, as a leader of the poor,

T—T.M.M.—E

made itself felt. Then we received more than respect; w
were handled with a mixture of awe, reverence and famili
arity, which was a degree more disquieting than simpl
hostility.

But my real troubles were at school. I had sought to sup
press my father and the life of my family. Now, like Ho
years before, I was betrayed; for me school could no longe
be a private hemisphere. Our traditions at Isabella Imperia
were brutal. Neither masters nor students in those day
worried about wounding anyone's racial or political sus
ceptibilities; the curious result was that almost no one wa
offended. A Negro boy with an extravagantly jutting hea
could, for instance, be Mango to everyone. So now I becam
Guru. Major Grant gave the name and popularized it. H
taught us Latin and wore a monocle, partly I believe as a
comic prop; he was a great manufacturer of names. I ha
learned that the only way to handle the Major was to b
brutal in return. So now the double act was forced on m
of dissociating myself from my father at the same time as
stuck up for him.

An old joke of Major Grant's was that a boy who di
badly at school could either join the staff of one of our news
papers – if he failed English, that is – or join the staff o
the City Council and ever after ride through the streets i
glory on his own blue rubbish-cart. For Browne, the singer
Major Grant had predicted not the *Isabella Inquirer* -
Browne's English was all right and this automatically dis
qualified him – but the blue rubbish-cart. He accordingl
called Browne Blue-cart Browne, and this over the year
had been shortened to Blue.

Browne came to school late one morning.

'Late this morning, Blue? Been making the rounds a
usual?'

'As usual,' Browne said. 'There was a lot of trash on
Rupert Street.'

A defeat for the Major: he lived in Rupert Street. He
tried to rally. 'Well, I am glad we are not all on *strike*.' He
got no response. He didn't wait; he went on, just teaching
now. 'A thing which many people don't know is that i

130

was our friends the *Ro-mans* who invented the *strike*.' It was his way of talking, laying stresses on words he considered important or funny, pronouncing them in what he considered a funny or foreign way, turning *t* and *r* into Spanish-sounding consonants. 'The first *strike* took place in 494 BC.' He got up and wrote the date on the blackboard. '494 BC 259 AUC. *And what, you may ask, is* AUC? And I will *tell* you, sir. *Ab urbe condita*.' He spat out the Latin, making it almost a single word. 'And they called their strike a *secessio*.' He wrote the word out, underlined the dates he had written, added in English *first strike*, and went back to his desk. 'Strikes were not invented, as some of us have begun to believe, by *Gu-ru*-de-va.'

He got his laughs and stared mischievously at me. A desk lid banged hard, twice. It was like a warning. It came from Browne. I wasn't looking for support there, I must say. Major Grant himself was taken aback. He was a harmless old soul whose jokes, by their fewness and badness, had become jokes, known to generations of Isabella Imperial boys. For the rest of the lesson he tried to pacify Browne. He addressed him gently and often as Blue and for stretches appeared to be talking to him alone.

'*Caeruleus*. When you see the word don't all reach for your *grubby* little pens and *scratch* "sea-blue".' He spoke the last word in falsetto, and continued in falsetto. '*Thaeruleuth*. It'h thea-blue, mummy. *Rubbish*, sir! *Caeruleus* simply means sea-colour. It might be blue, it might be brown, it might be green. It might even, Blue, be *black*.' He stopped abruptly, horrified at the unexpected twist of his words.

Amid the laughter Browne's desk lid banged again. He rose and walked out of the classroom without a word. Major Grant went red. He fitted his monocle carefully into his eye and looked down at his Vergil.

It was then that I saw that what I had thought of as my betrayal was no longer a betrayal. School had ceased to be a private hemisphere. The outside world, which we had denied for so long, had begun to invade it; and after Browne's widely reported gesture there was no need for me to fear ridicule. To many I became what I already was on our street: the son of the leader suddenly found. But I continued, as they say, to play both sides. With some boys I was as detached as before about my father's movement, though their criticism still pained me. And then I could not reject the conspiratorial devotion of the others. With them I was conspiratorial myself and behaved as though I knew of even greater things to come. For a time it did seem that greater things might be coming. The newspapers spoke about police reinforcements being 'rushed' to the hills; and there was a photograph of the Police Commissioner, pistol in hand, leading his apprehensive-looking men in a search of some building. It was strange how drama overtook certain areas, to which no one would have attributed romance or the possibility of adventure, and transformed them, so that even their names acquired a different flavour. Policemen watched our house; the fact was reported in the newspapers; I became a minor figure of drama myself.

It wearied and nauseated me, to tell the truth: the foolish drama, the foolish devotion so many offered me. If I try concretely to describe my reaction to what had overtaken our family – and at times, in lightheaded moods of withdrawal and shock, it was possible as after an accident to see the whole horror afresh, to compare past with present – I would say that the episode gave me a sensation of rawness and violation. It was as though I was chewing rubbery raw flesh and being made to swallow tainted oil. I had made my decisions to abandon Isabella, to eschew my shipwreck on the tropical desert island. But the island had been the island of *The Black Swan*, the fresh green island sighted at dawn, to music. Now it felt corrupted and corrupting. It was this corruption which I now wished to flee. I wished to make a fresh start in my own element; to rid myself of those relationships which it had solaced me to think of as temporary and unimportant, but which I now felt to be tainting.

Yet time, our life, passes. We cannot keep ourselves back for some tract of life ahead. We are made by everything, by action, by withdrawal; and those relationships, begun in corruption, which I thought I could shrug off when the time came, turned out in the end to be able to imprison. They grew on me; I did not look for them. But my failure was my silence. I was silent, to give just one example, in the geography class. It was a drowsy afternoon class. The master was reading from a dull book about the manufacture of sugar. At the beginning of the year, he read out, the ripened canes were cut. He had come to the end of a sentence; he sighed and added, still reading from the book, but it was like a personal interjection, that the cutters were paid by the root. 'Paid? Less than a cent a root!' It was Browne who had spoken. His voice was loud and precise; it silenced the drone and mutter of the master, who continued to look down at his book. In the silence many of the boys looked at me, as though I was campaigning for an increase in cutters' pay. The true embarrassment, I could see, was my presence in the class. I stared into space, giving away nothing. It was hideous and diminishing, this devotion, this assumption that I was *one of them*. I felt threatened. My chieftaincy lay elsewhere. But I was silent.

A movement like my father's could not endure. It was, as I have said, no more than a gesture of mass protest, a statement of despair, without a philosophy or cause. And the administration remained calm. A rash governor might have attempted to evict my father and his followers from their camp on crown lands; and then there might have been bloodshed and bitterness. As it was, certain necessary precautions were taken to prevent looting and arson in surrounding areas; the camp was guarded without being in any way harassed; and the frenzy was allowed to subside. Some acres of forest reserve were burned and some half-hearted planting of crops occurred. But the forests of glory did not yield food in four weeks or six weeks. People wearied of taking offerings to the camp and getting little in return; they wearied of idleness and the absence of drama. A drift began back to the city. It became marked when the dock strike was settled and the 'volunteers' were withdrawn. The union thus established plagued us ever after.

The camp in the hills became another fact of our island

133

life. For two or three days at a time the newspapers made
no reference to it. At school we – if I might detach myself
once more – gave it up as a source of drama. It was frustrat-
ing both to those who had hoped for some vague social upheaval and to those, like Deschampsneufs, who relished the
excitement. But we were not surprised. We accepted that on
Isabella we were a people of mainly domestic interests, incapable of supporting large events. Our attention turned
rapidly to other things. It turned, more characteristically,
to a slogan competition.

The slogan was for a brand of rum. The first prize was the
unheard-of sum of five thousand dollars, and the winner
was to be announced soon. Cecil had been ceaselessly inventive. Thousands and thousands of the coloured entry forms
had been showered on the city and our towns and villages
– you could see the pink, blue or green forms even in the
gutters – but Cecil was convinced that the prize was going
to be his. He said, impressively, that he 'needed' the money.
The name of the rum was Isabella Rum and Cecil's final
prize-winning slogan, which he publicized as soon as he had
sent it in, hoping no doubt to reduce the rest of us to
despair, was *At my parties I fly high with Isabella*. We had
all assumed that a reference to parties was the 'trick' require-
ment of the slogan judges: the drawing on the entry form
was of a party scene in a country of the North. I now believe
the drawing to have been an imported multi-purpose block.
It could have been used to advertise a dancer or dancing
school, a gala night at a restaurant or hotel, a tailoring establishment. But in all our slogans we assumed the role of
metropolitan party-givers. We did so easily; at Isabella
Imperial we were natural impersonators.

The slogan excitement, alas, ended as limply as many of
our other excitements. The result dismayed the school.
Many secret slogan-coiners came out into the open and
were as noisy as Cecil had been. We didn't think the judging
had been fair. For one thing the result came too soon after
the closing date of the competition. And we didn't think
much of the winning slogan. It was *Don't thank me, thank
Isabella*. The drawing that went with it showed a man in

evening garb of some sort showing his guests to the door on a night which, to go by the furs of the tall ladies, was wintry. He was speaking the words to his guests; and in a further balloon, attached to his head by a line of diminishing circles, to indicate unspoken thought, were the words 'Is a rum, Isabella!' For a week or so the newspapers carried the photograph of the very happy slogan-deviser. He was an old Negro labourer, one of those who worked on his own plot of chives or on a citrus plantation. He sat on a bentwood chair in front of his weather-beaten shack; before him was a table with bottles of Isabella Rum and tumblers on an embroidered tablecloth.

'I am not going to touch Isabella Rum from now on,' Cecil said. 'Let them drink their own rum. "Is a rum, Isabella." I don't call that a slogan.'

Deschampsneufs said, 'I don't know why you people worried your heads so much for. Of course they had to give it to a black man. And a black working man.' He had been sending in slogans like everyone else and was a little peeved.

'Eh,' Eden said. 'I don't see why for you grudge a poor black man. After all is they who does drink the blasted thing.'

'*Me* grudge. Is for *you* to grudge. Wait. You will see where you getting this *poor* and this *black* from. Poor black man! You call that a slogan? They call it a competition. But look at the prize-winners. They pick one in this part, one in that part, and they mix up the races to keep everybody sweet. And all of all-you was busting your educated brains. That is what is happening in this island. Wait. Just now they will have foolish black men like that one running the place. Not because they brilliant and so on, but because they foolish and they black. You just wait for this Royal Commission.'

'And a damn good thing too,' Eden said.

'You know, Eden,' Deschampsneufs said reflectively, 'the one thing I can't understand is why *you* didn't win this competition. You didn't have to send in a slogan. All you had to do was to send in a photo. In Technicolour.'

Eden was something of a buffoon. He was the blackest

135

boy in the school and for some time was known as Spit
because some boys said he was black for spite. His
reputation as a buffoon and his special relationship with
Deschampsneufs had been established early at Isabella Imperial. In a third-form science class one day the master held
up a simple device and asked whether we knew what it was
for. It looked like a two-pronged fork with a shiny handle
both prongs were hinged to a wooden or metal base. It might
have been a switch, of the sort scientists 'threw' in films
Deschampsneufs, sitting next to Eden, whispered, 'It generates electricity.' Eden whipped his fingers at the master
demanding to answer. 'Hush!' the master said. 'We are getting news from Adam. Yes, Eden?' 'It generates electricity
sir.' The master went wild. He threw the device on the floor
Then he took up everything within reach on the long lab
bench and let it fall. 'Let's drop it. This and this and this
and this. Let's drop everything.' He dropped two or three
light bulbs; he was like a man suddenly indifferent to his
personal safety. 'It generates electricity, sir. You get this
to generate electricity, Eden, and I will give you my salary
for the month. For the month? I'll give you my salary for
the rest of the year. For the rest of my life. I will give you my
pension. I will work for you in the evenings. I will send my
children to an orphanage and divorce my wife.' So it had
gone on, the agitated red man railing at the placid black boy
until glass shattered on the floor – a test tube or a light bulb
and as it shattered, the master bellowed: 'I will work for you
in *your* garden.' He had saved it for last, not only the familiar pun on Eden's name, but his statement, white man to
black boy, of what he considered Eden's true role, that of
garden-boy or yard-boy. It was cruel; it went too near the
truth; Eden's background was of the simplest. Our traditions were brutal; but now we all went still. Deschampsneufs stared down frowning at his crossed arms, like someone
sharing the abuse.

Later, when the incident had become a joke, Deschampsneufs claimed that he knew what the device was and had
deliberately misled Eden. I don't believe he knew, though.
I believe he was genuinely using or misusing a word he had

just acquired; and I believe his shock, at his error and the abuse that followed it, was as great as ours. But this became their relationship: Deschampsneufs the comic, Eden his willing straight man.

We were talking one day about marriage and the absurdity of the institution that would turn all the foolish boys we knew into husbands, lords and masters to girls, who, poor things, could not at that moment guess their maturing fate. We went on to talk about selective breeding. Deschampsneufs laid down the restrictions he would apply. On this subject he was allowed a certain authority. It was known that in the slave days the Deschampsneufs had kept a slave stud-farm on one of the islets off Isabella; the Negroes there were said to be a super-race still. Eden, attempting to clown and perhaps also looking for a tribute to his own superb physique, said, 'Champ, you would let me breed?' Deschampsneufs considered him. 'It would be a pity to let the strain die out,' he said. 'Yes, Spite. I think we will let you breed. But we will have to cross you with a damn intelligent woman.'

Much was forgiven Deschampsneufs because from the security of his aristocracy he mixed easily with the poorest and crudest boys; in this he was unlike the son of the English clergyman who, possessing only piety, didn't acknowledge black boys in the street, and thereby made himself ridiculous. A lot more was forgiven Deschampsneufs because he was witty and inventive. He loved, for instance, to put a price on a boy; but only he could have got away with it. Only he would have been allowed to say, of a boy he didn't like, 'He wouldn't fetch five dollars.' Outrageousness of this sort was required of him.

'All you had to do,' he now said to Eden, 'was to send in your photo. In Technicolour.'

But he didn't get his laugh. The moment was wrong. His tone was wrong; it was touched with a genuine bitterness. Browne didn't like it. Eden, taking his cue from Browne, didn't like it either. If they were younger they might have come to blows. Eden would have dumbly done what the new mood required of him. But not even angry words passed between them then. The teacher arrived; everyone went to his desk. The declaration of war was left unmade. In this new stage of the old war between master and slave it was left to me to have the fight with Deschampsneufs, a fight I never looked for. I had my own fantasies. I had made my decision to leave. It was horrible to me to be identified with those who struggled outside the gates of the *Cercle Sportif*.

My father's movement faded. Even in our house he faded. He had become a remote public personality, the possession of everyone; he was, occasionally, a name in the newspapers. I found I no longer tried to visualize his day concretely. Such private concern seemed unreal. At school there was no more talk of Gurudeva or riots or burnings; we all preferred for various reasons, to forget that frustration. The injustices of the slogan competition had also been forgotten. We had a new excitement: the Christmas meeting of the Isabella Turf Club. The *Inquirer* told us every day that racing was the sport of kings; and just as there were depressed boys who were prepared to talk endlessly with Cecil about models of motorcars they could never hope to drive, so now there were boys, in the Isabellan scale no higher than grooms, who talked endlessly about the sport of kings. They knew the names of horses, jockeys and trainers; they knew about pedigrees, past performances and handicaps. I couldn't believe in their interest myself. I hated racing; I hated the gambling that went with it. But even I was forced to learn a little.

The main race of the Christmas meeting was the Malay Cup. The *Inquirer* annually told the story of this cup. It had been given to the Turf Club at the turn of the century by the governor, Sir Hugh Clifford. Though it was on Isabella that Sir Hugh exercised his first colonial governorship, he regarded all his service in the Caribbean, in Isabella and elsewhere, as exile from Malaya, to which he was devoted; and he spent much of his time in Government House writing a book of Malayan memories called *Coast and Kampong* which, after an unfavourable review by Joseph Conrad, committed him to the further literary exercise of a lengthy correspondence, ripening to friendship, with the as yet little known novelist. The Malay Cup was Sir Hugh's parting gift to the island he had liked less than literature.

The favourite for the Malay Cup that year was a horse called Tamango. It belonged to the Deschampsneufs stables. Tamango was popular at school as well, for special reasons. Many boys claimed Deschampsneufs as a friend and therefore claimed a special interest in his horse. Then the name was African; and though the significance of the name was known to be ambiguous, the Negro boys were pleased. At Isabella Imperial we all knew where the name came from. Some people outside didn't know – so much we could gather from the sports pages, already notorious to us from the howlers Major Grant regularly culled from them; and this private knowledge made us more proprietorial. *Tamango,* in a simplified and abbreviated edition, was one of the French texts we used in the lower forms; we all knew that Mérimée story of the African chief, seller of slaves, himself treacherously enslaved, and finally a leader of revolt. It was typical of the coolness and ambiguity of the Deschampsneufs family to give such a name to a horse: they seemed constantly anxious to call attention to a past which they agreed had been disreputable.

The interest in his family's horse made Deschampsneufs insufferable at school. He came in in the morning smelling of horse, with his shoes and the bottoms of his trousers wet and dirty and stuck with bits of grass. He looked harassed, as though he had been up all night, a man with worries which the frivolous sporting world, mere watchers and gamblers, taking pleasure for granted, could never know or appreciate. He permitted himself no levity throughout the day, and as soon as the last lesson was over he was off again. His manner invited anxious questioning. But all inquiry or interest made him impatient and rude. He was especially brutal with those boys who, partly to please him, pretended to know more about horses than they did.

Then the horse called Tamango disappeared.

The reaction at school was strange. The correct thing to say was of course that it was a pity or, if you wished to use a newspaper word, an outrage. But there were undercurrents.

It was at once assumed that the horse would not be found; and it was also assumed that Deschampsneufs had in some way become vulnerable to further loss. His loss was tragic, but it made him ridiculous; and within two days the loss itself became something that could be justified. Boys who had put up with Deschampsneufs's brutality became retrospectively irritated; the merit of the horse was questioned; and the very name Tamango, to so many a cause for pride, was now seen as a provocation and an insult.

After about a week we heard that the horse had been found. It was dead. That was all we heard at first, and the news surprised no one. But what I next heard chilled and sickened me and gave me more strongly than ever the sensation of rawness and violation: rubbery raw flesh, tainted holy oil. It was more than a death. A charcoal burner had found the animal, garlanded with marigold and faded hibiscus, on a freshly prepared platform of beaten and plastered earth. Heart and entrails had been torn out; but there were flowers on the animal's mane, flowers woven into its tail; and the coat had been brushed as though by proud grooms. At the centre of the platform, on a smaller, shallow platform of its own, were the remains of a fire, still fragrant with burnt sugar, pitchpine, butter and coconut. Banana suckers had been planted at each corner of this smaller platform; and at each corner a swastika had been traced out in flour. *Asvamedha*: to myself alone I spoke the word. It filled me with unexpected awe and horror. An ancient sacrifice, in my imagination a thing of beauty, speaking of the youth of the world, of untrodden forests and unsullied streams, of horses and warrior-youths in morning light: now rendered obscene. My mind, at once literal and fantastic, created a picture of a deepening, endless tunnel: into this I felt I was ever descending, when all I wanted was to return to the light.

The killing of Tamango was inevitably linked with my father and his followers. The newspapers were outraged and called for action. But nothing could be established. The newspapers called for the destruction of my father's camp and his eviction from crown lands. The administration ignored this unbalanced and ill-timed advice; the governor continued to be cool. At school it was hard for me, though. I was at one with those who abused me. Their abuse was touched with fascination, but their sense of sacrilege was not greater than my own. I could not ridicule; I could not defend. I was sorry for Deschampsneufs's sake: the vindictive current still ran against him. I shared his anger, hurt and disgust. But when he challenged me to fight I fought.

I had never had a fight before and I was certain it would go against me. We were about the same height but Deschampsneufs was heavier. I thought that whatever I was going to do had better be done quickly; and I was as surprised as anyone when at the end of our first clinching I found that Deschampsneufs was on the floor and I was on top of him. That, I knew, was the limit of my success; through our unscientific tangling of arms and legs I could sense that he was recovering fast. I had a moment of alarm, and for an added reason. At the back of my mind was the thought that I had supporters. Now I saw that the battle was mine alone. And the defeated were always wrong. But our form-master was on the alert for just such a fight; the silence, unusual in a free period, warned him. He came and separated us. I was relieved. The boys who had offered me devotion before became more devoted now, they who were willing for me to have been alone.

In the history books, as I say, my father's movement is now made to appear just another part of a recognizable pattern of events in one region of the world. The mood is seen to have created both the leader and the special event associated with him. That event was not the exodus from the city, the march away from the troubled docks of both strikers and volunteers. It was the killing of Tamango. That was the movement's most famous deed, as central to it as the race-course suicide was to the suffragette movement in England. They are both events which, becoming history, lose their horror and obscenity and appear the natural, almost logical, expression of a mood; they are events which now seem oddly *expected* and dramatically right. In Jamaica, the regional history books now say, dealing with the disturbed prewar period, there were strikes and riots; in Trinidad there was an oilfield strike during which three people were shot dead and a policeman was burned alive; in Isabella they killed a racehorse belonging to an old French family.

So the deed becomes a crystallization of an existing mood. But my memory of those days tells me that the deed in such a situation is necessary; that without it a mood is useless and burns itself out. After this deed our island changed, though change was not to show for fifteen years. It was like the loaders' insulting of Cecil's father, the gesture which suddenly reveals society as an association of consent and teaches, dangerously for the future of all, that consent can be withdrawn. And I go back to the leader and the deed. The leader intuits the necessary deed. The killing of a racehorse, a favourite for the Malay Cup, was outrageous and obscene to everyone on that sport-crazed island. Yet it became an acceptable rallying point of righteous, underground emotion. The successful leader works by intuition; such is the degree of self-violation he imposes on his followers, whom he must never cease to surprise.

But for me there was something more. Primitive, bestial, degraded: these were some of the words used by certain sections of the island. I shared their horror, but I had my own reasons. *Asvamedha.* I had read the texts, I knew the word. The horse-sacrifice, the Aryan ritual of victory and over-lordship, a statement of power so daring it was risked only by the truly brave; purified by the tender Asoka; revived by those who came after; and performed, memorably, by the grandson of the general of the last Maurya to celebrate the expulsion of the Greeks from *Aryavarta*, the Aryan land. How had my father arrived at it? Was it simply the intuition of the leader? Was the act no more than what it was, accompanied by simple Hindu ritual which anyone might have observed and copied? Or was it an attempt at the awesome sacrifice, the challenge to Nemesis, performed by a ship-wrecked man on a desert island? *Asvamedha.* Tainted oil, raw flesh. Chieftaincy among mountains and snow had been my innermost fantasy. Now, deeply, I felt betrayed and ridiculed. I rejected the devotion that was offered me. I wished to fly, to begin afresh, lucidly.

4

I was relieved when the war came and my father was interned under some wartime regulation. In this internment he was fortunate. He disappeared almost as soon as he had made his mark. He left behind a reputation which memory could heighten; he was spared a slow neglect, leading to derision, which would certainly have come. With the war, with the arrival of the Americans in Isabella, the building of bases, with the money and prosperity and the urgency it created, with that new sense of nearness to great events, my father's movement would have died of its own futility. When he was released after the war he was no longer required. He was like a man who had been dead six years. This suited him. He wished to be alone; and after a week or so of mainly newspaper fuss he was allowed to live in quiet retirement. But he bequeathed me certain relationships.

With Deschampsneufs, in the first place. We had never been close. I remembered him on the beach pulling in the seine with the three corpses; I had tried then, for a reason I could never give, to hide from him. At Isabella Imperial there had not been anything like the belching competitions we used to have in our earlier school; the invitation to see his vine and Meccano set had not been repeated and possibly now lived in my memory alone. Our fight had only been an untidy scramble in a cleared space between desks; all I remembered of it was a confusion of limbs, the look of surprise on Deschampsneufs's face when he found himself on his back, and the dustiness of the oiled floor. But the cliché occurred: we were more friendly afterwards. He became less flippant with me. He told me some of his secrets. He too wished to leave Isabella. He intended to go to Quebec and paint. That he painted was news to me. He said he thought it was an interest which would be considered effeminate in Isabella; in Quebec, which was French and marvellous, they would understand. He also wished to get married, the sooner the better; he wanted to have ten children, so that he could 'sit down and watch those buggers eat'. I suspected this ambition: I heard the words coming from an older and more foolish person, some harassed poor relation at a Sunday lunch. I entered Deschampsneufs's world tremulously. I was not interested and I did not wish to offend. I felt I had little to offer in return. After all that had happened, his friendship embarrassed me; or perhaps I was embarrassed by what, on Isabella, his offering of friendship implied.

Browne offered me friendship of a different sort. He too had his secrets. His past as a clown and singer of coon songs tormented him, and he used me as his confessor. But I could not wash him clean. I remembered his delight – the delight of the dancing boy in a toy suit with a bowtie and straw hat and cane and painted red lips – and I remembered his parents' delight, and my envy of his fame.

> I like cake, I like honey,
> I am not the boy to refuse any money.
> I can sleep on a cotton bale,
> Or roost up a tree.
> Tell you what it is, boys:
> Nothing hurts me.

He blamed his parents – I remembered his father, in a heavy brown suit, leaning forward in his folding chair, and giving his cackling, squelchy, feminine Negro laugh, like a man about to spit – but he ought to have blamed our innocence. I wasn't sure what Browne required of me. Did he require my sympathy and anger? He insisted on the past and humiliation, but he appeared oddly indifferent to my response. And I didn't know what to say. Sympathy wasn't what I felt. It was more the nausea that came to me when I thought of what had overtaken our family. And just as I entered Deschampsneuf's privacy unwillingly, so I feared to hear more of Browne's interior life. It was not my past. It was not my personality. I lacked the equipment the Brownes carried, that innocence which, with the side of himself he now presented to me, he was trying to suppress.

I would look at our eastern hills, inescapable from the city, and I would imagine them the object of the gaze of those thousands who, from their fields, could look forward

144

to nothing but servitude and days in the sun. But this had to be stopped! This was not the way I wished to look at the island during the time on it that remained to me. I grew to fear Browne's fellowship. I grew to hate the very hills. It might have been the raw nerves of adolescence. How easily we forget the messiness of that process! There were days at this time when the sight of an automobile accident would make me want to fast out of sympathy for those who had suffered. And now through Browne I saw distress everywhere. See how I deal in paradoxes. See how, though rejecting my father's movement, I began to be contaminated by the attitudes he released in his followers.

Withdrawal: it became urgent now for me. Before it had been part of fantasy, part of the urge to escape shipwreck and to return to lands I had fashioned in my imagination, lands of horsemen, high plains, mountains and snow; and time had been as unreal as place. Now I felt the need only to get away, to a place unknown, among people whose lives and even language I need never enter. I transferred my urgency to others. There was a master whom I had startled in my first year at Isabella Imperial by going up to him at the beginning of a class and asking, 'Are you really a B.A.?' I had seen the tremendous fact recorded in the school magazine. He saw irony where I had intended only reverence and he chased me back to my desk; he was, in fact, sensitive about his university, which was Canadian and obscure. Now I startled him again by asking, during a relaxed period, 'How do you feel, sir, about living in Isabella?' He saw it as a political question. I had to explain. 'I mean you have lived in famous countries and seen famous cities. Don't you think you would prefer to live there?' He said, 'I've never thought about it. I used to go to England and the Continent before the war on leave. It was all right. I did the usual things. But I always felt that my work was here. I've never thought about it, really.' I didn't believe him. I remembered how one day he began to talk about the varieties of Canadian apples. I remembered him saying another time, 'You can go skiing in the Laurentians.' And then, as though talking to himself, as though seeing the white-and-blue landscape again, he had added, 'Mind you don't break your leg, though'; and the moment and the imagined landscape had been fixed in my mind forever. The Laurentians! Beautiful name for slopes of white, uninhabited snow! I longed in that barrenness to go skiing, even at the risk of breaking my leg. My element, and I feared I would be denied it. And there was the Belgian, of execrable accent, French and English, and almost no memories: a neat, bored and boring man in goldrimmed glasses. Even he had gone off one afternoon into chuckling, glazed-eye reminiscence: the subject, *la circulation*, not circulation but *traffic*: and suddenly we were with him in a taxi in a traffic jam, the meter ticking, the taxi-driver pulling his cap over his eyes, disclaiming all responsibility for his active meter. There, in Liège in a traffic jam, on the snow slopes of the Laurentians, was the true, pure world. We, here on our island, handling books printed in this world, and using its goods, had been abandoned and forgotten. We pretended to be real, to be learning, to be preparing ourselves for life, we mimic men of the New World, one unknown corner of it, with all its reminders of the corruption that came so quickly to the new.

My obsession took an odd turn. I developed the fear that our old timber house was unsafe. It was not uncommon in our city for houses to tumble down; during the rainy season our newspapers were full of such tragedies. I began to look for these reports, and every report added to my fear. As soon as I lay down on my bed my heart beat faster, and I mistook its throbbing for the shaking of the house. At times my head swam; ceiling and walls seemed about to cave in on me; I felt my bed tilt and I held on in a cold sweat until the disturbance passed. I was safe and lucid only when I was out of the house. So more and more I found myself abroad in that island whose secrets Browne was bent on revealing to me.

I had been able at certain moments to think of Isabella as deserted and awaiting discovery. Browne showed me that its tropical appearance was contrived; there was history in the vegetation we considered most natural and characteristic. About the bread-fruit and Captain Bligh we all knew. He told me about the coconut, which fringed our beaches, about the sugarcane, the bamboo and mango. He told me about our flowers, whose colours we saw afresh in the postcards which were beginning to appear in our shops. The war was bringing us visitors, who saw more clearly than we did; we learned to see with them, and we were seeing only like visitors. In the heart of the city he showed me a clump of old fruit trees: the site of a slave provision ground. From this point look above the roofs of the city, and imagine! Our landscape was as manufactured as that of any great French or English park. But we walked in a garden of hell, among trees, some still without popular names, whose seeds had sometimes been brought to our island in the intestines of slaves.

This was what Browne taught. This was the subject of his own secret reading. I thought his passion would resolve itself in a definition of a purpose or even an attitude. I was patient. But no definition came. He appeared to pursue the subject for its own sake. His friendship became a burden.

He cycled up to our house one Saturday morning and rang his bicycle bell from the street. Neither he nor any other boy from the school, except Cecil, had come to our house before. The visit showed to what extent we had abolished the private hemisphere of school, and I feel sure it was intended as a gesture. I was not in. My mother had not seen Browne before. She saw only an urchin of the people sitting on his bicycle saddle, ringing his bell and smiling. It was an unfortunate characteristic of Browne's – until in his thirties he grew a beard – that he always appeared to be smiling nervously. The skin from his lower lip to the tip of his chin was curiously taut and corrugated; it was as though he was holding back a laugh. At the very tip of this chin, accentuating the smile that wasn't a smile, was a wart; from a distance this looked like a drop of water and suggested that Browne had just washed his face and not bothered to dry it. All this gave him the comedian's appearance which his parents had exploited. My mother looked out from between the ferns on our veranda and asked what he wanted. He said he wanted to see me. But he used my last name. My mother thought he was another mocker of her husband and herself and drove him away as she would have driven away a street arab.

I was appalled when I heard. I knew where he lived and I went straight there. His house was as old as ours and of similar style. But it was on one of the busy streets of the city; it had no veranda and rose almost directly from the pavement, with a jalousied top half. A genuine old-time Negro, grey-headed and pipe-smoking, was leaning out of a window and vacantly regarding the crowded street. He wore a grimy flannel vest. A flannel vest was proletarian wear – flannel the favoured material of Negroes enfeebled by illness or old age – and I wished I had not seen it on Browne's father. Next to the house was a Negro barber-shop called the Kremlin – Negro barber-shops liked to attach such remote drama to themselves – with a caged parrot in the doorway.

I greeted the Negro in the flannel vest and, remembering Browne's misadventure at my house, hurriedly identified myself as a colleague of Browne's at Isabella Imperial. I also took care to ask whether 'Ethelbert' was at home. It embarrassed me to use the name. I never had before and as I spoke it I remembered what Browne himself had told me: that slaves were frequently given the names of Anglo-Saxon kings or Roman generals. Browne's father, he who had dressed up his son years before and taught him the words of the coon song, was at once attention. He grunted through his pipe, hurried to open the front door, and then was anxious for me to sit down. It was an honour not to me but to Isabella Imperial, the famous school, where a poor boy who behaves well and was attentive to his books could win a scholarship: this meant studies abroad, a profession, independence, the past wiped out.

There were two bentwood rockers in the front part of the room. He made me sit on one, called out 'Bertie!' and sat on the other, sucking at his pipe in old-time Negro fashion and staring at me while he rocked. Bertie! The home name! It was like opening a private letter. I felt that Browne wouldn't care for this visit, for the revelation of his father in his flannel vest, which was grimy with little rolls of dirt. It

148

was a narrow room, bounded by a maroon curtain whose reflection darkened the stained and polished floor. Beyond the rockers on which we sat four upright cane-bottomed chairs were arranged around a marble-topped centre table on three legs. The marble was covered with a white lacy material. On it was a brass tray with a stunted but still top-heavy palm in a tin wrapped around with crepe paper. At the top of the tin the crepe paper was finely fringed, almost minced, and fluffed out. On one wall, ochre-coloured with white facings, there were framed pictures of Joe Louis, Jesse Owens, Haile Selassie and Jesus. Against the opposite wall was a glass-doored cabinet with coloured tumblers, cherubs and pink-and-white ladies in glazed clay, three drunk top-hatted men in battered evening dress under a lamp standard, and a bouquet of paper flowers. Above this cabinet was a large photograph of a Negro man and woman, a girl, and a much bedecked boy whose tight chin with water-drop wart revealed him as Browne the comic singer, all standing before a painted backdrop of a ruined Greek temple. Browne's father followed my eyes. He was past pride; but in his look there was that satisfaction which comes to the old and foolish who feel they have done a lot by living long.

He called out again in his strangled voice: 'Bertie!' And presently Browne pushed through the maroon curtain. He was wearing washed-out and frayed khaki shorts; he was barefooted; his eyes were red. He had been having a Saturday afternoon nap. He didn't look pleased to see me. His father rocked, settling down to enjoy the dialogue between two scholars of Isabella Imperial. Browne barely greeted me and instantly pushed through the maroon curtain again. I had a glimpse of a small oval cyp dining table and some heavy polished chairs. I heard voices. Browne's was raised in irritation; I heard him say something about *that black jackass*. Then to him who had shouted 'Bertie!' there came a female call, pretending to be less than a shout, of 'Caesar!' and 'Caesar!' again; and Caesar Browne got up and padded carefully over the polished floor in his slippers, cut-down canvas shoes, towards the maroon curtain, from behind which he was given an invisible tug, so that he appeared

149

suddenly to have lost control of his limbs; and so, swiftly, h
vanished.

Browne himself, when he reappeared, had a shirt over hi
flannel vest. The tropics do impose on their inhabitants thi
recurring indignity of undress, which only above a certai
level turns to style. He sat in the rocker left empty by hi
father and yawned and passed his hands over his legs. H
aimed at casualness, but he was glum and less than welcom
ing. I said I had come to borrow his copy of *Peñas Arriba*. H
wasn't fooled. But it gave him something to do. He went an
got the book. It was the book of the careful student. It
covers were wrapped in brown shop-paper and were dark
furred and almost worn through at the edges where th
palm had closed over them on those sweaty journeys t
school. I thought it had a peculiar smell. I had nothin
more to say. Then Browne's sister came in with her boy
friend, from the police. The tiny room was suddenly alive
For a minute or so, with indefinable unease, I witnesse
actions and listened to talk. Then I left.

I ought not to have gone. I should have ignored Browne'
misadventure; I should never have let him know that I knew
We never forgive those who catch us in postures of indig
nity. That Saturday, with its two gestures, its two visits, it
two failures, marked the end of the special intensity of ou
relationship. I cannot deny that I was relieved. I had bee
choked in that interior, and not only by its smallness. Jo
Louis and Haile Selassie on the wall, the flannel vest, th
family photograph, *that black jackass*: it was more tha
an interior I had entered. I felt I had had a glimpse of th
prison of the spirit in which Browne lived, to which h
awakened every day. In those rooms he collected his facts
out of which he could make no pattern. I doubted whethe
he knew why he passed on those facts to me. He wanted m
to share distress. But, irritatingly, he stopped at distress. An
as I left the house it occurred to me that distress was part o
his reality, was nothing more, could lead to nothing. Int
that private horror I did not want to be drawn again. Pu
Eden in those rooms, and it would have been fitting and
comic. But Browne's nerves denied comedy. In that interio

150

ll the attributes of his race and class were like secrets no
riend ought to have gazed upon.

Our relationship ended. It had been unproductive; it left
no rancour. Yet its poison remained with me. It was with me
at school. Eden said he wished to join the Japanese army:
the reports of their rapes were so exciting. He elaborated the
idea crudely and often; it ceased to be a joke. He recognized
this; in his conversation he sublimated the wish to rape foreign women into a wish to travel. Deschampsneufs said: 'To
see, or to be seen?' He drew a grotesque picture of Eden with
cloth cap, dark glasses, camera and white suit leaning over
the rails of a ship, while sarong-clad Asiatics and Polynes-
ians, abandoning their dances, rushed to the water's edge to
look at the strange tourist. For Eden had fixed on Asia as the
continent he wished to travel in; he had been stirred by *Lord
Jim*. His deepest wish was for the Negro race to be abolished;
his intermediate dream was of a remote land where he, the
solitary Negro among an alien pretty people, ruled as a sort
of sexual king. Lord Jim, Lord Eden. Poor Eden. But, also,
poor Browne. How could anyone, wishing only to abolish
himself, go beyond a statement of distress?

At every reminder of our wide world I returned to that
front room, his security, which he yet hated, where his shop-
assistant sister brought in her young man, from the police,
and for a minute or so – unease later defining itself – were
like cartoon characters, exaggerating their roles: Browne
the younger brother, someone to be bribed and handled flat-
teringly, the young man modest and aggressive and slightly
ridiculous, the sister herself brisk and decisive and standing
no nonsense in her home. Perhaps I exaggerated. It was my
tendency at the time, part of my anxiety to put myself in the
place of those I thought were distressed; and perhaps, like
those misguided reformers who believe that for rich and
poor there is no reality but money, I failed to see much. I
minimized the quality of personality. But so it is when we
seek to forget ourselves by taking on the burden of others.
Was it only for Browne that I was concerned?

I had begun to spend much time in the cinema. It was my

own refuge. On week-days I went either to the late afternoon show or the evening show. On Saturdays I went to the one thirty afternoon show which some of the cheaper cinemas put on. It was the hottest time of day, but these shows were packed out by the young, attracted like myself by the atmosphere of holiday and licence. It was shockingly bright when we came out at about four; this was as dramatic and pleasing as the shock of true heat after an air-conditioned room.

I was at a one-thirty show one Saturday. It was very hot. Some of the rowdier college boys, mainly white and brown, took off their shirts. It began to rain. One or two groups continued shirtless, but they were noticeably quieter. The rain drummed on the corrugated-iron roof: that sound, comforting to us in the tropics, which people from other zones detest. Above the rain and the drumming came the sound of thunder, obliterating the soundtrack. The heavy curtains over the open exits flapped and the rain spattered in. The rain went on, gust upon heavy gust crashing from one end of the roof to the other. Soon the floor of the cinema was running wet. We willingly gave up the film. Our tropical days were even; we enjoyed it when they were dramatized. But then I thought of our house and the dangers of rain. On the screen the film ran on, but the exit curtains had been pulled back by those who preferred to watch the rain, and the picture was faint. The soundtrack was inaudible. The diminished, pointless gestures of the actors gave pleasure to a rowdy few.

I went out and stood in the tiled lobby among the boards which displayed the posters, tacky in the damp, for the afternoon and the evening shows. It thundered; lightning was fluorescent; the trees in the park before us rocked in the wind, which fell and rose. The gutters were already full and even as I watched, the pavements were covered. A cyclist went by. He was going nowhere in particular. He was simply cycling in water for the fun. More boys and girls came out and stood in the lobby to watch. We loved our bad weather. I thought of our house again, more urgently now; and, above drama, I felt alarm. A tree in the park groaned in a series of accelerating snaps and then slowly collapsed, rock-ng to rest on its branches. It was a great tree, one of those with a history. Its leaves were green and shining with wet, its hallow, lateral roots shaggy with earth.

I went out into the rain. The flooded pavement was indistinguishable from the road. Rain obscured our eastern hills and blurred all nearer outlines. Under shop eaves there were damp contemplative little groups. My mind played with images of disaster. It created a house reduced to rubble, embedded in rippled mud, like those tree trunks washed up on our coast. It created wet, isolated planks, crusted with old paint on one side, raw where newly exposed, twisted corrugated-iron sheets, death, the discovery later of little intimate things. Walking in the rain, I knew the panic I sometimes felt when I lay down to sleep.

The rain slackened. I felt the wetness of my clothes and the coldness of the coins in my pockets. And when I got to our street I found only calm. Through some engineer's skill this section of our city, though below sea-level, was especially well drained. There was no flooding here. The gutters were racing, but everything still stood, washed and shining with that newness which came to our roofs and roads and vegetation after rain. My mother was sewing. For her the rain had only been a Saturday afternoon drama, a cause for pleasant little shiverings in the cool. I was relieved. At least the discomfort and ridicule of disaster had been spared us. But, equally, I could not keep down disappointment: the disappointment of someone who had been denied the chance of making a fresh start, alone.

5

The house of my mother's family was solid. I tested it whenever I went there for the weekend. I jumped on the floors when I thought no one was looking; and sometimes I lay flat on them to gauge their level. I leaned against walls to assess their straightness. These precautions made me feel safe and sent me to bed without fear. I did not like returning to the physical dangers of my own house, about which I could talk to no one, and I longed for the time when I would not have to make that particular journey. I thought that this absurd disorder, of placelessness, was part of youth and my general unease and that it would go as soon as I left Isabella. But certain emotions bridge the years. It was unease of just this sort which came to me when I began this book. There was then no fear of the collapse of either the hotel or the public house between which I divided my time – as I still divide it – but I sickeningly recognized that sense of captivity and lurking external threat, that pain of a rich world destroyed and rendered null. Perhaps it was the effort of writing. The houses by which I was surrounded – like those in a photograph I had studied in a Kensington High Street attic during a snowfall and sought in imagination to enter, to re-create that order which, as I thought, expressed its sweetness in young girls and especially in one in a jumper in a sunny back garden – the red brick houses became interchangeable with those others in our tropical street, of corrugated iron and fretted white gables, which I had also once hoped never to see again. Certain emotions bridge the years and link unlikely places. Sometimes by this linking the sense of place is destroyed, and we are ourselves alone: the young man, the boy, the child. The physical world, which we yet continue to prove, is then like a private fabrication we have always known.

A solid house, however. It also offered freedom from the island of Browne and Deschampsneufs. My early attempt at simplification had failed; it had ended in this switching back and forth between one world and another, one set of relationships and another. My grandparents' house had changed. It had become a house of the young, mainly Cecil's friends, the sons and daughters of business families like his own. The community they formed was small and new. It took me by surprise. I have said I was not interested in the credentials of Deschampsneufs's family. But then I was not interested in the credentials of any family except my own. Outside school this had been my world, with Bella Bella and Coca-Cola its peaks. It had not occurred to me that there might be other families like mine with equal cause for self-love, people who made shirts or built roads and thought they were doing quite nicely. And it was disappointing, I must confess, to see the splendour of Bella Bella fade a little. These young people were like Cecil. They were not as extravagant, but they had the same capacity for talk about occasions they had just staged and occasions that were about to be staged. I could not feel for them the affection I felt for Cecil, who was my flesh and blood; and I could not feel I was part of their group. My sisters, though, fitted in easily. But if I was no longer completely at ease in the house, at least I found there no talk of past injury, no talk even of the past. These young people were of the new world. They made the photograph of Indian actors in the back veranda appear quaint and old; the prints, of gods and maidens and swings in the flower-spangled lawns of white palaces outlined in splayed perspective, were of an antiquated piety.

The house had another attraction. Sally had become my partner, Sally the stamper in a seersucker housecoat. Enemies as children, and bound by that special relationship, we had inevitably drawn closer in the changed house. No word was spoken. We simply came together; and nothing again was to equal that sudden understanding, that shared feeling of self-violation, which was for me security and purity. I could not conceive of myself with a girl or woman of another community or even of families like my own. Here for me was security, understanding, the relationship based on perfect knowledge, in which body of one flesh joined to body of the same flesh, and all external threat was diminished. Later I would have the reputation of a lecher and whoremaster. But in every relationship I would be aware of taint; I would recognize triumph or humiliation. There would be nothing again like this mutual acceptance, without words or declarations, without posturings or deceptions; and no flesh was to be as sweet as this, almost my own. I began to think of the world, which I had longed to enter, as the violation that awaited us both, inevitable but not the less painful; it was like growing old or dying. I felt I was losing the courage to enter that world. My longing to escape had turned sour; the

155

island had become my past. My world had narrowed. And at the same time I felt I was like the older people in this house now of the young. I was like my mother and her parents, who found themselves waiting for the end in a house that had grown strange.

I had left school. The war was still on, and it was impossible to travel. I took a job. So did we all. Eden, fulfilling Major Grant's prophecy about those boys who failed English, was snapped up by one of our newspapers. Hok – 'the exception that proves the rule': Major Grant's reported words, when he heard the news – joined the *Inquirer* as a feature-writer. His name presently began appearing above stylishly written articles, whose cleverness could still give me a twinge of jealousy, that jealousy – so easily converted into open admiration – which is the tribute we pay to the naturally brilliant. Browne worked as a clerk of some sort on the American army base. I heard he was writing a novel about a slave. Many people knew the plot: the slave leads a revolt, which is betrayed and brutally crushed; he escapes to the forest, reflects, arrives at self-disgust, and returns willingly to slavery and death. I saw a carbon of an early chapter, the second, I believe. The slaves arrive from Africa; they are happy to be on land again; they dance and sing; they beg to be bought quickly. The scene was all done in mime, as it were, and from a distance. It was brutal and disagreeable. I didn't want to read more. I don't believe more was written.

Deschampsneufs got a job in one of the banks. Those jobs in the banks! The resentment they aroused! They were reserved, quite sensibly, for those whose families had had some secure – rather than lustful and distant – experience of money; and these jobs had as a result acquired the glamour of whiteness and privilege. Eden met me one day on the street and told me enviously about Deschampsneufs's duties. It seemed that Deschampsneufs had *already* been put on to weighing coins. To Eden this casual, wholesaler approach to the coin of the realm – as though it was just another commodity like flour or peas – was maddeningly luxurious. This was the level of our island innocence. And I could see, too, that Deschampsneufs was still up to his usual mischief: consciously exciting envy by revealing what he thought were secrets to people who, he rightly judged, longed to know them from the inside. He had succeeded with Eden, who was delighted to know that coins were weighed, and infuriated that he wasn't allowed to do a little weighing himself.

I couldn't give Eden the sympathy he needed. I wasn't weighing coins. But I was doing an equally dreary job. I was working in a government department as an acting second-class clerk and writing out certificates of one sort and another by hand. The early months of any job are the longest, and I began to feel that I would never leave the department, that some disaster would occur and I would be compelled to stay there for the rest of my life. Pay-day was especially painful. Everybody came in frowning, in a simulated temper; no one spoke; and all morning subordinates and superiors applied themselves with every sign of pain to their duties, which on that day seemed especially onerous. At about ten the first-class clerk, like a man choking down rage, went off with a money sack to the Treasury; he came back an hour later and, losing nothing of his hangman's grimness, sat down at his desk and distributed the money he had brought into various envelopes. No one looked at him; everyone was furiously at work. Then he made the rounds, offering envelopes and a sheet for signature. Everyone signed; no one checked his envelope. The older men handled their envelopes most casually of all, tossing them to one corner of their crowded tables or into a drawer, and just letting them lie there. Half an hour later the trips to the lavatory started; one by one the envelopes passed out of sight, their contents checked. After lunch it was like a holiday. The men were red-eyed and high, giving satisfied little belches; the girls giggled in the vault, showing one another the purchases, usually of underwear, they had made during the lunch hour.

They were all people: I could see no reason why I should be spared. I began to envy the older clerks simply for having lived their lives through. I envied them their calm, their deep pay-day pleasures, their withdrawal from struggle. I envied them the age in their faces, the cultivated deliberateness of their gestures and movements. Cultivated, I now feel: those men were not as old as they appeared to me. I longed to be old. I feared to go out, to be by myself. I could not settle down to any reading. I required only the darkness that Sally provided. Part of my sickness, and I feared my sickness. But I hoped that such a fear would in the end be its own protection. Every weekend I went to the solid house and found Sally. The violation we feared, the violation I feared for her but recognized as inevitable: from this I rescued her, knowing that with every weekend the time for rescue and purity was narrowing.

For the sake of appearances I was forced to go on expeditions with Cecil and his friends and be the wild young man with them. Their wildness could be overdone. Cecil never ceased to enjoy his money and never lost the desire to startle the poor by his money. On a country road he would stop with a squeal of brakes just inches from some poor old woman selling bananas or oranges from a tray. He would shout, 'Get out! Go home, you ugly bitch! Leave that blasted tray this minute if you don't want me to break it on your head.' The terrified woman would make as if to obey; he would call her back angrily and give her ten dollars or twenty dollars, extravagant payment for the tray and oranges he didn't want but still took. Cecil still behaved as though smoking and drinking were vices he had discovered and patented. He visited degraded Negro whores. Pleasure for him appeared to lie in an increase in self-violation; he was like a man testing his toleration of the unpleasant. I believed in his high spirits less and less. But he communicated these to some of his friends and he communicated them especially to a Negro man of about forty whom he had attached to himself as a body-guard-companion-valet. He called this Negro Cecil. It might have been the man's real name; it might just have been Cecil's fancy. The Negro was illiterate and penniless and seemed to have no family. He depended entirely on Cecil and I got the impression that when they were together in public they liked playing a very dramatic master-and-servant, gangster-and-henchman game. I believe they both saw themselves acting out a film; the smallness of their activities must have been a continual frustraion to them. I thought they were both unbalanced.

From these expeditions it was good to return to Sally. It was a big house, but on weekends it was full of people. Discovery was inevitable. It was a visitor who found us. I had seen her around, somebody's mother or aunt, very old, very frail, with glasses that grotesquely magnified her eyes. I was totally blank: no shame, no guilt, no anxiety. I hated as the deeper intrusion the cross-examination that followed. It was detailed and I thought pointless; it reduced everything to absurdity. But for all the threats, there was no sequel then. The visitor's feebleness of sight and body seemed to be matched by the feebleness of her memory. When we next met at the house she had forgotten who I was.

At the house that Sunday was a young man I hadn't seen before. He was introduced as Dalip. He was well dressed and showed no uneasiness at being in a house of strangers. Cecil proposed that the three of us should drive to the beach before lunch. Movement was one of Cecil's ideas of fun; very often there was nothing to do when we got to a particular place. I was tired of these drives. But Cecil insisted, and Dalip was agreeable. We stopped in a side street not far away. Cecil sounded his horn and his valet came running out. He appeared to have been waiting; he always appeared to be waiting for Cecil. He had a bottle of whisky and a bottle of rum. He sat in the back with Dalip.

We were soon out in the country. We drove at great speed along narrow, curving roads. 'They know me, they know me,' Cecil said, as though this was going to keep us from an accident. He was pleased that I was uneasy. The valet grinned, hanging on to the strap. Dalip was relaxed. We came to an area of curves and hills. The car possessed the road right and left impartially, and once we came to a shocking halt before a bus that appeared round a bend. They celebrated by opening the bottles. I drank with them. The liquor was grateful. In the racing car it was not easy to pour or to drink. Rum and whisky were spilt. The car smelled of rum.

Cecil said, 'Open that glove compartment for me a little.' I obeyed. Among yellow cloths and grimy glossy booklets and pads I saw two pistols. One small, with an ivory

159

butt; one big, of pure metal. I had never seen a pistol before

'Take the big fellow out.'

I took out the big pistol. The car shot over the brow of a hill on the wrong side of the road. I had never held a pisto I had thought it was all metal, but now I saw that the but had wood facings, finely cross-hatched. I was astonished a the weight, astonished at the colour of the metal, the prec sion of the moulding. This precision was like beauty. I passe my fingers along the edges.

'A Luger,' Cecil said. 'Heavy, eh?'

In the back seat Dalip and the Negro grinned like men i a secret, who also knew about Lugers.

Cecil, staring ahead, one hand on the wheel, dipped int his shirt pocket with that elegant left-handed gesture, a flexible wrist, with which he usually fished out his packet c cigarettes. He pulled out a bullet. He said, 'This goes wit that.'

I put the Luger back. I took out the smaller gun. It wa old and smooth.

'Nice little thing,' Cecil said. 'It's Belgian. A revolver fc ladies. You can cover it in the palm of your hand. Try an see.'

I said, 'I prefer the Luger.'

I put the revolver back and closed the glove compartmen It was their idea of fun. The cigarettes, the drinks, the fa car going nowhere, the throwing away of money on frigh ened peasants. And now the guns.

An early Sunday morning, and the beach was deserte From the *cocoteraie* brackish streams ran under fallen tre into the sand. The sky was grey. It wasn't going to be a da of sunshine. We stripped. Dalip was plump and would soo be fat. Cecil was thin and stringy and strong as he ha always been.

The Negro had the physique of a weightlifter. We stri ped but did not go into the water. Cecil began to idle abo and we idled with him. How well I knew this idling about Cecil's! It was out of such idling that he fashioned his stori of wonderful times. He kicked sand and did foolish thing with coconut branches. The Negro did what he did. Dali picked up shells and sea eggs. But above all they drank. Soon they were talking with a sort of childlike philosophy about the sea. The sea. Not my element. Yet it entered so many of my memories of the island.

Suddenly, kicking his big toe hard into the sand, and looking up from the spattering sand to me, Cecil said: 'You never met Dalip before? You know who he is?'

I looked at Dalip. His easy-going face had altered. His expression was of pure hate.

Cecil roared with laughter in that breath-holding, neighing way he had – the nostrils that were so fine in his sister were on him slightly flared – and he said, slapping his thigh, 'Your brother, you damn fool!'

I knew at once what he meant. It was not pleasant. This Dalip was the son of the widow who had been living with my father after he had become Gurudeva and taken to the hills. I had hoped never to see her or the son of whom I had heard. But such a meeting had to come; the wonder was that it had not come before. We were a small community, our upper element crisscrossed with marriages, inbred already. There could be no hiding, no secrets. But now, looking at Dalip, soft and very pale, I again had that sense of being forced to eat raw flesh and drink tainted oil; and that sense of the obscene obliterated shame.

Dalip said, 'The son of Guru, eh?'

The Negro laughed.

Cecil leaned against the bleached trunk of a tree that had collapsed on some other island or continent and had been washed ashore here and anchored in sand. He set his mouth and looked hard at me. I understood. He held a bottle of Coca-Cola by the waist. The wrist-watch on his left wrist adorned his naked body.

My mind raced. It fixed on a word. I thought of the Luger and the single bullet, the Belgian ladies' revolver. It was so early in the morning. I thought of one word. Execution. It had occurred before. We were a small community and in a very deep sense we did not recognize the law of the desert island. Our code remained private and whole. Execution, then, on the hot sand on a Sunday morning. A family affair;

it could be concealed: such things had been done before. A disappearance; a gutted body sinking to the bottom of the sea beyond the reach of a fisherman's seine. Yet I couldn't believe in it. It would be foolish to behave as though this was about to happen. Nothing had been announced. I asked for a drink. They gave me rum. I would have preferred whisky. But I drank the rum. It was raw and sickening. I found, to my alarm, that I was passive. I was like the mouse or lizard mesmerized by the cat. I accepted. I was prepared to do what was expected of me.

The taunting, as I saw it, began. Dalip was red with drink and his face was swollen, the eyes heavy-lidded. He threw some sand at my feet and said, 'The son of the great leader. Well, let me tell you. I don't think he is any great damn leader, you hear. He is a skunk. A crook. A vagabond. They should have locked him up long time.'

Strange this taunting. What was said left me cold. Yet I responded to it because I knew it was taunting.

Cecil, reclined against the tree trunk, that silver strap so noticeable on his bare arm, grinned in his breath-holding way. His valet grinned with him.

I began a sentence: 'Who the hell do you think –' and then gave it up, overcome by the weariness of thinking out and speaking a sentence to its end.

'I will tell you something,' Dalip said. 'Your father owes me thirty dollars. *Thirty* dollars.'

When? Facing execution, my own helplessness, my own acceptance. When? I tried to imagine this other life my father had created, this rediscovery of himself and those gifts the missionary's lady had seen: that other life, with its own familiar bonds, so familiar that they might include a request for money. In weakness, as a suppliant? Or out of the prophet's strength and contempt for the things men held to be of value?

'Thirty *dollars*.'

Tears came to my eyes. So suddenly I had taken on my father's pain. It was a debt that had to be repaid, and in-stantly. Before the future took its course. Thirty dollars. What a sum! But it had once been needed. It had once been asked for. Poor Gurudeva! The tears were tears of my own humiliation as well. For all my wish to repay this debt, to wipe out this insult, I did not have this sum. But I ran to the car as though I had the money. I took out the dollar-notes from my trouser-pockets. Just about twelve. In the car, crouching over the seat behind the open door, I thought: the Luger. But I didn't have the bullet. I remembered: that was in Cecil's shirt. But I was unwilling to touch that shirt. Would I know how to insert the bullet? And perhaps the word and the horror lay only in my own mind. It was an absurd situation. The absurdity didn't lighten me. I would have to go laughing to my death, and up to the last I would have to pretend that death was in no one's mind. I left the Luger in the glove compartment. I ran back with the dollar notes and offered them to Dalip.

He said, 'That's not thirty dollars.'

'I will give you the rest later.'

'I just want my thirty dollars.'

I threw the notes at his feet. And of course, I thought, as they fell to rest on the dry sand, they won't stay there when this is all over.

He hit me. I hit him, though I wished to go without a fight. And he was drunk. Cecil and his valet, side by side now against the tree trunk, laughed. Dalip threw himself on me. He was heavy, uncontrolled. He missed me and stumbled. He lifted a twisted and polished piece of driftwood. With this he tried to hit me. It was too heavy for him. It fell of its own weight and I was able to get out of the way. Cecil threw some sand on me. His valet did likewise. They had come closer.

Cecil said: 'The Luger. The bullet in my shirt.'

And, really, I hadn't thought he had left it in his shirt. The Negro ran easily to the car, a man with much time. I ceased to fight. I let Cecil and Dalip hit me. They threw me on the ground and punched me and kicked me. And even then I could not be sure of their aim.

'Thirty dollars. Your father owes me thirty dollars.' Dalip repeated the sentence over and over.

And I only thought: the sea, the sand, the green waves, the breakers, the quaint ships with sails, the morning music.

Not my element, and I was ending here. And I had a vision of the three of us shipwrecked and lost, alien and degenerate, the last of our race on this island, among collapsed trees and sand, so smooth where no one had walked on it.

'A car,' Cecil's valet said.

I heard the wheels on coconut husks and sand. A door slammed. There were voices.

Cecil laughed and said loudly, 'But what the hell is wrong with this man on the sand?'

On a bank, just a few feet high, above the brackish fresh-water stream from the *cocoteraie,* I saw a white family. I got up. Dalip got up. He didn't laugh like Cecil and the Negro. He was still angry, still complaining about his thirty dollars. He still made attempts to fight. He was very drunk. Cecil and his valet kept on laughing, acting for the newcomers. I was forced to struggle with Dalip. The newcomers watched.

'Swim!' Cecil said.

The Negro ran to the water. Cecil chased him as if in sport. I threw off Dalip and followed them. He fell and remained where he fell. The family went walking on the beach, some in ordinary clothes, some in swimming costume. Dalip raised himself after a little and staggered to the car. He opened the door and appeared to collapse on the back seat among the clothes and the towels. I was at last out of the shallows. The water broke over me, the great breakers – the faded white board on the beach said in red *Danger* – and with every breaker I felt closer to myself. It was a coming back from far, as the hill people said. Whence had that mood of the previous minutes come? The sea and the sand. Oh, never again.

Later we found Dalip asleep and totally naked. He had tried to dress but had only got as far as taking off his swimming pants. He had tried to drink some more. The rum bottle was on its side and uncorked and almost empty; rum soaked and scented our clothes. He had apparently also tried to walk home. We followed his tracks through the dry hot sand below the coconut trees to the road. The asphalt was lumpy and rutted and full of holes, green at the base, in which water had collected. About fifty feet up the road he ad collapsed. Soft, pale flesh, innocent abused face, genitals polish and slack. We lifted him back into the car and put ome clothes on him.

We drove back at a rate. The car was damp and gritty ith sand and smelled of rum. We put Dalip down at his ouse. It was a large, clumsy, two-storeyed concrete dwell-ig, painted in vivid colours. I could see pictures of Hindu eities and Mahatma Gandhi in the top veranda. When we ot back to the house they were only reading newspapers. unch was to come. It was still morning, the adventure had een brief. The story Cecil told was the story of Dalip's runkenness. He referred to nothing else.

Some doubt remained in my mind. Some doubt remains ow. Dalip telephoned the next day and apologized. His oice was soft and winning. I told him not to worry. But I ook care not to meet him. We met again years later, after ve had both gone abroad and come back. By then the issue vas dead; accounts had been settled, down to the thirty ollars.

I never went back to Cecil's house. I never saw Sally again. They sent her off some months later to a girls' college in the United States. I knew she would never come back to Isa-ella. So she went out into the contamination of the wider vorld and was absorbed in it. And I was free to do the same. was as blank as I had been at the moment we were dis-overed. I went to my office and wrote out my certificates nd what grief I felt sank into the emptiness that had been vith me for some time. That did not lift.

I heard more about the Luger, though.

Cecil's father bought a cinema in the country. It was the ast thing he bought. It was not much of an investment from is point of view, and I believe that at the back of his mind here was the idea, of a perverted asceticism, that what was rivolity to the rest of the world was to him business. At the nd of his career he was back, in a way, and now from per-ect security, to 'fulling bottles with a funnel'. I also believe t was the last act of his special piety: the cinema showed nainly Indian films.

The cinema became Cecil's toy. It was Coca-Cola all over again: unlimited access to a delight for which the rest of the world had to pay. It was also another place to drive to. He was in and out of the cinema with his valet, harassing the manager; it gave him pleasure to be recognized in the village as the man who owned the cinema. He arrived drunk one evening, when a film was running, and ordered the manager to put on the house lights. There were shouts from the hall. He walked in, Luger in hand, his valet behind him. They climbed up to the stage. They were caught in the light of the projector and threw enormous shadows on the screen. He fired one shot into the floor and one at the ceiling. 'Get out! Take your money back and get out.' Some people lined up outside the manager's office, but most went home. The house lights were dimmed again. Inside Cecil sat, his feet on the seat in front, the Luger in his lap watching the film, alone with his valet, who didn't know the language.

I got the story from my sisters. They continued to live in the house. There they continued to meet the young men to whom they had become engaged. For them Cecil was now only part of the atmosphere of their romances; and this was just another Cecil story, like the famous one of his boyhood about the cases of Pepsi-Cola on the picnic launch.

I remained uncertain about that Sunday morning on the beach. But its revelation, its surprise, had been my sudden and intense sympathy for my father. Poor Gurudeva! There on the beach I had felt linked to his power, madness and humiliation. Thirty dollars. The time was to come when I could pay that sum ten thousand times over. But I remembered.

6

Just after the end of the war Cecil's father died. His disappointment in Cecil showed in his will, which was unexpectedly scattering. He left my mother enough money for her to say she was well off. He also left fair sums to my sisters and myself. In addition he left me some valueless land, which I tried in vain to sell. If Cecil was peeved he didn't show it. My grandfather used to say, proudly at first, later with resignation, that Cecil was born to give away. He was right. Within two years Cecil had run Bella Bella down and lost the Coca-Cola licence. Though even then, from what I heard, he lost nothing of his bounce, dramatizing his decline, seeing himself as a victim of fate alone and happy with his memories of childhood as the great days.

The last time I saw him before I left Isabella was on a Monday morning in our main street. He ran out from a bar and asked me to have a beer with him. His friendliness was so pure and anxious, and this made him so attractive that I agreed, although it was not yet eleven. He was wearing a brilliant white shirt and a tie. This was unusual. He said he was going to the bank. 'I need a few cents,' he said loudly. With his left hand he held his half-empty glass almost at the bottom and rapped it hard on the counter. 'I am going to ask them for two hundred and fifty thousand dollars. *Two* hundred and fifty *thousand* dollars, boy.' He gave a grunt. I didn't believe him; I thought he was only trying to impress the barman. But I was concerned for Bella Bella. He also said there was going to be some religious ceremony for his father at the house. He wanted me to come. I said I would. But I didn't intend to go, and he knew that. The house, now his, was no longer my place of escape: no more the glamour of Coca-Cola, or the security of level floors.

Consider me ungracious. But consider me perhaps also lucky, in that at a time of change I no longer needed these props. I was at last about to leave. I had written to colleges in various parts of the world and I had been accepted by the School in London. Many other people, of every sort, were leaving; the ambition, I now saw, had not been mine alone. The war had brought the world closer to us: the traffic jams in Liège, the white slopes of the Laurentians, the landscapes that imagination had filled out from the drawings by H. M. Brock in a French reader. A few more scholarships were being offered. Browne got one. He was going to London, to do languages: a disappointment to his family, who required

167

a professional man. I heard no more about his novel. Eden applied for a scholarship to study journalism in Canada and, to our horror, almost got it. His failure didn't worry him too much; he settled down happily to studying the movements of ships and passengers for his paper. Hok applied for nothing; a type of lethargy had come over him; he was also reportedly in love.

I used to meet Deschampsneufs from time to time. He was still in the bank and still painting. He had no immediate plans for travel. He said he didn't feel ready for Quebec or Paris just yet. I got the impression that he was enjoying his reputation in Isabella as a 'radical'. He had created a stir in our Art Association by painting either a red donkey in a green sky or a green donkey in a red sky. There had been letters to the newspaper, for and against, quoting all sorts of famous names; and at the end Champ had become a figure. He continued to treat me as a 'serious' person and we would have intellectual conversations. I believe we both enjoyed the idea of ourselves walking about the rundown colonial city and talking art and ideas. He was getting interested in religion and regarded me as an expert. I didn't think the reason was flattering – it seemed a curious tribute to my father – but I pretended to speak with the authority he required. These conversations were a strain; I think we were both always a little glad when they ended.

About a month before I left we met by chance in a café one lunchtime. We exchanged an idea or two. Then he said: 'I hope you can come home one day before you go.'

I was miserable with embarrassment. He spoke like one who knew that an invitation to his home was something which many people on the island would welcome. He also spoke like someone who knew he was exposing himself to a snubbing of sorts, since no one is as ready to snub as the oppressed and the powerless when they find themselves suddenly courted. And again he spoke like someone who was asking for both these considerations to be put aside. His invitation was his offer of reconciliation, his sealing of our stiff intellectuals' friendship.

I didn't want to go to his house. We could meet easily

168

only on neutral ground. But I didn't wish to appear snubbing. I played for time.

I asked, 'How is the vine?'

'A strange thing. It's been attacked by ants.'

The invitation hung in the air.

I said, 'What's a good day?'

We fixed an afternoon.

I had given up the island. But a family, especially if it is at home, can impose its idea of itself; and it was to this idea that I found myself reacting when I went to the house. Deschampsneufs's parents were there and his younger sister Wendy. The father was stocky and swarthy; the mother was pale and thin with no hips to speak of and a sharp worn-out face. Wendy was as thin as her mother but more engagingly ugly. She was at the rubbing-up, flesh-testing, showing-off stage. She climbed over me and my chair, stood on her head in another chair and generally asked for attention. I was told there was some trouble about getting her into a school.

Mrs Deschampsneufs said, 'She is a very intelligent child, though they don't seem to think so here. I took her to a psychiatrist in New York when I was there.'

I expressed my interest. I half-believed that psychiatrists existed only in cartoons.

'He said she was above normal. Very high I.Q.'

Wendy was standing on her head in a deep chair at the end of the room.

'And it wasn't as if he knew anything about us or anything like that.'

There were photographs on the walls of various members of the family, including one which I took to be of the great Deschampsneufs, the leader of the man without in 1877. There was also a very large oil painting of a woman in early nineteenth-century costume. The painting looked new and shiny and I thought it was appallingly done. There were also group photographs; pictures of the French countryside; one or two of French châteaux; and half a dozen old prints in old frames of Isabellan scenes: people landing on surfy beaches and being taken ashore on the backs of naked Negroes, forest vegetation, a waterfall, Negroes in straw hats

169

and striped knee-length trousers rolling casks of rum. There were also, on one wall, the photographs at which I feared to look: racehorses, Tamango no doubt among them.

'I hear that you are going to England,' Mrs Deschampsneufs said. 'I wonder how you'll like it.' She had been flattening out her accent; now she sounded like a woman of the people. I thought she was going to make some remark about the rain or the cold. But what she said, making a face, was, 'Whitey-pokey.'

Her husband raised a hand in tolerant reproof.

I was mortified. This was the term used by Negroes of the street to describe white people. To me it was as obscene in connotation as it sounded. I wondered whether I had always misunderstood the word or whether Mrs Deschampsneufs, attempting vulgarity, hadn't gone farther than she knew. By the judgement of the street she was whitey-pokey herself, very much so. But she appeared pleased with the word. She used it again. It occurred to me that this might be her attempt at the common touch: her statement, to the man she judged political and nationalist, that she belonged to the island as much as and perhaps more than anyone else. Her next sentence confirmed this.

'It might be, of course, because I'm French. But I don't think anyone from Isabella can get on with those people. We are different. This place is a paradise, boy. You'll find that out for yourself.'

Mr Deschampsneufs asked me, 'Do you like music?'

I made a noise which left the issue open.

He got up from his chair and, with Wendy clinging to his legs and impeding his passage, went to the bookcase. He opened the glass door and took two cards from a shelf.

'Here are some tickets for the concert at the Town Hall. We can't go. Champ doesn't like music, and I don't think they should be wasted. It isn't as if we get these things every day.'

'Roger is always being sent things like that,' Mrs Deschampsneufs said.

'Take them,' her husband insisted.

'Otherwise no one will use them,' she said.

Well, I took the tickets.

Mrs Deschampsneufs asked me what I intended to do in London. I told her about the School. But she was interested in smaller things. She wanted to know how I thought I would spend a Sunday, for instance. I didn't know what she expected. She pressed me. But I wasn't going to betray myself by fantasy.

She said, 'I imagine you'll be coming back with a whitey-pokey bride.'

Her husband said, 'But why do you want to arrange everybody's life?'

'Let me tell you, boy. Take a tip from somebody who has seen the world, eh. Don't.'

With that she left the room.

Mr Deschampsneufs said, 'What do you think you will do when you come back? I don't see much scope here for what you intend to do there.'

But I was still thinking about Mrs Deschampsneufs. She had been a little too aggressive, and I thought: goodness, she was aggressive because to her I was someone who was already abroad, no longer subject to the rules of the island.

Champ said, 'Who is arranging everybody's life? Why do you think everybody must pine so to come back?'

His father said, 'Oh, yes, we all want to get away and so on. But where you are born is a funny thing. My great-grandfather and even my grandfather, they always talked about going back for good. They went. But they came back. You know, you are born in a place and you grow up there. You get to know the trees and the plants. You will never know any other trees and plants like that. You grow up watching a guava tree, say. You know that browny-green bark peeling like old paint. You try to climb that tree. You know that after you climb it a few times the bark gets smooth-smooth and so slippery you can't get a grip on it. You get that ticklish feeling in your foot. Nobody has to teach you what the guava is. You go away. You ask, "What is that tree?" Somebody will tell you, "An elm." You see another tree. Somebody will tell you, "That is an oak." Good; you know them. But it isn't the same. Here you wait

171

for the poui to flower one week in the year and you don't even know you are waiting. All right, you go away. But you will come back. Where you born, man, you born. And this island is a paradise, you will discover.'

I said, feeling that he was seeking to drag me back into his world, where he walked with security, 'I am not coming back.'

He wasn't put out. 'It's what I always say. You fellows from the Orient and so on, ancient civilization etcetera, you are the long-visioned types. You give up too easily. Just the opposite of our Afric brethren. Short-visioned. Can't look ahead, and nothing to look back to. That is why I am sorry to say I can't see our Afric friends coming to much. Lot of noise and so on, but short-visioned. I'll tell you. You know those fellows in the South American bush, when they kill something, say a deer or something like that, you know they just sit down and eat out the whole damn thing, man. They not putting aside any for the morrow, you know.' He gave a little laugh as he broke into the popular accent.

I said, 'You mean the bush-Negroes?'

'Indians.' He gave another laugh. 'Amerindians. Bucks, you know. But a similar short-visioned type.'

He was launched on what was clearly a favourite theory. The example he had given, of the South-American deerfeast, had that feel, of a fact polished to myth by its frequent use in argument. In his own way he was a racial expert. His knowledge ranged wide and in some places touched my own, which I had thought personal and sufficiently recondite. The names of books he mentioned revealed him as an addict of racial theory. He rejected simple racial divisions as a crudity. Instead he divided nations into the short-visioned, like the Africans, who remained in a state of nature; the long-visioned, like Indians and Chinese, obsessed with thoughts of eternity; and the medium-visioned, like himself. The medium-visioned were the doers, the survivors.

'No great philosophy and so on, but we've survived. Goodness, how many revolutions?' He pretended to count. 'The French Revolution, for one. What happened? We came over to this part of the world, to Santo Domingo. And then there

as that revolution there. Let's not talk about Haiti. Ten
lorious years of revolution etcetera etcetera, but never men-
on the hundred and thirty, forty, years afterwards. Let's
ot talk about Haiti. Anyway, then we came here. *Tonnere!*
To sooner here than our friends the English take over. Look
t the result. Listen to me talking English in my low Isabella
ccent. Champ here can scarcely talk French.'

It was true. Champ's French was dreadful.

'But we're still around. That lady you see there' – he
ointed to the shiny and terrible oil portrait – 'was an an-
estor of this boy.'

'Not of yours,' Champ said. It seemed a family joke.

'She was born in Santo Domingo. It wasn't too bad with
ld Toussaint in the beginning. Then of course we all came
ere. She was still a child. When she was about fifteen she
ent to Paris. To be educated, to get to know people. You
now. She was very pretty, as you can see. She was a little
it wild too. I think you can see that too. Very popular and
ought after and so on. She used to stay in the house of a
oman called Clémentine Curial.'

I didn't know the name.

'Her husband was a general, a count. What I call Napol-
on brand. There was a man who was in and out of the
ouse. Ugly little fellow, full of talk. And not too well off
ither. He was about forty, and writing a lot of rubbish
obody wanted to read. Biographies and travel books and so
n. Fat little fellow. And you know what? She' – he pointed
o the portrait – 'fell for him. His name was Henri Beyle.'

I gave a start.

Mr Deschampsneufs lifted the palm of his hand, applaud-
ng my knowledge but asking to be allowed to go on. 'When
he came back to Isabella she had a stack of letters from
Ienri Beyle. Of course nothing had happened. The trouble
vith that fellow Beyle was that he was better at talking love
han making it. One day, I think it was in 1831, nothing like
Abolition or anything like that yet, she got a book from
'aris. It was called *Le Rouge et le Noir*. On the fly-leaf
Beyle had written the number of a page. She turned to this
age and saw that two short paragraphs had been marked.

173

When she read the paragraphs she tore up all Henri Beyle'
letters and destroyed the book.

We had studied *Le Rouge et le Noir* in the sixth form.
hadn't liked it. The language seemed to me crude, and
thought the story was simple and unreal, more like a fairy
tale than a story about real people. I said this to Mr Des
champsneufs.

'Well, it must seem like that to us out here. We don't hav
people like marquises and so on here or anything like thei
society. And we can't see the point of a man like Julien c
the Marquis de la Mole. But still, they tell me it's a grea
book.'

'I know. I had to write essays about it. What were th
paragraphs Stendhal marked?'

'The paragraphs. You know the story well? You remem
ber when Julien climbs into Mlle de la Mole's room at night
He went to the bookcase and took out a book. It opene
easily at the place he required. 'Julien has just thrown th
ladder and the rope down on the flowerbeds. You remember

'That was the sort of fairytale thing I couldn't appreciate

'Yes, yes.' He began to read from the book: '*Et commen
moi m'en aller? dit Julien d'un ton plaisant, et en affectan
le langage créole.*' Mr Deschampsneufs's accent was suit
ably broad. 'Suddenly, you see, that fellow Beyle throws in
reference to creole French. For no reason at all. It's a bi
moment in his story, and he goes and does a thing like tha
And then he puts in, in brackets, mark you: *Une des femme
de la maison était née à Saint-Domingue.—Vous, vous en alle
par la porte, dit Mathilde, ravie de cette idée.* For no reaso
at all. That bit of dialogue in creole French. Just for a pr
vate joke. And the joke was that he had exchanged thos
very words in the house of Clémentine Curial with tha
woman whose picture you see there.'

I was deeply impressed. I felt that Mr Deschampsneufs'
story had brought the past close. It was possible to believ
in the link between our island and the great world. My ow
dreams were rendered absurd. The outside world wa
stripped of its quality of legend and reduced to the compre
hensible. Grand figures came near. A writer accounted grea

had been turned into a simple man, fat and middle-aged and ironic. And nearness exalted; it did not diminish.

'A whole life. And that is all that remains. A little aside in a novel, a sentence in brackets. A little affectionate, a little mocking. *Femme de la maison*. Not true, not nice. What do you think? I don't know about you, but I feel it's more than I'm going to leave behind. This immortality is a funny thing. You can never tell who is going to get it. How many people who read that book would stop and think about what I've just told you, you think? She tore up all the letters. Do you think she was right to feel insulted?'

Another familiar topic, clearly. And, as with the first, I took no part. Shortly afterwards I left. Champ walked part of the way with me. I asked him whether it was true about his ancestor and Stendhal. He said, 'My father would kill himself if it wasn't true. I believe *Le Rouge* is the only novel he's read.'

It was the end of another of our Isabella days, the sun gone, the wind cool, the sky ablaze in the west with red-tinted clouds, and against this swiftly passing splendour the tall palmistes and branching saman were black, but with a suggestion of deeper, warmer tints. With Stendhal and the ancestor and the creole language of Santo Domingo in my head, I saw the scene as though I had already been removed from it and it was occurring in memory, in a book.

'The painting of the lady, is that old?'

'Don't try to be too polite with me. It was done by a man in Florida or Minnesota or some such place. He paints from photographs and my father sent him a sketch of some sort. There is another one, if you want to know, in my parents' bedroom. I made them put it there. Done on a dish, and glazed.'

I was carrying away more than a story of Stendhal and the lady. I was carrying away a memory of the absurdity with which the meeting had ended. Did old Deschampsneufs genuinely not see when I attempted to shake hands? I attempted twice, and when he did give me his hand it was only two fingers. The pointlessness of the insult had taken me by surprise. It was as if an unknown, unnoticed man whom

I was passing on the pavement had suddenly attacked me and walked on. So private! So much a thing to keep! And walking back through this horribly man-made landscape of which Browne had spoken, I thought, above Champ's talk: You do not care for what they stand or what they are and they have nothing to offer you. You are about to leave, you have left: the mother saw that. Why, recognizing the enemy, did you not kill him swiftly?

We underestimate or overestimate our strength always. We refuse to wound and thereby throw away our hand. We create problems for the future. *Le Rouge*. Our attention in class had been drawn to Stendhal's cleverness in making Julien, right at the beginning of the book, mistake water on a church floor for blood. This had seemed to me crude. But now, full of the closeness of Stendhal, I looked at the red sky and saw blood. And yet was glad I was leaving. Do not dismiss melodrama and style: they are human needs. How easy it is to turn that landscape, which we make ordinary by living in it and becoming part of it, into the landscape of the battlefield.

One journey had to be made before I left. It was to my father. Some months after the end of the war he had been released. For a few days the newspapers were interested. So too were some of our new-style politicians the Royal Commission had brought into being, businessmen and contractors who saw in politics a potentially rewarding extension of their private affairs. These men thought my father's approval was still important. But my father had not responded and they had gone away. My father did not go back to his camp in the eastern hills. He selected a wooded site in the south-west, near the sea. This was also on crown lands. But the government, I was glad to see, did not molest him.

I went with money in my pocket. I had a debt to repay. His camp was in a clearing off a track. It was an ugly clearing, a disfiguring of the woods. He, or the disciples he still had with him, had turned the ground between the tree stumps into mud; and on the mud they had laid passageways of planks and coconut trunks. The land was not cleared all the way down to the sea. A thin screen of woods hid the sea, as though that was a tainted view. At one end of the clearing was his hut, with mud walls and a thatch of carat palms. On a tree stump on a mound was what looked like a toy replica of this hut. The mound had been scraped clean of weeds and grass and had been plastered. The toy hut was obviously a shrine of some sort. Such childishness was not what I had expected from Gurudeva. Better the leader of the mob than this wasted, scruffily bearded man in a yellow robe who now, ignoring me, went to his shrine and rearranged his little bits and pieces, his stones and shells and leaves and roots and his coconut. The coconut seemed especially important. He had invented so much. His inventions had been so brilliant. Had the gift now been withdrawn?

I went to the larger hut. A woman dressed in white greeted me. She recognized me and I knew who she was. The embarrassment was mine alone. I said, 'I am leaving the island for good. I have come to see him before I go.' She spoke to me in Hindu: 'Have you come then for a sight of him?' She used a word with strong religious associations: *darshan*. I did not wish to lie. I said nothing, surrendering, as I had surrendered at the Deschampsneufs', to the woman's idea of herself, her concept of the holiness of her charge and the holiness of the ground. She was beyond the reproach of sex: this was the reproach I had feared to sense. She said: 'It is his day of silence. He has given up the world. He has become a true *sanyasi*.'

Sanyasi, yellow-robed, among woods! Woods hymned endlessly in Aryan chants and found here on an island surrounded by a brown-green sea. It was his day of silence. When he came back to the hut from his shrine he greeted me without recognition at first. But then he put his arms around me. I remembered the embrace of his arms before, the day he towed me on the crossbar of his bicycle. He was gentle and silent. He went to the inner room of the hut. The sympathy that remained was for the idea of him. Gurudeva, *asvamedha*: these were the inspired moments, the fulfilment in a few weeks of a promise that had festered long.

But I had also come to repay a debt. It couldn't really be

repaid, but the gesture was necessary. I said to the woman
'I would like to leave this for Gurudeva.' I gave her a prepared wad of a hundred dollars. Then I gave her three ten-
dollar bills. 'My father borrowed this from your son Dalip.'
Clad in white, the colour of purity, she took the money
showing no surprise.

Afterwards I went for a walk on the beach. The coast here
was wild and untidy. The water at times frothed yellow
with mud. The beach was littered with driftwood and other
debris from the mighty South American rivers which, in
flood, pushed their discolouring fresh waters as far north a.
this. The sand was black and pebbly and sharp. Another
cloudy day, the clouds as dirty and ragged as the sea and
the beach. I walked. The woods of crown lands gave way
to the mangy coconut grove of a rundown estate. The trunks
of the trees had orange blotches; beyond them were the
white wooden houses of the labourers, white distemper
streaked with the running salt rust of old tin roofs. There
was a car on the beach. And in a little huddle in the shallows,
as though in the vastness of sky and sea and sand they had
come together for protection, was a white family, made up
it seemed only of women and girls. A man, clearly of the
party, was standing on the beach. A man burdened by
women. We walked towards one another.

He said, as one sharing a joke, 'You went to Gurudeva's
camp?'

'I've just been to see him. I am his son.'

'Oh! Deschampsneufs told me you went to see him.'

'His son asked me to tea.'

He was not more than forty, but he had the used-up look
of a man who had found his niche early and could already
look back to a stupendous twenty years' experience.

'How did you like old Des?' he asked.

'He was all right.'

'He told you about his ancestress?'

'I heard about her.'

'Poor Deschampsneufs.'

'I don't see how anybody can call Deschampsneufs poor.'

'It's pathetic, really. He's got this French thing.'

'I know.'

'But of course, as you know, the Niger is a tributary of that Seine.'

The phrase came out whole: it had been used before. I felt choked. I wanted fresh air. I wished to be among people of greater fears.

'Des told me you were going abroad to further your studies.' He used the newspaper words. His thin hair fell crinkly and wet over his sallow forehead, above eyes hollow from glasses. 'You know, it's an odd thing. But I've never been abroad. All my friends they go abroad and come back and say what a wonderful time they had. But I note they all come back. I tell you, boy, this place is a paradise.' That word again. 'I suppose you going to do like all the others and come back with a whitey-pokey.' Again that word.

He lifted his hand to his forehead to push back the loose hair. I studied his veins. They were like the map of a river. Whitey-pokey: I had learned to read that word. The Niger was a tributary of that Seine, in paradise. Fresh air! Escape! To bigger fears, to bigger men, to bigger lands, to continents with mountains five miles high and rivers so wide you couldn't see the other bank, to journeys that took two days and a night. Good-bye to this encircling, tainted sea!

My friends from Isabella Imperial planned a dinner for me. I was overwhelmed by the gesture. It was sweet to find that after all the fumbling with relationships I had friends who wished to mark my going. Too sweet; too disturbing. When Hok came to take me in his car to the restaurant I made some excuse. I couldn't explain why at the last minute I no longer wanted to go. It was an impulse of childishness, no doubt: a fear of the big occasion, a fear of warmth and friendship, a poisoning feeling of inadequacy and the wish to be alone with that sudden, nameless hurt. I don't know. I was ashamed and regretful a moment after he had left, taking my excuse to the others. The next morning he brought the book they were going to give me. It carried all their stylish, evolving signatures. *Fête Champêtre: The*

Paintings of Watteau and Fragonard. I felt that the choice of book had been left to Deschampsneufs.

It was only on the ship, well on my way, that I came upon a narrow strip of paper between the pages. It carried an unsigned typewritten message: *Some day we shall meet, and some day.* ... I suspected Hok, because of the typing and because the paper was of the sort used for copy in newspaper offices. It was like that last family lunch my father had arranged. There is something after all in the staged occasion, the formal sentiment. It came to me on the ocean, this message ending in dots, telling me that all my notions of shipwreck were false, telling me this against my will, telling me I had created my past, that patterns of happiness or unhappiness had already been more or less decided.

I thought of Columbus as hour after hour, day after day – with no pause at night, as I had been half-expecting – we moved through that immense ocean. The wind whipped the crests of the waves into rainbow-shot spray. The sunlight grew paler and faded; the rainbows disappeared. I thought of that world which, as I was steadily separated from it, became less and less discovered, less and less real. No more foolish fears: I was never to return.

And witness me then, just four months later, standing in the attic of a boarding-house called a private hotel in the Kensington High Street area, holding a photograph of a girl and praying for a little bit of immortality, a prophylactic against the greater disorder, the greater shipwreck that had come to me already.

7

I wished then to go back as whole as I had come. But though a fresh start is seldom possible and the world continues our private fabrication, departure is departure. It fractures; the bone has to be set anew each time. I was in London, awaiting health, Sandra my luck, when I heard that my father was dead. The news came in a guarded letter from my sister. I went to the British Council reading room, to which I had been long a stranger, to look at our local newspapers. What was not even a paragraph in a London paper had made headlines in the *Inquirer*, with photographs of the camp I had seen once, now unfamiliar and oddly exposed with officials and policemen standing about. My father had been shot dead, and a woman with him. The weapon was a Luger. The news required a response. It required sentiment and the opposite of sentiment. I walked about the streets. Later I went with a prostitute. I was full of my news. But I saved it for the end. Her shallow whorish reaction, of sentiment and reproof, was all I could have asked for. Later, in the blackness of night, I cried on Sandra's breasts. And suddenly I discovered I was ready to leave. We left from Avonmouth. It was August but the wind was chill. Gulls bobbed like cork amid the harbour litter. We headed south and sailed for thirteen days.

Three

As I write, my own view of my actions alters. I have said that my marriage and the political career which succeeded it and seemed to flow from it, all that active part of my life, occurred in a sort of parenthesis. I used to feel they were aberrations, whimsical, arbitrary acts which in some way got out of control. But now, with a feeling of waste and regret for opportunities missed, I begin to question this. I doubt whether any action, above a certain level, is ever wholly arbitrary or whimsical or dishonest. I question now whether the personality is manufactured by the vision of others. The personality hangs together. It is one and indivisible.

Sandra saw in me a husband. She was right. She saw what was there. I think of the day she left. It was officially on a shopping trip to Miami. This was a pilgrimage our group was beginning to establish as fashionable. From these trips our women returned with large light parcels in unfamiliar wrappings and that day's edition of the *Miami Herald*: dramatic sunglassed figures as they stepped out of the Pan-American aeroplane. For me it was a moment of another type of drama: the aeroplane the cinematic symbol: Bogart in *Casablanca*, macintoshed, alone on the tarmac, the Dakota taking off into the night.

Afterwards I drove back to the Roman house. I walked round the central swimming-pool, the fountains splashing noisily into the blue water, no one now, I thought, to listen to them. I went to her room and looked through her cupboards. There was no sign that she intended to return. Some shoes she had left behind, abandoned for good, some dresses she hadn't worn for some time. I held a shoe and studied the worn heel, the minute cracks in the leather. I touched

183

the dresses. I was light with whisky; the gestures seeme
suitable for a moment of private theatre.

It was only later, minutes later, when the ceaseless splas
of the fountains became unbearable and the feeling of reli
I was stimulating suddenly vanished, that I knew that th
gesture, however self-regarding and theatrical, of handlin
Sandra's abandoned shoes and dresses, yet held somethin
of truth: as that other gesture, in London of the magic
light, on the day of my first snow, of holding the crease
photograph of an unknown girl and wishing for an instan
to preserve it from further indignity.

It is with my political career as with that gesture. I use
to say, with sincerity, that nothing in my life had prepare
me for it. To the end I behaved as though it was to b
judged as just another aspect of my dandyism. Crimina
error! I exaggerated my frivolity, even to myself. For I fin
I have indeed been describing the youth and early man
hood of a leader of some sort, a politician, or at least a dis
turber. I have established his isolation, his complex hun
and particular frenzy. And I believe I have also established
perhaps in this proclaimed frivolity, this lack of judgemen
and balance, the deep feeling of irrelevance and intrusion
his unsuitability for the role into which he was drawn, an
his inevitable failure. From playacting to disorder: it is th
pattern.

A name of peculiar power had been prepared for me. I
was a name I had sought to deny. It was the one thing I kep
secret from Sandra, feeling the name like a deformity t
which anyone might at any time refer. Now the name
claimed me. And with the name there came again that un
easy relationship with Browne which I thought I had lef
behind for good when I went to London.

We were in London at the same time. But our interest
never coincided – Browne, I imagine, was ferociously politi
cal and public-meeting and *New Statesman* – and I had
met him only once. It was near Earl's Court Station. He wa
in a great hurry, the macintosh flying behind him, and he
shouted out to me without stopping as we crossed, 'How

ow, man? You know what happen just now? A bitch spit
n me, man.'

'Spit on you?'

'Yes, man. Spit on me.'

We crossed; he was on his busy way; and that was all. It
as as if he had seen me a few hours before and was going
o see me again soon. He was very cheerful, considering the
ature of his news. I wasn't sure whether he had made up
he story; whether he had heard of my way of life and was
tending some irony; whether he had mistaken me for
omeone else; or whether the story was true and when he
aw me he was still in a state of shock. He was in a hurry,
s I have said. But I thought, even from that slight en-
ounter, that London had had an effect on him, as it had
ad on me. He was lighter and freer than he had been in
he sixth form.

Later, on the island, he had become something of a
haracter; and that glimpse of him in London fitted. His
haracter was of a special type. People like Browne were the
earest things we had to poets, renegades, interesting
ailures; they were people we cherished. He was a good ex-
mple of the type: a man of the people, a scholarship boy
ho had not quite made good and was running to seed. He
ad given up his teaching job and had become a pamphle-
er. He wrote articles for the *Inquirer*, had rows with the
ditor, and made these rows the subject of further pam-
hlets. He was an occasional publisher, an occasional editor,
nd a tireless talker in the middle-class bars.

He talked better than he wrote. He was always intense
ut always, oddly, negative. He analysed situations acutely
nd with relish. But he gave equal weight to everything. He
as content with a feverish analysis of each succeeding epi-
ode. He was saved by his ambivalent attitude towards the
ubject he most exploited: the distress of his race. He had
ritten a venomous little pamphlet, anti-everybody, about
he Negro skull, working out in this way some of the anger
e had felt about an article in an American journal. Yet
ne of his favourite bar stories – he liked doing the upper-
ass English accent – was of the bewildered but honest

English cricket captain who had cabled back to London i
the 1880s: *Beaten by local team whereof six were blac*
And it was Browne again who, while campaigning for th
employment of Negroes in the firm of Cable and Wireles
supported their exclusion from the banks. He used to sa
'If I thought black people were handling my few cents
wouldn't sleep too well.'

On the subject of distress he was serious, without a doub
But he was bitter only in his writings. He did not give th
impression, which many others gave, of regarding a secrete
and growing bitterness as a source of strength to come. Pe
haps in his conversation he was trying unconsciously
flatter his hearers; for Browne, more noticeably now tha
at school, preferred the company of other races. It mig
be that he required alien witness to prove his own reali
and make valid the distress he anatomized. Or perhaps
was that he feared to be alone with his distress, and coul
exercise his wit only with others. His frenzy seemed such
private thing. It was what we expected of our poets an
it might be, our clowns. It was attractive. There were alwa
people to support his most outrageous enterprises. I myse
had taken the back cover of his pamphlet on the Negro sku
for an understating advertisement: *Crippleville is a subur*

When he came to the Roman house to urge me to pr
claim my father's name he had grown a small beard an
was editing a paper called *The Socialist*. The beard we
well with his thin face and slender body. It hid the wart c
his chin and made him look less of a comedian. That wa
its sole motive. It had nothing to do with the paper which
after the first issue in which the policy was stated at lengt
contained little of socialism. Browne always stated the poli
of each of his papers at length. He was a pamphletee
Having stated the policy of his paper, he became bored wi
the paper; and most of his energies seemed to go in gettir
advertisements. What he wrote became increasingly bitt
gossipy and even disheartened; the reader got the impre
sion that the editor was having trouble not only in gettir
advertisements but in getting things to put between them.

The Socialist was at this stage when Browne came to s

e. He said he had a plan and an idea. The plan was that should put money in the paper, or in some other paper we ught start together. The idea was that *The Socialist* should celebrate the anniversary of the dockworkers' exodus from the city, and that I myself should write the main article bout my father.

Certain ideas overwhelm us by their simplicity. It was the roclaiming of the name first of all that appealed to me; then the idea of the magazine. My excitement astonished, then excited, him. He made those gestures I knew so well – the washing of the hands, the whipping of the right index nger, the great swivel in the chair as he made some telling oint. His interest in his own paper revived; he seemed almost ripe for another lengthy statement of editorial policy. His vision widened. He saw *The Socialist* as an international paper, and he talked about the need for a 'nationalist' publishing house in the region. This was one of the schemes he ften spoke about, and I knew it was just the sort of thing e might jump into. Even in my excitement, though, I could ee a pointless business proposition. I steered him back to *The Socialist* and the anniversary number.

And there in the Roman house – where I had prepared the scene for an occasion with an altogether different issue our agreement was made. The blue-and-white Hong Kong raffia chairs and table, the drinks, the illuminated swimming-pool, the Loeb edition of Martial: all this had been meant less to overawe Browne than to create the picture of man who, whatever might be said about recent events in is private life, had achieved a certain poise. The Martial an be easily explained. I had taken up my Latin again. It was my own therapy. The acquisition in easy stages of a recise, dead language, through an easy author, was curiusly soothing. It called for effort; it filled the time; it led rom one day to the other.

My mood might explain the excitement I felt, my ready acceptance of an idea which to so many on the island might ave seemed absurd and which to me a few months before ould have seemed affronting. But I was also a prisoner of my special relationship with Browne, that understanding

187

which began, continued and faded away in misunderstanding. A burdensome relationship, a boyhood uneasiness never quite forgotten when we met. Now it was flattering. He needed alien witness to prove his reality. For me a similar proof was offered by his literalness, which was like generosity. For him I had been, ever since Isabella Imperial, a total person. He remembered phrases, ideas, incidents. They formed a whole. He presented me with a picture of myself which it reassured me to study. This was his generosity; it was a relief after the continual challenge and provocation of relationships within the group that had been Sandra's and mine. So between Browne and myself the old relationship was resumed. He invited me to share distress. He presented me with my role. I did not reject him. How can I regard what followed as betrayal?

Even at that first meeting in the Roman house my uneasiness was not wholly suppressed. Where once I carried a name that was like a deformity, so now I felt I had a past to which Browne might at any moment refer. He asked me no questions about Sandra, though; and he made no reference to the Roman house. It was my own uneasiness which made me think, even while we spoke, how little I knew of his private life, how unable I was in imagination to see him at home, relaxed. One detail sharpened this. His beard appearing to be causing him some irritation. He wiped the bumpy skin around his Adam's apple with his handkerchief, placed it against his neck, and let the beard rest on it. A disturbing mannerism: the perspiration on my own neck began to smart. I made some remark about the beard. He dismissed it in his brisk, self-satirizing way as 'a Negro's beard'. I didn't know what to make of this. He then said that in his three years in London he had never been to a barber-shop. It had been no problem; hair like his never really grew long.

I thought he was joking. I still don't know whether he wasn't: it is hardly the subject for casual query. But with this amazement at a physical fact which would have caused no amazement to most of the people on the island which I was now claiming as mine, there went the dim knowledge that I was now committed to a whole new mythology, dark

nd alien, committed to a series of interiors I never wanted
o enter. Joe Louis, Haile Selassie, Jesus, *that black jackass,*
he comic boy-singer: the distaste and alarm of boyhood
ose up strongly. But already Browne had turned the talk
o his nationalist publishing house; the fountains splashed,
ecalling me to the solidity of the Roman house; the twinge
f tribal alarm passed. It was a detail, a drowning man's
econd: it stayed with me.

The essay about my father for *The Socialist* wrote itself.
t was the work of an evening. It came easily, I realized later,
ecause it was my first piece of writing. Every successive
iece was a little less easy, though I never lost my facility.
ut at the time, as my pen ran over the paper, I thought
at the sentences flowed, in sequence and without error,
ecause I was making a confession, proclaiming the name,
aking an act of expiation. The irony doesn't escape me:
at article was, deeply, dishonest. It was the work of a con-
ert, a man just created, just presented with a picture of
imself. It was the first of many such pieces: balanced, fair,
ith the final truth evaded, until at last this truth was lost.
he writing of this book has been more than a release from
ose articles; it has been an attempt to rediscover that
uth.

So, pettily and absurdly, with the publication of the
niversary issue of the new-look *Socialist,* our political
ovement started. Consider the stir we made. Consider the
culiar power of my name. Add to this my reputation as a
ndy and then the more forbidding reputation as a very
ung 'Isabella millionaire' who 'worked hard and played
rd'. Consider Browne's licensed status as a renegade and
mantic, a 'radical', for whose acknowledged gifts our
and provided no outlet. See then how, though as indi-
duals we were politically nothing, we supported one
other and together appeared as a portent no one could
smiss. Certain ideas overwhelm by their simplicity. In three
onths – just six issues of the new *Socialist,* its finances
d organization regulated by me – we found ourselves at
e centre less of a political awakening than a political

anxiety, to which it was left to us merely to give direction

It has happened in twenty countries. I don't want t
exaggerate our achievement. Sooner or later, with or with
out us, something similar would have occurred. But I fee
we might claim credit for our courage. The nature of th
political life of our island must be understood. We were
colony, a benevolently administered dependency. So long a
our dependence remained unquestioned our politics wer
a joke. A man like my father, extravagant as he was, ha
been a passing disturber of the peace. He fitted into the pa
tern of dependence, as did those who came after him, takir
advantage of the limited constitution we were granted ju
before the end of the war. These politicians were contracto
and merchants in the towns, farmers in the country, sma
people offering no policies, offering only themselves. The
were not highly regarded. Their names and photograph
appeared frequently in the newspapers, but they we
slightly ridiculous figures; stories about their illiteracy
crookedness constantly circulated.

To go into politics then was not as simple a decision
it might seem now. We might easily have made the error
appearing to compete with the established politicians. An
that would have been disastrous. We would have covere
ourselves with ridicule. Instead, we ignored them. We sa
they were dead and unimportant. We not only made publ
a public joke; we were a demonstration of what was des
able and possible. We had the resources, in intellect an
offers of support, to question the system itself. We deni
competition; and indeed there was none. Simply by comi
forward – Browne and myself and *The Socialist*, all togeth
– we put an end to the old order. It was like that.

Courage: this is all I would claim now for our moveme
in its early stages. It takes courage to destroy any syste
however shabby, which has permitted one to grow. We c
not see this shabbiness as a type of order appropriate to c
circumstances. That we were to see only when we had sw
it away. And yet, equally, this shabbiness did not represe
us; it could not have lasted. Did we then act? Or were
acted upon? When we were done it was no longer possi

r someone like my mother's father, his money made, to
a nominated member of the Council, to hold this posi-
n by being 'safe', in a situation which when all was said
d done called for little adventurousness; and from this
sition to strive, by charities and good works, after a
coration or a title.

I write, I know, from both sides. I cannot do otherwise.
y mother's father was no doubt an undignified figure, an
ject of easy satire. But at least at the end, within the
mework of our old order, benevolence and service were
posed on him. And he was never as totally ridiculous as
e men we put in his place: men without talent or achieve-
nt save the reputed one of controlling certain sections of
e population, unproductive, uncreative men who pushed
emselves into prominence by an excess of that bitterness
ich every untalented clerk secretes. Their bitterness
ponded to our appeal. And in this response we saw the
ccess of our appeal, and its truth!

Yet how could we see, when we ourselves were part of the
ttern? The others we could observe. We could see them
their new suits even on the hottest days. We could see the
blish stern faces they prepared for the public to hide their
easure at their new eminence. We could see them coming
t of restaurants with their 'secretaries'. We could see them
rtsleeved – their coats prominent on hangers – as they
re driven in government cars marked with the letter M,
which they had insisted, to proclaim their status as
inisters. The car, the shirtsleeves, the coat on the hanger:
e fashion spread rapidly down the motorized section of
r civil service and might be considered the sartorial
hion of our revolution. At sports meetings they went to
e very front row of the stands, and over the months we
uld see the flesh swelling on the back of their necks, from
e good living and the lack of exercise. And always about
em, policemen in growing numbers.

They were easily frightened men, these colleagues of ours.
ey feared the countryside, they feared the dark, they grew
fear the very people on whose suffrage they depended.
ople who have achieved the trappings of power for no

191

reason they can see are afraid of losing those trappings. The[y] are insecure because they see too many like themselves. O[ut] of shabbiness, then, we created drama. At least my mothe[r,] father, never requiring a vote, never required protectio[n.] At least he knew the solidity of his own position and unde[r]stood how he had got there.

Courage, I have said. It takes courage to destroy, for co[n]fidence in one's ability to survive is required. About surviv[al] in those early days I never thought. I never saw it as an issu[e.] When I did see it, it was too late. Because by that time I ha[d] ceased to care.

2

It has happened in twenty places, twenty countries, island[s,] colonies, territories – these words with which we play, thin[k]ing they are interchangeable and that the use of a particula[r] one alters the truth. I cannot see our predicament as uniqu[e.] The newspapers even today spell out situations whic[h,] changing faces and landscapes, I can think myself into. The[y] talk of the pace of postwar political change. It is not t[he] pace of creation. Nor is it the pace of destruction, as som[e] think. Both these things require time. The pace of events, [as] I see it, is no more than the pace of chaos on which stri[ct] limits have been imposed. I speak of course of territories li[ke] Isabella, set adrift yet not altogether abandoned, where t[he] controlled chaos approximates in the end, after the hea[ted] speeches and token deportations, to a continuing order. T[he] chaos lies all within.

I will not linger on the details of our movement. I cann[ot] speak of the movement as a phenomenon generated by m[y] personality. I can scarcely speak of it in personal terms. T[he] politician deals in abstractions, even when he deals wi[th] himself. He is a man lifted out of himself and separate fro[m] his personality, which he might acknowledge from time [to] time. I let Crippleville run itself; I gave up the study [of] Latin. I applied myself to *The Socialist* and our par[ty] rganization. It was the sort of administrative work for which I was born. But – in spite of what has gone before – I will be less than fair to myself if I do not say that my labours were sweetened by the knowledge that I had become a public figure and an attractive one. It was the personality Browne had seen: the rich man with a certain name who had put himself on the side of the poor, who appeared to have turned his back on the making of money and on his former associates, who appeared to have been suddenly given a glimpse of the truth: I was now aware of his attractiveness. So in unlikely circumstances the London dandy was resurrected. I knew the affection and kindly mockery he aroused, and it was pleasant in those early days just to be this self. I had known nothing like it.

Create the scenes then. Imagine Browne, the leader, in his shabby journalist's suit, energetic, enthusiastic, frequently breaking into the local dialect, for purposes of comedy or abuse. Beside him set myself, as elegant in dress as in speech: I knew my role. Imagine the public meetings in squares, in halls. Imagine the tours along dusty country roads in the late afternoon and at night, the headlights illuminating the walls of sugarcane on either side. Imagine the developing organization in the Roman house, the willing black hands of clerks from business houses and our civil service. Imagine the lengthening reports of our speeches in the *Inquirer*. Imagine that other mark of success: the policemen in heavy serge shorts, becoming less aggressive and more protective as their numbers grew. Their amiability was pathetic: it was like the amiability of the gangster who finds himself in polite society. Add an enlivening detail: the yellow light on shining black faces, an old crazed woman somewhere in the crowd proclaiming her own message of doom, and here and there the flambeaux on stalls which now, because they are part of the people, one and entire, the police will not move on or break up.

Add the smell of Negro sweat as, to applause, we make our way through our followers, shining eyes in shining faces, to the platform, they so squat and powerfully built, we so tall and slender. In this smell of heated sweat, once rejected,

I tried to find virtue, the virtue of the poor, the labouring the oppressed. Such is the vulgarity that mobs generate, in themselves and in their manipulators. The virtue I found in that acrid smell was the virtue of the protecting, the massed and heedless. It was Browne's privilege to be less sentimental. 'The old *bouquet d'Afrique*,' he would mutter. And sometimes, when we were on the platform: 'Did you get the old booky?'

It was genuine, this sentiment, part of his ambivalence. But it was also, increasingly, an attempt to reassure me, to tell me, in the shorthand of speech we had evolved for use in public, that we were as one. For other scenes have to be created, other details added: casual estate labourers, picturesque Asiatics, not willing to share distress, lounging about a country road at dusk, unaroused, polite only because of my name. Someone in our party struggles with a microphone or a pressure lamp. The impassive shopkeeper in his dark shop sells sugar or flour to a young girl, who is indifferent to our mission; as afterwards he sells us beer. Then comes the drive back through the still land: weak lights in silent houses. The mud and deep ruts surprise us. We are aware of the remoteness of the safe town and those facilities we have taken for granted. We sympathize silently with the picturesque people we have left behind. In this sympathy we feel confirmed in our mission and our cause. Time was all that we needed, to bind all in distress.

Fill the Roman house with people once again. Suppress all rowdiness and strenuous gaiety. But do not destroy the coldness that is the fate of houses which have been mentally abandoned by their builders before they are complete. Until they are warmed by new tenants these houses are never like places to live in. Remember the cold kitchen and the terrazzo of empty rooms where a lost girl, pure of body, walked about, thinking of other landscapes. Fill these rooms now with a new and more appropriate feminine atmosphere. It is the atmosphere of dedication and mutual loyalty, in which speech is soft, statements, however inexact, are never violently contradicted, and even drink, served by loyal women to deserving men, is taken sacramentally.

194

A court had developed around us. There was competition to serve; and among these helpers there was, as we knew, murder in the wings. Outside the gates strange men began to appear in the evenings. We thought at first they were from the police, and no doubt in the early days one or two were. But we got to know the faces. They were of people who had come unasked from the city to protect us. So with the court there came drama. Drama created itself around us. When reports came to us of violence, in various districts, the protection around the house increased.

What had begun could not, it seemed, be stopped. Were we in the court responsible? In the feminine atmosphere of the Roman house all was goodwill and dedication. A sacramental quality attached not only to food and drink but to the liaisons that had grown up among our courtiers, between handsome men and ugly women, handsome women and mean-featured men. Sex a sacrifice to the cause and a promise of the release that was to come: so different from the cartoon unreality I had found in the relationship between Browne's sister and her boy-friend, ugliness coming to ugliness in mock humanity, on the only occasion I had been to Browne's house, when we were both schoolboys at Isabella Imperial.

In the Roman house itself, then, those interiors I had feared to enter opened up to me. In this atmosphere delight could not be openly proclaimed. And I will say that the reports which increasingly reached us of violence, more and more racial in character, filled us with awe. We were already sufficiently awed at ourselves, sitting up in the still nights, the splashing fountains drawing attention to the silence, assessing our progress, writing speeches, planning tours. We felt we had discovered something good and true in ourselves. We, I say. We, I perhaps felt. But this awe was something which excluded me. For our courtiers, men and women in poor jobs in teaching and the civil service, it was awe of a sort I can only call holy. I write with control: this awe was moving and frightening to behold. It was the awe of the ungifted who thought they had, simply through enduring, suddenly discovered, in this response of the ungifted among their people, the source of the power and regeneration they had waited for without hoping to find.

I couldn't be sure where Browne stood in this. He was as dedicated as the rest. But he was more frivolous than any of us dared be. We met regularly, but we were never as close again as on that first evening in the Roman house. It was as though each had declared himself irrevocably then, and further probings were unnecessary. So that, absurdly, we became close again on the public platform, when we each became our character.

The awe of our court excluded me, I say. I sometimes thought: they are presuming, they are asking too much of me. But I could only assent, and the time soon came when I felt it was up to the others to make some worthy reassuring statement when an Asiatic vendor was beaten up in the name of our movement, or a white girl insulted. This had to be put aside. It was superficial. Those were my own words. I heard them echoed. The truth of our movement lay in the Roman house, the court inside, the guard outside. In my own silence and assent there was dedication to the organization I had built up. There was also vanity: the vanity of the prime mover who believes it is in his power to regulate what he has created. There was no self-violation in the article I wrote for *The Socialist*. I wrote that violence in the Americas was not new. It had come with Columbus; we had lived with violence ever since. The cry was taken up by the court. But I noted that they continued in their special awe.

The truth of the movement lay in the Roman house. It also lay in our undeniable success. We attracted support from all races and all classes. We offered, as it soon appeared, more than release from bitterness. We offered drama. And to our movement there was added a name which made mine fade a little. It was the name of Deschampsneufs: Wendy, indifferent to the recent past, heedless of rebuff, presuming on the eccentricity of an ancestor. What could I do? How could I put that relationship right? There was a welcome for her: she was right. She came to the Roman house and ruled it for two months, and I was helpless before her assur-

nce. She became the mother to us all in her brisk young-
irl way; she offered the final benediction of her name and
er race, both of which separated her from us. Ugly, flat-
)oted, squeaky-voiced!

Rumour did things to her. It attached her to dockers. It
ttached her to Browne. It finally attached her to me. It was
favourable rumour in the early days. Later it was one of
ie things to be used against me: it proved that even in the
eginning I had been corrupted by glamour and as such was
rompt to betray. Wendy relished every rumour. Whenever
ie were at a meeting together she did what she could to
uggest that our intimacy was of the sacramental sort I have
escribed. And the people were favourable. They adored
Vendy for her sacrifice. The squat men with bright eyes in
umb faces offered her the protection they offered the rest
f us. She moved among them like their ugly queen. And
s for me: it will come as no surprise that I became, at least
> far as appearances went, what others saw in me. It was
lay for me, play for her.

At the end of two months she pronounced herself bored
/ith the movement and bored with the island. Everyone
orgave her. She flew off to join her brother in Canada. And
rom Canada for the next year I received a series of letters
rom her brother. He was still painting and had just dis-
overed Hinduism. He set me the riddles of the universe and
f existence and asked in so many words for ancient wisdom.
did what I could.

A twinge of jealousy, an alarm of loneliness: this was
/hat I felt when Wendy left. I envied her her freedom and
aw her as the freest of us all. I was grateful to her too for
he relief she had provided from the intensity of those days.
t was an intensity made up of confusion, dishonesty, fear,
lelight, awe. My awe was not the awe of the others. It was
vonder and puzzlement at this suddenly realized concept of
he people, who responded and could be manipulated, for
vhom tactics of the broadest sort could be planned in the
Roman house. And with this wonder there went, I can con-
ess it now, a great awakening fear of those shining faces;
. fear just buried under the delight I felt at being protected

by this foolish strength, as virtuous as the smell of its sweat, a fear just under my delight as speaker and manipulator, the new possessor of the sense of timing, with the instinct now for the right place for the big word, to arouse that gasp of admiration, the instinct for the right place for the joke with which we abolished the past, the right place for the dandyism which, with me, was like the comedian's catch word when he plays to an audience who knows him well. And dishonesty: those speeches, whose brilliance so many commented on and travelled distances to hear, had as their basis contempt, the knowledge that it didn't matter what was said. The presence was enough. Whatever was said, the end was always the same: applause, the path made through the crowd, the hands tapping, rubbing, caressing my shoulder, the willing hands of slaves now serving a cause they thought to be their own.

Confusion: in the end it possessed us all. We were dazed by success. We didn't know whether we had created the movement or whether the movement was creating us. And I come back to the awe. When I examine myself I can think of no cause, no politician's speeches stirring enough or convincing enough to send me into the streets, to make me one of a manipulable crowd. We zestfully abolished an order; we never defined our purpose. And it has happened in twenty countries: this realization of the concept of the people, the politician's humanity, this bewildering proof of the politician's truth.

What did we talk about? We were, of course, of the left. We were socialist. We stood for the dignity of the working man. We stood for the dignity of distress. We stood for the dignity of our island, the dignity of our indignity. Borrowed phrases! Left-wing, right-wing: did it matter? Did we believe in the abolition of private property? Was it relevant to the violation which was our subject? We spoke as honest men. But we used borrowed phrases which were part of the escape from thought, from that reality we wanted people to see but could ourselves now scarcely face. We enthroned indignity and distress. We went no further.

I am not sure that the wild men of our party did not

peak more honestly than we did. They promised to abolish
poverty in twelve months. They promised to abolish bicycle
licences. They promised to discipline the police. They promised intermarriage. They promised farmers higher prices
for sugar and copra and cocoa. They promised to renegotiate the bauxite royalties and to nationalize every
foreign-owned estate. They promised to kick the whites
into the sea and send the Asiatics back to Asia. They promised; they promised; and they generated the frenzy of the
street-corner preacher who thrills his hearers with a vision
of the unattainable rich world going up in a ball of fire. We
disapproved, of course. But what could we do? We were
awed, I say. We were helpless with our awe. It wasn't dishonesty. Detachment alone would have shown us that in the
very success of our movement lay the pointlessness and
hopelessness of our situation. In our very success lay that
disorder which, daily, we feared more.

3

The election was at hand. The frenzy was heightened and
given acute point. To the victors would go the spoils:
further constitutional conferences in London and, after that,
independence. More night meetings, more processions,
demonstrations, motorcades; tedious journeys by motorcar;
late meetings in the Roman house. Among our supporters,
among our court, there were occasional alarms. We let them
play with visions of defeat which, in the frenzy, must have
appeared total; they were encouraged to greater effort.

It all led to the inevitable: the success of election night,
the cheering, the flag-waving, the drinking. It led to that
moment of success which, after long endeavour, is so shatter-
ingly brief: a moment that can almost be fixed by the clock,
and recedes and recedes, leaving emptiness, exhaustion,
even distaste: dissatisfaction that nags and nags and at last
defines itself as apprehension and unease.

Unease: with us, even during those first hours of victory

in the Roman house, this centred on Browne. The thought
came to us at intervals that in just a few hours, between the
colleague of the day before and the Chief Minister of a few
hours hence, he had been set apart. He had been set apart
by our efforts. The play was over. Exhilaration went. We
could no longer draw strength from one another. It was one
of those occasions when each person looks down into him
self and finds only weakness, sees the boy or child he was
and has never ceased to be.

From this awareness of weakness – strength only when it
was in combat with something we judged to be strong – we
arrived at dismay. It was as though, in a tug-of-war contest,
the other side had suddenly let go. It has happened in twenty
countries like ours: the sobering moment of success, when
playacting turns out to be serious. Our grievances were our
reality, what we knew, what had permitted us to grow, what
had made us. We wondered at the ease of our success; we
wondered why no one had called our bluff. We felt our
success to be fraudulent. But none of this would have mattered as much if we hadn't also understood that in the game
we had embarked on there could be no withdrawal. And
each man was now alone.

That morning saw the end of the life of the Roman house.
In the moment of success the feminine atmosphere vanished.
Everyone was easily irritated. Innumerable jealousies were
at last expressed. There were one or two open quarrels. The
wand had been waved: the prince had become a toad again.

On such occasions we look for someone to give the lead
and set the new mood. We looked to Browne. He made an
effort. He tried to heighten both aspects of his manner, the
authoritative and the colloquial. Selfconscious ourselves, we
studied him critically, and no more so than when he returned that afternoon from Government House after his
consultations with the Governor. We looked for weakness
and found it. It amazed us a little to find that he behaved
like a man socially graced. I knew that this was an extension
of the Browne who spoke with familiarity of the writers and
commentators who contributed to the journals he read. It
was part of his literalness and part of his enthusiasm, find-

ing something new to feed on. But it delighted the foolish women in our court for another reason. They saw in this a complete vindication of the movement, a triumph of the race, Browne their representative speaking on terms of equality with the representative of the ruling power. In normal circumstances Browne would have dismissed their pleasure as servile. But now he seemed not at all displeased.

He had an analytical mind that dealt in abstractions; he had no descriptive gift. Now he revealed a descriptive talent. His story of his encounter with the Governor reminded me of nothing so much as the talk of my mother's father after he had returned from an air trip to Jamaica. It was the first time anyone in our family had been in an aeroplane, and that too had made a dry man flourish.

Now Browne held us with his talk of furnishings and rituals, of views of our own city through windows and doors, of paintings. There was a moment when the Governor, leading Browne to an alcove, had said: 'But we rather like this little thing.' The little thing was a view of a pink-and-white Mediterranean fishing village, a gift to the Governor, mentioned by his first name, 'from Winston'. We shared Browne's admiration: this was an ennobling link with the world, with a great man and great events. Then Browne remembered his new role. Earnestness replaced delight.

'To think,' he said, in the pause our admiration had created, 'that decisions concerning our future have been made for so long in a room like that.'

It was disappointing. But I wonder whether we were right to be disappointed by Browne's delight or by his emphasis that day on legality and ritual. Our disappointment was part of our simplicity. Ritual was a link with the security of the past. Browne, like the rest of us, required reassurance; he too was made irritable by the thought that his behaviour might be misinterpreted. Later I was to say that my betrayal had been thought out beforehand, but I never believed this. We never operated with such sophistication.

A crowd had gathered outside the Roman house. Various businessmen came to pay their respects. There were also petitioners seeking better jobs or houses or the reversal of court decisions. We were quickly fatigued; we ordered that no more people should be admitted. But there was an old Negro who would not be denied. He shouted out slogans and added religious texts. He was crazed with distress and passionate for justice. He was almost in tears when he was allowed in.

He ignored us all and went straight to Browne, redeemer of the race. He unwrapped a parcel he was carrying and offered the contents: a small bookstand, which he said he had made himself. He began to tell his story. But his distress did not abate and his words could not always be followed. For years, he said, he had been working for an English contracting firm. For years he had been passed over when it came to promotion. Inferior Negroes were the ones his employers selected for promotion, to prove that Negroes couldn't do responsible jobs well. For years he had been subjected to insult and had kept his peace. Now he could speak. All the insults he had secreted over the years he now poured out, in proof of his virtue and merit. He had worked in the evenings on the bookstand; he had despaired of finding someone worthy to give it to. This was no longer so. Look: the bookstand was made of four interlocking detachable pieces: no glue had been used.

It was an old story, one we had hardened ourselves to. Even distress, if sufficiently repeated, becomes vulgar. But this scene was large and moving. The old Negro in his old suit, discoloured at the edges and under the arms, a man I could see cycling back from the humiliations of his office, hat on his head, the badge of respectability, cycling back to his street where he was no doubt respected and where perhaps he had created for himself the character of the wise old Negro who knew the ways of the white world but would speak only when the time came. The time was now!

Browne listened without irritation. When the old man was finished he said, 'You must leave this firm. It is the only advice I can give you.' The old man looked stunned. Browne waited, then went on, 'Look. I could take up this telephone here and get on to the Chairman. Tomorrow morning you would be sitting in the Manager's chair.' This directness in Browne's speech, this folksy creation of pictures, was new; it was as impressive as the confidence he showed in his own power. The old Negro looked abashed, playing with the idea of himself in the Manager's chair. We were all silent, studying Browne, the magician, the man now apart. 'But then what?' he asked abruptly, irritably. The old Negro looked down; he was going to say no more. 'Then what?' Browne said. 'You want me to tell you? Somebody in London would decide that they want to get this contract or that contract. And then what? Who would be the man they would send to ask me? To bribe me. Who?'

And the old Negro, playing the rhetorical game, answered with pride and satisfaction: 'They would send me.'

The audience was over. Petitioner and court were satisfied. And I thought: goodness, in a few hours consciousness of power has turned a semi-politician, a semi-ideologue, a joker, into a folk-leader.

He recognized our admiration. He said, simulating impatience, 'If I stay here these damn people will eat me up.'

And now I could no longer read his ambivalence.

Did Browne believe in his power? Was he overwhelmed by the despair that comes at the moment of success and the knowledge that success changes nothing? He had shown me the nature of the violation we had been exploiting. Did he feel, like me, that violation was violation and could not be undone, even from where he stood, the limit of his ambition? I could no longer read his ambivalence. All I knew was that the time came when he longed to step down, to return to the past we had so lightly destroyed. But how could such a man, who had revealed such power, be permitted to do so by those faceless men – M for Minister, M for master – whom we had created? Like me, he became a prisoner of his role.

So the Roman house died a second time. Browne presently moved into his official residence. There he was protected from mendicants, petitioners, lunatics and even his colleagues. He took to writing me letters. I thought at first they were meant to reassure me, like his whispers on the public platform. Then I began to feel that they were exercises. I caught his mood; my letters matched his. It was an undergraduate correspondence, somewhat pretentious, a little like that I was carrying on with Wendy's brother agonizing now in Quebec over a separate French state as well as Shiva's dance of life and death. Browne and I wrote as though for publication. We wrote about books we had read, ideas that had struck us; we wrote about everything except the work we had undertaken; and though in our letters we referred to our meetings, we never, when we met, referred to our letters. We continued, though less frequently, to appear together in public, each still being his role. But we were no closer there than we were in cabinet, where each man was alone, secretive, careful. The process of learning had begun, and each man was keeping his knowledge to himself.

We learned about power. We learned about our poverty. The two went together, but it was our poverty which made the understanding of power more urgent. In territories like ours the process of learning about power takes four years. Our constitutions usually prescribe an election in the fifth year; and it is in the fifth year that people begin feverishly to challenge the strength of their rivals or colleagues. Everyone's bluff is called, and the strong are revealed. There is an upheaval; the result often is that second elections are never held. Crunch-time came in Isabella and I was the one to go. I went like a lamb. I blame no one. It was left to me to act, and I didn't. I held a good many of the cards. I threw them away. My behaviour seemed logical enough to me at the time. Now it seems irresponsible.

It was part of our innocence that at the beginning we should have considered applause and the smell of sweat as the only source of power. It took us no time to see that we depended on what was no more than a mob, and that our hold on the mob was the insecure one of words. I went a little beyond this. I saw that in our situation the mob, without skills, was unproductive, offered nothing, and was in the end without power. The mob might burn down the city. But the mob is shot down, and the power of money will cause the city to be built again. In the moment of victory we had wondered why no one had called our bluff. Soon we saw that there had been no need, that our power was air. We had no trade unions behind us, no organized capital. We had no force of nationalism even, only the negative frenzy of a deep violation which could lead to further frenzy alone, the vision of the world going up in flames: it was the only expiation.

The situation was squalid. But we were among men to whom, in trips abroad at the invitation of foreign governments, in conferences in London, in the chauffeured Humbers and in the first-class hotels of half a dozen cities, the richness of the world was suddenly revealed. We were among men who felt more cheated, more bitter in their power than they had ever done before, men who feared that the rich world so wonderfully open to them might at any moment be withdrawn. Each man therefore sought to turn that airy power, which his anxiety rightly painted to him as insecure, into a reality. Some sought it in quick money. The emissaries of Swiss banks came to us: this corruption at the edges we were powerless to prevent. Some tried to become labour leaders. Some tried to subvert the police. To all, the proclamation of distress was necessary, with its complement of racial antagonism.

We were trapped in our situation. Each attempt at the establishing of a personal security prepared the way for further disorder. The vision alarmed me, to tell the truth. I prepared a five-thousand-word paper for cabinet on the reorganization of the police force. It was my aim to rehabilitate it socially, to rid it of its association with backyards; I wanted to see it integrated into such responsible elements of society as we possessed. I proposed to keep on British officers while we created our own officer class; there was to be no sudden promotion for the unqualified or the socially unacceptable. The paper made me suspect. It was dismissed as illiberal by the spokesmen for bitterness; nothing was done. I saw that in our situation the police force or the regiment might itself become a state, like its parent, in which power might change at any time, the soldier might refuse to obey, and indeed ten determined men might wipe out the leadership they refuse to obey because they see no reason why it should be obeyed.

I had never thought of obedience as a problem. Now it seemed to me the miracle of society. Given our situation, anarchy was endless, unless we acted right away. But on power and the consolidation of passing power we wasted our energies, until the bigger truth came: that in a society like ours, fragmented, inorganic, no link between man and the landscape, a society not held together by common interests, there was no true internal source of power, and that no power was real which did not come from the outside. Such was the controlled chaos we had, with such enthusiasm, brought upon ourselves.

The vision of hysteria, wrongheaded, criminally irresponsible: perhaps. But it weakened me. I was overwhelmed by the cruelty of what I saw. I withdrew into my role. So too did Browne, who had talked so much of distress and dignity as discoveries in themselves, but had not thought to go further. He never learned anything beyond that first day. He remained the folk-leader, waiting like me for crunchtime. His role was his strength. Mine exposed me to danger from my colleagues.

I continued to run *The Socialist* as before, proclaiming the dignity of distress. My speeches maintained their old tone of protest. I never abandoned the character of the dandy. In this was neither honesty nor dishonesty; it was the easiest way out. But I became identified in the public mind with a type of opposition from within, and this won me favour. Soon I saw how my blind consistency, my refusal to manoeuvre, my position, in the eyes of my colleagues, became one of strength and especially dangerous. I held too many of the cards. I could have got the big money on my side, to apply a squeeze here and there when necessary; I could have got the banks, the Stockwells, the bauxite companies; I could have got that middle-class to which by instinct I belonged; and I could have drawn numbers from the rural workers, picturesque Asiatics like myself, ever ready to listen to the call of the blood. I might have rescued myself from the falseness of the position of the simple sharer of distress: the convert, suspect to both the faithful and the infidel. The cards were all mine. I played none and puzzled everyone by my folly.

Like Browne, I was no politician. The prospect of power in Isabella fatigued me. Easier, much easier, the path that had been chosen for me. And there was my correspondence with Browne, and with Wendy's brother in Quebec. To one I wrote fanciful disquisitions about the cosmic dance. To the other I wrote more and more about history, with which I was becoming absorbed. I remember I wrote a long essay about the behaviour of Pompey during the Civil War, which had always seemed to me a puzzle – this was the sort of 'safe' subject Browne and I now corresponded about. I thought I kept up this correspondence for the sake of the people I wrote to and for the sake of that self they saw in me. But it had the effect of deepening my conviction that I had a secret, deeper life. Below the public dandy, the political manoeuvrer and organizer; below that, this negation. I distrusted romance. See, though, how I yielded to it.

A man, I suppose, fights only when he hopes, when he has a vision of order, when he feels strongly there is some connexion between the earth on which he walks and himself. But there was my vision of a disorder which it was beyond any one man to put right. There was my sense of wrongness, beginning with the stillness of that morning of return when I looked out on the slave island and tried to pretend it was mine. There was my sense of intrusion which deepened as I felt my power to be more and more a matter of words. So defiantly, in my mind, I asserted my character as intruder, the picturesque Asiatic born for other landscapes.

And then there was the madman's lure: my belief in my star, not the star of fortune, but the star that, if only I surrendered to situations, if only I did what I had been called upon to do, would take me to my appointed place. The compassion of the messiah, the man doing penance for the world: I have already explained the absurd sentiments which surprised me at the moment of greatest power and self-cherishing, the feeling that we were all riding to the end of the flat world: the child's vision, or the conqueror's, the beginning of religion or neurosis.

4

The child, driving with his grandfather along a country road on a day of rain, sees the sodden mud-and-grass huts of the estate labourers. He sees the labourers wading up to their shins in black mud which, drying, will cake white on their dark skins. He exclaims: 'Why can't they give them leggings?' His grandfather says, 'Leggings cost money.' It is a disappointing reply, the child feels; and when he sees the compound of the overseers' houses, ochre walls with red roofs, fair-haired children playing in the scruffy gardens, he is outraged.

The politician carries that sense of outrage as well. But sitting in the cabinet or debating in the Council, he has to see agriculture as an issue. He knows its value to the precarious economy of his country. He has the facts and figures; he knows the world price of sugar or copra; he knows who guarantees his export markets. He knows that peasant farming is uneconomical and land resettlement schemes quixotic. He knows that the interest of his country is bound up with that of the estates, and that the estates are on his side. He knows they are agreeable to some modification in taxation. He chooses to forget the figures wading in mud; he chooses to forget the outrage he felt at the overseers' compound. All this is superficial and irrelevant; but it was that that spurred him on. All his leadership lies in taking back this message to his people. He is a politician, a man lifted out of himself.

We began in bluff. We continued in bluff. But there was a difference. We began in innocence, believing in the virtue of the smell of sweat. We continued with knowledge, of poverty and power. The colonial politician is an easy object of satire. I wish to avoid satire; I will leave out the stories of illiteracy and social innocence. Not that I wish to present

208

im as grander or less flawed than he is. It is that his situation satirizes itself, turns satire inside out, takes satire to a point where it touches pathos if not tragedy. Out of his immense violation words come easily to him, too easily. He must go back on his words. In success he must lay aside violation. He must betray himself and in the end he has no cause save his own survival. The support he has attracted, not ideal to ideal, but bitterness to bitterness, he betrays and mangles: emancipation is not possible for all.

We had spoken, for instance, of the need to get rid of the English expatriates who virtually monopolized the administrative section of our civil service. We had represented their presence as an indignity and an intolerable strain on our treasury. They received overseas allowances; their housing was subsidized; every three years they and their families were given passages to London. Each expatriate cost us twice as much as a local man. One degree less of innocence would have shown us how incapable we were of doing without expatriates: they were so numerous that to pay them all compensation would have wrecked our finances for at least two years, and we were in no position to break agreements. Besides, not a few of the higher technical men, in forestry and agriculture, were subsidized by London, under a generous scheme for colonial aid.

We let the issue hang. We issued a statement about our confidence in the loyalty of the civil service; and from our own lower ministerial people there emanated from time to time disingenuous parables about the black and white keys of the piano working together to create harmony. In fact, we were beginning to discover in ourselves a deep reluctance to render the civil service more local. In the secretive atmosphere of our own power game some people preferred to be served by men who were no threats to them, who at the end of their service would return to their own country.

This did not satisfy the local men. They had been among our most intelligent supporters. Now they felt betrayed; and a man of fifty does not accept the message, however sympathetically given, that he will receive promotion after his superior of forty-five has worked out a life-contract.

There was much discontent. It crept into *White Paper*, the civil service journal which, until our advent, contained lists of appointments and transfers and retirements, news of people on leave, reports of salary negotiations, and sometimes a very carefully written short story which usually began with people drinking, elaborately, in a bar and one man being reminded of a strange incident. We decided to break one or two of the higher and more vocally disappointed local men. It was not hard. *White Paper* helped us. We contrasted the old acquiescence with the new irreverence and suggested that it was the new régime that was being affronted. The offending civil servants were coloured men; they spent their leaves in England and sent their children to English schools; they sought to keep their complexions clear and their hair straight by selective marriages. Their punishment was just. Nothing we said was untrue; the public approved.

From London there presently came more offers of technical aid and experts on short-term contracts. We gratefully accepted; so that in the end there were more expatriates than before. Some of our ministers took pains to be seen in public with their English permanent secretaries, who behaved impeccably. It was what these ministers offered their followers: the spectacle of the black man served by the white: the revolution we claimed to have created.

Satire creeps in. But understand the colonial politician. It might have been personal indignities that drove him on. He can reply in success only with personal dignity, and for some little time it satisfies his followers. He is a symbol; he holds out hope for all. It is part of his function then to turn to the trappings of power: the motorcar marked M, the suit on the hottest days, the attendant white men and women. Understand, too, his jumpiness. He knows his own futility and every time he returns from the rich world his delighted reaction to his country – 'At least this portion of the world is mine' – is quickly lost in the uneasiness he feels at the precariousness of his position. For the future he cannot read; he must lay up money; uneasiness turns to panic even on that ceremonial drive from airport to city which also takes im past the compound of the tall ochre-and-red overseers' houses. Understand the jumpiness, the sensitivity to criticism, the solitude.

Understand Browne's irrational, panicky behaviour, the disappearance of his frivolity, his angry descents among us and the people, and together with the assertion of his personal dignity, his proclamation now not of distress alleviated but of distress just discovered, and greater than before. He had settled in the role of folk-leader. He did not have the courage to go beyond that; he had come to terms with the bitterness and self-disgust his role must have brought him. His speeches altered, though to the public their substance remained the same. Whereas before he had spoken of distress as though speaking only to the distressed, now he seemed to be addressing the guilty as well. He shrieked at them, he lamented, he tried to terrify. His defiance became as shameful as the thing he preached against. He was, I saw, in competition with his inferiors. But it paid off. It made him into a figure of a kind; it won him paragraphs in weeklies of international circulation. The outsiders who would have been chilled by his earlier appeals to dignity and stoicism, because such appeals would have excluded them, were now flattered by the more recognizable anguish he proclaimed and were willing to recognize him as a leader at last. Even if there had been the will to go forward from the emptiness of his position, this recognition would have weakened it.

Our correspondence continued, that oblique irrelevant exchange which yet, as I can now see, revealed so much; and it was from this correspondence that I began to feel that more and more he would have liked to step down from the role that imprisoned him, as once his house next to the Kremlin barber shop had imprisoned him. In his letters he took me back to the past, back to London, back to the writing of his unfinished novel, back to Isabella Imperial and the days of my father's agitation, back to the child who had been dressed and powdered and, to the delight of his parents and envy of his schoolfellows, had sung that so successful coon song. From these letters I could gather not only his

contempt for our colleagues who were no longer made shar
by their personal bitterness; not only his contempt for th
endless stream of mendicants who appealed to him in th
name of their common race and their common past; I bega
to feel that I was entering a fantasy which was like my own
Here was more than longing for the past we had destroyed
of erratic magazines with statements of policy, of occasiona
pamphlets, of quick ideas worked out in bars. Here was
longing for different landscapes, a different world, where
child's first memory of school was of taking an apple to th
teacher and where, in essays at least, days were spent o
temperate farms. Here was a longing, like my own, for free
dom and what we considered the truth of our personalitie
In fantasy, perhaps, this truth was one of the things succes
ought to have brought; the disappointments of fantasy ar
not the less real. So we each to the other explained ou
actions or inaction – what else, I see, was the purpose o
my own ponderous essay on Pompey – while we continue
to be political colleagues, each supporting the other.

It was in the third year of our government that ther
occurred the incident which made Isabella notorious; an
yet it did not lessen our reputation outside for stability an
good sense. It was the tasteless idea of the *Cercle Sport*
to celebrate Browne's birthday with a fancy-dress ball, an
it was the tasteless idea of some people to turn up as Africa
tribesmen with spears and little beards. Word got to Brown
before the evening was over – a waiter at the *Cercle* ha
thought it his duty – and on the following morning instan
deportation orders had been served on everyone at the part
who could be deported. A number of expatriate civil ser
vants were caught in this way.

For two or three days Browne raved, in public meeting
in the Council, on the radio. He seemed to have gone of
his head. He was like a man anxious to stir up a racial up
rising. The newspapers at last objected. One ran a cartoo
showing our airport lounge with three doors: Arrival
Departures, Deportures. Browne instantly calmed down. H
issued a reasonable statement about his and the govern

nent's attitudes to racial clubs. There was no objection to them, he said, provided they were not maintained in any open or hidden way by public funds; there was no objection to the *Cercle Sportif* as such because it was no longer a place where 'decisions concerning the deepest interests of our country are taken over whisky-and-soda'. His outburst had embarrassed many of us. But it did him no harm. It strengthened his position and won him a good deal of sympathetic foreign press comment; his subsequent statement about racial clubs was considered statesmanlike by outsiders and 'diplomatic' by his supporters. Poor Browne! Into what a position had he manoeuvred himself? Did he still know what he thought about anything?

There was a sequel. About a month later there began to circulate an anonymous satirical tale called *The Niger and the Seine*. It was in English but so closely modelled on *Candide* it read like a translation from the French. Slavery has just been abolished, and the daughter of a French creole family comes home one day and announces that she is going to marry a Negro. Her worthy statement about her motives is cut short by her father, who embraces her. He not only agrees to the marriage but promises to do what he can to rehabilitate the Negro and the Negro's family. He will send his son-in-law to Paris and pay for his education. All this is done and soon there is established on the island a Negro family of some substance. Their descendants continue the practice of inter-racial marriage. So too do the descendants of the French family: their load of guilt is heavy and their liberalism is tenacious. In time both families undergo some degree of racial alteration. It happens, then, that one day the daughter of the Negro family, now indistinguishable from white, comes home and announces that she wishes to marry the heir of the French family, now totally black. Her father refuses; the air is blue with racial abuse. The girl kills herself. The liberal cycle is over; it has served its purpose; it will not be repeated.

The Niger and the Seine was a polished piece of work, fine, witty, piercing, almost unbearable in its cruelty. Nothing as outspoken had been written about Isabella since

Froude's visit. It brought to the discussion of racial attitude
a brutality that had been tacitly outlawed on our island
Out of violation there had grown a certain balance and
order. Now, with the fancy-dress ball, Browne's outburst
and this satirical pamphlet, it became clear that this order
was breaking down. And of course it was the intruders, those
who stood between the mutual and complete comprehen
sion of master and slave, who were to suffer.

5

So we brought drama of a sort to the island. I will claim
this as one of our achievements. Drama, however much we
fear it, sharpens our perception of the world, gives us some
sense of ourselves, makes us actors, gives point and some
times glory to each day. It alters a drab landscape. So i
frequently happens – what many have discovered – that in
conditions of chaos, which would appear hostile to any
human development, the human personality is in fact mor
varied and extended. And this is creation indeed! It migh
be that I write subjectively, from the order of this suburba
hotel set in the roar of this industrial city – once of such
magical light – whose busyness does not conceal the fact of
its death, revealed whenever an interior is entered and tha
busyness resolves itself into its component parts. *Who come
here? A Grenadier. What does he want? A pot of beer.*

The drama we created did buoy me up. It abolished for
me the tedium I had known in childhood and associate
with the landscape: those hot, still Sunday afternoons whe
my father wandered vacantly about our old wooden hous
and bare yard in his vest and pants and sometimes applie
himself to cleaning, meticulously, his bicycle for the drud
gery of the week ahead. And I will record the private gam
I played from the beginning. It was the game of naming
I would begin a speech: 'I have just come from a meetin
at the corner of Wellington and Cocoye Streets. . . .' Du
streets of concrete-and-tin houses; but it gave me pleasur

name them, as it gave me pleasure to name documents
statements after the villages or towns where they had
n first outlined. So I went on, naming, naming; and,
r, I required everything – every government building,
ry road, every agricultural scheme – to be labelled. It
gested drama, activity. It reinforced reality. It reinforced
t sense of ownership which overcame me whenever I re-
ned to the island after a trip abroad: do not think I was
mpt from that feeling. Drama buoyed me up in my acti-
y, and there was drama in that naming. Administration
l been unobtrusive before. Now we, the chief actors, how-
r powerless, however finally futile, were public figures,
narked on wherever we went. There was drama in that
ver game, from which I had withdrawn. There was one
el at which divisions and alignments were public pro-
ty; there was another level at which it was possible to
tend that they didn't exist. Drama walked with us; it was
displeasing. I will claim it as an achievement, though
consequences for me were far from pleasant.

Our energies went, then, on making public what already
sted. We were busy. We opened schools which before
uld have opened their doors to children without much
fare; we cut ribbons across brief stretches of country
d; we opened laundries, shoe-shops and filling stations.
were photographed with visitors from American or Ger-
n travel agencies, who said the correct things; we were
otographed shaking hands with the representatives of a
nch motorcar firm who had come to assess the potential
a regional agency. We attached ourselves to all the acti-
y of the island and to whatever, in a territory like ours,
ssed for industrialization or investment.

An English firm began making biscuits. Someone else
de toothpaste or brought down the machinery for filling
es with toothpaste. I am not sure now what it was they
. We encouraged a local adventurer to tin local fruit. This
s a failure. It hadn't occurred to anyone concerned to
d out whether local people wanted local fruit tinned; no
e else did either. The same man went in later for tinning
rgarine and was a success. The margarine was imported,

215

the tins were imported. Our effort was to operate a machi
that turned the flattened tins into cylinders. We capped o
end, filled the cylinder with the imported margarine, a
capped the other end. I remember the process well. I open
the factory. Our margarine was slightly more expensive th
imported tinned margarine, and had to be protected.
believe the factory employed five black ladies, whom
photographed looking grave and technical in white coats.

Industrialization, in territories like ours, seems to be
process of filling imported tubes and tins with various i
ported substances. Whenever we went beyond this we we
likely to get into trouble. There was, for instance, the plast
business, later the plastics scandal, to which my name w
attached. A Czech came to me one day. He represented hi
self as a refugee from a giant Dutch firm and proposed th
we should set him up as the head of a state-run plast
factory. He dazzled us with the possibilities of plastics; a
I must confess I was attracted by his nationality. In time
produced some plastic combs and plastic bowls. They we
a mottled brown or a mangy blue. But there was somethi
irremediably wrong with his process. Everything he ma
literally stank. Crunch-time was coming – let this be remer
bered in the midst of all these adventures, all this activi
and drama – and I have no doubt that the plastics affa
would have been used to weaken me, if there had n
occurred, at about the same time as the Czech was maki
his getaway, the great news about the bauxite contract.

We had committed ourselves from the outset to r
negotiating the bauxite contract. It was our only maj
resource, and its exploitation, in the late 1930s, was perha
the only thing that had rescued our economy from tot
ruin and saved our island from revolution. But many peop
were not satisfied; there was a widespread feeling that t
contract had been negotiated in anxiety and ignorance, ar
that we were not getting what we should. *The Social*
created brilliant pictures of what could be done with i
creased royalties. The trouble about bauxite, though, is th
nearly everybody in the world is a layman. The coloni
politician who vows to renegotiate a bauxite contract is

the position of a physics teacher who promises to make an atom bomb for his fifth formers. We were in trouble before we began. We had no knowledge and didn't know where we could get knowledge. London wasn't helpful. We wanted an expert; we were willing to pay. But there was apparently no such person as a bauxite expert who was free and willing.

I made official approaches to the companies. They replied with unofficial invitations to friendly barbecue parties beside swimming-pools. They were very friendly parties. The men had friendly rolls of flesh about their waist; they played with balls and dogs and occasionally dropped stern words to splashing children. Meat hissed over charcoal; laughing wives basted. In this atmosphere talk about bauxite seemed perverse, when it came from me, and threatening, when it came from them. A new arrival was greeted; a silent local housemaid appeared; someone laughed at a swimming dog. And I was being told that in South America bauxite, of excellent grade, lay below white sand, which had just to be hosed off; that in Jamaica the bauxite lay just below a couple of inches of stoneless earth; and that Australia was in fact a continent made entirely of bauxite. The bauxite of Isabella was difficult to mine and of indifferent grade. By making too much trouble we were gambling with our future; even as it was, there was little to stop all the companies leaving Isabella, and then the natives could play as long as they pleased with the red dust, as they had done before 1935. Besides, any degree of uncertainty about the future might lead to the abandonment of plans, well under way, for the establishment of an alumina plant. And that was an investment of some millions.

The case was overstated. I was not alarmed. *The Socialist* continued to express its resentment, but it seemed that that was all we could do. How can you negotiate about something whose value you don't know? To all our official approaches the companies replied with unofficial invitations. I believe some of the managers changed in my time, but the barbecue, family atmosphere remained the same and our conversations were the same. The companies didn't want to be rude to us. We were a new country and so on, and they were in our life and part of it – the theme of their soft-sell advertisements in our newspapers – but their line was that there was nothing to discuss. And we couldn't do a thing. There was no question of calling out the workers to support us. We had no control of that union. Besides, the companies' workers were the best-paid in Isabella – there was a continuous scramble for jobs with them – and so far as things like housing and recreation facilities went, they were model employers. So there we were. Another message to be taken back to the people, another exercise in leadership.

We were saved by Jamaica. They had more resources, a more experienced and energetic government, and more international contacts. They too had been exercised about their getting their bauxite, so easy to mine, renegotiated and at last they seemed to be getting somewhere. We merely followed their example and advice. The barbecue parties stopped. Instead we were photographed with our aides in a conference room, amid blank blotters and carafes and tumblers. We all looked stern and businesslike. From their advertisements, no one was happier than the companies.

It was a triumph. It was the peak of my political achievement. After this descent was to be rapid.

The smaller the society the more complex the issues: the hostilities and alignments in a parliament of six hundred are more easy to follow than those in a parish council of twenty. To me even now there is only a sequence of events. Everyone's motives remain unclear, and I doubt whether an impartial commission of inquiry will establish more than confusion, leading cloudily to a resolution of some sort. I am sure that motives and alliances shifted rapidly in the month after the renegotiating of the bauxite contract. Crunch-time was near; there was alarm and nervousness.

Coinciding with the flight of the Czech whose plastic stank, coinciding with the jubilation and publicity over the new bauxite contract, there occurred a great and continuing disturbance throughout the Stockwell sugar estates.

218

which our police force for almost a week was powerless to control.

See how the first two events had me as their centre; see how jumpiness linked me to the third. It was a movement of Asiatics, so cool to the idea of sharing distress. It was the first serious challenge to order we had had to face, and we recognized it as a show of true strength. It was the crop season. Ripe canes stood in the fields waiting to be cut; the loss from arson was immense. See how quickly jumpiness turned to alarm; see how many interpretations could be put on this disturbance, which at first seemed so unmanageable. See how many ways of action suggested themselves to men who distrusted each other and saw their own power as nothing more than bluff. There was the desire to win over and control this suddenly displayed strength; there was the desire to destroy it. There was talk of exploitation and absentee landlords; at the same time, here and there in towns, there were demonstrations of counter-violence, totally racial in character.

I was at the centre of events which I could not control. I was aware of feeling focusing on me. I was aware of every sort of rumour. Even those barbecue parties were being sinisterly interpreted: the delaying tactics of a man bribed, the delaying tactics of a man committed throughout his political career to the fortunes of his race. Easy to prove in a way, because *The Socialist*, against common sense, had continued to proclaim nationalization of the sugar estates as a desirable goal. It was part of my consistency, briefly my strength, and now the very thing to be used to destroy me.

Yet out of all the confusion, against daily reports of ripe burning canes and violence in the towns, this was the very cry that came out and was echoed from one end of the island to the other: nationalization. The estates had to be nationalized for the sake of unity, for the sake of that freedom from exploitation about which so much had been said. The estates had to be nationalized to balance the good fortune of the new bauxite contract. The estates had to be nationalized to prevent such threats to order in the future. I was at the centre; the task was mine. Browne spoke and was ambiguous: the task was mine. My supporters, and there were many, no doubt hoped for a miracle. Nationalization was as impossible as getting rid of the expatriate civil servants: so much London had made clear. A delegation to London was proposed. The expected reply came: there was nothing to discuss. But the cry did not die down on the island; I could not ignore it. Nationalization had become a word. It had no meaning. It held only Asiatic threat and Asiatic hope; to some it was a word of fulfilment and to others a word of revenge. Nationalization became less than a word: it became an emotive sound. The sugar-cane fields burned; two or three police stations in the country were overrun; in the towns shops and houses were looted. We were in the midst of a racial disturbance, but we spoke of it as nationalization. And to everything said by friend and enemy I was committed: to nationalization, to unity, to dignity, to the sharing of distress.

Once before, as a young man, I had been in a situation where I would have had to laugh my way to death by a Luger on a sunless beach; to the end I would have had to pretend that it was a joke, because it might have been. So now I found myself imprisoned in pretence, when it was so clear what was being prepared. On both occasions I might have cried out: 'No! You are not going to kill me!' On both occasions the reply might have been: 'But who is going to kill you?' Better the pretence, the joke.

Every day of drifting made withdrawal less easy. Every day of drifting weakened me. The strength was mine: control awaited me, awaited my plain statement. I do not exaggerate. In a confused situation my position was as clear as it always had been, and from the very falseness of this position I could have drawn together sufficient of the elements of our island to make my power certain and to restore calm. There were the ideologues to whom *The Socialist* had remained as an organ of internal opposition; there were those who had seen in the bauxite contract the only true achievement of our government; there was the middle class of all races, whom my presence in the cabinet had always reassured; there were the workers on the estates, who sought nly a spokesman for their strength. All these looked to me; ll these I let down. Control, the challenge to kill, was the nly alternative to pretence. But control, the prospect of ower, and its corollary, the prospect of keeping power in a tuation which would always turn to air in my hands, the rospect wearied me.

My sense of drama failed. This to me was the true loss. or four years drama had supported me; now, abruptly, rama failed. It was a private loss; thoughts of irresponsi- ility or duty dwindled, became absurd. I struggled to keep rama alive, for its replacement was despair: the vision of boy walking on an endless desolate beach, between vegeta- on living, rotting, collapsed, and a mindless, living sea. lo calm then: that came later, fleetingly. Drama failing, I new frenzy. Frenzy kept me silent. And silence committed e to pretence.

Nationalization? I would go to London. The idea of a elegation had been accepted: much work had been done ehind the scenes, by friend and enemy. In the fortnight I ould be away I would be undermined. Violence would be ustained; I would have nothing to return to. I began to now relief, to tell the truth; I longed to leave.

elief: I was astonished by the mood that settled on me. Departure had eluded me once before. Now at last, devi- usly, it was coming: fulfilment and truth. There would be return, of course; but that would be in the nature of a isit, an ascertaining of what I knew would be there. The ime before a departure is a splendid thing. I made my pre- arations slowly. My briefing was the least of my worries. had the facts at my fingertips and knew our arguments by eart. And London had made its attitude clear. It would ccept a delegation, but the delegation would not be re- eived by the Minister. London was playing the game up to point, doing us a favour.

Crop-time in Isabella, of the burning sugar-cane field[s]; early spring in London. The overcoat, then, which it h[as] always given me pleasure to hold over my arm in all t[he] light and heat of our airport lounge: the mark of the m[an] required to travel. On the road to the airport: houses [of] tin and timber, Mediterranean colours, fields, trees, sho[ps,] hoardings, the black face advertisements for toothpaste a[nd] stout: none of this would be seen with the eye of possessi[on] again. At the airport there was a demonstration. It surpris[ed] me, this thoroughness. It was of our movement, of cours[e;] it was favourable. I made a speech suited to the occasio[n;] it came as easily as the others. My last speech: I kept [my] style to the end. Presently we were sealed off, and risi[ng] above fields, rivers, roads and settlements whose logic h[ad] never been clearer.

Such a send-off; and an almost private arrival at Lond[on] Airport. This might have made me sensible of the path[os] of the politics of places like ours. But now it fitted my moo[d.] A representative of our Commission; junior officials fro[m] the Ministry; no newspapermen. But there was a motorc[ar] and a chauffeur; and, at the end of the journey, a first-cl[ass] hotel. There are few things as fine as an arrival at a fir[st] class hotel in a big city. One is luxuriously housed, with t[he] responsibility only of paying the bill. About one there i[s a] muted, urgent hum of activity: a score of services awa[it] one's lightest call. Glamour touches everyone: the chamb[er]maid, the telephone girl, whose accent and intonati[on] remain with one, the men at the desk, the girl at the new[s]paper kiosk. They are part of the fairyland, which contin[ues] as fairyland until one catches sight of the telephonist at h[er] winking board, the weary uniformed figures sitting slack[ly] on chairs in the laundry rooms, and one sees the pale nig[ht] clerk arriving in his shabby macintosh, until the structure [of] fairyland becomes plain, and the hotel becomes a place [of] work, linked not to the glamour of airline timetables in rac[e] but to houses such as those seen on the drive from the a[ir]port. This is the time to leave; this is when the days begin [to] race and grow tasteless. Until this time, though, the hotel [is] a place which radiates its magic to the city.

I was free. Such talks with officials as we had planned ere not to take place for a few days. I was alone. Many of y aides had disappeared into various corners of the city, eking pleasure or looking up friends and relations, students or immigrants, for whom they had brought gifts of m and cigarettes. How easily in this city they dwindled! A nk, this, with my own past in the city. But this was the city hich, exploring now from the hotel, I consciously tried to olish. I had dissected and destroyed the glamour of this ty; I had seen it as made up of individuals; I had ceased to e.

Now I tried to re-create the city as show: that city of the agical light in which I could walk without shadow. I tried rediscover the warm, sweetly pungent smell of tobacco- ists' shops and the acrid smell of the sooty cold air at dusk. I ied to be a tourist in the city which once had taught me the possibility of escape. And such was my mood, I succeeded. or three days I was completely happy. The days were not ite blank. Each day there was some event to which I could chor myself: a lunch with some businessmen; a dinner ith the London representatives of our Isabella newspapers; interview for the BBC's Overseas Service, recorded in sh House, in whose basement canteen Sandra, macin- shed, hysterical with a vision of the future she was afraid read, had proposed to me.

But there was the work of the delegation. The news from abella became worse; there was more violence; a para- aph appeared in the *Daily Telegraph*. We had our talks ith the officials. They said what they had said many times fore and what we expected them to say. They outlined early and concisely the consequences of nationalization. ur meetings need have lasted only a minute; we made them st three days and held daily press conferences which were nored by the London newspapers. Was it my imagination, ough, that detected a more than official hostility towards yself? I sensed that I was personally disapproved of, a cialist and a radical, a dangerous man, a troublemaker here there need only have been stability.

So the hardening of attitudes in Isabella, during my three

free days, was reflected in London. I could do nothing; I ha
committed myself to our game. And I could not help addin
to the unfavourable impression. The talks with the officia
ended in failure. I insisted on seeing the Minister: it was th
only thing left for me to do. My request was twice refused.
was told the second time that I could be invited to a lunch a
which the Minister would be present. I used the la
manoeuvre that remained to me: I called the representative
of the Isabella press and told them of my request. Two day
later I was told that the Minister would meet me, but with
out my delegation. It was better than nothing.

It was a brief, humiliating meeting. This man, whom i
other, humbler capacities I had met more than once befo
on various government trips to London and had thoug
affable and slightly foolish, now barely had time for the cou
tesies. His manner indicated clearly that our game had go
on long enough and he had other things to do than to assi
the public relations of colonial politicians. In about fort
five seconds he painted so lively a picture of the conse
quences of any intemperate action by the government
Isabella that I felt personally rebuked.

Then I spoke the sentence which tormented me almost
soon as I had said it. It was this which no doubt made th
interview so painful in recollection. I said, 'How can I tak
this message back to my people?' 'My people': for that
deserved all I got. He said: 'You can take back to you
people any message you like.' And that was the end.

I was shattered. I had entered the game so lightly. I ha
walked as a tourist about the Minister's city. Now I playe
but helplessly, knowing my own isolation, with visions
destruction. But all about me were signs of growth an
gaiety, reconstruction and colour. I felt the hopelessness
the wish for revenge for all that this city had inflicted on m
How easy it was to dwindle in this city! How easy to be th
boy, the student that one had been! Where now the magic
light? I walked about the terrible city. Wider roads than
had remembered, more cars, a sharper smell. It was to
warm for an overcoat; I perspired. I got into quarrels wit
taxi-drivers, picked rows with waiters and saleswomen. Ur

lignified, but I felt I was bleeding, with that second intimation of the forlornness of the city on which, twice, I had fixed
so important a hope.

Balm came from an unexpected source, from Lord Stockwell himself, whose estates were at issue. He wrote me a
letter in his own difficult hand – each letter separate but
barely decipherable – inviting me to dinner. I thought it
politic to accept, though it was not pleasant to contemplate
attending this celebratory dinner. So I thought it. I expected
something vaguely official; I felt sure that the Minister had
reported, with relish, our brief exchange. I began to secrete
bitterness and found that it gave me strength of a sort. And
it was in this mood, which had displeased me in others, that
I went. The mood held drama; it supported me in the dark
taxi-cab; I was prepared to assault the driver at the first sign
of deviousness. I was ripe for a full public scene. It was a
reaction of simplicity, based on an ignorance both of Lord
Stockwell and of the behaviour of the secure. I ought to have
known better; I knew better. I was astonished at myself, at
this example of derangement and coarsening.

The taxi-driver was not devious. We parted in silence. I
rang at the door. It was opened by a Southern European of
some sort, slum-faced, pallid, grave. I noticed little else just
then. I felt I had spent my life in interiors like these. It wiped
out, what at that moment it should have sharpened, memories of black mud and red-and-ochre overseers' compounds.
The man took my overcoat, folded it and put it on a chair,
below a Kalighat painting, momentarily disturbing because
so unexpected: Krishna, the blue god, upright, left leg
crossed in front of right, flute at his lips, wooing a white
milkmaid. A door opened, my name was announced.
Women, from whose faces I averted my gaze: the sudden
reassertion of childhood training; a small man, a very big
man moving towards me, very tall, a large paunch empha-
sized by a buttoned jacket, a heavy curling lower lip. I had
expected someone much smaller and neater.

The introductions were made. A woman's voice rumbled.
Something about the weather, perhaps; a query about what
I thought of London; something about the sunshine of

Isabella. I couldn't say. At the sound of the voice I close
my mind to what was being said; my mood tightened
dangerously, inside me. This time the enemy was going
be killed, and swiftly.

Then Lord Stockwell said: 'You'll never grow bald, that
for sure.' And the room became real again. I was impressed
I was pleased; I was relieved. This balm I sorely needed.
was foolishly grateful. Then Lord Stockwell added: 'You
father never did.' And left me to ponder afresh the name
carried. For a long time after that he said nothing at all.

The women took over. There were three women: Lad
Stockwell, her daughter Stella, and a woman of about fort
five whose name I didn't pick up throughout the evening
Much care had been expended on her characterless feature
she was attached to the small man, whose name and function
equally eluded me. Mine, happily, also appeared to elud
them. They intermittently showed me a courteous, incurio
interest and sometimes asked a question – was I in Londo
on business? – which in the circumstances was tactless; bu
generally they spoke to Lady Stockwell of common acquain
tances and private interests.

At dinner I sat next to Lady Stella. I put her in her earl
twenties. When her father went silent she appeared to re
gard it as her duty to entertain me. She was very bright.
must have been a strain. It took me some time to get used
her chirruping voice, so different from her mother's, whic
was harsh but clear; so that, while looking earnestly at Stell
and acknowledging the fact of her speech, I was in reality
for relief rather than interest, listening to her mother. Stell
seemed slightly frantic, but I did not feel I was in a positio
to assess anything; the evening was being conducted in
mode which was unfamiliar to me. I concentrated on he
voice, trying to disentangle words from the ceaseless tink
ling; and it was only when we were at the dinner table that
realized she was a beauty. Then I was disturbed and coul
no longer fix my eyes on her. It was a beauty of transpar
ence, of transparent skin, colourless hair and transparen
eyes. Perhaps it was her eyes that unsettled me; bright blu
eyes are to me empty and unreadable; when I look at them

ee only their colour. It might have been this, then, with the
difficult voice, that suggested frenzy.

She talked on. I picked up more and more of her words;
exchange became possible. She was asking me about the
books I had read as a child. I thought about *The Aryan
Peoples and Their Migrations* but suppressed it. She was
interested in children's books, and I had to confess that apart
from some stories by Andersen I had read none.

'No Henty or Enid Blyton or anything like that?'

I had to shake my head.

'No fairy stories or nursery rhymes?'

'I believe we had "Pat-a-cake" in one of our readers.'

She looked saddened and unbelieving. What she had read
as a child was important to her, and it was her theory that
understanding was impossible between people who had not
read the same children's books or heard the same nursery
rhymes.

Lady Stockwell said she disapproved of the cult of childhood and the cult of children's books; it was something else
that was being commercialized. She added that it was an
exceedingly English thing and that societies like my own, if
she could judge from what I had said, were wiser in encour-
aging children to become adults 'with all due haste'.

Stella's forehead twitched. She said to me: 'Do you know
Goosey-goosey Gander?'

I shook my head.

She said, 'Don't you know *Goosey-goosey Gander, whither
shall I wander?*'

Lady Stockwell said, 'I think it's obscene, putting all those
animals into clothes. I can't bear those bears and bunnies in
frills.'

'*Upstairs, downstairs, or in my lady's chamber?* Don't you
know it?'

'I can't bear those menus,' the forty-five-year-old lady
said. ' "Mushrooms picked in morning dew" or some such
thing. Why can't they just say mushrooms?'

'Milk from contented cows,' her companion said.

'*Cushy cow, bonny, let down thy milk,*' Stella recited, '*and
I will give thee a gown of silk.* Don't you know that one?'

'*I* don't know that one,' Lady Stockwell said. 'That must be something you got out of the Oxford book.'

'You must make them your constant study,' Stella said 'They're frightfully sexual.'

'I've often thought,' the forty-five-year-old lady said, 'that Jack and Jill are the most obscene couple in literature.'

'I don't know,' Lady Stockwell said. 'I've read that most of them were made up in the eighteenth century and were about real people.'

'It's the meaningless ones that are fascinating,' Stella said

Throughout this I was aware of Lord Stockwell gazing a me. From time to time I looked at him: his big sallow face small disturbed eyes below a large rectangular forehead. He didn't react to my own gaze. He continued to stare at me, his left hand moving steadily from his side plate to his mouth He was like a man eating nuts; he was in fact picking up minute pieces of bread crust and carrying them to his mouth but the gesture was large. I accepted his scrutiny, though about my father and my childhood and all those books and rhymes I had missed. It was more than wine and my own sense of release. The evening, I say, was being conducted in an unfamiliar mode.

He spoke again only when the women had left the room Then at least he had something to do. He offered brandy which he did not drink himself; he offered cigars, which no one smoked. He continued to eat bread crumbs.

I said, 'I never knew that you met my father.'

'I met him twice.'

I knew so little of my father; I had wished to know so little. Now there was something in Lord Stockwell's voice which told me that a show of embarrassment on my part would be out of place.

He said, 'The second time I met him he had given up politics. He had a little hut by the sea. Crown land, oddly enough. He had given up politics, but there was a little queue of people waiting to see him. He asked me what wanted. I couldn't tell him. He said, "All right, you just sit yourself down there." I sat myself down in a corner. It was very moving. These simple people came and told their roubles. The usual sort of thing. Job, sickness, death. While they were talking he was always doing something else. But at the end he would always speak a word or two, sometimes a sentence. It was marvellous. And sitting down, witnessing this, you felt immensely comforted. I couldn't leave.'

'Most extraordinary,' the small man said.

I felt uncomfortable. I asked, 'What sort of thing did he say?'

Lord Stockwell's forehead twitched, as his daughter's had done. 'Certain things are simple, banal. Some people make you live them, though.' He smiled; it did not become him. It's like the Highway Code. No good until you are on the road. Then it's a little bit more than logic.' He was disappointed in me; that I could feel.

I tried to look solemn. I said, 'I saw little of my father in those days.'

'Naturally. I will tell you something else about him. The second time I saw him he was just wearing a yellow dhoti. His chest was bare. His skin had a shine.'

We sat in silence for a little. The conversation turned to other things. I excused myself and went to the lavatory. I thought I was going to be sick. But it was just a momentary faintness. In that small room, coming to myself again, I could have wept for my solitude.

Just before I left Lady Stella said, 'Just a minute.' She ran out of the room and returned with *The Oxford Nursery Rhyme Book*. 'Have a look at this. I would like to know what you think.' I made some objection to taking the book; my stay was short and it might be difficult to return it. She said, 'Are you very busy? Couldn't you return it tomorrow or the day after?' It was not at all what I was expecting. I was tremendously flattered. A link with the past, with the city of magical light. We agreed on lunch. She had a flat of her own; she gave me the telephone number.

I walked back to the hotel. I smelled the cold sooty air. The sky was low; for just a little way above street level there was light, from street lamps and shop windows. The city was as if canopied; I had no feeling of being exposed. Around me the sky glowed. Well, it probably glowed in Isabella too,

229

for different reasons. It was past midnight. In the past
which my present mood was linked the city would have bee
still at such an hour; now the streets hummed with moto
cars whose red tail-lights were like warnings in the dark.
made no difference.

Holding *The Oxford Nursery Rhyme Book,* oddly sol
and scholarly in its bulk and feel, I entered the fairyland
the hotel. I had a hot bath; and, sipping the hot milk whic
awaited me every evening in a vacuum flask, I began to rea
I read, as I had been directed, as a child. It was no effor
Who comes here? A Grenadier. What does he want? A p
of beer. My mood was soft. And soon I was saddened, b
pleasurably, not only by the loss, in this roaring red city,
village greens and riders on horseback and milkmaids an
fairs and eggs in baskets and journeys by country folk
London town, but also by that limpid, direct vision of th
world, neither of which had been mine, neither vision,
delight, nor world, of order.

> But when they are clean,
> And fit to be seen,
> She'll dress like a lady,
> And dance on the green.

'Winnie the Pooh?' I said, passing the book back. 'I've ofte
seen it in bookshops and I've often seen it referred to. But
must confess I've never read it. I suppose the title has alwa
put me off.'

'*Ther* Pooh,' Stella said.

'Ther Pooh?'

'Don't you understand? I see this is something else I
have to read to you.' She sat up and pulled the sheet abov
her breasts. 'Are you ready? Then I'll begin.'

The delegation had gone back to Isabella. I stayed on
London. I no longer seek to explain; I merely record. F
eight days, during which whatever reputation I had left w
being destroyed, I stayed on in London, held by what I ha
detected in Stella's manner at our first meeting. Frenzy w
what I had first thought it to be; and frenzy it was, of a sor
It was a capacity for delight, such as I had found in Sandr

230

ut without Sandra's anguish. It was a coolness. It was more, much more, than Sandra's feeling for an occasion. It was a way of looking at the city and being in it, a way of appearing to manage it and organize it for a series of separate, perfect pleasures. It was a sustaining of that mood to which I feared to put an end, knowing it could never return. It was a creation, of the city I had once sought: an unexpected fulfilment. Perhaps I was deceived by Stella's manner and skills, which might have been the manner and skills of her class. But I was willingly deceived.

All this had to be paid for, though, in those afternoons in her flat. What I know of the sexual capacities of others I have learned from books. With this knowledge I cannot say that excessive demands were made of me, but I believe I have said enough in this narrative to make it plain that my sexual charge was low and unreliable. In fact I dreaded those afternoons behind drawn curtains; in the end they drove me away. They began on my second visit to her flat; she had promised to tell me some stories. She was wearing a quilted pink housecoat or dressing-gown. I kissed her lightly on the forehead. A disagreeable scorched smell, I remember: she had just been to the hairdresser's. Her expression didn't change, and I was not prepared for her acknowledgement. She said, 'Shall we go to bed?' I was struck by the contrast between the calm, childish voice and what it was proposing. But it was familiar; I remembered. 'Shall I show you my nude drawings?' The sentence held an equal guilelessness. There could be no refusal.

Our love-making was standardized. It followed the pattern of that afternoon. It was divided into two parts. The first was dedicated to me; the second Stella claimed for herself. For the first part she lay on her side and was passive. For the second she straddled me, leaning back, resting her hands on the bed or on my shins; she was all motion; her eyes were closed; her skin went moist. She made no sound, except once, when she said, as though to herself, 'Aren't bodies wonderful?' I did not share her view then; later I marvelled at her precision and honesty. Such small breasts as she leaned back! Such a private frenzy; I might not have been there.

She was a little alarming. For me this speechless, prolonged second part was torment and torture. I sent my mind off on to other subjects, with such success once that, taking up a large picture book from the bedside table – it was about the treasures of Tutankhamen's tomb, I believe – I heard myself saying, what I thought I was only thinking, 'So you've got this.' A swift, slight slap was the reply I received. I put the book down.

So now, with a sinking heart, I listened to the adventures of Pooh and Eeyore and Piglet, knowing that the moment would soon come when sterner things would have to be faced. The moment came. The sheet was thrown off, the book put aside, and I lay patiently on my back. The book was within reach; I longed for nothing more than to be allowed to continue quietly reading. I studied the jacket. It remains imprinted on my mind and whenever I see it I am irritated by a little feeling which presently defines itself as deprivation. Then the inevitable happened; I had feared that it might. I began to fail. The figure above me was pathetically frenzied; I wished I could help her. Later, when failure was absolute, the childish face was blank with disappointment and unforgiving anger. It was the end. No relationship, especially a play-relationship like ours, recovers from such a failure.

And really it was time to go, to leave the city of fantasy, to leave the fairyland of the hotel, no longer fairyland. But it was a good thought of Stella's to send the paperback of *The House at Pooh Corner* to my hotel.

7

It was time to leave. But there was no need for me to return to Isabella. That, however, I didn't see until it was too late, until, in fact, our aeroplane was a few minutes from Isabella and we were fastening safety belts. The city and snow, the island and the sea: one could only be exchanged for the other. So my mind ran; departure implied a destination.

vas calm. It was the calm that comes to so many in moments f crisis; and I was still infected by Stella's attitude to experience, her special hubris, as I saw it, the gift perhaps of her class or race, her prodigal's conviction that what is will ontinue to be. Fulfilment creates its own illusions. Sandra ad been made careless of the wealth she had longed for; how I easily turned my back on the city which I had at last been to glitter. It was only at the airport, where I had arrived n good time, that I became aware of my calm. And instantly began to question it. Error! Questioning, self-examination, reassurance: the process quickly became continuous, and I feared I was launched on the familiar switchback of neurosis. It seemed to me at the time it was this fear alone which vas working on me. I feared and saw that my fear was justified. Within minutes my world was spoilt – so recently whole – and my calm was gone.

Even then I did not ask myself whether a return to Isabella was necessary. I wished only to delay it, to make a detour, to have a momentary escape. To recover my calm and hat limpid vision of the world: this was now all my concern. Everything else dwindled: Stella, Isabella and what awaited me there. I was a student in the city again. I needed new sights, new landscapes, an unfamiliar language. Northern Spain in a snowstorm, the brown earth whitening, the light suddenly grey; Provence on a sunny morning, green and yellow and hazy, the big Wagon-Lit coffee cup kept steady by a heavy spoon.

Stopover: the word from the airline advertisements came to me. Not easy at this stage. But my frenzy ignored rebukes and overcame difficulties. And a few hours later I was walking, as in a dream, through the streets of a city, I thought I didn't know, which yet now revealed little points of familiarity, abrupt half-remembered areas: so that reality was disturbed, sounds curiously muted, and for stretches I had the sensation of witnessing and performing actions for the second, third, fourth time. I drank the drinks I had first tasted twelve years before, nibbled at the same savouries; they rested as heavily on my stomach. A glimpse of sawdust on a tiled floor of a familiar pattern, the eye-straining fluorescent light in a dark corner, a face, snatches of conversation in a language I could only partly follow: my disturbance was complete. For the second time that day I was frantic with airline officials. But there were no aeroplanes to Isabella that day. Tomorrow, yes: a fresh sticker was gummed to my ticket. Sixteen intransit hours awaited me.

I went into bookshops and looked through expensive, difficult-to-handle editions of the country's classics until assistants became over-attentive. Then even the shops closed and the streets had nothing to hold me. I dawdled about the hotel, in the lounge, in my room. On the cream-coloured plastic bell-push a flat-footed maid stared placidly and slender steward raced, tray aloft, coat tails flying. Promise of delight! I rang for snacks I didn't want and drinks I couldn't finish. I exhausted the services of the hotel. I had a bath and got into bed. After some time I got out of bed. It was only nine o'clock. I dressed with an effort, and went out into the streets.

I took small drinks from tired barmen in little tiled bars, each drink added to the weight in my stomach. A conjunction of streets, a building, a slope, a turning: a remembered area. A woman walked slowly ahead of me and turned into a café entrance. Memory stirred. I followed the woman through the revolving door. I was strained with more than drink; I was exhausted; it was the last thing I was looking for. But my stomach lightened with an old excitement. I felt I had been guided to this place: the light, the low tables and low chairs, the slender half-filled glasses, the solitary intense young men in double-breasted suits, the carefully made-up women, in twos and threes, so cool, concealing such skill, such energy.

It is for faces I go on such occasions. The body doesn't interest me, one body being so much like another. The excitement I feel is enough; what follows is perversity or, oddly, duty. I went for a fresh, appealing, witty face, unusually thin for the country, though to this face was attached a body as plump as any. She was friendly and gentle, as such women invariably are; and as we left the café on foot for the hotel she chatted of this and that with such ease that the observer

234

night have believed we were old friends. Her good humour was not out of place even in the hotel. The thin elderly lady at the desk, though businesslike and brisk in her starched apron, greeted my companion effusively. She said it was good to see my companion again, and looking so well; was she better? My companion replied that she was. The lady at the desk, studying the register I had signed, said that she was not surprised; she playfully reproached my companion with her earlier despair and said that in all circumstances we would be wiser to leave everything in the hands of God. And so we went up the dimly-lit carpeted stairs. No word had been said to me, it being the gracious custom of the ladies of these hotels to pay no attention to the clients of their clients. My smiling companion, appreciating my un-spoken alarm at the talk of illness, explained that she had been slimming. Making a face of satire, and holding her hands wide apart, she said she had been fat, oh, but enor-mous.

The curtained room was warm; red-shaded bedside lamps made it cosy; at the same time it was somewhat surgical with its white, polished wash-basin, two small towels lying across its spotless bidet, and other towels lying neatly folded on the edge of the bed. I paid my companion the sum we had laughingly agreed on in the café. She stroked my cheek and said she didn't like taking money beforehand – it was modern and rapacious – but she had had unpleasant experiences. Her courtliness delighted me. She left the room, doubtless to hand over some fraction of the sum I had given her to the lady of the hotel; I heard animated conversation between them. Presently my companion returned, somewhat out of breath, apologizing as to a child for her absence. I had un-dressed and was lying on the bed. I was beginning to know the depth of my exhaustion. Whatever excitement I had felt on entering the cosy, surgical room had subsided; and the smiling willingness of the young girl to please – I now saw that she was young – seemed remote, slightly touching, slightly absurd.

Without her outer garment – which she hung carefully over the back of the chair – she all at once appeared bigger

235

than I had thought. She exceeded the generous standards of
the country. Her arms were wide and slack. Her breasts had
been pulled tightly upwards and flattened against her chest;
even so they had appeared full and large. Now, with a sigh
from my companion that turned into a laugh, these breasts
were released. They cascaded heavily down. They were
enormous, they were grotesque, empty starved sacks which
yet contained some substance at their tips, where alone they
had some shape. She unbound, untied, released herself.
Flesh, striped, indented, corrugated, fell helplessly about
her. Below those breasts, wide flabby scabbards which hung
down to her middle, her dimpled, loose belly collapsed;
flesh hung in liquid folds about her legs which quivered like
risen dough. She was ghastly, tragic, a figure from hell with
a smiling girl's face, the thin starved face of the slimmer.
Tormented by flesh, she offered knowledge of flesh. *Fat, fat*
she kept on saying, smiling, tragic; and courtesy, compassion
answered for me, *No, no*. I knew I would never touch; and
feared being touched. Yet I never moved. Flesh, flesh,
thought: how could I disdain? How could I even judge?
She lifted herself off the bidet and sat on the bed, liquescent
flesh running laterally, her breasts touching what passed for
thighs. I closed my eyes and waited.

No damp, flat, smothering embrace came; only the softest
of words, the sweetest of breaths, a brushing – of those
breasts? – against my nipples, the barest touch of a fingernail
circling my areola. I never touched; my hands still lay at my
side. Yet I was already turning in on myself; judgement was
disappearing. Nails, tongue, breath and lips were the instruments of this disembodied probing. Two light lines
drawn down my chest, a quick tongue against the side of my
belly, and my tense abdominal muscles quivered, rippled,
liquefied. The probing went lower; no effort of concentra-
tion was now required, no need to shut out the world, the
liquid sighs and sounds. Judgement disappeared, I was all
painful sensation. Flesh, flesh: but my awareness of it was
being weakened. I was turned over on my belly. The probing
continued, with the same instruments. The self dropped
away, layer by layer; what remained dwindled to a cell of
236

perception, indifferent to pleasure or pain; neutral perception, finer and finer, having validity, existing only because of that probing which, growing fainter, yet had to be apprehended, because it was the only proof of life: fine perception reacting minutely only to time, which was also the universe. It was a moment that was extended and extended and extended. There could be no issue; it was a moment which, when release without fruition came and perception widened again, defined itself as an extended moment of horror. It is a moment that has remained with me. After three years I can call it back at will: that moment of timelessness, horror, solace. The Highway Code! Through poor, hideous flesh to have learned about flesh; through flesh to have gone beyond flesh.

But, monstrous, she was in despair. The smile, of hysteria, was replaced by tears; she reproached herself for my failure. I comforted her; at that moment I was genuine. *Fat, fat,* he said, lifting her breasts, lifting her belly; and I said *No, no.* She began to smile again; she rinsed out her mouth, made up her face, rearranged her hair. We talked, imperfectly, in her language. She misunderstood something I said. She said, as though replying to a question, 'During those moments I never open my eyes. I never think.' I was too moved to speak. I watched her re-erect her body for the café without disdain or judgement; it was all I could offer her. I walked her back to the revolving door. Less than an hour had passed.

In the hotel that night I was awakened by a sensation of sickness. As soon as I was in the bathroom I was sick: all the undigested food and drink of the previous day. My stomach felt strained; I was in some distress. On the plastic bell-push the chambermaid still stared and the waiter still paced. But it was just past three; the hotel was still. I began to wait for morning. I had not slept well. In a serial dream I had found myself on my back, on my belly, in a London street or tunnel through which red underground trains careered on crisscrossing tracks. Beyond the trains I could see Sally, Sandra, my father, Lord Stockwell, anxious to come to me, who could not move towards them. As I slept and awakened, waiting for the light to come to the fantasy city, known and unknown, memory and the dream flowed together. When the light came I was weak and ill. The stopover was at an end. It was necessary to rise and prepare for another departure.

8

My arrival was quiet. I was not expected. My stopover arrangements of the previous day had given rise to the rumour that I had disappeared or fled. It was as a private person, then, that I took a taxi to the Roman house. I required sleep. The drive was swift; it was later represented, not unjustly, as furtive. Indeed it astonished me that, on an island where I had needed notice and drama to sustain me, I should now relish privacy. For a little I played with the idea of the impossible, of prolonging this enjoyment by resignation and silence. It was impossible, of course, in the nature of our political life.

I was not allowed to be a private person for long. News of my return quickly spread. In the morning there was a police guard outside my house. The guard was needed. My stopover had frustrated a demonstration that had been arranged to meet me at the airport; public feeling was aggravated. I learned that at this airport demonstration I would have been allowed to make a statement and answer questions; it would have been part of the show. But I was not allowed to speak at the meeting which was now hurriedly called. I was not even invited to attend.

At this meeting a massive, contradictory but satisfying case was made against me. My private life – my methodical making of money, the racial exclusiveness of my development at Crippleville, my marriage to Sandra, my relationship with Wendy, my escapade with Stella – all this was used to heighten the picture of my public imposture. I had sold out on the nationalization issue; it was my playboy attitude to distress. At the same time my steady advocacy o nationalization, of benefit mainly to Asiatics, had been an attempt to create racial divisions to ensure my own continued power. My attitude to distress had always been equivocal. I had joined the movement, had helped to create it, only to destroy what it stood for. I had even tried to gain control of the police and had secretly recommended that it should remain under British control. It was a massive charge, as I say. In the hysteria of a public meeting it must have been overwhelming. It could not be answered reasonably, and from a position of weakness, because it contained too many points of truth. It could be answered only with a challenge, and from a position of strength.

But no one was interested in my answer. In a month I had thrown away my power. In a month I had been discredited. The newspapers were free, but no one spoke up for me. No restriction of any sort had been placed on me, but no one came to the Roman house and I never left it. We had created drama, an awareness of strength and vulnerability; we had created an unwillingness to offend. My mother came to see me, and my sisters and their children. We splashed about in the swimming-pool. Strange this privacy that had been granted me, whose misdemeanours filled the newspapers. I read them every morning like any other private citizen. I soon ceased to react to the sight of my name; it was no longer something I could attach to myself. I followed the fortunes of others. I read the announcement of Wendy's engagement in Montreal to someone with a French name. A photograph, affectionately captioned. The medium-visioned, the surviving!

I had written to Browne. He had not replied; and now, reading the newspapers, I felt I had not paid sufficient attention to his silences. He had not been at the public meeting which condemned me. It presently came out that he had not been asked; there were vague suggestions that we were too close. Then I saw that my return to Isabella was not only unnecessary, it was even more irresponsible than my departure had been.

I had already seen Browne, as black folk-leader, incapable of breaking out of that sterile fate, in competition with the faceless men we had made. Whether I had returned or no[t] that competition would have continued, and at that leve[l] In our movement power was to be redefined, and its tru[e] possessors revealed. I was out of the running, for all th[e] newspaper space I occupied. But by returning, by puttin[g] myself at the passive centre of events, by being the dand[y] the picturesque Asiatic, I gave direction of a sort to the strug[g]le. My presence made the struggle more plausible, made i[t] more than one of personalities. It dictated the terms in whic[h] that struggle, irrelevant to myself, was to be fought out; i[t] suggested the way in which faceless men, by creating dis[-]order, might demonstrate their power. And the foreign pres[s] always conventionally sympathetic to proclamations of dis[-]tress, was approving! What could I do? I had my polic[e] guard. I stayed in the Roman house.

For the calamity that came – there is no other word fo[r] open racial conflict in a small territory – I must bear muc[h] of the responsibility. It was a responsibility that began wit[h] that moment of return to the slave island, that moment [of] morning stillness; it continued to the moment of my fina[l] departure. Do not think, the acceptance of guilt being easie[r] than action and in some ways more satisfying, that I see[k] simply to heap guilt on myself. The faceless men, who ou[t] of disorder of this sort rise to the top and are briefly glor[i]ous, are never guilty. They play with incurable distress fro[m] within. They are made by distress and are part of it. Th[e] same will be true of their successors.

Do not yet think that I speak calmly from the position o[f] the secure, the physically safe, the man who has found refug[e] thousands of miles away in this suburban hotel, where ever[y] evening I dine below the portraits of the man and woma[n] whom we here regard as our protecting lord and lady. M[y] inactivity and folly amounted to cruelty. But I was a help[-]less spectator of this cruelty. Helpless; yet I cannot say tha[t] at the time I felt guilt. I lived; I passed the days. Everythin[g] in the Roman house continued to work. The water in th[e] swimming-pool continuously changed, continuously passe[d] through the filter. If the machine had failed for thirty-si[x] hours that blue pool, restlessly webbed with light through[

out its depth, would have become as still and milky green and opaque with minute vegetation as a pool in the jungle. So the water-jets splashed; and every morning, beside them, I sat in the shade at my breakfast table – avocadoes, fried plantains, cinnamon-scented chocolate, white tablecloth, ironed white napkin, a small bowl of fresh flowers – and read the newspapers.

When the organized violence began, when men distraught with anger and fear and outrage, who considered themselves betrayed by me yet saw that in their predicament they had no one else to turn to, when these men, braving the city streets, came to me at the Roman house with tales of Asiatic distress, of women and children assaulted, of hackings, of families burnt alive in wooden houses, I closed my eyes and thought about the horsemen riding to the end of the world. The details of physical suffering entered into me. In a book about Japanese prisoner-of-war camps I had once seen a photograph: an Australian, blindfolded, on his knees, far from home, about to be beheaded. Heroic this central figure had seemed to me, in my quick fear: heroic and very private, and by this privacy ridiculing the ridicule of his tormentors. Now I asked my informers to give me no more details. I offered them the comfort I offered myself. I said, 'Think about this as something in a book, in a newspaper. Do not give me names. Do not tell me how people died. Say instead, "Race riots occurred". Say, "There was loss of life".'

One poor man had brought a stone stained and sticky with blood and fine hair, the hair perhaps of a child. What could I do with his evidence, his witness? I tried to get him to enter my mind, to ride with me to the end of the empty world. His grief made him, as it had made others, receptive. It was night. I took him to the garden of the Roman house and asked him to drop the stone. He was glad to obey. The link between us then was more than the link of speech. The comfort I offered him was the comfort I offered myself, to destroy the images of vulnerable flesh. Was this cruel or fraudulent? The gift of comfort which at that moment I discovered in myself, this ability to transmit my own vision of the world, this was something I could have worked miracles with, I know, even at that late stage. But this would have required an assurance of imminent order, and to a belief in that I could lead no one. The call to action and self-fulfilment was the necessary complement to the vision I offered; without this the gift was useless, destructive. So the gift, at the moment of its discovery, was abandoned. I became a leader too late.

And it would not surprise me to hear that that very man, whose face in the dark garden I couldn't even see, turned on me a week later when he heard that I had accepted, from our new leaders, the offer of a free and safe passage, to London again, by air, with sixty-six pounds of luggage and fifty thousand dollars. A fraction of my fortune. My irresponsibility extended even to myself: I had not taken the proper precautions. They were simple, frightened men. I am sure they had no wish to harm me. But in their situation they could no longer trust themselves; they offered me only what they hoped they might themselves be offered when their time came.

Perhaps, then, I was a betrayer. But not in the way that was said. This was not something that could be explained to a reporter, if there remained any who wished to interview me. And my acquiescence, again in a role that was given me, need not be wondered at.

9

I thought when I began this book that it would be the labour of three or four weeks. Memories of my fluency, on *The Socialist*, in cabinet, were still fresh; the five-thousand-word paper on the reorganization of the police, not a negligible document, had been the concentrated work of an evening. After eighteen months of the anaesthetizing order of life in this hotel, despair and emptiness had burnt themselves out. And it was with a delicious sense of anxiety and of being employed again that I got the hotel to give me a writing-table, set it beside the window, and composed myself to work.

It was just after breakfast. The pleasant middle-aged Irish chambermaid had got my room ready early and was going to bring me coffee at eleven. My mouth felt clean; my arms were strained and tingling with excitement. At the appointed time the coffee came. My excitement had turned to a type of irritable fatigue; I had written nothing. The wallpaper, in grey, black and red, had a pattern of antique motorcars; the curtain, which hung beside the table, was of a heavy red rep, brownish where it had been handled, discoloured along the folds exposed to the sun; the window, in a modern metal frame, was low, offering a view of the hotel's putting green, bounded at the far end by a wall of brick, pale-red, washed-out; beyond this, more red brick, warehouses, garages, houses, just a segment of the city. I was overwhelmed as much by the formlessness of my experiences, and their irrelevance to the setting in which I proposed to recount them, as by the setting itself, my physical situation, in this city, this room, with this view, that lustreless light. And it was not until late afternoon, excitement gone, the light faded, the curtains about to be drawn, my stomach, head and eyes united in a dead sensation of sickness, that the memory at last came which, forcing itself to the surface all day, had kept the first page of the Century notebook blank except for the date: the memory of my first snow and the memory, incredulously examined, of the city of the magical light.

Fourteen months have passed since, in a room made over-dry by the electric fire, I re-created that climb up the dark stairs to Mr Shylock's attic to look through a snowfall at the whitening roofs of Kensington. By this re-creation the event became historical and manageable; it was given its place; it will no longer disturb me. And this became my aim: from the central fact of this setting, my presence in this city which I have known as student, politician and now as refugee-immigrant, to impose order on my own history, to abolish that disturbance which is what a narrative in sequence might have led me to.

In Isabella in the early days I spoke as much as anyone about culture and the need for a national literature. But, to

243

tell the truth, I had no great regard for writers as men, much as I might have enjoyed their work. I looked on them as incomplete people, to whom writing was a substitute for what it then pleased me to call life. And when I settled down to this book, the labour of three or four weeks, as I thought, I was looking beyond to other things. The financial uplift at the end would be small, I knew. But I thought there was a good chance that publication might lead to some form of irregular, agreeable employment: reviews and articles on colonial or 'third world' matters, calls from Bush House to prepare talks and even on occasion to indulge in the harmless banter of a radio discussion, and perhaps, after a year or two of this light underground labour, some little niche in television: the colonial expert, keeping his own counsel, calmly leaving his suburban hotel and returning later, in the taxi for which others have paid, to find himself the object of an awe which he will not of course acknowledge. This last, I must confess, was a recurring daydream. Nothing was known about me at the hotel. I had unwisely represented myself as a businessman; and my inactivity, extending over eighteen months, had begun to excite suspicion.

It never occurred to me that the writing of this book might have become an end in itself, that the recording of a life might become an extension of that life. It never occurred to me that I would have grown to relish the constriction and order of hotel life, which previously had driven me to despair; and that the contrast between my unchanging room and the slow progression of what was being created there would have given me such satisfaction. Order, sequence, regularity: it is there every time the electric meter clicks, accepting one more of my shillings. In fourteen months the meter has swallowed hundreds of my shillings, now with a hollow sound, now with a full sound. I have seen the putting green in all weathers, preferring it best in winter, when our middle-aged ladies, mutton dressed as lamb, as our barman says, cease to sunbathe, and our homeless men no longer appear on it at weekends in sporty clothes and make hearty conversation.

I know every line on the wallpaper above my table. I have

244

seen no deterioration, but there is talk of redecorating. And the table itself: when I first sat at it I thought it rough and too narrow. The dark surface was stained and scratched, the indentations filled with grit and dirt; the drawer didn't pull out, the legs had been cut down. It wasn't part of the standard hotel furniture. It had been provided specially; it was a junkshop article, belonging to no one, without a function. Now it feels rehabilitated and clean; it is familiar and comfortable; even the scratches have acquired a shine. This is the gift of minute observation which has come to me with the writing of this book, one order, of which I form part, answering the other, which I create. And with this gift has come another, which I least expected: a continuous, quiet enjoyment of the passing of time.

I have fitted into the hotel; the fact has been remarked upon. Suspicion has disappeared; it had nothing to feed on since I learned to fill my day. I have breakfast. I work in my room. I walk to the public house for lunch. The beermats never change. *Who comes here? A Grenadier.* Sometimes in mid-afternoon I go to a restaurant where frying oil hangs in the still air like a mist; beyond the streaming glass the lorries, buses and motorcars pass ceaselessly in their own blue haze. I have tea and read an evening paper. On Sundays we all have tea in the lounge; it is the custom then for the ladies to serve the men. The older folk play cards; the rest of us read the newspapers. I read the characterless hand of a lady, lower-middle-class but nice, who was in India until 1947; now, after Kenya and Northern Rhodesia, her husband dead, her family scattered, she has given up the Empire. Like me. I frequently go down to the bar before dinner to have a drink and watch television. It is a private bar; postcards and souvenirs from residents who have gone abroad are reverentially displayed. I have my own table in the dining-room. It is behind a square pillar, clad with varnished pine. I like being behind the pillar. It is as wide as my table and gives me privacy of a sort. It also enables me, without giving offence, to observe the hands of the man I think of as Garbage.

Garbage also sits behind a pillar. His hands are all I can

245

see of him. They are long, middle-aged, educated hands: and their primary concern appears to be to convert a plate of meat and vegetables into a plate of acceptable garbage. While chaos comes swiftly and simultaneously to other plates; while meat is hacked and pushed around and vegetables mangled and scattered on a spreading, muddy field of gravy; while knives and forks, restlessly preparing fresh, mixed mouthfuls, probe the chaos they have created, and cut and spear and plaster; those two hands are unhurriedly, scientifically, maintaining order, defining garbage, separating what is to be eventually eaten from what is to be thrown away. What is to be thrown away is lifted high and carefully deposited on that section of the plate, a growing section, which is reserved for garbage. It is only when the division is complete – most of the other plates abandoned by this time and ready for surrender – that the eating begins. This is the work of a minute; the plate is ready for surrender with the others. The waitress passes. Stiffly, dismissingly, the outstretched hands offer up their labour: a neat plate of garbage. I feel I have witnessed the first part of some early Christian ritual. For this is not all. After the plate of garbage comes the slaughter of the cheese. The big left hand arches high over the block of cheddar; thumb and middle finger find their hold and press lightly; the right hand brings down the curved, two-pronged knife. But at the last moment the hands pretend that the cheese is alive and getting away. The cheddar shifts about on the oily slaughter-board; there is a struggle; thumb and finger release their hold, but only to press down more firmly; instantly, then, the knife falls, in a strong clean stroke that continues until the cheese is truncated and still. And I almost expect to see blood.

So the time passes. There are occasional incidents. Some one objects to the way a deaf diner scrapes and taps his plate with his knife; he, unlike Garbage, likes to offer up a clean plate. The barman gets drunk; a waitress leaves after a quarrel. Sometimes I have to endure a difficult week or two when the double room next to mine is taken by male employees of a nearby factory which, I believe, ceaselessly converts American maize into glucose; then I have to listen to a constant stream of churlish chatter, pre-public house, post-public house, always vapid, always punctuated by that even, mirthless, four-beat laugh which I detest.

But such people come and go and are quickly forgotten; they form no part of the life of the hotel. When I first came here I used to think of this life as the life of the maimed. But we who belong here are neither maimed nor very old. Three-quarters of the men here are of my age; they have responsible jobs to which they go off in their motorcars every morning. We are people who for one reason or another have withdrawn, from our respective countries, from the city where we find ourselves, from our families. We have withdrawn from unnecesssary responsibility and attachment. We have simplified our lives. I cannot believe that our establishment is unique. It comforts me to think that in this city alone there must be hundreds and thousands like ourselves.

We have our incidents. But we also have our events. The most important is of course Christmas. That truly separates the faithful, who stay on, from those who, steadfast throughout the year, at last reveal other, saddening loyalties. Among the faithful the event is spoken of weeks before. A subscription list circulates: we exchange presents with our lord and lady on the day, just as they exchange presents with the staff. There is much half-bantering, half-serious talk of precedence; for on the day the tables are joined together to form an E, and we eat together, lord and lady and faithful, and he who is the newest among us finds himself farthest from the centre.

I have moved up year by year, but I know I will never sit at our lady's right hand. That position is reserved for a man who has been here twenty-three years, a shy, gentle, delicately-featured man, still quite young-looking, so unassertive in hall and bar and putting green that his eminence on the day comes as a surprise to many. It is a sincere occasion. Nothing is skimped, and no extra charge is made even for the wines and liqueurs which are liberally served. But we are grateful for more than the dinner. We are celebrating our safety, and our emotion is profound. It is intolerably moving when the kind and aged waitress who represents the staff on these occasions comes out from among her uniformed colleagues at the kitchen entrance and, in silence, makes her way to the centre with a large cellophane-wrapped bouquet which, after a brief, faint, stumbling speech that contains not one false word, she presents to our lady. I must confess that last year when, for the first time, the toast was made by our lady to 'our overseas guest' and all heads turned towards me, tears came to my eyes. And I was among those who, unashamedly weeping, stood up at the end and applauded our lord and lady all the way out of the hall. And really, I thought, in the French patois of the cool cocoa valleys of Isabella, *je vens d'lué*. I had come 'from far', from the brink.

So this present residence in London, which I suppose can be called exile, has turned out to be the most fruitful. Yet it began more absurdly than any. I decided, when I arrived, not to stay in London. It had glittered too recently; and I wished to avoid running into anyone I knew. I thought I would stay in a hotel in the country. I had never done this before, in England or anywhere else; but after recent events the conviction was strong that I was again in a well-organized country. I made no inquiries. I simply chose a town I had visited as a student in a British Council party. My imagination, feeding on the words 'country' and 'hotel', created pictures of gardens and tranquillity, coolness and solitude, twittering hedgerows and morning walks, spacious rooms and antique reverences. They were what I required.

But it was holiday time, as I quickly discovered: the season of ice-cream tubs and soft-drink bottles, pissing children and sandwich wrappings. Hotels were full and squalid or half-full and very squalid; they all buzzed and shrieked with the urgent sound of frying. Ceilings were decayed, cramping, partitions paper-thin, forty-watt light bulbs naked; and always in tattered sitting-rooms there were tattered copies of motorcar magazines, travel magazines, airline annuals. Country roads were highways and gardens car-parks. Tall hedgerows, which prevented escape from packed holiday motorcars, turned narrow lanes into green tunnels of death.

248

nd destruction; broken glass was crushed to powder at
ntersections. And there were the inns of death itself, areas
f complete calm, where the very old had gathered to die.
Iere food was liquid and medicinally tinctured, each aged
ater sat with his transistor radio linked, like a hearing-aid,
ɔ his own ear, and the tiny plastic extractor fans were pro-
elled, in gentle silent spasms, by warm air alone.

Daily, by erratic bus services, making difficult connex-
ɔns, I travelled from small town to small town, seeking
helter with my sixty-six pounds of luggage, always aware in
he late afternoon of my imminent homelessness. I consumed
he hours of daylight with long waits and brief periods of
ravel. Money, of which I was at last aware, was leaking out
f my pocket. Laundry was about to be a problem. At the
nd of a week I was exhausted. Even then I did not give up
ɪy quest; I was too dispirited to make that difficult decision.

did so on the eleventh day, when laundry had become a
roblem. I decided to go back to London. But again I did
ɪot take into account the holiday, which had apparently
eached its climax on the day of my decision. I did not take
nto account the irregularities and excisions which on such a
lay turn railway timetables into guides to nightmare.

I made an early start. Afternoon found me at an unknown
mpty country station, hours from London. The tall trains
rent by and did not stop for me. They were long trains, and
acked; people stood in the corridors. Tomato sauce and
ravy and coffee stained the tablecloths in the restaurant car.

knew. Hours before one such train had brought me to this
tation. I was waiting for another to take me away. Early
mpatience had given way to despair, despair to indifference,
ndifference to a curious neutrality of perception. The con-
rete platforms were white in the sun, the diagonal, length-
ning shadows sharp and black. Heatwaves quivered up
rom the rails and their level bed of dry, oiled gravel. In the
ushy field beyond, pale green blurred with yellow, white
nd brown, junked rusting metal was hot to look at.

I was fighting the afternoon alarm of homelessness, an
nseparable part of the gipsy life that had inexplicably be-
allen me. But this was the limit of desolation. The moment

linked to nothing. I felt I had no past. Nothing had happene[d]
that morning or yesterday or the last eleven days. T[o]
attempt to explain my presence in this station to myself, o[r]
to look forward to the increasingly improbable search tha[t]
awaited me in a London to which I was drawing no neare[r],
to attempt to do either was to be truly lost, to see myself a[t]
the end of the world. The green doors of the buffet wer[e]
closed. Three circular sticky tables, a very narrow stick[y]
counter, a sticky floor; the glass cases empty, even the plast[ic]
orange at rest in the orange-squash vat of cloudy plastic.

The tall magenta trains passed, summer clothes abov[e]
black, busy metal below, and blinded me with their racin[g]
rippling shadows, that fell on me, on the platform. 'Standin[g]
by himself on Swindon station.' They were the words of M[r]
Mural, breeder of boy scouts. Poor emperor, I had though[t]
subject to such witness. I had seen him, though, standing o[n]
Swindon station as he had stood in the photograph i[n]
Browne's house: in his cloak, his head thrown back, dignifie[d]
aloof. Such was the exile of Mr Mural's witness; and dignit[y]
and aloofness implied an audience. It wasn't like this: a ma[n]
sitting at the limit of desolation with sixty-six pounds of lu[g]
gage in two Antler suitcases, concentrating on the momen[t]
which he mustn't relate to anything else. And who will late[r]
give me even Mr Mural's proof of this moment? It was [a]
moment of total helplessness. It occurred on an afternoon [of]
sunshine, while the holiday trains passed.

That was a long time ago. Such a moment cannot retur[n].
It is the moment which really closes that section of my lif[e]
which I have been chronicling these past fourteen month[s].
An absurd moment, but from it and by it I measure my re[e]
covery. *Je vens d'lué.*

It does not worry me now, as it worried me when I bega[n]
this book, that at the age of forty I should find myself at th[e]
end of my active life. I do not now think this is even true. [I]
no longer yearn for ideal landscapes and no longer wish t[o]
know the god of the city. This does not strike me as loss. [I]
feel, instead, I have lived through attachment and freed my[-]
self from one cycle of events. It gives me joy to find that in s[o]

doing I have also fulfilled the fourfold division of life pre-scribed by our Aryan ancestors. I have been student, house-holder and man of affairs, recluse.

My life has never been more physically limited than it has been during these last three years. Yet I feel that in this time I have cleared the decks, as it were, and prepared myself for fresh action. It will be the action of a free man. What this action will be I cannot say. I used to think of journalism; sometimes I used to think of a job with the UN. But these were attractive only to a harassed man. I might go into busi-ness again. Or I might spend the next ten years working on a history of the British Empire. I cannot say. Yet some fear of action remains. I do not wish to be re-engaged in that cycle from which I have freed myself. I fear to be continually washed up on this city.

Nine or ten months ago, when I was writing about my marriage and had written myself back into my aching love for Sandra, I used to ask myself what I would do if suddenly one day, from behind my pillar, I saw her enter the dining-room alone. I know of course what I would have done then: the question was no more than a wish. But now I find I have gone back to something closer to my original view. I once again see my marriage as an episode in parenthesis; I see all its emotions as, profoundly, fraudulent. So writing, for all its initial distortion, clarifies, and even becomes a process of life.

I do not believe I exaggerate either about Sandra or my mood. Last Saturday there was much excitement in the hotel. We, through our lord and lady, were being honoured by the attendance of a young but distinguished financier at the local branch dinner of some international brotherhood. The dinner took place in one of the upper rooms reserved for wedding luncheons. We, staff and faithful in the dining-room, studied the guests as they were received and went up the stairs. Our guest of honour arrived, with his wife. Lady Stella. I pulled my face behind the pillar and studied Gar-bage bringing his two-pronged knife down on the strug-gling cheese. *Dixi*.

August 1964 – July 1966

More About Penguins

Penguin Book News, which appears every month, contains
details of all the new books issued by Penguins as they are
published. From time to time it is supplemented by
Penguins in Print, which is a complete list of all books
published by Penguins which are in print. (There are well
over three thousand of these.)

A specimen copy of *Penguin Book News* will be sent to you
free on request, and you can become a subscriber for the
price of the postage – 4s for a year's issues (including the
complete lists). Just write to Dept EP, Penguin Books Ltd,
Harmondsworth, Middlesex, enclosing a cheque or postal
order, and your name will be added to the mailing list.

Some other Penguins by V. S. Naipaul are described on the
following pages.

Note: *Penguin Book News* and *Penguins in Print*
are not available in the U.S.A. or Canada

Also by V. S. Naipaul – two travel books

The Middle Passage

V. S. Naipaul, the distinguished Trinidadian novelist long resident in England, writes about his impressions of five societies in the West Indies and South America – Trinidad, British Guiana, Surinam, Martinique, and Jamaica.

'It belongs to the same category of travel writing as Lawrence's books on Italy, Greene's on West Africa, and Pritchett's on Spain' – Walter Allen in the *New Statesman*.

'Where earlier travellers enthused or recoiled, Mr Naipaul explains. His tone is critical but humane, and he tempers his inevitable indignation with an admirable sense of comedy' – James Pope-Hennessy in the *Observer*.

'*The Middle Passage* would be hard to beat for descriptive power and cool assessment of the situation there . . . He unfolds the picture with irony and pity' – Anthony Powell in the *Daily Telegraph*.

An Area of Darkness

Coming from a family which left India only two generations ago, V. S. Naipaul felt that his roots lay in India. But the country and its attitudes remained outside his experience, in an 'area of darkness', until, with some apprehension, he spent a year there. He arrived at Bombay, then travelled as far north as Kashmir, east to Calcutta and south to Madras, taking in a pilgrimage to a holy cave in the Himalayas and a stay on the Dal Lake. With his novelist's perception and sense of comedy he both describes the places, people and incidents, and manages to convey the meaning which lies behind them. He shares his experience of India generously and gives the reader deep insight into a country and a writer's mind.

'Tender, lyrical, explosive . . . excellent' – John Wain. 'Most compelling and vivid' – V. S. Pritchett.

Not for sale in the U.S.A.

Also by V. S. Naipaul

The Suffrage of Elvira

'I promising you,' said Mrs Baksh of the Elvira district election in Trinidad, 'for all it begin sweet sweet, it going to end damn sour.'

And she was right. Surujpat Harbans, the candidate, had to square Chittaranjan, the goldsmith, to get the Muslim vote and Baksh, the tailor, to get the Hindu vote. *And* he had to woo the negro vote away from his coolly eloquent rival, Preacher.

Petrol vouchers for taxi-drivers, more vouchers for Ramlogan's rumshop, a loudspeaker van . . . Harbans' expenses rocket. And his path to the Legislative Council is further complicated by two pretty Jehovah's Witnesses and a dog thought to be an evil spirit.

'Elvira,' said Harbans, summing up his constituency, 'Elvira, you is a bitch.'
Sweet, sweet . . . sour, sour.

And

A Flag on the Island (*Short Stories*)
The Mystic Masseur

Not for sale in the U.S.A.